Praise for *The* NOBLE GUARDIAN

"Michelle Griep has done it again! *The Noble Guardian* is well written and filled with plenty of action, danger, and romantic tension to keep the pages turning. Her admirable and appealing hero will win readers' hearts."

—Julie Klassen, bestselling author of
The Bride of Ivy Green

"I love this author! Ms. Griep just keeps getting better and better. *The Noble Guardian* is my new favorite novel! You can't go wrong with an alpha-male hero who is a protector, noble, and yet flawed in a way that touches your heart, and a heroine who is strong, independent, but in desperate need of love. The story moves along at a good pace with lots of nail-biting action and intense emotional scenes, only to culminate in a highly satisfying and happy-tears ending!"

—MaryLu Tyndall, award-winning author of
The Legacy of the King's Pirates series

"Remarkable! Griep creates alluring characters woven into unforgettable stories. Samuel is her best hero ever!"

—Elizabeth Ludwig, HOLT Medallion winner for
A Tempting Taste of Mystery

"The dark, brooding Samuel Thatcher gets his story at last in this third of Michelle Griep's Bow Street Runners, and it does not disappoint! Griep delivers once again with an endearing heroine, a heart-wrenching dilemma, and her usual cast of vivid characters. As always, she excels at bringing this time period to life."

—Shannon McNear, 2014 RITA® nominee and author of
The Cumberland Bride

"With her signature spice, Michelle Griep takes us on a rollicking ride across Regency England in *The Noble Guardian*. But beware! Just when you think you've met her most dashing hero yet, Captain Thatcher steals your heart. Add an endearing heroine who is equally adventurous and the wee gem t   , and you have all the makings of a fabul   ners series."

                                      ira Frantz, author of *A Bound Heart*

"*The Noble Guardian* is full to the brim with rich details, delightful romance, and page-turning intrigue. Readers who enjoy Regency novels will fall in love with the strong but wounded hero, Samuel Thatcher, and the charming and spirited heroine, Abby Gilbert. The extra touch of suspense will keep readers up late turning pages until the satisfying ending."
—Carrie Turansky, award-winning author of
Across the Blue and *No Ocean Too Wide*

"Packed with heart and hope, *The Noble Guardian* is sure to take historical romance fans on a journey they won't want to end. Endearing characters, a page-turning plot, vivid prose, and timeless truths make this novel a true pleasure to read."
—Jocelyn Green, award-winning author of *Between Two Shores*

"A rich and rare glimpse into Regency England, *The Noble Guardian* catapults readers into the bold and breathless era of the Bow Street Runners, London's first police force, where love conquers all—but just barely! Truly a regency unmatched, Michelle Griep has penned a plot so unique and compelling, pages will fly and sleep will be lost."
—Julie Lessman, award-winning author of *The Daughters of Boston*,
Winds of Change, and *Isle of Hope* series

"A stunning read! With tender moments and powerful romantic tension, Griep takes readers on another adventure through historical England in her latest Bow Street Runners novel. Vibrant chemistry abounds between this courageous heroine hoping for love and the jaded yet incredibly valiant guardian who comes to her rescue. Touching, engaging, memorable—*The Noble Guardian* is a book you won't want to miss!"
—Joanna Davidson Politano, author of *Lady Jayne Disappears* and
A Rumored Fortune

"There's something about a dark and brooding hero that makes me swoon. But add the undertones of thwarted love to a story cloaked in intrigue, and I'm a goner! Griep proves why she's an award-winning author, for Samuel Thatcher may be a lawman, but he has hijacked my heart!"
—Jaime Jo Wright, author of *The Curse of Misty Wayfair* and
Christy Award-winning *The House on Foster Hill*

The NOBLE
GUARDIAN

MICHELLE GRIEP

SHILOH RUN PRESS
An Imprint of Barbour Publishing, Inc.

© 2019 by Michelle Griep

Print ISBN 978-1-68322-749-6

eBook Editions:
Adobe Digital Edition (.epub) 978-1-68322-751-9
Kindle and MobiPocket Edition (.prc) 978-1-68322-750-2

This book is a work of fiction. Names, characters, places, and incidents are either products of the author's imagination or used fictitiously. Any similarity to actual people, organizations, and/or events is purely coincidental.

Cover Design: Kirk DouPonce, DogEared Design

Published by Shiloh Run Press, an imprint of Barbour Publishing, Inc., 1810 Barbour Drive, Uhrichsville, Ohio 44683, www.shilohrunpress.com

Our mission is to inspire the world with the life-changing message of the Bible.

 Member of the
Evangelical Christian
Publishers Association

Printed in the United States of America.

In memory of my sweet friend,

Bilinda Kelly
April 3, 1964–December 30, 2017

A stalwart warrior of the faith and
one of the most noble women I know...

And as always, to the Author of my faith and
noblest guardian of my soul—Jesus

Chapter One

Was it wicked to say goodbye with a smile? Wrong to feel happy about leaving one's family behind? Surely only a sinner's heart would harbour such uncharitable emotions. . .wouldn't it?

Stepping into the corridor, Abigail Gilbert closed her chamber door, shutting off such reproachful thoughts. This was a day of celebration, not bleak ponderings. Not anymore.

Hand yet on the knob, she hesitated a moment and angled her head. The usual morning sounds—servants bustling, trays rattling, feet padding to and fro—were absent. She'd heard them earlier while she'd sat at her dressing table. Why not now?

But no time to ponder such oddities. She scurried along the corridor to her stepsister's room, tightening her bonnet ribbons as she went. Her other half sister, Jane, would be down to breakfast already, but not Mary. Never Mary. The girl was a perpetual slugabed.

"Mary?" Abby tapped the bedroom door and listened.

No answer.

"Sister?" She rapped again, louder this time. "Are you still abed?"

Pressing her ear to the wood, she strained to hear some kind of complaint, or at least a pillow thwacking against the other side.

And. . .nothing.

Turning the knob, Abby shoved open the door, expecting a darkened room. Instead, brilliant sunbeams landed on a very empty bed. The light needled her eyes, and she blinked. Odd. Mary up so soon? How unlike her, unless—

Abby's breath caught in her throat. Perhaps she'd been wrong, and

Mary truly *did* care she was leaving. Even now her youngest sister might be waiting along with Jane in the breakfast room, teary-eyed and saddened to say farewell. La! Abby gave herself a silent scolding. She was a bad sister to assume the worst.

Lighter of step and of heart, she darted back into the corridor and sped down the grand stairway—despite years of reprimands for such hasty movements. Even now her stepmother's voice scolded inside her head.

"Fast feet fly toward folly."

She frowned. Surely that was not what she was doing. Any woman would hurry to be with the man who loved her. Still, she hesitated at the bottom of the staircase and smoothed her skirts before proceeding in a more ladylike manner.

She glided into the morning room, all grace and smiles, a pleasant *adieu* ready to launch from her lips. But her smile froze. She stopped.

No Jane.

No Mary.

Not even any breakfast dishes upon the sideboard. Would there be no one to wish her well on her journey?

Her throat tightened. But perhaps her sisters were already waiting outside by the coach, desiring a last embrace and wave of the hand as she disappeared into the land of matrimony. Everyone knew sisters should part in the best of ways, even Mary and Jane. Abby pivoted, intent on sharing a merry goodbye outdoors with them.

But first she must find Father and give him a final embrace. Besides her stepsisters, he was the last person to bid farewell, for she'd taken leave of her stepmother and stepbrother the night before.

Across from the sitting room, the study door was closed. One more curiosity on this momentous day. Pipe smoke ought to be curling into the hall by now, the scent of cherry tobacco sweetening the morning. Once again, Abby knocked on wood.

"Father?"

Without waiting for a response, she entered.

"What are you doing here?" Her stepmother frowned up at her from where she arranged lilies in a vase on Father's desk. It was a frivolous task, for Father cared not a whit about such trivialities, yet her stepmother insisted the touch added a certain *richesse*—as she put it—to the home. . .though Abby suspected it was more to remind her father what a doting woman he'd married so he wouldn't be tempted to look elsewhere for companionship.

Abby pulled her spine straight, a habit she'd developed as a young girl whenever in her stepmother's presence. "I came to say—"

"You should be gone by now!" Her stepmother crossed to the front of the desk and narrowed her eyes.

"I—I. . ." Her words unwound like a ball of yarn fallen to the floor, rolling off to the corner of the room. Not surprising, really. Her stepmother always effected such a response.

"I asked you a question, girl. Why are you not on your way to Penrith?"

Abby's gaze shot to the mantel clock. In four minutes, the hour hand would strike eight, her planned departure time. Was her stepmother confused—or was she? But no. Father's instructions had been abundantly clear.

Even so, she hesitated before answering. "I am certain that I am not to leave for Brakewell Hall until eight o'clock."

"Do not contradict me." Her stepmother clipped her words and her steps as she drew up nose to nose with Abigail. "Seven, you stupid girl. You were to depart at *seven*."

Abby bit her lip. Was she wrong? Had she misunderstood? Twenty years of doubting herself was a hard habit to break. Yet if she closed her eyes, she could still hear old Parker, her father's manservant, saying, *"Coach leaves at eight bells, miss. Young Mr. Boone will be your driver until you swap out at Tavistock. Charlie's to be your manservant."*

She stared at her stepmother. This close up, it was hard not to. A tic twitched the corner of the woman's left eye, but even so, Abby did not look away. To do otherwise would earn her a slap.

"I am sure of the time, Mother, yet I wonder why you thought otherwise. I am surprised you are not yet taking breakfast in bed. Where is Fath—"

A slap cut through the air. Abby's face jerked, and her cheek stung. She retreated, pressing her fingertips to the violated skin.

"Do not shame me. Curiosity is a vice of the ill-bred. Of all your faults, you cannot claim a mean upbringing, for you have been more than blessed."

The heat radiating on her cheek belied her stepmother's logic. She was blessed to have lived beneath this woman's iron hand for two decades? Abby drew in a shaky breath yet remained silent.

A smile spread like a stain on her stepmother's face, her teeth yellowed by age and far too much tea. "I suppose I might as well tell you, though it's really none of your affair. Your father is taking your sisters and me abroad to see off your brother on his grand tour. They are all out even now, the first to look through a recently arrived shipment of silks and woolens. I expect each of them shall make fortuitous matches as we summer amongst the elite in Italy, surpassing even the arrangement your father made for you."

Abby pressed a hand to her stomach. Gone? All of them? When they knew she was leaving?

Her stepmother clicked her tongue. "What's this? You didn't actually expect anyone to see you off, did you?"

For a moment, her heart constricted. Of course she'd known. She was an outsider. A stranger. She knew that as intimately as the skin on her face or the rift in her heart. A loving family was nothing more than a concept, an idea—one she'd have to learn, for she had no experience of it. Her lower lip quivered.

But she lifted her chin before the trap of self-pity snapped shut. "Of course not." She flashed as brilliant a smile as she could summon. "I merely wanted to thank Father one last time for arranging my marriage to Sir Jonathan, but you can tell him for me. I am grieved you shall all miss the ceremony."

Brittle laughter assaulted the June morning. "Oh Abigail, don't be ridiculous. We have other things to do. Now that we have your association with a baronet, the chances of my daughters marrying better than you are within reach. There is no time to waste."

The words poked holes into her heart. Why had she been so foolish to expect anything different? Abby whirled and ran from the house, praying it was no folly to escape such a hateful woman.

Outside, Mr. Boone stood at the carriage door, ready to assist her, but he was the only one in sight. Her maid, Fanny, was likely already seated inside, and old Charlie, who was to accompany her for the entire trip, was nowhere to be seen.

Mr. Boone held out his hand, but she hesitated to take it. "Are we to wait for Charlie?"

Red crept up the young man's neck, matching the hue of his wine-coloured riding coat. "Pardon, miss, but he will not be attending. It was decided he was more needed here."

Here? When the whole family would be absent for months? Anger churned her empty belly. This smacked of one last insult from her stepmother. If Jane or Mary were traveling cross-country, besides a maid and manservant, the woman would have sent a footman, a coachman, and a hired guard for good measure. Abby frowned. Should she wait for Father to return? He might rectify the situation, provided her stepmother didn't make a fuss. Or should she forge ahead?

She glanced back at the house, only to see her stepmother glowering out the window.

Abby turned to Mr. Boone and forced a small smile. "Well then, let us begin our journey, shall we?"

She grabbed the servant's hand and allowed him to assist her into the coach, then settled on the seat next to her maid. With Fanny and a driver, it wasn't as if she were traveling alone.

"Ready for an adventure, miss?" Fanny nudged her with her elbow. "Soon be queen of your own castle, eh?"

"Yes, Fanny." Cheek still stinging from her stepmother's slap, she turned her face away from the only home she'd ever known. "I should like to be a queen."

Hounslow Heath, just outside London

Gone. For now. Like a demon disappeared into the abyss. Samuel Thatcher shaded his eyes and squinted across the rugged heath kissed brilliant by the risen sun. Shankhart Robbins was out there, all right. Somewhere. And worse—he'd be back. Evil always had a way of returning bigger and blacker than before, singeing any soul it touched. After ten years on the force, with five in the Nineteenth Dragoons before that, Samuel Thatcher's soul was more than singed. It was seared to a crisp.

Behind him, Officer Bexley reined in his horse. "We lost Shankhart's trail nigh an hour ago. What do we do now, Captain?"

Aye. That was the question of the hour. Shoving his boot into the stirrup, he swung up onto his mount and turned Pilgrim about. "Go back."

"You're giving up?"

"Didn't say that." He rocked forward in the saddle. Without a word, his horse set off into a working trot, though she had to be as bone weary as he. Tired from a sleepless night. Tired from humanity. Tired of life.

An hour later, he pulled on the reins, halting in front of a gruesome sight. Draped over the hindquarters of his men's horses were the bodies of two women and two men, covered haphazardly with black riding cloaks. The other two horses, taken down by the highwaymen's shots, lay beneath a gathering swarm of blackflies. Who in their right mind would allow women to travel across this stretch of scrubby land accompanied by only a postilion? And by the looks of the overturned carriage, an inexperienced one at that.

Colbert and Higgins, the officers Samuel had left behind, rose from near the felled chaise, their red waistcoats stark as blood in the morning light.

Colbert turned aside and spit. "No luck, eh?"

Next to Samuel, Bexley dismounted, working out a kink in his lower back the second his feet hit the ground. "It'll take more'n luck to bring down that lot."

The men recounted once again how the attack must have played out, shuttlecocking ideas back and forth. For the most part, their conjectures were plausible. Even so, Samuel gritted his teeth, suddenly on edge. But why? The sky was clear. The weather temperate. And Shankhart was gone for now, so there was no imminent danger to them or any other passing coaches.

All the same, he stiffened in the saddle and cocked his head.

And. . .there. He angled Pilgrim toward a tiny mewl, not unlike the cry of a rabbit kit caught in a snare. Bypassing the ruined chaise and giving wide berth to the downed horses, he followed a small path of disturbed bracken, barely bent. Easy to miss in last night's gloaming, when they'd happened upon the scene. Yet clearly something had traveled this way.

He lowered to the ground, following the delicate trail on foot. The cry grew louder the farther he tracked. So did the alarm squeezing his chest. *Oh God. . .if this is a baby. . .*

Upping his pace, he closed in on a small rise of bracken and rock. Tucked into a crevice, a child, two years old or possibly three, whimpered for his mam—a mother who would never again wipe the tears from the lad's smudged cheeks.

Though relief coursed through him that the victim was not a babe, his lips flattened. One more piece of his charred heart crumbled loose, leaving his faith more jagged than before. It wasn't fair, such suffering for a little one—and he knew that better than most.

Reaching into the cleft, he pulled the child out. Teeth sank into his forearm. Nails surprisingly sharp ripped some of the skin off the back of one of his hands, and kicks jabbed his stomach. Despite it all, Samuel straightened and soothed, "Shh. You're safe now."

The lie burned in his throat. No one was safe, not on this side of heaven. He closed his eyes while the child squirmed.

Lord, grant mercy.

Lately, that prayer was as regular as his breath.

He retraced his route and hefted the child up into the saddle with him. He held the lad tight against him with his left arm, and gripped the reins with his injured right hand, blood dripping freely from it.

By the time he returned to the men, they were mounted as well. Bexley's brows lifted. The other two officers clamped their jaws and averted their gazes. To say anything would only magnify their failure to discover the lad sooner.

Samuel scowled, as much at his own deficiencies as theirs. If no family could be found, the child would end up in an orphanage. Even so, God knew it could be worse—*he* knew it could be worse.

Bexley edged his horse closer and lowered his voice for him alone. "Don't go too hard on the men, Captain. It were an easy oversight on such a long night."

He'd have to mete out some kind of censure. Good Lord, if he hadn't discovered the child and they'd left the youngling behind—but no. Better not to think it. He shifted the child on his lap, digging out an elbow shoved into his belly, then wiped the blood from his hand on his trousers. He'd come up with a discipline for Colbert and Higgins later, when his bones didn't feel every one of his thirty-one years and his soul wasn't raging at the injustice of the world.

"Move out." He twitched the reins, and Pilgrim lifted her nose toward London.

Bexley fell in beside him. "You've got that look about you."

He slid a sideways glance at the man but said nothing.

"You're not long for the force, are you?"

He did look then, full-on, studying every nuance of the stubbled face staring back at him. "What makes you say that?"

Bexley shrugged. "It's no secret your contract is up in a month."

So everyone knew. But did everyone also know he didn't have enough money yet to purchase the land he wanted? He turned his gaze back to the road.

"Why, Captain?" Bexley gnawed at the subject like a hound with a bone. "You're the best officer we got. You know this road will be more dangerous without you."

He grunted. With or without him, danger would prevail.

"Where will you go?" Bexley asked.

"Far."

"What will you do?"

"Farm."

"You? A farmer?" Bexley's laughter rumbled loud and long. "No. You'll miss this. The action. The adventure. Farming's too dull and lonely a life for you."

"Exactly." He pushed air through his teeth in a sharp whistle, and Pilgrim broke into a canter, leaving Bexley behind.

That was exactly what he wished—to be left alone.

Chapter Two

Abby's eyelids grew heavy as the chaise rumbled along. After only two days of travel, the tedium of the journey wore on both her and Fanny. Even now her maid's head drooped sideways onto Abby's shoulder, the woman's breathing thick and even. Abby shifted slightly, easing into a more comfortable position. It wouldn't hurt to close her own eyes. They still had Hounslow Heath to cross before stopping for the night. There'd be nothing to see but rain-dampened flatlands anyway.

Her chin dropped to her chest, and she gave in to the jiggle and sway of the carriage. For the first time since her father had remarried, she could finally fully relax. No more cutting remarks from her step-mother. No cross looks from her sisters. It was a welcome feeling, this freedom. Decadent and heady.

And horribly shame inducing. She ought to be missing her family, not reveling in their absence. She ought to be praying for them each night as her head hit the pillow, not dreaming of her new life with Sir Jonathan Aberley. As she bobbed along with the rhythm of the rolling wheels, she vowed to be more diligent in prayer for them. Starting tonight.

Guilt assuaged—for the moment—she purposely tuned her thoughts to memorized portions of the Psalms, losing herself in still waters and green pastures. . .one of her favorite ways to drift into sleep.

But a sudden stop jerked her back to reality. Groggy, she fumbled at her bodice for the watch she wore pinned to her spencer, then blinked at the tiny numbers. 'Twas only half past two.

Gently pushing Fanny aside—who mumbled something about

scones and jam, or maybe pudding and ham?—Abby unlatched the door and peered out. The postilion had already dismounted from his perch on the lead horse and was brushing mud flecks off his blue jacket as he strode over to lower the steps. He'd stopped the chaise in front of a building that brightened the dreary day by virtue of its whitewashed stones and the lit lanterns in the windows. Above the front door of the inn, gilt letters, chipped and crooked, spelled out THE GOLDEN CROSS. Abby reluctantly took the driver's offered hand and lowered to the ground. Surely the man couldn't be thirsty nor the horses tired when they'd taken a meal not two hours ago. "Why are we stopping?"

Brown eyes stared directly into hers, for the fellow was her height. Though she'd interacted now with many postilions when they changed horses and drivers at every inn, she'd still not grown accustomed to men no taller than herself. A boon for the horses, not having to haul large frames, but unnerving for her to stand eye to eye with a man.

"Ground's a muddy mess, miss. It'll take too long to cross the heath with the roads such as they are. We'd never make it across by nightfall, and the heath's no place to be caught in the dark. It's better to give it a go early in the morning."

Behind her, feet splatted onto the wet ground. A moment later, Fanny's whisper warmed her ear. "Is there a problem?"

"The roads are too wet. We are stopping for the night."

"Ahh, good. Then you could order us some scones and jam, eh?"

Stifling a retort, Abby gathered her skirt and lifted it slightly. It would do no good to reprimand the woman for such impertinence. It was Fanny's way. The maid's insolence was likely the reason her stepmother had chosen her for Abby in the first place. Still, for all of Fanny's peculiarities, the woman had a pleasant way about her. . . especially when food was involved.

Stepping on flagstones too far apart for comfort, Abby gathered her gown a bit higher and focused on the precarious walkway leading to the door of the inn. A full day of mist coated the world in slippery dampness. The promise of hot tea lured her to up her pace, but a glance at the mucky ground tempered that urge. Sitting with wet shoes would be bad enough. Adding a muddied gown to the mix would prove intolerable.

Inside, she and Fanny stopped at an ancient slab of a bar, darkened by centuries of spilled ale and the elbows of patrons too many to count. Behind it, a round fellow, wiping off the rim of a mug with the corner of his apron, glanced over at them. "What'll it be, ladies?"

"We need a room for the evening and tea for now." Abby dabbed away the moisture on her cheeks with the back of her hand. "For two, please."

"Aye. Room four is yours. I'll have a boy fetch yer belongings." He set the mug down then tipped his head toward an open door across from the bar. "Find a table in the front room, just through there. Tea will be out shortly."

"Thank you." Abby offered the man a smile, then turned and strode through the door. Only one of the five tables was unoccupied, the one nearest the window. The space was likely drafty, but once their hot drink arrived, it wouldn't matter.

Abby sank into the chair, thankful for a seat that wasn't jostling and juddering, then untied her bonnet and lifted it from her hair.

Fanny did the same but stretched her neck to glance around the room. "Quite the full house for this time of day."

"I suppose, with the weather, we are not the only ones holding off our jaunt across the heath." Abby's gaze shifted to the window. Tiny droplets gathered together, forming great tears that wept down the glass. It was sound judgment to stop here for the night, but even so, a growing anticipation needled her for the wasted time.

The closer they drew to Penrith, the more anxious she was to see Sir Jonathan again. She'd met her intended only once, at a dance crowded with people—and even then merely in passing. 'Twas a miracle he'd offered for her. There'd been other beautiful, eligible hands he could have requested. A small smile rippled across her lips. Sir Jonathan must have truly been taken with her to have approached her father before leaving that night.

"Miss?" Fanny's urgent murmur cut into her sweet ponderings. "I don't like the way the fellow at the table behind you is looking at us. Perhaps we should take tea in our room."

"But we are already seated. Do you really think it necessary?" She studied her maid's eyes, trying to detect how much anxiety swam in those brown depths or if the woman was merely angling for a good lie down. Besides food, Fanny's other penchant was napping, and a champion she was. The woman would've made a proficient lapdog.

Fanny leaned across the table, speaking for her alone. "I wager that fellow is eyeing us up for the pickings."

Real fear pinched the sides of Fanny's mouth, and Abby reached out to pat the woman's shoulder. "Do not fret. I am sure brigands have better things to do at this time of day than take tea."

Fanny's gaze burned into hers. "I've heard it said ol' Dick Turpin used to meet with his gang 'round here, maybe even at this very inn, planning his vile attacks. Oh!" Fanny gasped, her voice dropping to a ragged whisper. "He's coming over."

Biting her lip, Abby straightened in her chair just as a tall man pulled up to the side of their table. She lifted her face to a whisker-jawed fellow in a cutaway dress coat, smelling of onions and blue stilton.

"Pardon me, ladies. I am Mr. Harcourt, a local constable in these parts." He hitched his thumbs in his lapels. "Might I have a word with you?"

"You may." Abby snuck a glance at Fanny. The maid leaned as far back in her chair as possible, as if the man might pick her pocket at any moment.

Abby turned back to Mr. Harcourt, preferring to give him the benefit of the doubt. "Is something amiss, sir?"

Mr. Harcourt shook his head. "Not at all. I simply noticed the two of you are traveling alone—unless your gentlemen are joining up with you later?"

For a moment she studied the fellow. He seemed upright enough, with his cream-coloured cravat tied neatly and his silver-streaked hair combed back in a tidy fashion. Still, constable or not, it wouldn't do to admit she and Fanny were alone. She lifted her chin. "Pardon me, but I do not see how that signifies."

"Only that if my summation is correct, and you are planning to cross the heath, then I'd like to offer you my services."

Fanny narrowed her eyes. "What services might those be?"

"Sharpshooting, miss."

Abby pressed her lips flat to keep her jaw from dropping. *Sharpshooting?* Did the fellow think they were off to net big game? "Thank you for your offer, Mr. Harcourt, but we are on a simple journey, not a hunting foray."

"You may not be hunting, but Shankhart Robbins is."

Abby couldn't help but bunch up her nose a bit. Was that a name of a man or an animal? "I beg your pardon, sir?"

"It's like this." Mr. Harcourt cleared his throat and clasped his hands behind his back, as if he were about to launch a tale while employing great oratory.

Abby shifted on her chair, just in case he was.

"A fortnight ago," Mr. Harcourt began, "two women, such as yourselves, set out across Hounslow with naught but a wee lad, a manservant, and a single driver as accompaniment. I warned them against such a rash venture. Why, they sat at this very table when I approached them just like this. I said to them, 'Ladies—'"

"Highwaymen got them," Fanny cut in. "Am I correct?"

Mr. Harcourt's brows sank into a thick line. "I was about to get to that, but yes. Only the lad came back. 'Twas a grisly murder scene, I'm told. Robbins. . .well, he's a blackguard who takes more than gold. He takes everything." He stretched the word so that his meaning couldn't be denied, then he drew back and sniffed. "And that's why you need a hired gun to see you safely across the heath. Three guineas ought to cover it."

Across the table, Fanny's worried gaze met hers. Mentally, Abby tallied her remaining traveling allowance. Paying this fellow would dip deep into those coins, so much so that by the end of the journey, she might have to use the funding given to her by her father for her last-minute wedding needs.

"I, uh. . ." She licked her lips, praying for wisdom.

"Well, what's it to be?"

Mr. Harcourt's bass voice pulled her from her conjecture, and she smiled up at him. "Thank you for the information, Mr. Harcourt. I shall consider your offer."

"As you wish, but don't think on it too long. I generally take the first offer." He slipped a glance at the rest of the occupied tables. "And as you can see, there may be others who will want my services."

"I understand. Good afternoon, sir."

Mr. Harcourt stepped toward the next table but then suddenly turned back. "Oh, and miss? Even if you do have gentlemen meeting up with you, unless they are familiar with a gun and the heath, you ought still to consider hiring me on. Robbins is no respecter of fools. He eats them for dinner and spits out their bones."

Rain drizzled from clouds low enough for a man to reach up and yank down. On a good day, London streets were crowded and smelly. But with the addition of the sooty mist coating one and all, today was a bad one. Not that Samuel minded. The grey June afternoon was a big shadow—and that suited him fine. It felt like home, this murky obscurity.

Rounding the corner, he turned onto Bow Street. Many feet had trod this path to the magistrates' court entrance, usually with trepidation. His steps were no different. Would the chief magistrate grant his contract renegotiation, extending it for only a month instead of the required two more years? Just four weeks more and he'd have money enough to buy the parcel of land that Lord Mabley, needing to raise cash, was selling over in Burnham. Hopefully Magistrate Conant was in a charitable mood, for if he wasn't. . .

Lord, grant mercy.

He flexed his hand and scowled at the remains of the deep scratch from the orphan boy atop it. The gash should've been sewn up, but what was one more scar? The last ten years on this job had been nothing but wound upon wound, in more ways than one.

He reached for the door—just as two hulking shapes stepped out.

The flaxen-haired figure—former Officer Alexander Moore—clapped him on the shoulder. "Speak of the devil—"

"And he doth appear, as I said he would." The darker of the pair, Officer Nicholas Brentwood, shifted his hawklike gaze from Moore to Samuel. "If I don't miss my mark, you're on your way to see Conant. Though judging by the looks of you, you're running a bit late due to an overturned cart loaded with an apothecary's delivery. Am I correct?"

Samuel's scowl deepened to a glower. How in all of God's green earth would Brentwood know that? Narrowing his eyes, he glanced down at his trousers, and. . .yes, there, clinging to the hem and the top of his shoes were small splotches of yellowish goo, too thick and sticky to have been washed away by the drizzle. Hang the man for his overly observant ways.

Part nudge, part shove, Moore turned Samuel about and herded him down the street—away from the courtroom's door. "Come. I've not much time before I must meet up with my wife. I don't often get to London anymore, so this round is on me."

Samuel shook his head. Likely a fruitless rebuff, knowing Moore's penchant for a tall mug and a good jawing. Blast! This would be his only chance for the next week to meet with the chief magistrate, for he was slated to ride the heath again tomorrow. He stopped in his tracks. "I'll catch up. First I must—"

"Don't bother." Brentwood clouted him on the back, bookending him between the two and pushing him into motion. "Conant isn't in, as usual."

Moore cocked a brow. "Not like the old days, eh?"

"Not at all." The words were more of a growl in Brentwood's throat, yet he was right. Things had never been the same since Ford resigned and ran off to Sheffield with his new bride.

"You can tell Ford he is still sorely missed," Brentwood added.

"What, and give the old duff a fat head?" Moore chuckled. "No, thank you. He's barely tolerable when he and Johanna's mam come for a visit. It's all *I'm the best grandfather this'* and *'never better grandchildren that.'* The man's pride of family is enough to choke a horse."

Samuel stared at his friend, baffled. "Oughtn't you be glad of it? It is your family he's proud of, after all."

"I suppose, though it would be easier to bear were he not as domineering in his child-rearing advice as he was with his former directives. You'd think I'm still a runner under his employ instead of his son-in-law." Moore shoved open the door of the Blue Boar pub and barreled ahead, glancing over his shoulder. "And then there's old Nutbrown, thinking he knows all there is about children just because of his ridiculous puppeteering. . .though I do admit his theatre group keeps the little ones entertained in Dover and beyond."

The reek of ale and sausage wafted out the door, and as Samuel stepped inside, the additional stench of dampened wool and body odour blended with the mix.

Moore hailed the barkeep with a wave of his hand. "Three mugs, over here."

Instinctively, the three of them gravitated to a table in the far corner, each of them vying for the choice seat against the wall with a view of the entire room. But where Brentwood excelled at observation and Moore the use of his cunning tongue, Samuel slid fast and silent into the prized chair. A small victory, but one he'd hold on to with both hands.

Doffing his hat, Moore shook the extra droplets from the ends of his hair, not unlike a great Saint Bernard. And like the big dog, everything about him was powerful yet even-tempered. Samuel would never forget the good days he'd spent in Moore's company.

As if reading his mind, Moore voiced the same sentiment. "As happy as I am in Dover, I have missed you two renegades, though I won't own up to it in a court of law." He chuckled as Brentwood snorted. "But I am glad to find you both hearty and hale."

Accepting a mug from a serving girl, Brentwood took a draw, then swiped his mouth with the back of his hand. "Emily would kill me were I to take a bullet, so don't worry on my account. I'm not much on the streets anymore. With my seniority, the more lucrative security jobs are mine for the picking—which is a boon considering I've got four extra mouths to feed at home. No, Moore, it's this one who ought to concern you." Brentwood's dark gaze slid to Samuel, and he lowered his voice. "Word is Shankhart Robbins is gunning for you. You've been interrupting his business on the heath these past two weeks, and he's none too happy about it."

Samuel grunted. Despite his best efforts, the blackguard was still at large.

"I'm a little in the dark here." Moore slugged back a large swig then set his mug on the table. "Who's Robbins?"

"A dead man, should I find him." Samuel shoved his mug away, thirst for justice stronger than his need for a drink.

Moore's brows shot high. "Must be quite the swine to have you so riled."

"He's vile, I hear." Brentwood leaned forward, an underlying rage deepening his tone. "Sparing no one, not even children. That boy you found a fortnight ago, Thatcher, was a lucky one."

Lucky? Hardly. With no identification, the lad had ended up in an orphanage, just as he'd expected. Perhaps they'd eventually find the boy's father, but each day that passed without a lead, the slimmer the chance.

Tipping back his head, Brentwood downed the rest of his ale, then stood. "Well, as much as I'd like to stay and hear of your plans for capturing Robbins"—he turned his face to Moore—"or your innkeeping exploits in Dover, I must be off on an adventure of my own. Guarding an overnight load of munitions down at Wapping, and it pays to do a preliminary survey."

Moore frowned. "Can't you get Flannery to take care of that for you?"

"Flannery's gone. Back to Ireland to tend his ailing mother. I'm on my own now." He shrugged. "Give my best to Johanna. I suspect next time we meet, you'll have more than two daughters and a son, hmm?"

Moore winked. "I'll get right on that. Godspeed."

"You as well. And Thatcher"—Brentwood paused, his gaze piercing in the dim light of the taproom. "For once, take a care for yourself. Don't let Robbins be the end of you."

Samuel said nothing—for there was nothing to say. Of course he wouldn't go looking for death, but it would come eventually. And he could think of no better way of dying than in the pursuit of justice.

Brentwood's dark form hardly made it out the door before Moore turned to him, all mirth fleeing from his blue eyes. "Look, Brentwood may be a lifer, but you're not. Get out while you can, man."

He rolled the mug between his palms. "I intend to."

"Flit! Life's too short for intentions. Brentwood says you've got only a few weeks left on your contract. Ride it out here. Don't go back on the heath, not with this Robbins fellow at large. You've served too long to be taken out at the last minute."

Setting down his mug, he met Moore's terrible gaze and matched it with one of his own. "You think that frightens me?"

"No. I do not." Moore leaned back in his chair. "And that's what frightens me."

Chapter Three

Sunshine mottled Abby's closed lids, and she fluttered her eyes open. For a moment, dust motes mesmerized her while she swam from the depths of a hard-won slumber. All the talk last evening of brigands and highwaymen, coupled with the jabs of Fanny's elbows and knees—for the woman was a rampaging bed hog—made for a long night. But at least she'd managed a few hours of sleep. Maybe. Reaching for her watch brooch on the small table next to the bed, she glanced at the numbers, and—

Sweet heavens! She flung off the counterpane and shot to her feet, clutching the timepiece. Nine o'clock. They should've been on the heath hours ago.

"Fanny, wake up." She scurried over to a washbasin and splashed water on her face, then darted back to the bed and jostled her maid's shoulder. "Fanny! We are running late. Please, get moving."

"Hmm?" Fanny pushed up on her elbows, blinking. "Oh...aye, miss."

By the time her maid finally shimmied into her own gown, Abby had hers buttoned, hair gathered up into a loose chignon, and hat ribbons securely tied beneath her chin. Snatching up her reticule, she strode to the door, then on second thought, turned back to face Fanny. If she didn't spell out the woman's instructions, there was no guarantee her maid might not dillydally over a cup of tea.

"Please see our baggage loaded as soon as you leave the room. I shall secure a driver and arrange for an on-the-road breakfast to make up our lost time. I will meet you at the front door."

"Very well, miss." Fanny glanced at her as she tucked in a last hairpin. "What about Mr. Harcourt? Did you make a final decision?"

"I have." How could she not? She'd been weighing the benefits and deficits of the man's offer ever since he'd proposed it the previous evening. "For our safety, I think it best to employ him, but I had better make haste. Hopefully no one else has hired him. I shall see you outside."

Urged by her own words, Abby hurried out of the room and dashed down the corridor, slowing only to descend the stairs into the taproom.

Behind the counter stood the same burly fellow of the night before, wearing the same stained apron. Upon closer inspection, his shirt was the same too, albeit more creased. She wrinkled her nose. He smelled a bit riper as well. Had he slept in those garments?

"Good morning, miss." The innkeeper dipped his head. "I were just about to fetch a maid to see if you ladies be planning on spending another night."

"No, sir. We are simply getting a late start." She fished a coin out of her small purse and set it on the scarred wood. "Would you wrap up a few rolls and some hard-cooked eggs or cheese that we may take along?"

"Aye. I'll have it packed and sent out to your carriage in a trice." His big fingers scooped up the money, and he turned to open a small strongbox on a shelf behind him.

"Very good. I am also seeking Mr. Harcourt, the tall fellow with side whiskers who took tea yesterday. Have you seen him this morning?"

The man swung back to her. "Mr. Harcourt left with a party earlier, near on two hours ago now. You ladies are the only guests remaining."

She couldn't stop the frown that weighted her brow. If Mr. Harcourt was already hired, were there even any drivers left, or would she and Fanny be forced to tarry another day?

"Oh dear," she breathed out.

"Not to worry, Miss Gilbert. All is not lost. There's still a driver available if you're wanting to cross the heath yet today. One of our most experienced, matter of fact. You'll find Mr. Shambles in the coach house."

Lifting up a small prayer of thanks, she smiled at the man. "Thank you, sir. You have been most hospitable."

The innkeeper tugged his forelock. "Godspeed and safe travels to ye."

Once outside, Abby couldn't help but lift her face to the brilliant June sky. She'd learned long ago to openly savor glorious mornings. And this time there'd be no scolding from her stepmother for such careless behaviour. How grand it would be—it *will* be—when she could greet each morning thus, walking hand in hand with her new husband.

Sighing, she stepped into the cool shadows of the coach house, breathing in horseflesh and leather. Perched on a stool in front of a long workbench was a man-sized grey toad. The fellow's hoary head dipped to his chest, and small snores issued with each inhale.

Abby pivoted in a circle, searching for the experienced driver the innkeeper had spoken of. Yet no one else was in sight. The only movement was the quiet rustle of straw beneath horses' hooves.

She turned back to the old fellow, hating to disturb his rest, but there was nothing to be done for it. "Excuse me, sir. I loathe to bother you, but—"

A great snore ripped out of him, cutting her off and waking him up. With a jerk, he snapped up his head, and she stifled a gasp. Indeed, he was a toad, for a plentiful crop of wartlike growths dappled his face. Bulging black eyes—set wide and somewhat milky—stared back at her.

"Eh? What's that you say?"

Lowering her gaze, Abby focused on the man's faded blue neckerchief instead of his face. "I beg your pardon for disrupting you, but I am wondering if you could direct me to a Mr. Shambles?"

The old fellow chuckled, the movement hunching his back all the more. "Why, that be me, miss."

This was Mr. Shambles? She pressed her lips tight, stopping a moan.

"You be needin' a driver, miss?"

"Y–yes." She stumbled over the word, her admission indicting her for having slept so late. Had she not been such a layabout, she'd have had a better pick of postilions.

"I'm yer man." Mr. Shambles edged off the stool, he and the tall seat tottering a bit. "I'll bring a carriage 'round to the front."

Swallowing her dismay, she forced a smile. "Thank you."

She left the coach house behind, pretending all would be well. And likely it would. It wasn't as if she'd be stuck with Mr. Shambles for the rest of the journey to Penrith. Only across the heath and to the next inn.

Leaving the stable yard, she spied Fanny waiting by the front door—chewing on an apple, her munching and crunching competing with the *chek-chek* of a warbler. A lad loitered nearby, ready to heft her trunk and their traveling bags into the carriage.

Fanny eyed her as she drew near. "Where's Mr. Harcourt?"

"He was not available."

"Hmm." Fanny took another great bite, and after a few lip-smacking seconds, she swallowed the mouthful. "Shouldn't we wait until he is?"

Abby feigned a confident smile. "That could be days from now. We need to move on. I cannot be late for my own wedding."

Tossing aside the apple core, her maid turned to her, worry creasing her brow. "But do you think it's safe?"

Abby pressed her lips flat. Her opinion of the matter didn't make the journey any more safe or dangerous. Still, if she didn't quell Fanny's fears, the silly girl would conjure all sorts of ghastly stories of highwaymen—not the sort of traveling conversation she'd like to hear for the next several hours.

"It is a bright morning." She schooled her voice to a cheerful tone. "We shall cross in plenty of time before dark. And I have been assured that we have hired the most experienced driver the inn has to offer."

Just then, their carriage rolled up. Mr. Shambles sat upon the lead horse. Barely. The hunchbacked man canted a bit sideways, his leather gloves clinging desperately to the reins.

"Pah!" Fanny spit out. "Experienced? Is the old fellow up to the task?"

The question buzzed like a hornet, stinging Abby's good sense. Still, what choice did they have?

"There is one way to find out." She lifted her chin and strode to where the lad had lowered the steps, then gripped his hand as she ascended.

Outside, Fanny hesitated near the door, but eventually she acquiesced—right after the lad hefted up a cloth-covered basket of food.

The coach rolled off, and after stopping at the tollgate to pay the crossing fare, they rumbled into the wilds of the heath.

Fanny heaved a satisfied sigh between bites of cheese and cold meat. "Well, this doesn't seem so bad. Hounslow isn't nearly as frightening as I imagined."

While the maid tucked the basket into a corner on the floor, Abby glanced out at the passing landscape. Scrubby shrubs dotted the expanse. Here and there, rangy trees bold enough to withstand the ever-present wind bowed in deference. Sunshine gilded the grassy plain, and yellow gorse flowers added to the golden effect. Fanny was right. It truly wasn't a frightening scene.

"It is quite beautiful," Abby murmured. "In a primal sort of way."

"It surely is different from Southampton. I wonder what our new home in the north will be like."

She turned back to her maid and studied the woman's brown eyes. "Are you nervous?"

"Not really." Fanny shrugged. "Truth is, with your Sir Jonathan Aberley being a baronet and all, I expect life will be better than ever."

Abby nodded absently. Yes, it would be far better to live with someone who wanted her around. Someone who'd listen to her, *really* listen. Someone who didn't expect her to blend into the background but would cherish her for herself and would love her for who she was, just as her real mother had, God rest her.

With a sigh, Abby turned to thoughts of living in a manor home with a handsome husband. Of candlelit dinners and walking hand in hand. Sharing whispers in the dark. A brazen smile twitched her lips. How long would it be before children came laughing and crying into their world? Would they have her brown eyes or—

Gunshot cracked the air, shattering her daydream. Fanny screamed. So did the horses.

Abby's breath stuck in her throat as she stared out at the nightmare through the window. Mr. Shambles fell sideways, and for one horrifying moment, his boot snagged on the cinch strap. The top half of his body dragged along the ground, bumping and scraping his torso over rocks.

Abby slapped a hand to her mouth, stopping a shriek.

The old fellow's body broke free then, rolling like a thrown sack of potatoes. Abby jerked her face to the side window as they passed him. His eyes were open. So was his mouth. Mud covered half his face. Blood the other.

And then he was gone.

But there was no time to mourn. The horses bolted, and the chaise careened to one side. Abby flailed for a grip as she slid sideways and crashed into Fanny. Without a driver, the carriage bounced wild, the wheels gaining momentum as the horses broke into a run.

Abby clawed her way upright, but only for a moment. Her head hit the glass, her face mashed against the window. Pain smacked her hard.

And the horses picked up speed, smearing the outside world into a blur.

Samuel slid off Pilgrim and looped the horse's lead over a picket, then turned and strode into the Golden Cross on silent feet. Not that he needed to be stealthy this brilliant June morn. No brigand in his right mind would be kicking back with a brew and kidney pie this time of day. Moving as a spectre was simply his way, a habit so engrained, he could no more stop doing it than he could quit breathing.

He slipped into the shadowy confines of the taproom and angled toward the bar. Behind it, innkeeper Willy Gruber worked a rag around the inside of a tankard.

"Mornin', Gruber."

Willy spun, and the mug flew from his hands. The earthenware hit the counter with a crack, then plummeted to the floor, splintering into shards against the greasy oak planks.

"Thatcher!" Willy spat out his name like a curse. "Why the flippity-flam can you not warn me when you come through the door? That's the fifth mug in the past fortnight you've ruined. I oughtta start chargin' ye. Aye, I'll keep a regular tally, I will, chock-full o' numbers. Send it right down to Bow Street and have 'em dock yer pay, that's what."

Samuel held his tongue. Giving in to Willy's drama only frothed it up all the more.

"Bah!" Willy flicked his hand in the air, swatting him away. "Off with ye. Yer men been here and gone already."

He grunted. He hadn't really expected his squad of officers to still be here, though it would've made for an easier ride. "How long ago?"

"Near on an hour and a half now, I figure. Maybe more." Willy tucked his rag into the apron tied around his big belly, then cocked a brow at him. "I were surprised to see you weren't with them."

"Cinch strap broke."

"Well, no doubt the poor sot what fixed it worked at breakneck speed beneath your devilish stare."

His mouth twisted. Willy was right. The *devilish stare* he'd perfected had served him well while facing Mahratta chieftains back in '03.

"Which route did they take?" he asked.

"Din't say, but I'm guessing the Exeter Road. That were the direction most o' last night's guests were headed, leastwise all those what had set out right before yer men arrived. Knowing that horse o' yours, ye'll catch up to 'em in no time."

No doubt, for off the top of his head he could think of at least three different shortcuts to make up for lost time—or more, if he cared to put his mind to it. Which he didn't.

Giving Gruber a sharp nod, he turned to go, but something dragged his steps. Something not quite right. Like the unsettling creak of a floorboard when sitting alone in an empty house.

He reached for the door—then drew back his hand. "*Most* guests?"

Willy flinched at his voice, for he'd already turned to grab another mug. At least this one stayed in the man's meaty paw. Breathing out curses that would redden a smuggler's ears, Willy swung back to the bar where Samuel had backtracked. "Aye, most. Had a few ladies set off not long ago, headed north."

"Who accompanied them? Harcourt?"

"Nay. He were employed by one o' the two coaches what left afore 'em."

Samuel frowned. "Any men with them? Husbands? Escorts?"

Willy shook his head. "Only Shambles."

Scarpin' bodgers! Those women would be easy prey should Shankhart be on the prowl. He tipped his hat and headed for the door.

Willy's voice followed. "And next time, rattle the doorknob or stamp yer feet. I'm done with yer slinking about!"

Samuel waved him off as he strode outside. Willy nagged more than a fishwife. Grabbing hold of Pilgrim's lead, he swung up into the saddle and turned the bay around. Once past the tollhouse, he cut loose onto the northern road. With any luck, he'd find old Shambles and the ladies in one piece.

Gusty breezes tried to steal his hat, but Samuel tucked his head into the onslaught, his worn black felt as much a part of him as his arms and legs. The heath whooshed past. Green. Yellow. Brilliant. Mornings didn't get any better than this.

Or did they? What would it be like to finally trade in his tipstaff for a hay rake? How much more peaceful? No more chasing cullys and killers. No more blood. Or death. As the world rushed by in a smear of green and gold, a small smile tugged his lips. Soon, God willing. Twenty-five pounds more and he'd have enough to—

A gunshot fractured the air, violating the summer morn. Judging by the echo of the report, not too far away. He dug in his heels, urging Pilgrim to top speed.

The wind whipped. Grit blasted his face, and his eyes watered. Samuel dropped closer to the horse's neck, cutting resistance and letting Pilgrim take the brunt of the breeze.

Leaning into a curve, he rounded a stand of gorse bushes, then spied a black lump ahead. Man-sized. Unmoving. Sprawled at the side of the road like a dumped heap of rubbish.

Samuel slowed his mount only long enough to identify the unmistakable face of Mr. Shambles. Part of it, at least. Blood hid the rest, having poured from an entry wound gaping at the side of his temple.

Yanking out a gun, Samuel urged Pilgrim onward, righteous fury burning in his gut. Either this was Shankhart Robbins's day to die. . .or his.

Lord, grant mercy.

Again the road curved, skirting a small rocky rise. When the trail straightened, Samuel growled. Twenty yards ahead, horses screamed to a stop. Barely. Whoever handled them didn't have the sense of a gnat. Another man stood at the side of the chaise like the grim reaper about to call. One hand on the door handle. The other gripping a pistol.

Samuel yanked on the reins. The instant Pilgrim stopped, he sighted the man with the barrel of his gun and fired.

The scoundrel fell. The horses bolted. And the carriage lurched into motion.

Pushing air through his teeth, Samuel jabbed his heels into Pilgrim's side, but truly neither was needed. After ten years, the horse knew the routine.

The chaise bounced like a child's toy dragged by a tether. Samuel sped past it, gaining on the blackguard who drove the lead horse.

"Stop!" he roared.

Dark eyes swung his way.

So did a gun.

Chapter Four

She could die here, in this rocking four-wheeled casket—and Abby wasn't ready. Not yet. Not now.

God, please!

The wheels hit hard, and Abby's teeth snapped shut on her tongue, filling her mouth with the taste of copper. She could barely breathe, let alone cry out.

Next to her, Fanny shrieked, her flailing elbow punching Abby in the cheek. The carriage jolted faster, tilting one way, then back the other. Flying up. Crashing down. Abby's fingernail tore as she scrambled for a hold on the seat, the side, anything.

Despite her desperate clutching, her shoulder smacked against the wall, and her bonnet slipped forward, covering her eyes. She batted it away in time to see the galloping hooves of yet another horse streaking past the window. Atop it, a man in a muddied black cloak brandished another gun.

Dear God, is there no end? Save us!

But the chaise rumbled on. The men roared. So did the crack of a shot. The man driving the carriage listed sideways. With a yank on the reins, the man in the black cloak veered his horse into him, knocking the driver to the ground. Before Abby could suck in a breath or Fanny could scream again, the newcomer leapt from his saddle to the carriage horse. The wild ride slowed and, an eternity later, stopped.

That's when the shaking started. Somewhere deep and low. Spreading up Abby's legs to her belly to her arms. As the black-cloaked man dismounted and stalked toward the door, she trembled harder with each of his steps. What was to become of them?

She scrambled like a cat across the seat, crashing into Fanny, both shrinking away from the door. Fanny whispered a ragged rendition of the Lord's Prayer, her breath hot against Abby's ear. Abby bit her lip—heedless now of the blood—wishing she could pray, scream, run.

But all she could do was stare at the latch. It jerked down. The bolt scraped back. The door opened. A shadow-faced highwayman jumped up, blocking light and air and hope. His black gaze violated hers, and she quaked all the more.

He was night, this man. His dark hair hung wild to his chin. His darker hat shaded his eyes, so that all she saw were the sharp angles of his cheekbones, the cut of his nose, the strong mouth flattened to a grim line. Without a word, he stretched out his hand.

For her.

This was it, then. The end of innocence. The end of life—and just when love and belonging were within her reach. It wasn't fair, this ripping away of the gift she'd not yet opened.

And she'd have none of it.

She flattened against Fanny, flung out her hands for balance, and kicked like a wild donkey.

A heel caught Samuel's jaw, jerking his face sideways. Pain shot to his temple. Sweet blessed heavens! Must every person he tried to help lash out at him? The tear on his hand from the orphan boy was not yet completely healed.

Lurching back from the thrashing wildcat, he held up a hand. "Peace!"

The word thundered loud, startling the woman midkick.

"I won't harm you," he murmured, cautious and low, all the while edging slowly toward her. "You need to get out. The horses may bolt again."

God help them all if they did.

Indeed, God. A little help, if You please.

Keeping track of the woman's feet, he once again offered his hand.

Her gaze bounced between his face and his outstretched fingers. Blood trickled down one of her cheeks, marring the porcelain skin. The other woman, ashen-faced and scowling, shoved her forward. And no wonder, for it was a miracle the woman behind the wildcat could even breathe the way she'd been mashed against her.

The chaise rocked, the horses clearly spooked and willing to charge at the slightest provocation. Blast! He didn't have time to coddle frightened women.

Setting his jaw, Samuel reached for the wildcat, prepared for a biting, screaming mass. But she gave way without a fight and, in fact, gripped his hand with nary a complaint. What the deuce?

He helped her to the ground, then turned back to collect the other woman—yet no need. That lady shoved past him and flew from the chaise like a sparrow set free from a cage.

He jumped down after her, his boots sinking deep into the softened muck. Stretching out his arms, he shooed the women away from the road, toward the grassy bank, then gave them each a quick once-over for signs of injuries.

The wildcat stared back at him, quietly indicting him as a rogue, her brown eyes as dark as her scowl. She was a fighter, this one, which was a curious contradiction to her petite form. Or maybe not. Perhaps she'd learned at a young age to defend herself. Other than a swollen lip and the blood riding the curve of her cheek, she appeared to be unharmed.

He shifted his gaze to the bird woman who'd flown from the chaise. No cuts. No abrasions. Except for her rumpled gown, she looked well enough. But all the same, she doubled over, pressing one hand into her belly. "I'm going to be ill."

Samuel wheeled about and followed the crazed carriage tracks carved into the soft ground. Let the wildcat deal with her sick friend. It might work off some of her fury.

Ahead, the man he'd shot in the leg clutched his thigh, his moans an ugly blemish on the brilliant June morning. He tried to scramble away, but with that wound, he wasn't getting very far. The closer Samuel drew, the more frantic his thrashing and the louder his outrage.

"I'll kill ye for this! Ye hear me? Yer a dead man." Groans punctuated the blackguard's threats, rendering them moot.

Samuel reached for his neck cloth, and the man flinched. Samuel smirked. Not that he denounced the fellow for fearing a quick choking, but truly, if he had meant to kill him, the man would already be dead.

"Don't move," he ordered.

He crouched next to the grunting fellow and worked to tie the cloth around his leg, staunching the flow. "Who are you with?"

"I ain't talkin' to the likes o' you, ye filthy runner."

Samuel yanked the knot tighter than necessary.

"Shove off!" the man growled and followed his words with a host of vile epithets.

Rising, Samuel planted his feet wide and stared down at the villain, reminding himself that this was why he was out here. Stopping the wicked. Protecting the vulnerable. A noble endeavor. A needed one. But Lord, he was weary of it.

He turned his back on the scoundrel and continued following the ruts of the carriage wheels. Hopefully the man's partner yet lay in the dirt where Samuel had shot him in the leg. If he'd missed his mark and only grazed the fellow with a flesh wound, no doubt he'd already hied it out of there to attack again another day.

Squinting, he scanned the road as far as he could see. Just beyond a slight bend, a mud-splattered shape hunkered. This one not thrashing about. Who knew? Maybe this fellow would be more cooperative and talk—though it didn't really matter. Whether they admitted it or not, he'd wager his last breath these men belonged to Shankhart Robbins's gang. . .which meant that other members might very well be lurking close by. He upped his pace. It wouldn't be soon enough to his liking to haul in the pair and get the women to safety.

But his steps slowed as he drew near the other man, his gut twisting. Not so much as a twitch riffled the man's coat. No curses sullied the air. He didn't even turn his head to watch Samuel approach.

Something wasn't right.

Five yards away, Samuel stopped. Blood bloomed around a hole in the man's calf, where the gunshot had hit. Not a triviality, but also not an injury to keep down such a strapping fellow. Samuel's gaze followed the deep rut of the carriage wheel—right to where it dug into the man's neck. That hadn't been simply a nasty fall from the chaise door.

It had been a deadly one.

He stomped around to the other side of the body and stared into the empty eyes of the dead man. . .then blew out a long breath. By all that was holy, he truly might have a death warrant on his head for this. That glassy gaze belonged to Pounce Robbins.

Shankhart's younger brother.

Closing her eyes, Abby lifted her face to the sun and, for one sanctifying moment, gave in to its warmth while everything in her yet shook. Maybe this was naught but a dream. It might be, especially with all the talk of guns and highwaymen the night before. She could awaken at any moment to the grumbling of the carriage wheels as she had so often done over the past four days. Yes, of course. That was it. This was just a great, awful nightmare. Nothing more.

"He's coming," Fanny hissed. The maid's clammy fingers wrapped around hers, pulling her back to reality. "I told you we should've made a run for it."

Abby frowned at her maid. "And go where? We are no match for a man with a gun. It is better not to anger him. We shall lead him to believe we will cooperate. Then when help is near, we will flee."

The man in the black riding cloak strode toward the carriage, two lengths of rope coiled in his hand. He pulled something big behind him, and judging by the way he strained with each step, something quite heavy. Two objects, rather flat and long and rustling the grass. He stopped far enough away that she couldn't quite make them out, but they appeared to be man-sized.

"Turn around," he bellowed.

That didn't sound good. She didn't know much about men and violence, but it seemed one ought to always keep an enemy within sight. Just because he hadn't harmed them yet didn't mean he wouldn't. Summoning her courage, she lifted her chin and stared the man down.

"What are you going to do with us?"

His dark gaze met her challenge, the set of his jaw stating he'd not be trifled with. "I'll take you to the next inn. Now, do as I say."

She slipped a sideways glance at Fanny, whose brow wrinkled as much as her own. He'd take them to the next inn? As if he were naught but an escort instead of a highwayman? Or was that where he'd meet up with his gang and. . .

She swallowed. Better not to think beyond that.

"I'm waiting," he rumbled.

Fanny turned, and with a huff, so did she.

The man's heavy steps neared, the grass swishing and crackling beneath his boots. Closer and closer. Then his feet stopped. Some grunts. Thick breaths. A thud, accompanied by creaking leather on the back seat outside the chaise. And again. Then more footsteps—slowly fading.

Abby whirled to see the hem of the man's riding cloak swinging in the breeze as he stalked away.

Next to her, Fanny craned her neck toward the back of the carriage. "What did he. . . ?" She stepped closer, angling for a better view.

Abby planted her feet. Though trouble often had a way of finding her, there was no sense in hastening toward it.

"Why, it looks like— Oh! That's Mr. Shambles." Fanny spun, slapping a hand over her mouth. She darted back to the grass and once again doubled over.

Abby turned her back to the chaise, unwilling to witness whatever gruesome sight had sickened Fanny. Even so, the sounds of the maid's heaving and the thought of what she might have seen made her own stomach churn. With stilted steps, she approached Fanny and slowly rubbed circles on the woman's back. "It is going to be all right. We have to stay strong. Surely God is watching over us."

Her chest tightened. He was, wasn't He?

She shoved down a tide of rising doubt and rubbed all the more. "We cannot let that man know he frightens us."

Fanny stiffened beneath her touch. "I am frightened!"

"So am I, but if you show fear, it will only incite him." A bitter frown weighted her brow. How well she knew that truth, branded into her soul by a stepmother who thrived on fear.

Fanny shuddered one last time, then straightened.

Abby reached into her pocket and pulled out a handkerchief. Fanny had already ruined her own. "Here."

"Thank you, miss." The woman accepted her offering with shaky fingers and dabbed the corners of her mouth.

They both turned back to the road when boot steps thudded.

Without a glance their way, the black-cloaked fellow lugged past them a man bleeding from his leg. Vulgarities spewed out of the injured man's mouth, especially when he was hoisted atop a mount. The horse stamped and puffed a harsh breath, no happier than he.

Fanny edged behind her as the other man turned toward them and closed the distance with the stretch of his long legs.

He stopped near the door, the gleam in his dark eyes a wearied sort of dangerous. A crescent scar marred the skin high on his cheek near his left eye. Not surprising, for he'd certainly shown he was capable of violence. How many other marks did that riding cloak of his hide?

He tipped his head toward the carriage. "You ladies need to get in the chaise."

Abby shook her head. He could take them anywhere. Do anything, for he'd shown what he was capable of. But she'd be hanged if she made it easy for him. "We are not going with you."

He rolled his eyes and swung out an arm, indicating the bleeding man who was hog-tied on the horse. "I'm not one of these wretches. If I were, you'd be dead by now."

She gaped. That was supposed to be reassuring? "Surely you do not think I am naive enough to fall for such glib falsehoods."

His lips flattened into a straight line, and he reached inside his coat.

Fanny gasped. So did she. Had she pushed him too far? Would the barrel of a smoking gun be the last thing she saw on this earth?

Slowly, he pulled out a wooden-handled baton, brass at one end and ornamented with a small crown. Abby stared at the tipstaff. Could he truly be a lawman? Or had he stolen that from the body of one?

Her gaze drifted from the truncheon to the man's face. Nothing had changed in his fierce appearance—yet everything had. A gleam of pure veracity shone in his eyes. Not one speck of anything sinister swam in those brown depths. Not a jot of wickedness or cruelty. For the first time, she thought that maybe, perhaps, he could be trusted.

He jerked his head toward the open door of the carriage. "I am a Principal Officer operating out of Bow Street. Now get in the carriage. You're safe as long as I'm with you."

Safe? She trapped a retort behind her teeth. He may be an officer of the crown, but there was nothing safe about him.

Chapter Five

The Laughing Dog was a ramshackle hovel, barely clinging to the turf at the far end of the heath. It stood like a drunkard, leaning hard to the east, pushed cockeyed by wind and years of neglect. Samuel frowned as he stopped the carriage. This wasn't his first choice of refuge. It was his only one. Turning back to the Golden Cross would've doubled the time, and the next inn wasn't for another fifteen miles.

"Stay put," he growled at the villain on the horse next to his. Likely the command was unnecessary, for the ride had drained the fellow. He merely sat there, stoop-shouldered and ashen-faced, his trouser leg soaked with blood.

Samuel swung down into a thick patch of mud, and a scowl etched deep into his brow. A pox on Skinner for being such a cinch-purse of a proprietor. Two coins out of the innkeeper's profits would dump a load of wood shavings on this mess. And by doing so, perhaps more savory patrons would frequent the place instead of the usual riffraff that congregated beneath the inn's crack-shingled roof.

He rounded the side of the carriage, opened the door, and yanked out the stairs. Without a word, he lifted his arm and offered his hand. Silence proved best in dealing with frightened women, for they often read too many sinister meanings into the most innocent of remarks. And no doubt these women were frightened. They'd seen enough today to make a grown man's bowels turn to water. He coaxed his mouth into a semblance of a smile, especially when the wildcat peered down at him.

Her small fingers pressed against his as she descended. She'd tucked up her loosened dark hair, blown wild by the winds of the heath, but several curls refused capture and dangled free. Her gown was wrinkled, the hem caked with mud. Her crushed bonnet dangled from its ribbons like a dead cat down her back. She'd fit right in with the clientele of the Dog.

But despite her ruffled appearance, she smelled of lavender and something more. Something sweet. He inhaled as she swept past him. Citrus, perhaps? Orange blossom water, if he wasn't mistaken.

He lent his hand to the other woman, and then the wildcat turned to him. "Where are we?"

"North side of the heath, the Laughing Dog Inn."

"What is to become of us now?"

Oh no. He'd not fall for that one. Fluttering eyelashes were sure to follow. Then coy blushes and flattery. He'd seen it before. Women always got far too attached to whoever helped them in a time of need.

"That's up to you, miss."

He stalked toward the inn, his boots sinking into the mud. Lighter footsteps squashed and sucked behind him, the noise kindling a fire in his gut. These ladies should not be here, stamping through the filthy mire. Who in their right mind had sent them out on their own? Allowed them to travel without a manservant? Without any kind of protection whatsoever?

He shoved open the door with more force than necessary, and a belch of smoke from an ill-drafted hearth greeted him. Thin blue haze hovered below the rafters in the small room, stinging his eyes as he entered. Opposite a bar scarred from one too many knife fights, three tables graced the tiny public area. A single window shed light through sooty film. Even on a brilliant afternoon such as this, the Dog lived and breathed in perpetual twilight.

Samuel stalked past a man nursing a mug at the bar—or rather the mug nursed him. The tankard propped up his shaggy head as he snored with an open mouth.

"Skinner?" Samuel called.

A mousey man scurried out of the kitchen door. Skinner's shorn head and clipped beard resembled a pelt of grey fur. His clothes had been washed so many times they were now a perpetual shade of dingy. He twitched when he walked, and his voice squeaked in an off-key pitch. "Aye, Cap'n! Why, I ain't seen ye in awhiles. Got ye some pretties, have ye?"

He didn't have to look behind to know the women stood close at his back. Despite the smoky air, he breathed in a faint whiff of orange blossoms. "These ladies need a place to refresh. Give them your best. I'll need a bed and a surgeon for one man. A gravedigger for the other two."

Skinner cocked his head. "Hit a patch o' trouble, did ye?"

"You could say that."

The little innkeeper darted a look about the taproom, then jerked a step closer. "Were it Robbins?"

"One of them."

The man's eyes widened, black and beady. "Which one?"

"Pounce."

"Pounce!" Skinner jumped back. "Don't tell me I'll be housin' that devil."

"You won't." Thank God. The world would be a better place without that scoundrel. Samuel rolled his shoulders, working out a knot. "Pounce's thieving days are done."

Behind him, the ladies conferred in whispers—hard to make out with Skinner's low whistle filling the small room.

"There'll be a price on yer head, Cap'n. Shankhart will hunt ye down, and that's God's truth." Skinner's nose wrinkled. Were he truly a mouse, no doubt his whiskers would be trembling. "Ye know that, don't ye?"

Of course he knew it—and had since he'd first stared into Pounce's glassy eyes. "Won't be the first time."

"Always were one to live on the edge, eh?" The little man chuckled. "You be riding back today, Cap'n, or staying the night?"

"Depends upon what the surgeon says, how soon that villain out there can ride." He hitched his thumb over his shoulder. "Have someone haul him in, hmm? Oh, and send a lad to see to the ladies' belongings and to my horse."

Skinner's head bobbed. "Aye. I'll have Blotto heave in the ol' carp and the baggage, and I'll send my lad Wicket to tend yer mount. Set yerself down. I'll bring ye a whistle wetter while ye wait."

Samuel took the table in the corner, shoving the chair so his back would be against the wall. Pulling off his hat, he scrubbed a hand over his face, wiping off some of the grime, then winced as his fingers hit the sore spot on his jaw from the woman's kick. Lord, but his bones ached. His muscles. His soul. He was getting too old for this.

Heated whispers floated on the air, somewhere in the cloud just above the heads of the two women. Colour rose on each of their cheeks. Were they sisters? Cousins? Rivals or friends?

The wildcat shook her head then spun toward him. Her steps clipped on the wooden planks, little clods of mud breaking loose from her hem and littering the floor. She stopped at his table, her brown eyes a fierce sort of velvet, far too bold. And worse, far too comely. He shuddered inwardly at what Pounce would've done to such a beauty had he not come upon the scene.

She bobbed a small curtsey. "I wanted to thank you, sir, for your aid. I realize now that you are a noble man of integrity."

He studied her for a moment. What was she angling for with such flattery? Slowly, he shook his head. "No thanks needed, lady. It is my job."

"Even so, you have my gratitude. I am Abigail Gilbert, and this"—she lifted her hand, indicating the woman standing at her shoulder—"is my maid, Fanny Clark. Might I ask your name, sir?"

He stored the information in a mental file. Not that he intended to ever use it, but one never knew when a name might need to be retrieved. Leaning back in the chair, he eyed her, debating if he ought to part with his own name or ignore her. Normally, he didn't engage on such a personal level with those he aided—or anyone else, for that matter.

But then normally women tended to shrink from his scrutiny. Not this one. Miss Gilbert didn't flinch beneath the weight of his gaze, and in fact, tilted her head and stared right back as if she'd spent years facing dragons.

Unbidden, words flowed past his lips. "The name's Thatcher. Captain Thatcher."

"Pleased to meet you, Captain." Her lips curved into a pleasant smile. "I am wondering if, once you are refreshed, you would consider employment as our escort for the rest of our journey."

"The *rest* of your journey?" Sweet heavens! The little wildcat had narrowly missed death only hours ago, and now she was ready to continue on as if the experience had been nothing more than an afternoon ride through Hyde Park?

He set his jaw to keep from gaping. "Lady, you shouldn't be journeying anywhere. Go home, wherever that is. And this time, take a public coach. They are guarded."

The woman at Miss Gilbert's back nudged her, and though she spoke in a whisper, her words sprayed down on the wildcat's head like a curse. "I told you!"

Miss Gilbert brushed at the wrinkles in her gown, ignoring her maid's impertinence. Strange. Why would she do that? Most gentlewomen wouldn't suffer such cheek without censure. Samuel folded his arms, pondering the odd pair.

"Yet if you would consent to hire on as our escort, Captain Thatcher," Miss Gilbert continued, "then we would be guarded every bit as much as a public coach. Would we not?"

He stretched his neck sideways until it cracked, relieving a wicked kink—but it did nothing for the unease that the woman's determination stirred up. Could that same determination be the reason she'd been out on the heath undefended? He pinned her down with a direct stare. "Why are you out here alone, traveling without a manservant or any sort of protection?"

"As you can see, I am not alone." She swept her hand toward her maid. "And not that it signifies, but I am on my way to be married."

"That doesn't answer my question."

Her eyes flashed as if he'd probed too deep. A small satisfaction, that, for truth often welled from the deepest of cisterns.

"If you must know, Captain, at the last minute my family's

manservant was needed at home, and there were no more servants to spare."

He shoved down a grunt. Some family. Likely a brood of selfish rich toffs bent on meeting their own needs and forsaking those of others. But if they were wealthy. . .

He studied her all the more. "Why didn't your family hire a guardian, then?"

"Oh, well. . ." She fluttered her fingers—no doubt trying to distract him from the spreading flush on her face. "They have likely even now left for the continent. There was no time to acquire one before I departed. So you see, Captain, that I am in need of your services."

He smirked. She was an unwavering little firebrand, he'd give her that. Spunky too. Still, he shook his head. "No."

"But you have not yet heard my terms."

"'Ere we are, Cap'n." Skinner leaned around the women and thwunked a mug onto the table in front of Samuel, foam sloshing over the rim. "Be right with ye, ladies. Just scrapin' a bit o' muck out of a back room for ye. Got a pot o' tea on for ye as well, and being as yer friends o' the captain, I'll see if I can scare up a dainty or two to go along with it."

The innkeeper darted off before the ladies could reply.

Samuel collected his mug and slugged back a drink, secretly hoping the women would retire to a table of their own and reconsider taking a coach from here on out.

But Miss Gilbert didn't move. Not a whit. She stood there waiting, as if by merit of her presence alone he might change his mind.

He eyed her over the rim of his mug. "Go home, lady. It is foolish to travel alone."

She tilted her chin. "You will be paid handsomely, Captain. I can give you twenty-five pounds up front, and when you deliver me safely to my intended at Brakewell Hall in Penrith, he shall reimburse you another hundred pounds. Or more. What do you say to that?"

He choked, but not from the smoky air. One hundred twenty-five pounds? He didn't earn that in an entire year of hauling in cutpurses and killers. The sum was enough to not only buy the patch of land he desired but put up some outbuildings and purchase more seed than he'd need for two years. At a good pace, he could get them to Penrith in a little over a fortnight—which would also put a bit of distance between him and the heath. . .where Shankhart would be gunning for him.

The front door slapped open, drawing his gaze. Blotto, Skinner's man, wrapped a beefy arm around the highwayman's shoulders, shoring up the injured criminal as he stumbled across the floor. Reminded of his duty, a great glower pressed deep into Samuel's brow. As much as he needed Miss Gilbert's money, obligation to the crown came first—and that meant seeing the highwayman hauled into goal until a trial could be held.

He tossed back his mug, swallowing the last dregs. The aftertaste was bitter, both from the rotgut and from knowing how he must answer the lady. He reached for his hat, then stood and gazed down at her. "My answer is no, Miss Gilbert. Stay the night here, then take the coach first thing in the morning."

Her chin lifted ever higher. "Very well, Captain. You have been most helpful."

But the sparking gold flecks in her brown eyes and the taut line of her shoulders belied her words. If he didn't miss his mark, the woman had no intention of heeding his counsel. . .and he rarely missed his mark.

Sidestepping the ladies, he stalked off, more rankled than when he'd first entered the Dog.

The woman—Miss Gilbert—was entirely too much like himself.

Abby eased the hem of her gown off the taproom floor, tucking the extra fabric between her legs and the chair. Only God knew the origins of the oily brown residue near her feet. While she and Fanny had frequented a fair number of inns on their journey, the Laughing Dog was by far the foulest. Why had Captain Thatcher brought them here?

Her eyes watered and her lungs were beginning to burn, both from the smoke and from not wanting to breathe. The whole place smelled of cabbage gone bad. Very bad.

Seated across from her, Fanny folded her hands in her lap, the beginnings of a fierce frown brewing. For hours now, ever since the failed conversation with Captain Thatcher, her maid had made clear her stance on wanting to take the public coach back home. But each time Fanny brought it up, Abby refused to yield. Not that her opposition had stopped the woman, though. And now, as the maid leaned forward and parted her lips for yet another shot, Abby steeled herself to take the next round.

Thankfully, the proprietor skittered up to them, bearing two steaming bowls. "Here ye be, ladies."

Mr. Skinner set their meals on the crusty tabletop. Abby frowned at the washcloth tucked into the man's waistband. Did he not know how to use it? Or did he not own a chisel? For that's what it would take to chip away the dried remains fossilizing atop the table.

His face squinched into a broad smile, somehow making his pointed nose seem even longer. "Made this meself, I did. Thought you ladies might appreciate something other than a shank bone."

Abby smiled at the man's thoughtfulness. "Thank you, Mr. Skinner."

With a nod, he darted off, disappearing behind the bar where the broad backs of four men hunkered on stools.

Fanny took a bite, screwed up her face, then set down her spoon and shoved away her bowl. "You should have withheld your gratitude."

Abby couldn't help but sigh. The maid had been nothing less than tetchy since they'd arrived. "Oh Fanny, I know this has been a trying day, but are we not in God's debt for even a mean bowl of pottage? And should we not share that thankfulness with the hands that made it? After all, Mr. Skinner did go to the effort of preparing this especially for us."

"Go on, then." Fanny fluttered her fingers toward the bowl. "Take your own bite and see if your sentiment changes."

As Abby lifted her spoon, the rotted cabbage odour intensified, and suddenly she understood the source of the stench. Even so, she determined to give the stew a fair shot. But as the stringy broth landed in her mouth, it took all her willpower to swallow the swill and not spew it out.

Fanny cocked her head, arching an I-told-you-so brow. "Perhaps we should retire. The first coach leaves at dawn, so we'll have an early morning."

Abby set down her spoon. "We are not taking the coach."

"Didn't you listen to what the captain said earlier?"

"We have been over this before." Several times, actually. And with her shoulder yet sore from the crack against the side of the chaise, the repeated dialogue had made for a long afternoon. "Sticking to coaching routes will add over a week to our journey."

"I understand," Fanny clipped out. "But you'll have a whole lifetime with your baronet. Why the hurry?"

"Sir Jonathan is expecting me, and I cannot keep him waiting. Besides, if you were the one on your way to the man of your dreams, would you not also make haste?"

"Not if it cost me my life."

She couldn't stop the roll of her eyes. "Save your drama, Fanny. We have already crossed the most dangerous leg of our journey."

The maid threw up her hands. "And been accosted while doing so!"

"Yes, yet lightning does not strike twice in the same spot."

Three pairs of eyeballs turned their way from the nearest table, and Abby lowered her voice. "Listen, if it makes you feel any better, I will find someone to ride along with us. Surely Captain Thatcher is not the only available guardian for hire."

"That idea is even more dangerous than riding alone. Do you see the men in here?"

Her gaze slid around the ragtag collection of patrons gracing the taproom. Several stared back, interest gleaming in their eyes—the cold and calculating kind. A beast of a man in the corner looked as if, among other things, he wanted to kill her just for the pleasure of it. The rest were so busy wooing their cups, the walls could've collapsed around them and they'd never notice.

She pursed her lips to keep from sighing again—and to keep from admitting aloud that Fanny was right. Not one of these men would be suitable to hire. She and Fanny would be safer on their own.

Turning back to her maid, she curved her lips into a confident smile. "We shall simply travel on to the next inn and employ a manservant there. It will only be another fifteen miles or so on our own. After all, we have made it this far without a hired gun."

Slowly, Fanny shook her head. "While it pains me to do so, miss, if you refuse to take the public coach, I feel I must resign as your maid."

She stiffened. Surely she hadn't heard correctly. "What are you saying?"

"Unless you relent"—the maid pressed her hands onto the table and bent forward—"I will be forced to take the morning run back to Southampton and search for other employment."

Abby drew a sharp breath. "You would leave me to journey on alone?"

"Beg your pardon, miss, but I must. Your determination will not be my downfall." Pushing up, Fanny stood. Without a backward glance, the maid hastened across the small room and vanished up the stairwell.

Of all the arrogance! Abby gaped. Fanny had been the closest thing to a sister she'd ever had. . .and now even she would turn on her? Would this horrid day never end?

Across the room, a dark shape stepped out of the shadows. Captain Thatcher's burning gaze met hers, and her breath hitched, for he looked into her very soul. The man couldn't possibly have heard all that was said between her and Fanny, but all the same, she got the distinct impression that he knew—which both frightened and strengthened her in an odd kind of way. God had provided the captain at just the right time today. Surely He would continue to provide tomorrow.

Abby drove back her chair and rose. If Fanny wanted to return home, then so be it. As for her, she would travel on to the next inn and hire a guardian there. Whatever the cost.

Hopefully it wouldn't be more than she could afford.

Chapter Six

Morning fog muffled everything. The jingle of tack. The nickers of the horses. Even the loading of Fanny's baggage onto the coach was nothing more than a muted scrape followed by a subdued thud. Abby stood silent, watching the action with an equally dull gaze. It seemed like a death, this parting. How fitting that the mists of dawn distorted the world into the unnatural.

Turning to her, Fanny laid a hand on her sleeve. "Are you certain I can't persuade you to join me?"

A sad smile flitted across her lips. As much as she hated to see her maid go, there was no turning back. Not to a stepmother who despised her and half sisters that scorned. The scars of the past were still too raw and fresh, and she had a sinking feeling they would always be so.

Facing Fanny, she forced a measure of courage into her voice that she didn't feel. "I will not return home. Ever."

"Very well then, miss. May God bless you." Fanny's fingers squeezed her arm—and then she let go. "Goodbye."

The woman turned and fled up into the hulking coach before Abby could respond. Her throat tightened against a sob. It was a strange, wonderful, terrifying thing to lose this last connection to her past. So many conflicting emotions squeezed her heart that she could barely breathe. Of course she was doing the right thing. Wasn't she?

Am I, God?

Unwilling to witness the fog swallow her last glimpse of the coach, she whirled—then startled. A pace away from her stood Captain Thatcher, sporting a grim-set jaw and a gaze that penetrated even through the mist.

His eyes flicked from her to the retreating coach, then back. "Why are you still here?"

She chewed the inside of her cheek. How was it that this man could instantly make her feel as naught but an impish schoolgirl?

Stifling the urge to retreat a step, she smoothed her hands along the damp fabric of her skirt. "I will not be here for long."

His head lowered, and his dark eyes studied her from beneath the brim of his hat. "You should be on that coach."

His tone of authority rankled, as irritating as the cold moistness seeping in near her collar. Or was it the way he looked at her, as if his gaze alone could cut through any façade?

Despite the wrinkles she'd create, her fingers bunched handfuls of her gown. "Thank you for your concern, but I have rented a perfectly good traveling chaise, Captain."

He shook his head. "Lady—"

"I have a name, sir. It is Miss Gilbert, not *lady*." The words flew out before she could stop them. La! After all the years she'd spent mastering her tongue in front of her stepmother, why could she not tether her speech with this man?

One of his eyebrows raised. Barely. Had she angered him? Amused him? Given him reason to slap shackles on her wrists and haul her in? Hard to discern by the way his lips tightened into a straight line.

"Don't tell me you intend to journey on by yourself, *Miss Gilbert*."

Ignoring the way he pushed her name through his teeth, she lifted her chin. "I do not see how that is any of your business, for as I recall, you refused my employment."

He blew out a long, low breath. Were the man not already employed by Bow Street, he'd make a daunting head schoolmaster.

"Everyone who travels the roads hereabouts *is* my business. I cannot allow you to—"

"Thatcher! Thank God." The words boomed, nearly drowning out the muted thud of horse hooves and clinking of tack. A grey-cloaked man emerged from the fog astride a strawberry roan with a blaze on its nose. He slid from the saddle and clapped the captain on the back.

Abby used the distraction to whirl and scurry back to the inn. While the captain may be a man of integrity—though she wasn't quite sure of that yet—he certainly had a way of making her feel jittery.

Inside, behind the counter, the mousey barkeep glanced up at her entrance, his dark little eyes widening. "What, you still here miss? I thought ye and yer companion were off this morn."

"I am, or more like I shall be." She loosened the strings of the reticule secured to her wrist. "I should like to hire a postilion and inquire about a possible manservant as well. Someone well acquainted with the roads and able to use a gun."

"Well, miss. . ." The innkeeper paused to scratch a spot behind his ear, loosing a powdering of dandruff onto his shoulder—thank heavens it wasn't lice. "We're a small operation, ye see. Not a regular coaching inn. Still, I suppose I could part with my boy Wicket to ride ye to the Gable Inn, near abouts ten mile off or so, long as he's back afore dark. Can't rightly help ye with a manservant, though."

"I can." A deep voice rumbled at her back.

She clenched her jaw. Why had Captain Thatcher made it his duty to badger her into doing what he thought best? The man was more determined than her stepmother to have his way. She turned, prepared to confront him.

But cold, green eyes—lizard-like and unflinching—stared at her from beneath a shaggy set of brown eyebrows. A wiry man dipped his head toward her, not much taller than herself. He was all sinew and tendons. The type of fellow that could spring up the trunk of a tree before you knew he'd even thought to do so. She remembered him from the evening before as one of the men who'd slipped glances at her from his stool at the bar.

He touched the brim of his hat and gave a slight nod. "Ezra Thick at your service, miss. I heard you be needing a man to hire as guardian. I'm available, if you like."

Though this was what she'd wanted, every muscle in her tensed. He seemed polite enough, his speech respectful, but was it wise to hire a man to guard her when she didn't know if she ought to be guarded against him?

She glanced back at the innkeeper, hoping to find either acceptance or alarm at Mr. Thick's offer. But the mousey man had disappeared through a back door, apparently done with the both of them. She frowned. Surely if Mr. Thick were a rogue, the innkeeper would've warned her. . .wouldn't he?

She turned back to Mr. Thick. "You heard correctly, sir. I do need a manservant, but only until we reach the Gable Inn." Where hopefully she'd find a more respectable fellow. Her shoulders sagged. What if she didn't? Oh, why hadn't she hired Mr. Harcourt when she'd had the chance?

"Then I'm your man, miss. I know these roads like none other." He shuffled his feet, then lowered his voice. "I'll take my pay up front, though. No disrespect intended, but I've been cribbed a time or two."

Her reticule weighed heavy in her hands. If she gave him the full amount, what was to prevent him from simply running off? She fished around for only two coins and held them out. "I shall pay you half now and the rest when you see me safely to the Gable. Take it or leave it."

"Business woman, eh? I like that. I like it a lot." An oily smile slid across his face, and he snatched the gold from her palm. "I'll ready my horse and meet you outside. In the back."

Her heart sank as he bypassed her and vanished out the door. Had she made the right decision?

Samuel gritted his teeth as Officer Bexley's cuff on the back rippled through him from spine to ribs. The man didn't realize his strength—or his insubordination. Samuel let it slide, though. Despite Bexley's poor judgment, the fellow meant as much harm as an overgrown bear cub.

"It were a devil of a ride to track you down, Captain. Had me frettin' like a fishwife when you didn't check in last night." Bexley elbowed him, his blue eyes twinkling brilliant through the mist. "The boys were placing bets that ol' Shankhart had got to you."

"Waste of good money. Hold on." He pivoted to launch a final admonition for Miss Gilbert to reconsider taking the next public coach—only to find the patch of muddy ground empty.

He bit back an oath. Foolish, strong-headed woman! While she hadn't actually admitted she'd be traveling on alone, neither had she denied it. And if she did venture out unaccompanied, a comely young woman such as herself wouldn't stand a chance against any hot-blooded man crossing her path, cutpurse or not.

"What kept you, Captain?"

Despite his unease over Miss Gilbert, Bexley's voice turned him back to his duty. He'd have to see to the woman later.

"Two of Shankhart's gang accosted a carriage." Fog droplets collected into one big splash dripping from his hat down to his cheek. He flicked it away with the back of his hand, annoyed at the damp and the memory of the postilion's body lying dead on the heath. "One of the blackguards didn't make it. The other wasn't ready to travel—till now."

"Humph." Bexley pushed out his lower lip as he digested the information. "Then we'll haul him in together, eh?"

"Maybe." He wheeled about and stalked toward the inn, heels digging deep into the softened ground. He didn't need Bexley to hold his hand while bringing in a prisoner—and in truth, it might endanger his fellow officer's life. Word about Pounce Robbins's death could have already reached Shankhart's ears.

Bexley fell into step beside him, his horse clomping along at their backs. "What aren't you telling me?"

For the love of women and song! After serving so closely for the past eight years, Bexley knew him well. Too well. He upped his pace.

So did Bex. "You know I won't be put off so easily, Captain."

Just before the door of the Laughing Dog, he stepped aside, folded his arms, and faced the man. Better to hash this out here than in the taproom, on the off chance that what'd happened to Pounce hadn't been spread far and wide yet.

"Well?" Bexley's blue eyes searched his.

He looked away, to the eerie mist hovering over the land. It didn't bode well, this chill settling deep in his bones. "It's best if you turn around now. You shouldn't be seen with me on the heath."

But Bexley wouldn't give. Not an inch. The man merely widened his stance. "Why's that?"

It was more a grumble than a question. The tone he'd use himself had he ridden hell-bent across the heath with naught but leftover moonlight shrouded in a rising haze.

He swiped the brim of his hat, warding off any future drips. "It wasn't just any man I took down out there." He met Bexley's gaze. "It was Pounce."

Bexley spit out a curse, loud enough that his horse tossed its head and stamped a hoof. "As if Robbins didn't have enough reasons to kill you, you had to go and give him one more?"

Samuel stared him down, saying nothing.

"What a mess of rotten kippers." Bex blew out a long breath, his cheeks puffing. "Yet there's naught to be done for it now, I suppose. Tell you what, I'll take your brigand in myself. You stay put. Or better yet, move on a bit farther. Go north. Hie yourself up to St. Albans. Stay at the Gable Inn for a while. Give ol' Shankhart plenty of time and space to cool off."

His brows lifted. "Robbins, cool off?"

Another curse cut through the air. "Well, what then? Anything short of you crossing that stretch of land without an armed guard is suicide."

"I won't hide." He shrugged. "Nor will I endanger others."

For a moment, Bexley's jaw worked, then he turned aside and spit. Slowly, he ran his hand across his mouth. "Not surprised. And neither should you be when I say I'm going with you. You know Shankhart's penchant for cat-and-mouse torture. He'll toy with you if you're on your own. Play his wicked games. Drag it out before he strikes. The man ain't right in the head."

Bex folded his arms, leaving no room for argument. A bold move, considering Samuel outranked the man in seniority and position. Bexley was a brave one, he'd give him that. Occasionally foolhardy, yet one of the best on the squad. And he was right on all accounts about Shankhart.

Samuel gave him a sharp nod. "Suit yourself."

A smile slid across Bexley's face, and he looped his horse's lead around a nearby picket. "Come on, then. Let's have us a drink and be on our way."

Samuel squinted into the fog. The first half circle of a sun barely cut through the gloom. Hardly morning, and Bexley wanted to drink? Samuel shoved open the door to the Dog and held it for his friend. Still, he wouldn't think less of the fellow if Bex felt the need for a mug or two before they left. It would take a stout amount of courage for Bex to be seen with him when any manner of killers could be lurking in the mists, all mad-dog possessed to bring Samuel's head in to Shankhart.

Chapter Seven

Skirting the side of the inn, Abby clutched her small travel bag in one hand and, with the other, held the brim of her hat against a gust off the heath. Between the wind and the hazy outline of a half-circle sun now climbing on the horizon, the fog would be gone in no time. The first smile of the morning lifted her lips. Good. Clear skies would make for safer travel—for her and for Fanny. Wherever she was. *Oh Fanny. . .Godspeed to you.* As cantankerous as her former maid could be, Abby already missed the woman's banter. It would be strange to ride silent in the chaise.

Behind the Laughing Dog, the ground churned up in a sea of mucky gouges and rises. Several chickens strutted about, pecking earthworms too slow to take cover. Near the stable, the yellow carriage she'd rented stood at the ready. At the front of it, a lad bent, checking buckles on the horses.

Abby's smile slipped off as she approached him. The boy could be no more than ten, if that. Surely he wasn't the driver the innkeeper had assigned. Hopefully not, at any rate. "Excuse me, but could you tell me where to find Mr. Wicket?"

The boy straightened, a chip-toothed grin running pell-mell across his face. "Ha! That's a good one. Why, I'm Wicket, m'um. Ain't no mister about me. Not yet, anyways."

"Very well, Wicket." She forced a pleasant tone to her voice— quite the feat when the urge to rail against the universe welled up. Must everything about this journey be ill-fated? "I understand you are to drive me to the Gable Inn. Could you tell me how long of a ride I should expect?"

"Well. . ." His face screwed up, little wrinkles bunching his nose nearly into a bow. "Looks like this fog'll burn off. Roads might be a bit o' a slog yet, though. I reckon. . ." Apparently deep in thought, he angled his head, his lips quirking one way, then the other.

Abby couldn't help but smile at the boy's serious expression.

"I reckon," he continued, "near about two hours. Three tops. Which is good, since my pap expects me back by dinner. We'll be ready to go in a trice. Might wanna heft yerself up to yer seat."

"Thank you." Swiveling her head, she glanced about for the wiry Mr. Thick, but her hired manservant was nowhere to be seen. She turned back to the boy. "Excuse me, Wicket, but have you seen the gentleman, Mr. Thick? He is to accompany us."

"Oh! Aye." The boy smacked the heel of his hand against his brow. "Near forgot. He asked you to meet him in the stable."

She frowned at the odd request. "Whatever for?"

The boy shrugged, the movement dipping his flat cap down over one eye. "Somethin' about needin' to purchase more oats for his horse." He shoved the hat back into place. "Says ye must front him the coin afore we can leave."

Wicket pivoted back to the lead horse.

And a good thing too, for that way he'd be spared the glower that dug deep into Abby's brow. The nerve of the man! Asking for more money before they'd even left the Gable. Hefting her skirts, she stomped over to the chaise and hoisted in her bag, then whirled. She'd have to nip off Mr. Thick's beggarly ways here and now or suffer his continual petitioning until they parted ways.

Rounding the back of the chaise, she followed the edge of the stable. It was a long building, as windblown and leaning askew as the inn. She stopped just inside, breathing in horseflesh, leather, and the pungent odour of manure. "Mr. Thick?"

A stack of hay lining one wall muffled her query. To her right, the workbench sat unattended, assorted currycombs littering the top of it. She strode in farther and peered down the shadowy corridor of stalls, irritated that the man wasted her time by thinking to pinch more pennies off her. "Mr. Thick, are you in here?"

Far down in the dark recesses, something shuffled in the straw, followed by a low moan. A man's moan. . .Mr. Thick's. Abby huffed, feeling like moaning herself. Some guard she'd hired. How was he to protect her from ruffians if he couldn't keep himself from getting kicked or stamped on by a horse?

"Oof! My bleedin' foot."

Oh bother. Abby ducked back outside, intent on collaring Wicket to help her aid the man, but the boy was gone. The yard was empty, save for her carriage and the two horses.

Behind her, another moan leached out from the stable.

She blew out a sigh. There was nothing for it, then. She hurried back inside and darted down into the row of stalls. "Mr. Thick, are you—?"

A hand clamped over her mouth from behind. An arm wrapped around her stomach, pulling her backward, into an empty stall. Hot breath hit her ear. "One scream and I cut your throat, aye?"

Tears burned her eyes. Fear. Anger. Stupid! Why had she been so daft as to wander in here alone?

She managed a nod, barely.

"Good."

The hands dropped, and she spun. Mr. Thick's green gaze speared her in place, the whites of his eyes stark against the stable's gloom. He shoved out his palm, and she flinched.

"Now, I'll be taking the rest of that coin you've got jingling in your bag there." He indicated her reticule with the tip of a knife.

Her stomach clenched, the milk she'd taken with her breakfast curdling. What would she do without money? Mr. Thick's brows pulled into a solid line, his scowl deepening, and she trembled. Slowly, she unlooped the small bag from her wrist and handed it over.

A grin slashed across his face as he tucked her coins inside his greatcoat. "There. That weren't too hard, eh?"

She edged sideways, ready to make a run for it. Maybe if Captain Thatcher was still about, she could enlist his help to get her money back.

But Mr. Thick closed in on her, forcing her to retreat. Perspiration beaded on her forehead. He had his money. Why didn't he leave?

Mustering her spare reserve of courage, she lifted her chin. "Let me pass."

His grin grew, a macabre sort of grin, that which belonged carved into a gourd to frighten off evil spirits. "Not so fast, missy. A thank-you is in order, I think. Other men would've lifted far more than your coins." His gaze shot to her skirts. "But I'll only take a kiss."

He advanced, shoving her back against the stable wall.

"Please." Her voice shook, and she swallowed. "Don't do this."

He leaned in, running his nose along her neck up to her ear. "Mmm. You smell nice. All flowery and fresh."

A layer below her fear, a keen rage kindled. She'd put up with torment from her stepmother for so many years, and now that she was finally free of it, she'd be given even worse? No. *No!* Not if she could help it.

She snapped up her hand and dug her nails into his cheek, slicing lines across his flesh. His head jerked aside, and she bolted.

Only to be yanked back by her arm. He whipped her around and crushed her body against his. "So, you like to play rough, do you? Good." He rubbed his bloody cheek against hers. "I like that better."

Samuel followed Bexley into the taproom but only so far as the bar. Bex passed him up and settled at a table.

From his vantage point close to the door, Samuel swept a gaze from wall to wall, hoping to spy the green skirts of Miss Gilbert. He'd not quite finished with his admonition for her to take the next coach, though why he felt such a keen need to do so rankled him. Why should he care what the woman did or didn't do? He'd carried out his responsibility to her by seeing her safely to this inn. His obligation was finished.

Skinner scurried in from the kitchen door, caught sight of him, and darted over to his side of the bar. "Ye be needin' something, Captain?"

"A drink for my friend over there." He nodded toward Bexley. "And I'm wondering about the lady, Miss Gilbert, is she upstairs?"

"Nay." The man shook his head as he retrieved a mug. "She set out not long ago."

"Alone?"

"She hired a fellow to ride along."

Unease crept up the back of his neck. "Who?"

"Ezra Thick."

"And you let her?" The question roared out of him, drawing a raised brow from Bexley way across the room. Did Skinner not have a brain in his head? Ezra Thick was a known lecher!

The barkeep retreated a step, clutching the mug in front of him as a shield. "Weren't none of my nevermind, Captain. Besides, Wicket's driving. He won't let no harm come to the lady."

He squeezed his eyes shut for a moment. It was either that or lunge over the slab of wood and throttle the man.

Turning back toward Bex, he grumbled under his breath, "That boy doesn't even have chin hair yet."

Bexley's gaze cut from the barkeep to him. "What was that all about?"

Ignoring the chair Bexley kicked out, Samuel planted his feet. "Your offer to haul in my prisoner, does that still stand?"

"Aye. Why?"

"Something's come up."

Bexley pinched the bridge of his nose. "Why do I get the feeling this something will be more dangerous than if you invited Shankhart Robbins to tea? And even if you do take my suggestion and hole up at the Gable, he's got men from here clear up there and beyond to torment you."

He fixed the man with a pointed stare. "You worry too much."

Bex threw up his hands. "What do I tell the magistrate? When will you be back?"

"Not long." Hopefully. But the thought stuck in his gullet. His gut told him the lady might be more trouble than she was worth. "I'll send word from the Gable Inn."

Bexley's complaints followed him out the door. Nothing new. The man never agreed with the way he handled things.

But as Bexley's voice faded, a simmering fire kindled in Samuel's gut, burning hotter with each step toward the backyard. He didn't have time for this, truly. Instead of playing mother hen toward Miss Gilbert, he ought to be helping Bex haul in Shankhart's man. Snipe! The woman was a magnet for trouble, sticking her nose into things she had no business getting involved in. She could have no idea what Thick was capable of once he got her alone.

A yellow carriage stood ready to go in front of the stables, already mud splattered. Wicket, the barkeep's son, stood leaning with his back against it, a clay pipe sticking out of his mouth. As soon as the boy laid eyes on him, the pipe disappeared behind his back. Samuel rolled his eyes. He had bigger concerns than a lad bent on smoking.

The horses stamped at his approach. "Where is Miss Gilbert?"

"In the stable, Captain."

His frown deepened. "Why?"

Wicket shrugged. "She and Mr. Thick are havin' a few words afore we leave."

His earlier unease prickled over his whole scalp. Surely Thick wouldn't be so bold as to accost the lady here. . .though admittedly he'd seen stranger things.

Bypassing the boy and the carriage, Samuel strode to the stable door that gaped open near the end of the slap-hazard building. He entered the work area on silent feet and, finding it empty, paused and listened with his whole body.

Straw rustled down the confines of the horse stalls. Not unusual. But a muted cry was.

A lady's.

He took off at a dead run, pulling out a knife as he sprinted.

Four stalls down, he slowed, then peered around the edge of the next open pen. Two figures scuffled in the scant light. Shadows outlined the wiry frame of Ezra Thick, his body pressed tightly against a skirt. A green one.

Miss Gilbert's whimpers ignited a scorching rage in Samuel's gut. Were there no righteous men left on all of God's vast earth?

Without a sound, he crept into the pen. Then sprang. He grabbed Thick's arm and wrenched it behind the man's back, yanking upward until he felt a pop in the rogue's shoulder.

Thick roared and spun—which gave Miss Gilbert the opportunity to dart away.

With the lady out of the line of danger, Samuel raised his knife—just as Thick lunged with his own blade. But too late. With a wild swing, Samuel cracked the hilt into Thick's skull. Ezra's knife dropped. So did his body.

Chest heaving, Samuel turned to Miss Gilbert. Her hat was askew—again. Several locks of dark hair hung ragged against her cheek. Blood marred the pale skin of her cheek, but judging by the transparency of the smear, it was not her own. A torn collar on her spencer and a missing button appeared to be the sum of Thick's attack. Outwardly, at any rate. Lord knew what kind of anguish was going on behind those brown eyes. The lady stood still as a pillar, save for the slight ripple of her skirts. She stared, wide-eyed and unblinking, like a lost little girl. Did she even see him?

Slowly, he tucked away his knife, then held up his hands. "You're safe now. See?"

A shudder ran the length of her. "Yes," she whispered, then she straightened her shoulders and lifted her chin, drawing from some hidden reserve of bravery. "And I am in your debt, once again. Thank you."

He lowered his hands, surprised at her show of strength. Most women would've plowed into him by now and soaked his shirt through with their tears. Despite her small stature, this one was a fighter—which he admired and pitied all in the same breath.

"Come." He swept his hand toward the open gate. "Let's get you out of here. You have a carriage waiting."

She advanced a few steps, then hesitated at the side of Thick's sprawled body. What the devil? Quick as a flash of ground lightning, she bent and snatched a small bag out of the man's pocket.

Samuel quirked a brow. Not that it was surprising Ezra had purloined the woman's coins. No, it was Miss Gilbert's boldness that stunned. Though it shouldn't have, considering her determination to continue her journey alone after yesterday. What a curious lady, indeed.

He led her out of the stable and into the first true light of morning.

"You were right, Captain." She peeked up at him. "I should have taken the coach. I tremble to think what might have happened had you not stepped in."

So did he. Yet chastising her now would only add to the shame in her voice. He cleared his throat, unsure of how to encourage her. "You did the right thing in hiring a manservant. You just happened to choose the wrong man."

Nearing the open door of her chaise, he turned to her. He might regret what he was about to say, but then he stockpiled regrets as avidly as some men collected fine paintings. "I know someone for hire at the Gable Inn. Someone I'd trust with my life. I will take you there."

Chapter Eight

Samuel swung off Pilgrim and patted her on the neck. The mare's flesh was warm, but not sweaty. She bobbed her head, then tossed him a saucy look, her front hoof stamping the ground. After this morning's leisurely pace, she was anxious for a real leg stretcher, not a rest stop at the Gable Inn.

"I know." He gave her a final clap. "Not much of a ride, eh girl? And thank God for that."

An ostler approached, nodding a welcome. The young man was so lean, he was hardly more than a collection of twigs wrapped together in a shirt and trousers. Either Hawker was working his men hard or the inn didn't include meals with their wages.

"See to your horse, sir?"

He handed the fellow Pilgrim's lead. "Have her ready in an hour. Oh, and tell me, is James Hawker still the stable master here?"

The man blinked at him. "Aye, sir."

He gave the fellow a nod of his own, then turned at the sound of carriage wheels crunching along the gravel. Miss Gilbert's yellow traveling chaise, dappled with mud and listing to one side on the uneven ground, halted in front of the Gable.

Before the postilion Wicket could dismount, Samuel strode to the door and flipped down the stairs. Lord knew if the boy would even think to perform such a nicety before scampering off for a draw on his pipe.

The lady grasped his outstretched hand, her grip firm as she worked her way down. Her hair no longer hung to her shoulder, which strangely felt like an unaccountable loss. Her spencer was straightened. Her gown smoothed. And when she turned to him, the wild look in her brown eyes and heightened colour of her cheeks had all calmed. Apparently Miss Gilbert had used the placid ride to her advantage.

Late-morning sun, having burned off the earlier fog, shone brilliant against her smile. "Thank you, Captain. I suppose this is where we part ways." She loosened the strings of her reticule and fished out some coins. "I am much indebted to you. Will this cover your service?"

He shook his head. "No payment required."

Gold flecks of determination flashed in her brown eyes. "But I insist."

"As do I." He closed her fingers over her offering. While the few coins would be a boon toward buying his piece of land, it didn't feel right taking her money. He'd long been meaning to get up here to see Hawker. Too long. Miss Gilbert's need had been a means to that end.

He pulled away. "Use your money to purchase some refreshment while I arrange for a guard to see you to Penrith."

"But I. . ." Whatever opposition she'd intended to lob at him blew away on the next gust of wind.

Her gaze met his, direct and unwavering, and the thought struck him like a slap that this might be the last time he ever saw the woman. That rankled. . .yet why the devil should it?

She raised her pert little chin. "I thank you, Captain Thatcher. For everything. God bless you in your service. You are a good man."

He sucked in a breath, her praise stunning and pure—heating him in places he never knew were cold and barren.

Shoving her coins back into her small bag, she whirled and crossed to the front door of the inn, her green skirts swaying. He couldn't help but smile as she marched off alone into the unknown. He watched until she disappeared into the Gable, and curiously, for a few moments after.

Lifting his hat with one hand, he raked his fingers through his hair, then stomped to the back of the inn. Soon, Miss Gilbert would be nothing more than a memory, and the thought stuck sideways in his craw.

Behind the Gable, a long, wood-and-stone structure lined one side of the big yard, large enough to house horses and coaches alike. Several outbuildings dotted the rest of the perimeter. Samuel glanced about for Hawker. By the inn's back door, a few workmen bantered near a barrel. Crossing the yard, two fellows hefted a large pail between them, but neither sported a shock of red hair beneath their caps. A maid hurried past him, an armful of wildflowers cradled close to her chest.

But no Hawker.

No surprise, really. His friend was likely in the stable. Samuel swept through the big open doors, and after a thorough search and several queries, he again turned up nothing. Odd, that. Why was the man not seeing to his duties?

Back outside, Samuel followed the length of the barn to a small lean-to added onto the end, situated on the side nearest the horse pen. He rapped on the door. "Hawker?"

No answer, but the door edged open a bit. The stench of rum and bodily waste wafted out.

Samuel eased through the narrow opening. Dim light angled in along with him, cutting a triangular swath and exposing a broad-shouldered lump hunched over a bottle-strewn table. The man didn't move. Didn't see. Didn't hear. His meat-hook hands cradled his head—a head topped with coppery hair.

Samuel's throat closed. The strong stench of spirits and urine in the small room went down sideways and unearthed ugly memories. Change the man's hair from red to dirt and Samuel was an eight-year-old boy again, sneaking away from his drunken father before another beating ensued. Thank God Hawker didn't have a son of his own on which to take out his demons.

"Hawker!" The name flew out harsher than he intended.

"Wha—?" Like a lazy lion, the big man's head swayed as he looked up. His eyes narrowed to slits, then widened. "Well, I'll be a pig's uncle. Thatcher? Can it be?"

Leastwise that's what he might've said. Hard to tell with all the slurring.

Samuel frowned. "Aye. It's me."

"Come. Come!" Hawker reached for the bottle near his elbow. "Have a drink, for pity's sake."

In three strides, Samuel snatched the bottle away. "What's gotten into you?"

"'Bout a pint o' rum. Mebbe more." A belch rumbled out, and Hawker dragged his sleeve across his mouth. "Not less, though."

Setting the bottle down—well beyond the man's reach—Samuel grabbed a chair and sat opposite his old friend. He'd known the man to imbibe on occasion, but never like this. Not during the day. And especially not when he should be working. "What's happened?"

Hawker swiped for a different bottle, tipped it up and found it empty, then glowered and threw the thing to the floor. Glass crashed. Hawker roared an obscenity. "You wouldn't understand."

Samuel leaned back in his seat. "Try me."

Hawker reached for another bottle—and Samuel blocked his hand.

The resulting scowl could've stopped a battalion of armed dragoons. Hawker's red-rimmed eyes pierced him through. "You ain't no saint."

"Never claimed to be." With a sweep of his arm, Samuel knocked all the bottles to the floor, done with the man's antics. "And I'll have the truth of what's put you into such a sorry state. Now."

Hawker shot to his feet, his big hands curling into fists.

Reaching for his knife, Samuel bolted up as well. He'd hate to hurt his old friend, but the man outweighed him by at least seven or eight stone. And with the liquor skewing Hawker's mind, there was no telling what the crazed bull might do.

Hawker growled, enlarging the red veins in his eyes. His jaw worked for quite some time, his Adam's apple bobbing in his throat. But eventually, the man slumped back into his chair, and a single word oozed out of him like a draining sore. "Tia."

"Tia?" Samuel couldn't help but repeat it. Was that drunken babble or some sort of code word he didn't remember from their service days? Regardless, he tucked away his blade and reclaimed his chair.

"Wish to God I'd never. . ." Hawker's eyes glistened, and two fat tears broke loose. Before long, the man dissolved into a blubbering mess.

Samuel stared, dumbfounded. A charging Hawker he could deal with, but this? What was he to do with this weeping, rum-soaked wreckage? His gaze drifted to the ceiling, and he lifted up a desperate prayer.

God, grant me some wisdom here.

He leaned forward, and employing the same voice he'd used to calm the women the day before, he pulled encouragement from years past. "Remember that time back in Poona? Those were the days, eh Hawk? I thought I was done for when the Peshwa's forces captured me."

Hawker stilled.

Good. This might work. Samuel continued, "But then you came, sporting nothing but a crack-barreled Bess and a six-inch blade. . .that and your own blazing boldness. Ahh, but you were a force to be reckoned with."

With a shudder, Hawker pulled his big hands from off his face and stared into space.

Samuel rolled up his sleeve, the movement drawing his friend's gaze, and pointed at a jagged scar on his forearm. "I made it out of that hell hole with naught but this, and all because of you. You, Hawker. So pull yourself together, man. Whatever's happened to you, you're better than this. You hear me?"

Slowly, Hawker shook his head. "Not this time," he drawled. "You don't understand. Florentia was my world. My everything."

Sudden understanding washed over him. Of course. He should've known this kind of breakdown was because of a woman. He shoved down his sleeve, keeping his voice low and even. "Tell me about her."

"Tia?" Hawker's face lit, and a sad smile rippled across his lips.

"She were light and air. A regular flower, she was. Married her, a year ago now."

"You? Wed?" So, it *had* been longer than he'd reckoned since he'd seen Hawk. This big oaf was the last man he'd expect to settle down. He scrubbed a hand over his face. "I never thought to see you take vows."

"Din't think to, not at first, not till a child were on the way." Hawker's face folded, and for a moment Samuel feared the man's tears would flow again.

Hawker cleared his throat. Several times. "Tia died in childbirth."

Samuel sat silent, refusing the platitudes or prayers others might offer. Nothing he could say would bring the woman back. Fix what wasn't fixable. His years on the force had beat that lesson into him time and again.

Lord, grant mercy to this man.

"You know what I wish?" Hawker rasped out. "I wish I'd told her I loved her more. Wish I'd held her in my arms every chance I could, kissed her sweet lips as if it were the last time. Oh God, if I'd known we'd have only those few short years together, I'd have made *every* minute count. Every last one. I'd have spent less time with the horses and more precious hours with her."

Hawker leaned forward, his eyes burning embers. "Promise me, Thatcher! Promise you won't do the same. When you find a woman you love, you'll not waste one second. You'll go after her with all your heart because one day, ahh, one day. . .it will be too late, and you'll be left with nothing but regrets."

Slowly, Samuel nodded, storing away the man's advice, though he'd likely never need it. "Aye."

"Good. Good. . ." Hawker's words trailed off, and he stared into nothingness, memories flinching across his face. Samuel waited him out. He'd come around, eventually.

With a great inhale, his friend finally rolled his shoulders and refocused on Samuel. "Well, don't s'pose you rode all this way to hear me bawl. What are you here for?"

He blew out a long breath. There was no way he could ask his old friend to accompany Miss Gilbert, not with a grief so large and a powerful thirst to drown it out. Blast! Hawker had been the one—the only—man he'd recommend Miss Gilbert hire.

Samuel clenched his jaw, shutting down the host of ugly words begging for release. Suddenly he knew how Jonah felt, prodded into a mission he never wanted to take in the first place. But was this a task from God or a fool's errand?

He leaned back in his chair, considering seriously for the first time the possibility of guarding Miss Gilbert. The money would be more than enough to buy his land. He knew the route. The magistrate would understand his need to avoid the heath until Shankhart cooled down.

So why the foreboding deep in his gut? He curled his hands into fists, fighting the urge to pick up one of Hawker's bottles and guzzle a swig. Somehow he knew, without a doubt, that if he took on the guardianship of Miss Gilbert, it would leave a mark. A deep one.

But if he didn't, that would leave the lady—clearly prone to attracting trouble—to travel on her own.

Rock. Stone wall. And Samuel between.

Pushing back his chair, he stood before he changed his mind. "I'm on my way to Penrith. Thought I'd stop by, but time's wasting. Till next time, Hawk. And lay off the—"

"Penrith?" Hawker bolted out of his chair and advanced so fast, Samuel couldn't reach for his knife.

"Say you'll go through Manchester." The big man grabbed him by his shoulders. "Say it!"

This close, Samuel choked on Hawker's stench. "I could, I suppose," he eked out.

Hawker's hands dropped. So did his eyelids as he lifted his face to the rafters. "Thank You, God."

Samuel clenched his jaw to keep it from dropping. Hawker praying? Something big was up for that man's crusty soul to seek the Almighty. "Why Manchester?"

"My sister lives there." Hawker's gaze met his. "I need you to see my sister."

All this for a family member? Was the woman near death? Samuel narrowed his eyes. "What for?"

"I've got something you need to bring to her. Something I can't. . . Oh God, I can't." Hawker's eyes watered again. "Promise me. Promise!"

Gunshot. Wails and screams. Cannon fire and shouted orders all barreled back from his time in the Indies. Samuel swallowed down the memories. He owed this man his very breath. Whatever it was Hawker wanted him to bring to his sister, how could he refuse after Hawker had saved his life? "All right, you have my word. What is it you want me to deliver?"

Once again, the man's face crumpled, horrific pain etching lines into his brow. Hawker shuffled like an old man over to the only other door in the room and shoved it open. "In here."

Samuel strode to the small chamber, but when his feet hit the threshold, he stopped. Unable to move. Unable to breathe.

In the center of the room sat a cradle, the child inside it bouncing and mouthing on a dried crust of bread. A dirty pink cap dipped low over one of the baby girl's big blue eyes.

Cold sweat broke out on Samuel's forehead. Instantly he was ten years old again. . .the day he'd said goodbye to his little sister.

Forever.

The sweet scent of fresh pastry greeted Abby as she stepped into the Gable Inn. Pausing just inside the doorway, she breathed deeply. Quiet chatter and the tinkle of teacups set to saucers filled the large public room. Sunlight peered through the mullioned windows, bathing the patrons in a cheerful brilliance. Now this was how an inn should be run. The Laughing Dog could learn a thing or two from this establishment.

One of the liveried servants approached her, his blue topcoat and beige waistcoat both ironed crisp and not a stain marred the fabric. "May I help you, miss?"

"Some tea, please."

"Of course. Follow me." He wound a path around the other diners, leading her to a small table in the back corner, perfect for one. He held out her chair, and when she sat, he asked, "Perhaps a slice of gooseberry pie as well, miss?"

She smiled. Who could say no to that? "Yes, thank you."

While she waited, her gaze drifted around the room and landed on a couple near the window. Judging by the way the man leaned forward and whispered tenderly to the lady, they were clearly newly wed. A pretty shade of red bloomed on the woman's cheeks. She gave him a playful swat on the arm, her laughter merry amidst the din of low conversation. His gaze held hers as if she were the only one in the room. His dearest love. His own. Abby's chest squeezed. Soon that would be her. Sir Jonathan murmuring intimate endearments for her ears. Her feigning embarrassment while cherishing his words. His look of complete adoration—for her alone.

"Here you are, miss." The servant appeared with a thick slice of pastry and a steaming pot of bohea.

"Thank you."

She picked up her fork, but after her first bite, she nearly called the fellow back to *really* thank him. The crust melted on her tongue, and the sweet yet tart filling blended into a heavenly mixture. After the terror of yesterday, this was a welcome change. Things were definitely starting to look up.

Soon only crumbs remained on her plate. Not long after, she drained the teapot as well. The couple near the window departed, as did the other patrons, leaving her in an empty room. Glancing at her watch, Abby frowned. Nearly an hour had passed. Ought not Captain Thatcher have arranged for her new manservant by now?

She pushed back her chair, about to go look for him, when the blue-coated waiter approached her once again.

"You're wanted outside, miss."

She gnawed the inside of her lip. Why hadn't Captain Thatcher come to retrieve her himself? Better yet, should he not have brought her new guard in here to discuss traveling details and expectations? Being summoned like a common criminal wasn't very orthodox—or courteous—but truly, having spent the past twenty-four hours in the captain's company, was it any surprise?

"Very well. Thank you." She paid for her refreshments then traded the dining room for the brilliance of the June afternoon. Her chaise stood in the yard, horses hitched, a thin man checking the buckles on a harness. Captain Thatcher's bay stood nearby as well. But that was it. No other horses and no new manservant.

She strode over to the scarecrow of a postilion, for there was no one else around who could have possibly summoned her. "Pardon, but did you wish to have a word with me?"

The fellow turned, the sharp bones of his face looking as if they might break through his skin. "It weren't me, miss. I believe it were him." He tipped his head, indicating the yard behind her.

She pivoted. Marching across the gravel, boots pounding and face shadowed by the brim of his hat, Captain Thatcher advanced like a man set for battle—holding out a small child in front of his body like a shield.

Abby cocked her head at the curious sight. "Captain?"

"Here." He pressed the baby against her, so that she had no choice but to grasp the wriggling child.

"Why are you handing me. . . ?" Her question faded as she held the youngling up, face-to-face. Deep blue eyes sparkled wide above chubby cheeks. A smudged pink bonnet sat askew on her head, a few wisps of downy reddish hair peeking out. The little girl kicked her feet and cooed, her cherry lips parting into a huge smile. Five pearly teeth appeared on mostly barren gums, three on the bottom and two up top. She couldn't be quite a year old yet, but was likely close to it. One plump hand reached out and snagged a piece of Abby's hair. The girl giggled, and Abby's heart melted. "What a sweet darling!"

Captain Thatcher grunted. "Her name is Emma."

Abby lifted a brow at the man. "What is this about, Captain?"

His gaze met hers, his thoughts unreadable behind his dark eyes.

"I've decided to accept your offer to see you safely to Penrith, with a brief stop at Manchester along the way."

"That's—oh!" Little fingers yanked her hair, the sharp pain as stunning as the captain's declaration. She pried open the babe's clenched fist and flung back the loose tendril, then speared Captain Thatcher with a pointed stare. Hundreds of questions bombarded her, but only one sailed out. "Why?"

He shrugged as if she were a half-wit. "That's where I'm to deliver the child."

Until this moment he couldn't be bothered with escorting her, and now he wanted to take on both her *and* a child? She frowned. "Why the sudden change of heart?"

From this angle, light accentuated the strong cut of his jaw, stubble darkening the length of it. A muscle jumped on his neck, yet he said nothing. What on earth was he thinking?

Finally, he spoke. "You need me, and I need the money."

No shame rippled at the edges of his words. He didn't even bat an eye. The captain's blunt manner, while refreshingly honest, was astounding.

The girl wriggled, her little hands grasping for more hanks of hair. Abby turned the baby to face the captain. A delighted squeal cut the air, and the child bounced up and down. Suspicion curled through Abby like a waft of smoke. Did he need the money to hire someone to pay for the child's care—*his* child's care?

"Is this child yours, Captain?"

"No!" Despite the denial, red crept up his neck, and he cleared his throat. "Emma belongs to the stable master here at the Gable. I owe him a favor, and it's his wish the girl be delivered to his sister. That's all. So do we have a deal or not, Miss Gilbert?"

The babe swiveled her head side to side, squirming for release—and driving home the scope of what Captain Thatcher was asking of her. Abby gripped the girl tighter before Emma slipped from her hands. When her sisters were little, she'd looked after them on occasion, but this was a far different venture. She'd be a nursemaid, trapped inside a chaise with a wiggly bundle of energy all the way to Manchester, which had to be nearly two hundred miles from here. By the time she finally made it to Sir Jonathan, she'd be a wreck. No, this was out of the question.

She shook her head and held out the child. "I think not. Perhaps you ought to find someone else to accompany you, as will I."

He gathered the girl with one arm, the child looking impossibly small and fragile next to his worn riding coat. Was he disappointed? Angry? Frustrated? Hard to decipher with that even stare of his.

"Good day, then, Miss Gilbert. I bid you Godspeed." Wheeling about, he stalked to his horse. He shifted little Emma to his other arm, clutching her tight to his chest, then reached up to the saddle with his free hand and hoisted them both atop the big chestnut bay.

As the captain settled her in front of him, the girl's mouth opened wide, and a wail crescendoed into a screech—cutting sharply into Abby's heart. It would be a cruel ride for so young a child to travel on naught but horseback. Abby gnawed the inside of her cheek. Should she let the rough-and-tumble captain fend for a little one on his own for so long a distance? Was it really any of her concern? Or had God put her here for such a time as this?

Frustration and guilt nicked her conscience, and she stifled a wince. Truly, she'd be no kinder than her stepmother to ignore such an outright need.

"Wait!" Against her better judgment, she gathered up her skirts and dashed over to Captain Thatcher. She might regret this later, but for now, it seemed the right—the *only*—thing to do.

She lifted her hands. "It appears, sir, that you need me as much as I need you. Hand Emma down and let us be on our way."

Chapter Nine

Abby fought a yawn and shifted on the bench in the entryway of the White Horse Inn. It wouldn't be too soon to lay her head on a pillow this night—if Captain Thatcher could secure her a room. Though this particular coaching inn boasted three floors of lodgings, judging by the hubbub of horses and people in the front yard and the loud chatter floating out from the public room, many others sought a night's stay here as well.

She glanced down at the child in the basket next to her on the bench. Long lashes fanned against cherub cheeks. Good. Asleep at last. While little Emma was a pleasant child and had already wormed her way into Abby's heart, her suspicions had been correct. The girl had squirmed about in the carriage all afternoon, eager to explore every last inch of it, with a particular interest in pulling herself up to the window. Absently, Abby rubbed the sore muscles in her left forearm, the one that had repeatedly shot out to catch Emma before the youngling toppled headlong to the floor. The child would be walking in no time—and then trouble would begin in earnest.

Stifling another yawn, Abby pressed her fingers to her lips and lifted her face. Captain Thatcher stood in front of her, and her breath caught. How did he do that? Appear without a sound? The man was more ghost than human.

He held out a key. "Last room."

A frown weighted her brow as she accepted his offering. "And you?"

His dark eyes flashed. "Didn't want to leave my horse anyway.

Come. There's an open table."

He strode off before she could comment. She picked up Emma and followed his black riding cloak into a boisterous taproom, the weight of her charge slowing her somewhat. He led her to a table in the back of the room, nearest the door where servants buzzed. Abby took the chair farthest from the opening and tucked Emma between her and the wall, praying that the babe would continue to sleep.

Captain Thatcher dipped his head toward her. "Good night, then."

Her jaw dropped as he turned to go. "Wait! Will you not dine with me? And see me to my room?"

He glanced over his shoulder, the shadow from the brim of his hat hiding most of his face, but there was no mistaking the distinct disapproval in the tone of his voice. "I don't think that would be a good idea, Miss Gilbert."

The babe rubbed a fist against her cheek and squirmed in the basket—though her eyes remained closed. For now, at least. Yet there were no guarantees. Abby's stomach cramped when a waft of stew hustled by, clutched in a servant's hands. Were Emma to wake, dinner would be impossible.

"Please, Captain. At least stay until I have had a few bites to eat, in case Emma awakens."

He stood still a moment longer, a statue in the midst of the humming activity. Before she could blink, he dragged the table away from the wall and scraped a chair behind it, sitting with his back against the stones. . .as far from Emma as possible.

Abby couldn't decide if she should thank him for staying or ask the cause of such skittishness. In the end, she chose neither and remained silent. She could only hope Sir Jonathan wouldn't be as restless around babes—but of course he wouldn't be, or he'd not have asked for her hand in the first place. Marriage was always the precursor for children. No doubt Sir Jonathan wanted as many little ones as she.

A waiter approached, his apron straining around a potbelly. Apparently the food at the White Horse was good. "Evenin' sir, lady." He nodded toward them both. "We've got a nice kidney pie with mash on the side. Or Cook's made a lovely dish of boiled swedes and roasted up some stubble goose. Can't go wrong with either one. So, what's it to be?"

Abby's mouth watered. "Pie, please."

"The same," Captain Thatcher said.

The waiter dashed off, leaving them alone in a room full of chattering diners. Abby watched the merry travelers, raising glasses and sharing banter. Captain Thatcher watched them as well, but considering the guarded clench of his jaw, he didn't see the same cheer. And for some reason, a great sadness draped over her shoulders. How many burdens did this man carry? What had he seen in all his years to make him so hesitant to smile? A curious desire welled to be the one to put a grin on his face, to lighten the heavy weight—whatever it was—that he carried.

"So, Captain." She curved her lips upward, as if he might follow her example. "How long do you figure until we reach Brakewell Hall?"

His gaze continued roaming the taproom even when he answered. "Little over a week, God willing."

Her brows shot up. *God* willing? This rugged man, lantern light even now glinting off the gun handle peeking from inside his coat, professed such faith? "I did not take you for a religious man."

"In my line of work, you run either from God or toward Him."

Of course. By necessity, being an officer would mean he'd seen things—and likely done things—better left unspoken. Perhaps that was the cause for his restrained personality.

"It must be dreadful," she murmured. "Always seeing the worst in humanity."

His dark eyes shifted to her for a moment before resuming surveillance of the room.

"Have you any family, Captain Thatcher?" The question flew out before she could stop it, and she pressed her lips shut. It wasn't any of her business, not really.

But if he thought her curiosity forward, he didn't let on. He merely said, "No."

She studied him closer, noting for the first time the frayed collar on his dress coat, the missing button on his waistcoat. His shaggy hair was in need of a good trimming, and his skin had the weather-worn look of a man who spent far too much time in the sun. Then it dawned on her. This was a man who had no home to welcome him. No arms to hold him when the brutality of his job got to be too much.

Her heart squeezed. "How lonely for you."

"Loneliness is a state of mind, nothing more."

She leaned back in her chair, astonished by his sentiment. Did he really believe his own words? "Well, thankfully, I will not have time for such a '*state of mind*,' as you put it, but rather one of happiness and fulfillment once we reach Penrith. Sir Jonathan Aberley and I are to be wed straightaway."

His gaze shot to hers, an indecipherable gleam burning deep in his dark eyes. "Is that so? Tell me, how long have you known this man? This *Sir* Jonathan Aberley?"

He spit out the title like a piece of rotted mutton. Did he carry a grudge against the gentry?

She offered a smile to the waiter as he set a mug in front of each of them, and waited until he scurried off before answering. "I met my intended at a ball earlier in the spring."

He snorted then slugged back a drink. "That can't be more than a few months ago. I suspect, lady, that you have no idea what you're getting into."

She clenched her jaw, trapping a retort—a skill she'd honed and employed often with her stepmother. The nerve of the captain. He was the one with no idea of what lay ahead of her. She straightened her shoulders, intent on educating him. "May I remind you, sir, that my name is not '*lady*,' and the truth is that as a baronet, Sir Jonathan is a very busy man. He doesn't have time to waste, so it is no surprise our courtship is a whirlwind."

"Courtship, you say?" The captain folded his arms. "Your man is up north in Penrith. You are coming from the south. How much of a courtship could you have possibly had?"

Her stomach turned—and this time not from hunger. He was right, and that chafed. She straightened on her chair, careful not to bump the basket near her feet. "Admittedly it has not been much of courtship, what with the distance. Yet it is not the length of the relationship that matters, but the depth. Do you not agree?"

His lips twisted into a semblance of a smile. "I suppose you expect to live happily ever after, then."

"I do. Oh, of course I know there shall be hardships, mind you, but with Sir Jonathan at my side, I am certain we shall face each trial as a united front."

"Really." He unfolded his arms as the waiter set down a plate in front of each of them, and when the man had departed, he leaned closer to her. "What do you know of the man, other than he's busy?"

His question was neatly tied with a thick cord of cynicism. Abby closed her eyes and bowed her head, thanking God for the food and asking for strength to keep from snapping back at the infuriating man dining with her. Why had she asked him to stay?

She picked up her fork and jabbed at her pie. "Sir Jonathan runs a lovely estate just outside of Penrith. I am told that Brakewell Hall has two hundred acres. His is one of the oldest families in the area, their baronet title dating back to King James." She popped a bite of kidney pie into her mouth, satisfied with the flavor and with having put the captain in his place.

He merely stared. "And?"

She swallowed. Was that not enough information? But. . .oh. Of course. The captain was an officer of the law. It made sense he'd be more interested in a physical description. "Sir Jonathan is tall, broad of shoulders, with. . ." She stabbed another piece of pie. What colour hair did Sir Jonathan have? Brown? Black? It wasn't flaxen, at any rate. And had his eyes been dark as well. . .or had they been more of a hazel shade? No, they were blue. She was certain of it. Mostly.

She set down her fork and picked up her mug, gazing at the captain over the rim. "He has dark hair and blue eyes."

"And?"

Without so much as a sip, she set the mug back down. "What do you mean '*and*'? I have just told you."

"What you've given me, Miss Gilbert, is a physical description of the fellow and the state of his affairs, neither of which tells me about the man himself."

Frustration roiled the one bite of pie she'd eaten. He was right. She didn't really know much about Sir Jonathan, but living with him had to be better than abiding with her hateful stepmother and stepsiblings in Southampton.

"If you must know, Captain, Sir Jonathan is compassionate, kind, forthright, and generous. His sense of justice is acute, and he is above reproach in all matters. Not to mention he is as handsome as a Beau Brummell fashion plate. There." She lifted her chin. "Does that answer your question?"

"No man is that perfect." A slow smile lightened his usual brooding countenance—and she recanted of ever having wished to be the one to put it there. "You are a starry-eyed dreamer, lady."

"And you are a dour old naysayer," she blurted, then immediately slapped her fingers to her mouth, horrified. What had happened to her years of reserve? Her ability to withstand verbal jabs with nary a retort but a kind word? She wouldn't be surprised if he simply shot up and walked away, never to look back. But his response, when it finally came, was even more astounding.

Captain Thatcher's shoulders shook, a low, pleasant chuckle rumbling in his chest.

A pretty shade of pink blossomed on Miss Gilbert's cheeks. Mortification radiated off her in waves, which amused Samuel all the more. So the little miss wasn't nearly as prim as she let on, eh? And bold. Most women would've run off in tears by now, yet here she sat, not only dining with the likes of him but having invited him to join her in the first place.

Slowly, she lowered her hand and dipped her face to a sheepish tilt. "Forgive me, Captain Thatcher. I had no right to say such a thing."

"No apology required. I stand guilty of the charge, for you see"— he bent closer, speaking for her alone—"I *am* a dour old naysayer."

Her jaw dropped, accompanied by a sharp intake of breath.

Fighting another urge to chuckle at her astonishment, he speared a bite of kidney pie and shoveled it into his mouth. Miss Gilbert was a pleasant young woman, to be sure. Entirely too easy to amuse. He hadn't enjoyed a laugh so freely in years, not since. . .

All his humour faded, blotted out by ugly memories rising from the past. Gunshots. Blood. Death. Who was he to enjoy dinner and laughter with a beautiful woman when his former partner William would never get the chance?

He shoved in another mouthful and went back to surveying the room. One never knew when trouble would walk through the door. Not that he expected it—but more often than not, that's when an enemy struck.

"Tell me, Captain." Miss Gilbert's voice pulled his gaze from the door to her sweet face. "What will you do once you receive your final payment from my intended? A hundred pounds is no small sum."

It wasn't. It was more than he'd prayed for. Once again he silently thanked God before answering. "I intend to purchase a piece of land."

"You would leave the force?"

Hah! He should've left years ago, before he'd been gutted of hope and stained with indelible cynicism. He slugged back a drink of ale, then nodded.

Finished with her pie, the lady pushed aside her plate and dabbed at her mouth with a coarse table napkin. "And what will you do with your land? Horses? Farming? Sheep, perhaps?"

He studied her for a moment, trying to decipher if her enthusiasm was true or merely an attempt to while away her time. Nothing but interest gleamed in her brown eyes, as if she were truly fascinated by what he might say.

"Oats and hay," he answered at length. "After my years spent with horses, I've come to value reliable provender. I aim to produce the best possible feed at an affordable price."

A brilliant smile lit her face. "A noble effort, Captain, but be careful. You are dangerously close to sounding like a starry-eyed dreamer yourself."

Once again the strange desire to chuckle welled in his throat, but he swallowed it. Joy was a habit he couldn't own, not yet. Not when there were still criminals to haul in and brigands to put down—and deep in his gut, he sensed one nearby.

His gaze shot to the door. Steel-grey eyes met his from across the crowded room, hooded eyes, set deep beneath a forehead puckered with a scar stretching from one side to the other, like the man had barely escaped death from a sharp blade.

The same blade now tucked inside Samuel's boot.

Thunderation! Samuel jerked back into the shadow of a passing waiter, but not fast enough. Recognition flashed across the big man's face. Noddy Carper, one of Shankhart's gang. Carper's nostrils flared, hatred purpling his flesh like a bruise.

Then he turned and fled.

Bolting upright, Samuel leapt sideways, causing the table to jiggle—and crashed into another waiter coming through the kitchen door. Bowls plummeted. Soup sprayed on impact, burning through the fabric of his trousers. The waiter barely kept from toppling as he teetered on one foot.

But no time to apologize. Samuel dodged around the man and shot forward. If Carper got away, Shankhart would know where to find Samuel. . .and Miss Gilbert and the babe. None of them would be safe.

"Captain?" Miss Gilbert's voice followed him across the room. So did the other diners' eyes. He could feel the stares, and no wonder. It wasn't every day a man broke into a sprint between bites of kidney pie.

He barreled out of the public room and dashed through the smaller reception hall, banking hard to the right as two gentlemen swapping stories turned toward him. Pulling out his pistol, he reached for the front doorknob—then jumped back as it swung open.

A lady entered, and when her eyes landed on the gun in his hand, she screamed as if he'd shot her.

"What the devil?" shouted the man behind her as Samuel shoved past.

This time he did apologize. "Pardon."

He tore past them both into the night. Torches lit the front yard, casting a ghoulish flicker on the back side of a black horse and big rider galloping out of sight.

Chest heaving, Samuel slowed to a stop. By the time he saddled Pilgrim and tried to follow, Carper would be long gone and untrackable in the black of night. Of all the rotten turns of luck! He'd just have to gain as much ground as possible tomorrow, putting more space between him and Shankhart—or Shankhart would be breathing down his neck with a gun in hand endangering Miss Gilbert and little Emma.

"Captain?"

He turned. Miss Gilbert stood bathed in torchlight, Emma's basket clutched in one hand, the other fluttering to her chest. "Are you all right? Are you ill?"

He grunted. He was ill all right. Sick at heart that Carper had gotten away. Sick of murderers and thieves.

Sick of it all.

Chapter Ten

After two days of traveling—albeit slowed with a woman and child in tow—the uneasy knot in Samuel's gut ought to be loosening. All told, he'd put nearly a hundred miles between himself and Shankhart. That should be a load lifter in and of itself.

But it wasn't.

As he rode through the midlands, sometimes scouting ahead of the carriage, other times—like now—behind, he couldn't help but feel like a coward for running off. He should be back there on the heath, hunting down that killer beast Shankhart, not playing the role of nursemaid and guardian. Should be. Sweet heavens, but he hated *shoulds*.

And worse, the twisting in his gut tightened with each thud of Pilgrim's hooves. Something wasn't right.

Pulling out his pistol, he cocked the hammer and veered off the road, guiding his mount into the tree line. Then he doubled back, scanning the endless maze of ash trunks and ivy carpet. June sunshine filtered through the canopy, painting bright stripes of light. Were they being followed? Easy enough to spot anyone lurking about, yet no dark shapes darted from tree to tree or belly-crawled through the foliage. Nothing but a few random squirrels scampered about.

Blowing out a long breath, he tucked away the gun and chided himself for becoming a skittish old—

"Stop!"

Though faint, Miss Gilbert's voice strained through the trees. Samuel kicked Pilgrim into action, every muscle on alert. By the time he reached the carriage, the postilion had just pulled down the stairs.

Samuel swung off his horse, gun drawn. "Is there trouble?"

The man glanced at him, the whites of his eyes growing large as his gaze landed on the pistol. He threw up his hands. "The lady asked me to stop, sir. That's all I know."

Miss Gilbert's pink-cheeked face peered out the open window of the door. She acknowledged the gun with a sweeping glance yet did not shrink back. "Emma's made quite a mess of herself, more than I can care for in a moving carriage. Would you be so good as to put away your gun, Captain, and hold her while I step out?"

A soiled baby? He'd tensed to kill for nothing more than a fouled clout? If Brentwood or Moore heard of this, he'd be laughed out of service.

But as Miss Gilbert handed Emma down, he suddenly understood the urgency of the lady's request. The babe's gown was sopping, and the stink of it watered his eyes.

He handed the child back to Miss Gilbert as soon as her feet touched ground. Then he turned to the postilion. "Grab the child's bag and spread a blanket over there." He indicated a relatively flat swath of clover next to the edge of the woods.

Before either Miss Gilbert or the driver could move, he strode off to inspect the area. Nothing dangerous met his eye, only robins flittered atop some low-lying branches and rabbits ruffled the undergrowth beneath.

"Are you expecting trouble, Captain?" Worry thickened Miss Gilbert's usual cheery tone.

"Just taking precautions." He turned to find her big brown eyes seeking his. "That's what you're paying me for, isn't it?"

"Yes, I suppose I am." Her lips curved into a brave smile, and she nodded at the postilion as he set down a satchel and shook out a blanket. "Thank you, Mr. Blake."

Miss Gilbert laid down the fussing child, knelt, and set to work. Samuel kept a watchful eye on their surroundings, yet more often than not, his gaze drifted back to the woman. She was an oddity, in a surprisingly pleasant way. Not many gentlemen's daughters would've taken on the charge of a child not quite a year old. And none would deign to clean a squalling, filthy babe, not even if the child were flesh of her flesh.

That's what servants were for, yet Miss Gilbert not only snubbed such convention, but pushed up her sleeves and cared for the little one in a way that squeezed Samuel's chest. Judging by the loosened hair trailing down Miss Gilbert's neck, she'd endured quite a ride thus far.

At last, the lady stood and held out a fresh—yet still crying—little one. "Would you please mind Emma while I tidy up? I will only be a moment."

Before he could respond, Miss Gilbert pressed Emma against his chest, and his arms flew up in reflex to grasp the wriggling child. Without a word, Miss Gilbert began collecting the dirty cloths.

Emma's wide blue eyes met his, her lips opening to a big O. For a moment, the crying ceased—then a fresh wave of tears sprouted and the child cried all the harder. Samuel blew out a disgusted breath. There was nothing to be done for it, then.

"Shh," he soothed and started bouncing, startling himself that his muscles still remembered how to calm a wee one. He turned Emma around, cradling her against his shirt, and patted her back. Unwelcome memories rushed him, nearly buckling his knees, especially when the babe burrowed her face into his collar and her soft cheek brushed against his neck. How many tears had he calmed those many years ago? If he listened hard enough, could he yet hear Mary's cries mingled with this little one's?

Somewhere deep inside, an old folk tune rose up unbidden and, before he could stop it, emerged as a low humming in his throat. Emma stilled at the noise, and he swayed from foot to foot to prevent a fresh bout of wailing. One of her little fists broke loose and she clung to his arm, nuzzling her face against his shoulder. He sucked in a breath. This time the memories would not be stopped, though he closed his eyes against them. Mary had been such a frail child. Small. Too small. Definitely not sturdy enough to withstand his drunken father's careless fist when he'd swung for his mother and missed.

"Captain?"

His eyes popped open to Miss Gilbert's raised brow. Clearing his throat, he handed Emma back to her.

But she didn't retreat. She stood there, her brown eyes searching his. "You surprise me, sir. You obviously have some experience with little ones, yet you claim none of your own."

He shrugged. "I don't only rescue fair maidens, Miss Gilbert. Sometimes children are involved."

She pursed her lips, the dimple on her chin scolding him with suspicion. "It is more than that, though, is it not?"

Thunder and earth, but the woman was perceptive. He sidestepped her and stalked toward Pilgrim, who pulled with her teeth at the clover nearby.

Miss Gilbert's voice followed at his back. "This child may not be yours, but I suspect you have lost one very dear to you, have you not?"

He wheeled about, his hands curling into fists as he studied her. How could she possibly know that?

Her brow creased, her brown gaze glinting with compassion. "I do not mean to offend. I merely wish to help, and I am well practiced with a listening ear. Past hurts often lose their sting when shared with others."

He smirked. "There you go again."

"What?"

"Being a starry-eyed dreamer. And you're wrong." His tone lowered to a bitter growl, completely unstoppable. "Some hurts never go away." Well did he know that truth. Some were so deeply engrained, not even a well-meaning woman could uproot them. Once again he turned from her, and in three more strides, he bent and snatched up Pilgrim's lead.

Footsteps patted the dirt behind him. "Who was the child, Captain? The one your heart yet mourns?"

He stiffened. How the deuce could she see into him like that? In all his years on the force, not one of his fellow officers nor his brothers-in-arms back in India had ever guessed as much.

Why her, God? Why now?

"You do not have to tell me, but it might help if you told someone." Miss Gilbert's voice was a sweet addition to the June birdsong. Lord, but she was persistent.

She stepped closer, the scent of orange blossom water wafting over his shoulder from her nearness. "I hate to see you so tortured every time you take Emma into your arms, and we still have a long way to go with her. Should you not make peace with whatever demon it is from the past that yet haunts you?"

He clenched the leather lead in his hand. Should he tell her to mind her own business, or just walk away?

But instead, unbidden words launched from his tongue. "I had a sister."

Stunned, he clamped his lips tight. Not even Moore or Brentwood knew that bit of information. By all the stars in the heavens, what had made him reveal such a personal thing?

"Ahh, I see. . . . Emma reminds you of her. Is that what pains you?"

He gritted his teeth. The woman was more persistent than a sailor bent on a rum run. He stalked over to the carriage, Pilgrim in tow, and called over his shoulder. "It's time we leave, Miss Gilbert."

And it was. Stratford-'on-Avon wasn't far off, and sitting too long in one place was asking for trouble. . .so was answering too many questions.

Abby whispered one more ragged prayer for Emma to go to sleep before pushing herself upright on the bed. But the child continued to cry. It wasn't working. *Nothing* was working. Emma fussed just as much—if not more—than when she'd laid the child down in the little box bed nearly a half hour ago. Abby relit the lamp at her bedside, allowing a sigh to deflate her lungs. Apparently neither of them would rest this long night, and after a hard day of travel, every muscle tight from the jostling carriage, her own sob rose in her throat.

Lord, give me strength.

"All right, my love." She forced her tone to a lilting coo as she padded over to where Emma should be sleeping. Of all the ways she'd imagined how this faery-tale journey to her new husband's waiting arms might be, bouncing a fussy babe into the wee hours of the night had never entered her mind.

"Shall we take a turn about the room and—"

Abby dropped to her knees. "Emma?"

A swath of lamplight stretched out a long finger, pointing at a blue rim spreading in a circle around the little one's lips. Gooseflesh prickled Abby's arms. This was no ordinary illness.

She shot to her feet and grabbed her dressing gown. Pausing only long enough to shove her arms into the sleeves and tie the sash, she whispered one more prayer.

"Lord, grant mercy."

Throwing aside propriety, she dashed down the corridor. She stopped at a chamber just past hers and rapped on the door. "Captain Thatcher?"

A breath later, the door flung open. The captain stood, feet planted wide and muscles straining against the thin white fabric of his shirt. Dark hair peeked out on his chest, just below his collarbone, matching the dark stubble on his clenched jaw. A muscle jumped on the side of his neck. The fierce look in his eyes made her want to run and hide, but she forced herself to remain steady for Emma's sake.

"I fear Emma is ill."

He dipped his head, his voice low. "Take me to her."

Whimpers leached into the corridor and grew louder as Abby re-entered the room. The captain brushed past her and bent over the box bed. Then he knelt and pressed the back of his hand to the little one's forehead.

It was strange to witness the big man so gentle with his touch— and even stranger to see him in naught but his shirtsleeves, half-untucked and spilling over one side of his trousers. His feet were bare. Abby leaned back against the wall, heat rushing to her cheeks. It felt indecent, hosting a half-dressed man in her bedchamber.

But the next whimper pealing out from little Emma banished such embarrassment, as did the flash of concern in the captain's gaze as he stood and faced her. "She needs a surgeon. Keep her cool until I return."

And then he was gone like a ghost into the night, the only evidence of his presence the riffling of her hem from where he'd passed by her in a rush.

The next several hours stretched into an unending routine of dipping a cloth into a basin, wringing it out, then pressing the damp cloth against Emma's skin.

Dip.

Wring.

Press.

Again and again, yet it did nothing to stop the burning, the whimpers, the thrashing. Where was Captain Thatcher? Lost? Hurt? Tired of her and the crying child? Abby smoothed a loose hank of hair flopping in her eyes and stood, arching her back. Her sanity was leaching from her, bit by bit. Perhaps some tepid tea for her and a spot of milk for Emma. It would be good for the girl to drink something...wouldn't it?

Her shoulders slumped. What did she know of sick babies? She trudged back to the basin and retrieved the pitcher next to it. If nothing else, some fresh water was in need. Having already traded her nightgown for her traveling dress, she snatched up a shawl and wrapped it about her shoulders, then ventured out into the corridor and down the stairs into the public room.

At this time of night, no patrons remained. A few vigil lanterns burned from hooks on the wall, casting long shadows from the tables and chairs. Abby glanced around the room. Several doors might lead to a kitchen, but which one?

She bit her lip, debating which to try, when the front door opened and two dark shapes entered—one carrying a bag, the other a scowl.

The captain reached her in two long-legged strides, bringing with him the scent of horse and leather and man. The brim of his hat shaded his eyes, but she didn't need to see them to discern the worry clenching his jaw. "Is the child—?"

"She is much the same."

He brushed past her and disappeared up the stairs on silent feet, leaving her and the surgeon blinking.

"Your husband is a determined man, a noble trait in this instance, for I was out on a call and he hunted me down. I am Mr. Harvey, surgeon"—the man tipped his hat without pausing, the spare light glinting off the glass of his spectacles—"and I am guessing your daughter is up those stairs, so if you wouldn't mind leading the way?"

Husband? Daughter?

"I—I. . .er. . ." All the words she wanted to say bunched in her throat. There'd be no setting the man straight without a lengthy explanation. She turned and fled up the stairway before he could see the flush on her cheeks.

Inside the room, Captain Thatcher had lit all the lamps, flooding the room with light. Abby gravitated toward where he stood, near the bed yet back far enough to give Mr. Harvey clear access to Emma.

While the surgeon knelt at the child's side, Abby looked up at the captain. His dark hair, damp and clinging to the skin near his temples, tossed wild to his shoulders. His riding cloak draped over his shoulders, unbuttoned, half of his collar blown back. Mud dappled the top of his boots. It must've been some ride.

"What were you doing in the taproom?" the captain rumbled low.

"I went downstairs, looking for fresh water," she whispered.

He glanced down at her, his face unreadable as his gaze drifted over her face. "You're weary. Go get some rest in my room. I'll stay with the child until morning."

Her brows shot to the rafters. *He* would tend to the sick girl on his own? "And if Emma should need changing?"

"I imagine I've seen worse on the battlefield."

Her gaze drifted to the crescent scar high on his cheekbone. So, he was more than a man of law, though truly it didn't surprise her that his background included military service. Not with the way he commanded attention simply by merit of standing in a room.

Emma wailed as the surgeon lifted her and laid her on the bigger bed. The little one's mewling cries crawled into Abby's heart and squeezed. While she appreciated the captain's offer to escape to his room, there was no way she could accept it. She cared too much about Emma to leave her.

Clutching her hands in front of her, she lifted one more silent prayer for the surgeon's wisdom before she answered the captain. "Thank you, but I will not sleep until I know how Emma fares."

"Mr. Harvey will soon have her to rights."

Was he speaking to her or to himself? Both, likely, for the pinch on his brow did not go away.

He tipped his head toward her and lowered his voice. "Go. Sleep."

The urgency in his voice, the very thought of stretching out on a counterpane, was tempting. Merely the idea loosened some of the tightness knotting her shoulders. It had been a long day. A never-ending one.

But then Mr. Harvey turned from the bedside and faced them. "It is too soon to tell what is at the root of this distemper. At best, it may only be the beginnings of croup."

Captain Thatcher jutted his chin. "And worst?"

Mr. Harvey's blue eyes darted to Abby, then back to the captain. He beckoned for Captain Thatcher to follow him, then strode to the side of the room.

A flash of anger burned from Abby's belly to her chest as the men left her behind. After caring for the child for hours on end, cleaning and cooling and cooing, did they really think her so weak of heart? She crossed to them with clipped steps. "I am not a frail flower, Mr. Harvey. Whatever you need to say can be spoken in my presence."

Something flashed in the captain's eyes. Censure or admiration? Hard to tell, but he nodded his consent toward the surgeon.

"Very well." Mr. Harvey rolled his shoulders. "Then I shall give it to you straight. The child exhibits the first symptoms of putrid throat."

Abby's heart stopped. So did her breaths. The awful diagnosis stealing both for it was the foulest of thieves—the very one that had taken her mother's life all those years ago.

She swayed, but the captain's strong grip on her arm shored her up.

The surgeon held up a hand. "It may not be, and I pray that it is not, but even so, for the benefit of the public, I shall take her with me at once."

"Take her?" Abby squeaked out, leaning hard on the captain's strength. "What do you mean?"

"Your child, madam, needs to be quarantined until further notice." Mr. Harvey studied them both over the rim of his spectacles. "And at the first sign of any pain in your own throats, you will need to be confined as well."

Chapter Eleven

Horehound and vinegar. Blood and despair. Abby wrinkled her nose, though that did nothing to lessen the strong odour. While she'd expected the surgeon's office to have a stringent scent, it didn't make the smell more bearable.

She shifted on the small bench in the waiting room, fighting a yawn. After snatching a few hours of sleep, she'd persuaded Captain Thatcher to escort her to Mr. Harvey's office. It hadn't taken much coaxing, though. The lines on the captain's brow had confirmed he was as worried about the baby girl as she.

Fixing her gaze on the door between the anteroom and surgeon's office, Abby willed the thing to open. But it did no good. The oak slab remained shut. She glanced down at her watch brooch, then frowned. The captain had been in there at least fifteen minutes. He'd insisted she wait for him instead of meeting with Mr. Harvey herself, and she hadn't argued. But as the minutes ticked on, she wished she'd put up more of a resistance. She shifted once more, knowing all along that fussing likely wouldn't have done any good anyway. Though she'd known the captain for only five days, she'd learned one thing. When the brown of his eyes deepened to a flinty black, the man would not be moved.

For at least the tenth time in as many minutes, she lifted her fingertips to her throat and swallowed, probing to detect any pain or ache. Just thinking about the possibility of falling ill made little twinges tighten the muscles beneath her touch. But that was all. No tenderness. Just a scratchy feeling on the inside from forcing herself to swallow so many times.

Just then, Captain Thatcher stepped out.

She shot to her feet before he closed the door behind him. "How is Emma?"

"Much the same."

"Is that good or bad?"

He shrugged and donned his hat. "We should know more tomorrow."

The captain strode past her and held open the door, but Abby hesitated to follow. How could it possibly have taken a quarter of an hour simply to find out Emma fared no differently than when they'd last seen her? Was there something he wasn't telling her?

Narrowing her eyes, she studied the man, looking for clues, but he just stood there. Waiting. The sunlight streaming in from outside painted him in golden light, a chiseled, marbled statue—albeit a bit worn about the edges.

With a last glance at the surgeon's closed door, she exited onto the High Street of Stratford-'on-Avon. The captain fell into step beside her, putting himself between her and the road. Despite the shadow of worry about Emma, Abby lifted her face to the sun and allowed the golden warmth to soak in for one blessed moment. It was a glorious June day. Quite the contrast to the rattling walls of the carriage or the darkened timbers of the inn's public room.

She glanced up at the captain. "Would you like to take a turn about the town? This is, after all, the birthplace of the great playwright William Shakespeare. Perhaps we might take in a bit of history. At the very least, the fresh air would do us both some good."

"It's safer to remain at the inn," he rumbled, his tone as dull as the wheels on a passing dray.

She quirked a brow at him. "Do not worry, sir. I shall protect you."

While she appreciated that he took his role of guardian to heart, could the man not permit himself to enjoy a few brief moments?

His dark gaze snapped to hers. No smile curved his lips, but all the same, amusement sparked in his eyes. Though unspoken, she got the distinct impression her retort had pleased him—which unaccountably heated her face more than the sun.

She looked away, and her step faltered. Then she stopped altogether. After the fear-filled night she'd spent caring for Emma, her mind consumed with worry and flashes of despair, she'd almost forgotten the reason for her journey. There, inches behind the window of a seamstress shop, a beautiful gown made of cream-coloured silk draped over a dress form. Hundreds of embroidered roses in golden thread swirled up from the hem, climbing a vine of small seed pearls. The bodice fit tightly, with no ruffles or braids. Near the shoulders, the sleeves puffed a bit, then followed the arm in a sleek line. This time Abby's throat did ache—with longing. This gown was a dream. *Her* dream. Completely unlike the flouncy gauze and taffeta creation her stepmother had insisted upon and persuaded her father to purchase for Abby's wedding day.

"Oh my," she breathed out. "The woman who wears a gown such as that will be a picture of elegance."

"Waste of money," the captain grumbled beside her.

"How can you say that?" She flung out her arm as if to uphold the gown and her opinion in the palm of her hand. "Anyone wearing a gown like that would surely be the most beautiful bride in all of England. Would you not wish your future wife to be so adorned on your wedding day?"

"What makes you think I'm not married?"

"But you said you had no family!" Her brows knit into a knot as she tried to decipher the captain's question. Had he lied to her before? To what end? Yet all she'd experienced from this man for the past five days had been nothing but honor. Why would he—

She gasped as a sickening truth sank to her belly. "Oh! How careless of me. You *were* married, were you not?"

His eyes actually twinkled. "No." Half his mouth curved into a faint smile. "Never have been. You are entirely too easy to tease, Miss Gilbert."

The rogue! Her fingers curled into fists to keep from swatting the amusement off his face. Captain Thatcher was as incorrigible as her younger stepbrother. In fact, the softened lines near his eyes and jaw made him look almost boyish—and entirely too handsome.

She pinched her lips into a mock scowl. "Why do you torment me so?"

He leaned closer, angling his head. "Why do you fall for it?"

Her scowl slipped, giving way to a small chuckle. "Fatigue, I suppose. And it is unfair of you to take such advantage."

She turned back to the gown for a last look, powerless to stop a sigh from barreling out. "Simply lovely," she whispered.

"You don't need a gown to make you beautiful."

She jerked her gaze back to him, only to see his long legs already striding down the pavement. Had that been a compliment? From the dour captain?

Lifting her hem, she dashed to catch up. "Thank you, Captain, but I hope you do not think I was fishing for praise. There are simply certain expectations of how the bride of a baronet should present herself. Sir Jonathan Aberley will wish me to play the part, and I intend to meet his expectations."

"Sounds like a production on Drury Lane." He glanced at her sideways. "What kind of man cares more about the wedding than the marriage?"

"I am sure it is not like that at all. Of course the baronet cares about the marriage, about me, not just the ceremony."

A breeze kicked up a puff of dirt from the road, and the captain angled to block her from it, his head shaking as if he didn't believe a word she said.

She frowned, determined to change his obvious sour opinion of the man she was to marry. "Sir Jonathan Aberley is the highest-ranking landowner in the area. A man of his station must maintain the decorum people expect."

His eyes narrowed. "Are you marrying for a title, then, Miss Gilbert?"

"No!" How dare he even voice such a question? Was he teasing her again? She cleared her throat and forced a pleasant tone, unwilling to take his bait. "It is a love match."

"Love?" He scoffed. "You've only met the man once. You hardly know him, nor he, you. Not a very solid beginning to a marriage. Such a union can only be ill-fated."

She stopped and popped her fists onto her hips. Many the time had she sparred with her stepmother, but never did anger burn so fervid within her chest. This was beyond teasing. "Must you always expect the worst, Captain?"

His dark gaze challenged her in ways she couldn't begin to comprehend. "Must you always expect the best?"

She stared right back, refusing to be the first to look away. His assumption was wrong—*completely* wrong—for at this moment, she was having a hard time expecting the best of him!

Samuel's mouth twitched, a smile threatening to once again break loose. This was new. Entirely new. He couldn't remember the last time a lady inspired so much amusement—if ever. Then again, Abigail Gilbert was no ordinary miss, the way she held her ground, neither shrinking nor wavering. How tenderly she cared for little Emma, concerning herself for the child's well-being. The easy manner with which she'd laughed off his teasing. Was this how it had been for Moore or Brentwood when they'd first met their respective brides-to-be?

Gah! What was he thinking?

Miss Gilbert was right. If she could blame fatigue for her skewed thoughts, surely he could as well. He turned on his heel, calling over his shoulder as he resumed stalking down the High Street. "Come along, Miss Gilbert. I daresay neither of us will change the mind of the other."

Rows of dark-timbered storefronts rose up on each side of the road, standing shoulder to shoulder, like comrades bellying up to a bar. Halfway down the block, a crowd began to gather, forming a ring around a scuffle. He glanced into the road to cross, but coming up from behind them, a lacquered carriage pulled by four high-steppers clattered down the lane. He'd have to wait until it passed before leading Miss Gilbert to the other side.

But apparently the woman hadn't noticed his hesitation, for she continued on.

"Miss Gilbert, wait."

He darted after her, nearly crashing into her back when she stopped at the edge of the onlookers.

At the center of the ring of spectators, two men circled each other, knees bent, fists up. The smaller of the two struck first, uppercutting with a strong right hook to the jaw. The bigger man staggered—a bit too theatrically—then whumped to the pavement, eyes closed.

Samuel shook his head, disgusted. If the Stratford constable didn't put a stop to this kind of crowd gathering, the whole village would soon fall to cutpurses and pickpockets galore.

Miss Gilbert's big brown eyes lifted to his. "You are a man of the law. Can you not do something?"

Her fresh-faced innocence was beguiling. Sweet mercy! How he hated to be the one to introduce her to the ways of this conniving world. But so be it. He lifted a finger and gently pushed her chin for her to witness what would happen next.

The victor raised his fists into the air, strutting rooster-like around the inside of the circle. Behind him, the fallen man sprang to his feet. The crowd gasped, likely expecting the smaller bully to take a good cuff to the back of the head.

Miss Gilbert clutched his arm. "Captain Thatcher! You must stop this before one of them gets seriously hurt."

Her confidence in his ability to break up such a brawl did strange things to his gut, but he set his jaw. "Keep watching," he ordered.

With one meaty hand, the big man swiped blood from his split lip. With the other, he pulled out a cloth banner from his waistband. Snapping it open, he held it up for all to read a painted advertisement for Jack Henry's Boxing Club. "Don't take a beating like I did, mates. Learn to fight back. A new bout of lessons starts today, on Quigley and

Main. Affordable and necessary, aye Billy?"

The short man grinned back at him. "Aye!"

Miss Gilbert, pretty little lips parted, stared up at Samuel. Ahh, but he could get used to that look of reverent amazement.

"How did you know?" she whispered.

"Part of the job," he murmured, then swept out his arm. "After you."

She paused a moment more, other questions surfacing in the lines on her brow, much like a curious tot marveling over the discovery of a world beyond her chamber door. Then she turned and began weaving her way through the dispersing bystanders.

He followed, until a small child scampered between them. Samuel stopped to avoid kicking the lad with his boot.

The child stopped as well, blinking up at him like a fawn to a hunter. Slowly, the boy's face squinched into a wicked grin, then he bolted, laughing as he tore between pedestrians. What the deuce? Why would a boy—?

Gut sinking, Samuel jerked his gaze to Miss Gilbert. Sure enough, a tattered old woman held on to her sleeve, swaying on her feet. The woman's words screeched a layer above the din of the remaining people.

"My pardon, a thousand times o'er! Why, I ne'er meant to bump into so fine a lady as you, miss. Don't be cross, miss. Don't be cruel."

"Of course I shall not. It was only an accident. Go in peace." Miss Gilbert's innocent voice stabbed him in the heart. She had no idea.

Samuel shouldered his way past the few dress coats between them.

"God bless ye, mum." The old woman turned.

But Samuel flung out his hand and grabbed her arm, yanking her back. "Not so fast."

Miss Gilbert frowned up at him. *Him!* Not at the old woman who deserved her scorn. After years of such looks, he'd built up a rawhide skin to misunderstanding scowls, but this time, from this woman, it stung like a slap to the face.

"Captain Thatcher! How can you be so harsh? Release that woman at once."

Ignoring Miss Gilbert, he shoved his hand out toward the old thief. "Give it back."

The woman, surprisingly agile, wrenched one way then another, wriggling to break free. Satan himself couldn't have spewed such vile obscenities.

Samuel dug his fingers deeper into the fleshy part of her arm. "Mind your tongue, woman. There's a lady present."

"Pah! Lady or no, I'll say what e're I flip-flappity want to say, ye gleeking gudgeon. I ain't done nothing. I'll call the law on you, that's what. Now let me go, ye hedge-born clotpole!"

Her grey eyes widened as he shoved his greatcoat open with his elbow, exposing the brass end of his tipstaff.

"Now," he growled. "Hand it over."

One more curse flew out, but so did the old woman's hand. Miss Gilbert's golden watch brooch sat atop the thief's gnarly palm.

Miss Gilbert sucked in an audible breath as she snatched it away. This time when she gazed up at him, sheepish repentance shimmered in her eyes, and something more. He sucked in his own breath when he realized what it was.

Admiration.

"How did you know?" Miss Gilbert clutched the pin to her chest. "And do not tell me it is part of the job."

"Sometimes, Miss Gilbert, it *does* serve to expect the worst."

Still gripping the old woman, he fished around in his pocket and retrieved a farthing, then held it out to her. "See that you hold on to this coin instead of busying your fingers with other people's property, or next time I won't be so lenient."

He let go. The old woman narrowed her eyes for a moment, then seized the coin and darted off.

Frowning, he turned to Miss Gilbert. "Tuck your brooch away. Such a valuable keepsake ought to be kept out of sight."

Her eyes widened, glistening with unspent tears. "How do you know it is a keepsake?"

"One doesn't weep for the loss of a simple brooch. Where did you get it?"

"It was my mother's. And you are right. There is nothing simple about it. This is my last connection to her." She clutched the pin in a death grip. Clearly there was more attached to that bauble than grief.

Sighing, he softened his tone. "You know, Miss Gilbert, someone once told me that past hurts often lose their sting when shared with others. You rarely speak of your family. Why is that, I wonder?"

"There is not much to say. My mother died when I was five. Father gave me her watch shortly before he remarried. And a good thing too, for my stepmother would have cast it out of the home as she did with all of my mother's belongings." Miss Gilbert ducked her head, the dimple on her chin curving into a frown. "But enough about me. I. . .I owe you an apology, sir. I had no right to question your abrupt handling of the old woman, for you are far wiser than I."

A twinge of compassion squeezed his chest. Miss Gilbert couldn't possibly look more like a forlorn little girl if she tried.

"You owe me nothing, Miss Gilbert, save for my payment when we reach your baronet's manor. I pray your future husband is more educated in the ways of the world than you are, for your own safety."

Scarlet brushed her cheeks, almost feverish in intensity. While he'd meant no disrespect, had she taken his words the wrong way? Then again, such heightened colour could be the remnants of excitement from the near-robbery. A distinct possibility. Or. . .

His throat tightened. It could be Miss Gilbert was starting to exhibit the first signs of illness.

He blew out a long breath and offered his arm. Despite saying otherwise to the lady, he was tired of expecting the worst.

Chapter Twelve

Pins. Needles. Abby sat up in bed, her heart sinking as she swallowed again, and this time shards of glass scraped the inside of her throat. Heart sinking, she eased back against the pillow, her pulse beating loud in her ears. She'd been trying to ignore the increasing ache all night. But now, with morning light seeping between the cracks in the drapery, there was no more denying the truth.

Whatever illness little Emma suffered, she now had it.

Dragging her body from the bed, she went through the motions of dressing, all the while vainly trying to hold worry at bay. It could be nothing, as the surgeon had said of the babe yesterday. A trifling malaise of some sort, or naught more than a seasonal discomfort.

Or it could be putrid throat, the killer. The murderer.

Abby's fingers faltered as she cinched the front of her bodice. Even were she stronger than her mother and survived such a dreaded disease, the illness and resulting recuperation would add weeks, if not months, to her journey. Must everything impede her from reaching the man who would love her forever? She'd already tallied several extra days to her journey. Was Sir Jonathan even now so concerned that he'd send out a search party?

She sat on the small stool in front of the dressing table and pinned up her hair, peering at her face in the mirror as she worked. Scarlet didn't flame across her cheeks, nor did her skin pale to a deathly hue. Heat didn't burn through her, and she didn't shiver with chills. Those had to be good signs. Didn't they? But what if they weren't? What if those symptoms crashed down upon her all at once, any minute now?

This was ridiculous. She pushed the last hairpin into place then bowed her head. She'd learned long ago while enduring the hurts of her stepmother that only through prayer would she find peace.

Lord, I confess I am anxious and fretting and altogether not trusting in Your great providence. It is not You who are in my debt, but I in Yours. . . for everything You give. If this be putrid throat, then I will trust You for the best outcome, whatever that may be, for I can do no more. But even so, Lord, I pray You would grant healing for little Emma and for me.

She lifted her face, then on second thought, once more dropped her chin to her chest.

And keep Captain Thatcher hale and hearty as well. Amen.

Trying not to swallow, she rose and collected her watch brooch from off the bedside table. This time—and forevermore—she'd pin it on her gown and wear her spencer over it. Reading the time would be a bit more inconvenient, but the placement would also serve to confound thieves.

She fastened the golden keepsake to the fabric, then absently rubbed her finger over the tiny glass face. The captain had brushed off her gratitude and praise yesterday, saying he was only doing his job as her guardian, but he could have no idea how truly thankful she'd been to keep this treasure. If it hadn't been for his fast action, all her tangible ties to her mother would be gone.

She pulled her spencer from off a peg on the wall and shoved in her arms, then tied on her bonnet, taking care to keep the ribbon from digging into her neck. Though she hated to admit to the captain that her throat ached, there'd be no hiding it if Mr. Harvey's worst suspicions proved true.

Leaving her chamber, she padded down the corridor to the captain's door, prepared to suffer his censure for not telling him sooner. But after three raps, he still didn't answer.

"Captain Thatcher?" She knocked again.

No response. Strange. He always answered her call barely before the words left her mouth.

Leaning her ear to the wood, she listened for any sign of movement.

But there were no footsteps thudding. No rustle of clothing. No anything. Just the low chatter of morning patrons climbing up the stairs from the taproom below. Where could the captain be at this early hour? Unless he'd gone down to breakfast?

Of course. She should've thought of that sooner. She descended the stairs and paused on the last one, gaining a wide view of the public room. Her gaze drifted from table to table, but no strong-jawed, dark-haired man looked up at her—as Captain Thatcher always seemed to do whenever she entered a room. Well, then. She clutched her reticule with both hands and stepped off the last stair.

She'd simply go see Mr. Harvey alone.

Sun and wind. Air and light. Samuel bent and gave Pilgrim free rein. The horse surged into a gallop. Here in the English countryside, the world blurring into a green line, God spoke in the roar rushing past his ears.

"Peace. Be at peace, My son."

The words goaded him, and he dug in his heels, ramping Pilgrim into a frenzy. For a few breathless moments, Samuel gave in to the solid muscles beneath him, carrying him far and fast. Trying to forget. Straining for that peace.

And failing miserably.

As he neared the Stratford outskirts, he slowed the horse, but the same burdens weighted his shoulders. The latent anger simmering in his gut—so much a part of him he didn't know how to live without it—flared hotter. How was he to grab hold of peace when so much responsibility bound him tightly?

Swinging off Pilgrim, he seized the horse's lead and walked the rest of the way to the inn's stable, cooling down his mount and himself. He rebuffed the stable boy with a scowl, preferring to see to Pilgrim's care on his own. After watering, untacking, and a good brushing, his old friend nudged him in the shoulder with a playful nose jab.

Samuel patted the bay on the neck. "Yes, my friend. It was a much-needed ride, though I don't think it did any good for me."

He strolled from the stable to the inn, purposely restraining his stride to a slow gait—despite the urgency to discover if Miss Gilbert was up and about yet. The desire to see the woman's smile etched a frown on his face. Why care a whit about a woman betrothed to another man? He wouldn't. He didn't. But all the same, he stomped up the stairs to his room, completely distracted by glancing down the corridor to her chamber. She'd not been in the public room. Was she even now lingering over a cup of tea in her bedchamber, her dark hair undone, in naught but her dressing gown?

Bah! He'd spent far too much time in Moore's and Brentwood's company, their soft tendencies toward their wives influencing him overmuch. He stopped in front of his own door, shoved the key into the lock and turned it. The movement rotated without friction. The tumbler didn't click. Clearly the thing was already unlocked—and he *always* secured his room.

Tensing, he reached for his gun.

But not quick enough.

The door flew open, and Noddy Carper's hulking shape barreled out. His beefy forearm slammed into Samuel's windpipe, cutting off air and driving him back. Before Samuel could react, the back of his head smacked against the corridor wall. Pain seared into his wrist, splaying his fingers. His gun fell with a sickening thud.

The world blackened at the edges. Samuel jammed his knee up, hoping to connect with soft tissue. But once again he was too late. Carper wrenched aside, sticking out his leg and ramming Samuel in the shoulder, toppling him off-balance to the floor.

Samuel gulped in air, coughing—until a sharp crack hit his skull.

This time the world did turn black.

Seconds later, his best guess, the fuzzy outline of his bedchamber furniture sharpened into view. A rough grip yanked the back of his collar, hauling him to his knees. Pain bounced around in his head like a steel ball gone wild. Sucking in a breath, he pushed upward.

Then stopped breathing altogether.

An arm's length in front of him, a ruddy-skinned monster sat on his bed. A slow smile opened his big maw, revealing yellowed teeth clinging to mottled gums. Dark hair stubbled over the beast's shorn head, misshapen from years of hard living and too many blows. And in the brute's lap, a knife lay gripped in one hand, the blade cradled in the other. Sunlight glinted off the freshly honed metal, impossibly sharp.

Despite the cold gun barrel shunted against the back of his head, Samuel squared his shoulders and faced his nemesis.

Shankhart Robbins.

This time when Abby entered Mr. Harvey's outer foyer, she was prepared for the vinegary scent. But as she stepped into the surgeon's office, nothing could have readied her for the sights. As a gentleman's daughter, she'd never had cause to visit a working surgeon's theatre. Now she understood why the captain had commanded she wait for him on the bench the previous morning. She could only imagine the suffering the yellowed walls in here had witnessed.

At the center of the room sat a raised wooden slab, long enough for a body, darkened and splotched from years of blood. Small divots were worn into the edges, right about where hands had likely clutched and squeezed and clawed in pain. Various saws and pincers of assorted sizes hung from hooks on one wall. Bottles filled with different liquids stood on a nearby table. A large velvet-lined box yawned open on that table, and though she didn't want to, Abby couldn't help but stare at the large syringes lined up inside, ready to pierce flesh.

"Ahh, Mrs. Thatcher." Mr. Harvey glanced over his shoulder as he hung a stained apron on a peg. "I was just finishing up and about to make a call on you and your husband. You've saved me a trip."

Heat rose up her neck, and she thanked God the surgeon yet had his back toward her.

"Oh, he is not my—"

She bit her lip. Which was worse? Allowing the man to think she and the captain were married, or refuting him when Mr. Harvey had clearly seen them together in her bedchamber?

"Hmm?" Mr. Harvey turned.

She smoothed her skirts, giving her hands something to do other than flutter about from mortification. "I. . .uh. . ." Despite the biting pain in her throat, she swallowed. "I am glad I saved you the trouble, sir. I came to inquire after little Emma and also to ask, if you have a spare moment, if you might look at my throat?"

His brow folded, dipping his bushy grey eyebrows into his spectacles. "I was afraid of that. Let's see what the trouble is."

He advanced, sidestepping the table, and with a gentle touch to her chin, guided her face upward into a ray of sunlight beaming in from one of the many windows. "Now then, Mrs. Thatcher, open your mouth and say ahh, if you please."

She obeyed.

He mm-hmmed immediately.

"Yes. Yes, I see," he murmured while tipping her face to one side and peering closer. Then he released her and stepped back. "Thank you."

He said no more, but something flashed in his eyes. Concern? Worry? Frustration over how to tell her she'd succumb to a mortal disease within hours?

Clutching her skirts, she braced herself for the worst. "Your verdict, Mr. Harvey?"

"Unfortunately, I'd say you're well on your way to feeling as poorly as your little girl."

Her hand flew to her throat. "Is it. . . ?" But she couldn't bring herself to even think the words let alone say them aloud. She swayed on her feet.

"Now, now, Mrs. Thatcher. Don't go swooning in a surgeon's office, though I suppose if you must, this would be the best place for it, eh?" He guided her out to the waiting room with a gentle nudge to her back and led her to the bench.

She sank, grateful for the support and to be away from the operating room.

"Allow me to put your fears to rest, madam. Your daughter

suffers from a bad case of the croup, not the putrid throat. And neither do you."

She snapped her face up to his, relief pumping through her veins with each beat of her heart.

He reaffirmed his words with a nod. "I suspect you've contracted some form of the girl's ailment, though it will likely pass from you much faster than it will for little Emma. Some white horehound syrup for the both of you, and you'll be on the mend in no time. The girl will likely fuss a bit longer, but she should be back to rights within the week. Wait here, please, while I retrieve her for you."

Mr. Harvey disappeared through a different door, and Abby sank back against the wall, sighing. Thank God! No deathly illness for her or little Emma. She'd collect the child and they could be on their way this very morning, incurring no more delay.

Wouldn't Captain Thatcher be surprised when she showed up back at the inn with the babe in her arms?

Chapter Thirteen

Staring at death was nothing new. It was a way of life. A companion Samuel frequently clasped hands with. In a freakish sort of way, he was comfortable knowing each breath might be his last, for he'd been facing his own demise since the day he'd screamed into this world. No, the sickening clench of his gut had nothing whatsoever to do with the possibility of dying. It was that he'd slipped up. Been caught unawares. Fallen headlong into his enemy's snare. And that rankled more than the ugly grin slicing across Shankhart Robbins's face or Carper's gun drilling into the back of his skull.

In front of him, Shankhart's big hulk sagged the mattress in the middle, where he sat on the bed, defiling the counterpane beneath him. A breeze wafting in from the window directly behind him carried his sweaty taint.

"Well, well. If it ain't my old friend, Sam'l Thatcher. Thing is, though, I have to keep asking myself. . ." Shankhart's misshapen head hinged eerily sideways, as if it might topple off. "I say, 'Self? For the love of money and women, why would Thatcher go and kill my own brother?'"

Ignoring the gun Carper jabbed into his head, Samuel locked gazes with Shankhart. "'Cause *you* weren't within reach at the time."

"I am now." The man blinked, his eyelids never quite shutting. It was an unsettling defect, the moist crescent of his eyeballs showing at all times. God only knew how many victims had stared at those lizard-like slits as he sliced their throats.

Shankhart tapped his blade against his palm in a deadly rhythm. "Looks like I'll be the one doing the killing today."

"Have at it, then." Samuel lifted his chin, the muzzle sliding to a higher point on his skull. "If you're able."

Coarse laughter rolled out of the highwayman, jiggling Shankhart's meaty shoulders. "Big talk for someone down on his knees."

He had a point. Samuel clamped his jaw shut while mentally ticking off any possible assets to use for his escape. White muslin curtains riffled in the breeze behind Shankhart. The window he usually kept shut was now open—likely reserved for Shankhart and Carper's exit. But it could prove useful to him. To his left, a pitcher sat on the washbasin, a formidable weapon if shattered against one of these brute's faces. And he still had his boot-blade tucked away. All in all, if the timing were right, he stood a chance, albeit a very slim one.

"I won't be here for long." He forced confidence into his tone—more than he had a right to own at this moment.

Shankhart sucked in his lips, then released them, making a smacking noise. "Not to be difficult, Captain, but I beg to differ. This could take all day. You see, I'm going to carve you up, bit by bit, piece by piece. Real slow," he drawled.

Samuel steeled every muscle as Shankhart lifted the knife. But the big man merely raised the blade to his own chin and scraped the sharp edge lightly against his dark stubble. Again and again. The rasping noise more unnerving than when the blade slipped and opened a small line of red on the man's jaw.

Shankhart's lips curved as he studied the blood on his knife, tilting it one way then the other in a ray of sunshine beaming through the window. Then he lowered the weapon to his lap and skewered Samuel with a pointed stare. "Oh, I know. I see it in your face. Anxious for the revelry to start, are you? Not yet, though. Time's not right. You wanna tell him why, Carper?"

The gun dug into the back of his skull. Carper's snicker was as foul as his breath, wafting thick upon Samuel's head. "We bein' gentlemen, and all, why we gots to wait on that lady of yours."

The words slammed into him like a hammer blow. They knew of Miss Gilbert?

God, have mercy.

Shankhart chuckled. "That's right. We know about the woman you're running off with. It pains me you never told your ol' friend about the bit o' skirt you've taken up with. Never introduced us proper like." Shankhart leaned forward, close enough that Samuel could feel the heat of him. "And a child too. My, my, but you've been a busy boy, chasing me down by day and tumbling yer doxy by night."

Samuel's hands curled into fists, the slur to Miss Gilbert lighting a wildfire in his chest. "Leave her and the child out of this. Your quarrel is with me."

"You should've thought of that sooner," Shankhart growled. "Things changed when you killed my brother. It's only justice that your loved ones should be taken just as you've taken mine."

"Justice?" Samuel snorted. "You don't know the meaning of the word."

"What I know is that you've been a thorn in my flesh for far too long. This ends now."

Lifting a last, frantic prayer, Samuel ground out, "So be it."

He lurched sideways. Carper's gun fired.

The shot lifted the hair on the side of Samuel's head as the ball passed. A hot trail grazed across his temple—but sank into Shankhart's chest.

Shankhart roared, the bullet punching him back.

Victory—maybe. No time to gloat.

Samuel jumped to his feet and lunged for the pitcher in one motion. He swung the heavy porcelain at Carper's skull. But the man twisted at the last moment, the vessel shattering against the brute's shoulder instead of his head. Before Samuel could regain his balance, Carper drove his elbow into his face. Cartilage gave. Blood flowed. Pain stabbed.

So, this was going to turn ugly, then.

Samuel swiped for his blade—but Carper's boot cracked into his forearm. He stumbled from the force, then pivoted back with an uppercut to Carper's jaw.

Carper grunted.

Followed by a sharp rap on the door.

"Captain?" A feminine voice leached through. "Are you all right?"

Samuel's heart skipped a beat. *God, no!* Not Miss Gilbert. Not now. A wicked grin split Carper's face, and he lunged for the doorknob.

Samuel sprang. If he didn't take Carper down before the man grabbed Miss Gilbert, there was no telling what violence she might suffer.

He snagged Carper's arm and yanked him back, wrenching the man's elbow upward so sharply, his wrist nearly connected to his armpit.

Carper howled.

Before he could swing around, Samuel shoved his foot in front of the man's boot, knocking him off-balance, then thrust him to the floor, riding the villain down.

Jamming his knee against one of Carper's arms, Samuel ground his forearm against the man's neck and cut off his air supply. Carper writhed. Samuel held. Just as the body beneath him slackened into unconsciousness, Samuel shot back to his feet and whirled, snatching out his knife. If Shankhart were still alive, the fight was only beginning.

The curtains fluttered like unmoored ghosts. Blood smeared across the counterpane in a deadly line toward the window.

The bed was empty.

Samuel ran over to the window. No wounded body lay on the ground. No corpse. No Shankhart.

Just a bloody trail that ended where horse hooves had dug into the ground.

An anguished cry rumbled behind the closed door, the low growl terrible and altogether too familiar. Abby's pulse thumped loudly in her ears. Something was wrong. Horribly wrong. She clutched little Emma tighter with one arm and pounded her fist against the wood. "Captain! Please answer."

Boot steps thudded, and the door yanked open. Captain Thatcher stood, chest heaving, dark hair wild and hanging over one eye. Blood oozed down his temple and snaked out of his nose, running over his lips before it dripped from his chin. He swiped the offense with his sleeve, as if the flow were no more than a mild inconvenience.

She gaped.

He frowned—then winced. "Why do you have Emma?"

"You are hurt!" she cried. "What happened?"

Behind him, a body on the floor moaned.

The captain glanced over his shoulder, then his dark gaze shot back to hers. "Go to your—"

Feet pounded behind her, the heavy wheezing of the innkeeper rattling off the walls. "What the briny carbuncle is going on up here? Ye don't pay me enough to be shootin' the place to bloody ribbons."

Captain Thatcher tipped his head toward her chamber. "Go to your room, Miss Gilbert. I'll meet you there straightaway."

"But—"

"Now." His voice was flint. Arguing was out of the question. And as the bloodied man behind the captain groaned louder, she wasn't so sure she wanted to put up a fight anyway. Clearly enough battle had already taken place.

Emma shifted against her shoulder, and with one last look at the wearied captain, Abby turned away. For the child's sake—and hers—it was likely best to obey his command.

Once inside her chamber, she laid the babe in the middle of her bed, grateful Emma had slept through the commotion. Abby untied her bonnet, fingers trembling, then sank down next to her, more shaken than she cared to admit. First her carriage had been attacked, then that awful man at the Laughing Dog had cornered her in the stable. Now this. Maybe she should've gone home with Fanny.

Forcefully shoving her doubts away, she straightened. No sense wallowing in maybes or what mights or should haves, a lesson she'd learned long ago when her stepmother took over the house. Oh, the long nights she'd spent in vain weeping as a child, wishing for her real mother, craving for arms that would hold her. But Father had been too preoccupied with his new wife, and her stepmother truly had only space for one love in her heart—herself.

Abby glanced up at the ceiling, as stained and cracked as she felt on the inside, and closed her eyes.

Lord, give me strength.

Rising, she retrieved a leftover cup of cold tea from the bedside table and gulped the remains, somewhat calming the fire in her throat. She set the cup down and picked up her small book of Psalms, then settled on the only chair in the room. Peace came slowly, but it did come. And the longer Abby read, the more it seeped into her soul. At last, fully relaxed and replenished, her head bobbed. She laid the book in her lap and closed her eyes.

Knuckles rapping against her door jerked her awake, driving the Psalms to the floor. Retrieving it, she set the book aside then crossed to answer.

Captain Thatcher's big frame filled the doorway. No more blood flowed from his wounds, though splotches of deep red marred his skin where it had dried.

His brown eyes blazed into hers. "The child, how does she fare?"

Here he stood, beaten and worn, and his only thought was for little Emma? What kind of man was Captain Thatcher?

She narrowed her eyes. "What happened to you, Captain?"

His jaw clenched, his only response. He was quiet for so long, she was sure he wouldn't answer.

"Nothing to concern you," he said at length.

Nothing? Did he really expect her to believe that?

"The man I hired stands at my door a bloodied mess, and you think it does not concern me?" With a sigh, she stepped aside and swept out her hand. "Come in and use my basin, sir. I will consider it a fair trade to tell you of Emma's condition if you tell me who that man was in your room."

He didn't move. Not directly. But eventually, for a reason she couldn't guess, he strode inside as if he owned the room and stalked over to the washbasin. His footsteps roused little Emma. For propriety's sake, Abby left the door open wide and collected the child. No more fever burned Emma's brow, nor did she cry, but a cough rumbled in her little lungs. Abby propped the child upright against her shoulder and patted her back as Emma barked in spasms.

The captain filled the basin then shot her a raised brow. "The babe is still ill. Why did you bring her back here?"

"I went to see Mr. Harvey this morning because my own throat started to ache and he—"

Captain Thatcher slammed down the pitcher and faced her. "Are you ill too, then?"

His tone was harsh, and his brows pulled together into a fierce line. An angry façade, but just a veneer, she suspected.

Abby shifted Emma to her other shoulder, glad when the child's coughing eased. "I am fine, Captain. A few days' discomfort and I shall be right as rain. Apparently little Emma suffers from nothing more than a bad case of the croup, hence the cough she has developed. She is not to be exposed to night air, and I purchased an ample supply of horehound syrup to keep her comfortable during the day."

The lines of his face softened—mostly—yet the grim set of his jaw remained. "So, neither of you are in danger?"

"No, we are not." She lifted her chin. "But clearly you have been."

He turned his back to her and bent, cupping his hands and splashing water. A small smile twitched her lips. Did the man really think she'd be put off that easily?

She padded over to the washstand, keeping a firm grip on Emma. "Why did that man attack you?"

After a few more splashes, the captain reached for the drying cloth. He dabbed at his temple and nose before answering. "A few unwelcome visitors came to call. Nothing more."

She frowned. Did he harbour some dark secret, or was he trying to protect her?

Emma squirmed in her arms, and once again she shifted the child. The babe would be hungry soon, which would cut a swift end to any conversation she hoped to have with the captain, for she'd have to go in search of milk and porridge.

"There's more to it than that," she persisted. "You and I both know it, and I take you for an honest man. So tell me, Captain, what transpired in your room?"

He balled up the cloth and dropped it onto the washstand. Then, blowing out a long breath, he faced her. His nose was still swollen, but no more blood leaked out. "It isn't a burden meant for you."

A bitter laugh welled, but she swallowed it—despite the pain in her throat. Would that her stepmother had owned the same sentiment.

"I respect your caution in sparing my sensibilities, sir, but I believe God provides us with fellow sojourners to help lighten our heavy loads through prayer and encouragement. And for the time being, we are fellow sojourners, are we not?"

He recoiled—or was that a wince? Hard to say, but the cloth of his suit coat tightened across his broad shoulders. Either she'd surprised him or he completely disagreed with her theology. She stood silent, awaiting his verdict.

Finally, he spoke. "You are a singular woman, Miss Gilbert."

"Is that good or bad?"

A small smile ghosted one side of his mouth. "I haven't decided yet."

Slowly, he folded his arms and widened his stance. "All right, since you insist, but remember, you pushed for this information. The man who attacked your carriage—the one who didn't make it—was the brother of a very powerful highwayman, who is now out for revenge. I am the target."

The knowledge wasn't surprising, but it was heavy, and her shoulders sagged, jostling the babe. How many times in the captain's life had he fought off violence of such magnitude? Her gaze drifted over his face. His features had no doubt been handsome once, a strange mix of boyishness and masculinity. But now, after years of weathering the darkest whims of man, he wore the scars of past battles, from the swollen, purple bump on his nose to the angry red abrasion cutting a line at his temple. Her own awful upbringing began to pale in comparison. Verbal jabs were one thing, but the scrapes and bruises marring the captain's flesh were quite another.

"I see," she murmured.

"No, lady, you don't." His gaze sharpened into a dagger, slicing into her in ways she couldn't understand. "The man gunning for me is a killer of the worst sort. He'll stop at nothing to hurt me—*nothing*—including going after you or the child. It would be better, Miss Gilbert, if we parted ways."

The harshness in his voice shivered through her—as did his words. He was right. After witnessing the effects of the beating he'd suffered, it would be better for her if she found a different guard and made haste to Brakewell Hall.

But why did the thought of saying goodbye to this rough-and-tumble man feel like lightning struck her soul, leaving behind a hollowed trunk that might not stand without him?

Chapter Fourteen

Each jolt of the carriage over the rocky road magnified the pounding in Abby's head. Pressing her fingertips to her temples, she tried to shove back the pain, but to no avail. The veins beneath her touch pulsed with a crazed beat. Apparently this grand and glorious headache had unpacked its bags and moved in, settling for a lengthy stay no matter what she did to evict it.

The carriage tilted to the right, and Abby grabbed the side of the large basket at her feet to keep it from banging into the wall. Emma had finally fallen asleep, and thankfully, her eyes remained closed as she lay nestled in her blanket. Small rattles wheezed with each of her exhales. Just thinking about tending to Emma once she did reawaken made the ache in Abby's head throb all the more.

Leaning sideways, she glanced out the window at the passing greenery, hoping for a glimpse of the upcoming inn. Surely they would be arriving soon. . .wouldn't they? She'd trade her life for a hot cup of tea right now, and the hotter, the better, judging by the next shiver that shook her bones. Despite the sunshiny day, she was cold. So cold. Tea would be just the thing to warm her, and maybe a scalding drink would burn away the pain raging every time she swallowed.

But staring out the window didn't make an inn appear. Only rows of trees passed by, their trunks lined up like soldiers at attention. Abby frowned. Perhaps it had been a mistake to continue traveling after the trauma of the morning. Yet remaining in the same building where the captain had been attacked was out of the question—especially knowing the villain had gotten away and might still be lurking about, injured or not.

The coach lurched over a bump. Flinging out her hand lest she crack her head against the wall, Abby turned away from the glass and glanced down at Emma. The sweet girl rubbed one chubby fist against her cheek yet did not open her eyes.

Sighing, Abby sank back against the seat. Only God knew if she'd made the right decision to remain with Emma and the captain—leastwise until they reached Manchester. She'd been too weary to choose otherwise, even when the captain had insisted on finding her a new guard. The mere idea of hiring another man had drained the last of her strength. Even now her eyelids grew heavy and her chin dipped with the thought of it. Perhaps if she just gave in to exhaustion, the headache would go away, and she'd be able to think more clearly.

Seconds later, the carriage stopped, and her head jerked backward. Groggy, Abby fumbled for her watch brooch, then blinked at the glass face. She'd been wrong. It hadn't been seconds but nearly a half hour since she'd last checked the time.

The lowering of the stairs rattle-clunked outside the door, and she straightened on the seat. Every muscle screamed to be left as is—then screamed louder as she bent to pick up Emma. Just before scooping up the babe, another shiver rattled through her, and she pulled back. She hated to admit it, but she simply didn't have the strength to lift the girl. It would do neither of them any good if she tumbled out of the carriage with Emma in her arms.

As soon as the door opened, Abby peeked out. Shadows from the captain's hat shaded his eyes and covered the wound on his temple, but nothing could hide the jagged abrasion ripping across his nose. Though she was loath to trouble him more than necessary, the weakness in her arms reminded her this *was* necessary.

"Would you mind retrieving Emma after you help me down, Captain? She is asleep in her basket, but she will wake soon enough."

His dark gaze drifted over her face. Many a time her stepmother had studied her as intently, but beneath the captain's searching, compassion surfaced in his eyes, so genuine that it stole her breath. Heat flashed through her—a welcome warmth.

With a nod, he held out his hand.

His fingers wrapped around hers and she stepped out, his strength a bulwark to lean on as the world swirled and her head pounded. When her feet hit the ground, she planted them firmly to keep from swaying, then pulled away. Or tried to.

The captain held on with an unrelenting grip.

She arched a brow at him. Why would he not release her?

His brown eyes merely bored into hers, offering no explanation. Then, as suddenly as a spring tempest, he let go.

"We'll stay here for the night," he rumbled.

She glanced at the sky. No storm clouds sullied the horizon, nor did the sun lay low. Puzzled, she met his gaze. "But we can easily reach the next inn."

"Not with your fever."

Fever? Her fingers flew to her forehead. A bit moist, but the skin surely didn't feel any hotter than her hand. She'd confess to a headache and sore throat if need be, but not to a fever.

She dropped her hand and smoothed her damp palm along her skirt. "You are mistaken."

His trademark smirk lifted one side of his mouth. "Your hot skin says otherwise."

There'd be no arguing the point with him, not the way his jaw hardened into a strong line. La! What was she thinking? She didn't feel up to arguing, anyway.

She forced a small smile, for she'd learned long ago how to hide her true state. "I am certain that after a cup of tea I shall be fine. Besides, we have lost enough time already."

"Then it won't matter if we delay further."

Stubborn man. She'd stamp her foot if she knew the jolt wouldn't climb up her leg and join the throbbing inside her skull.

"While I appreciate your concern, Captain, I assure you I can manage a few more miles today. After all, a bride cannot be late for her own wedding."

He grunted. "I'm sure your Lord Fanciness won't mind."

"It's Sir Jonathan *Aberley*." She scowled—then repented of it as the movement heightened the pain behind her eyes. "And of course he will mind."

"Not if he knew you were feeling poorly." The captain folded his arms, his black riding cloak stretching taut at the shoulders. "If the man is worth his salt, he'd insist you rest for a while."

Would he? What a lovely thought, to be so cherished that time and schedules could be tied up and placed on a shelf, awaiting her renewed strength. But—illness or not—one simply didn't keep a baronet waiting.

She shook her head. Bad idea. The world spun, and she flung out her hand to shore herself up against the carriage. "I can rest as easily in the carriage as I can at an inn."

"Hogwash."

One of the horses whickered, apparently as astonished as she. Why was the man so unyielding? She blew out a sigh. "Fine. Then think of yourself. That man, that highwayman, he is still out there. We have not traveled very far from Stratford. You need to put space between him and...and..."

Her words trailed off as the world tipped. Strange, that. She angled her head, straightening things out for the moment, leastwise visually. Her thoughts, however, would not be as easily ordered. What had she been saying?

The captain narrowed his eyes, then unfolded his arms and offered her a hand. "Let's get you inside. I'll come back for Emma once you're seated."

She stared down at his outstretched palm, mesmerized at the way the darkness closed in around it. Like the drawing shut of a great set of draperies, daylight slowly vanished. She blinked, unable to think why or how or—

"Miss Gilbert?"

Her name was an annoying blackfly, buzzing around her head, adding to the pounding inside. She reached to swipe it away—then tilted sideways.

Oh dear.

Something wasn't right.

Strong arms broke her fall, lifting her up against a chest that smelled of leather and horses and man. Her face pressed against a warm neck, and for the first time in her life, she felt safe. Protected. As if the arms of God Himself held her aloft. Ahh, but she could live here.

Slowly, the wooziness ebbed away, and as it did, the pounding in her head crept back. So did light and the sound of Captain Thatcher's low voice.

"...a room. Now!"

She winced. Why was he so loud? Who was he upbraiding? Summoning all her strength, she lifted her head. The blurry outline of a public room sharpened into focus, as did a pungent waft of ale. Her stomach flipped, and she laid her head back down.

The ends of the captain's hair brushed against her cheek as he strode across the room and mounted some stairs. Somewhere toward the back of her mind—far, *far* back—she knew she ought to protest this cradling of her body against a man who wasn't her intended. But he was so warm. So solid. The captain's sturdy embrace held her together and mended holes in her heart she hadn't known were torn.

Still, that didn't make it right.

Once again she forced her head up, immediately regretting the loss of the comforting nook between his neck and shoulder. "I can walk on my own, sir."

"You can fall on your own too." His voice grumbled against her ear.

His boot kicked open a door, and several breaths later, he laid her down on a cloud. Her eyelids drooped. It would be so easy to give in to this pampering. To lie about like a queen with this handsome knight to do her bidding.

Heat jolted through her, and her eyes popped wide. Handsome? Captain Thatcher? Her gaze sharpened on the worried brown eyes staring down at her, the swollen nose, the scars and lines. His was no conventional beauty, but that didn't make him any less striking. Indeed, she'd never seen a more attractive man.

The thought burned through her from head to toe. What kind of bride was she, thinking so fondly of another? She pushed up to her elbows, and the ceiling spun in a wide circle.

"Be at ease, Miss Gilbert." The captain's big hand guided her back to the counterpane. "I'll get you to your baronet soon enough. I vow it."

"But I. . ."

She what? The draperies began to pull shut again, making it hard to see and even to think. Yet she had to tell him. Something urgent. Something important. . .but what was it she wanted to say?

"Shh," he murmured. "Rest now."

"You are so kind," she whispered. That was it! He *was* kind, despite his gruff exterior. And now that she'd told him, she could let go.

So she did.

Women had called Samuel many things over the years. Cold. Taciturn. Cagey and evasive. But kind? He frowned. Miss Abigail Gilbert could see the best in a baited bear about to rip off a man's head.

Fine dots of perspiration glistened on her fair brow, and he clenched his fingers to keep from brushing back the damp tendrils sticking to her temples. Even ill, the woman was a beauty. Almost angelic the way her long lashes curved shut against her pink cheeks. His gaze drifted, pausing for a moment on the full lips so easy to coax a smile from, on to the fine line of her neck, then swept the rest of her body. Alarm rose in increments the longer he studied her. She was still. Too still. Sweet heavens! Was she yet breathing?

He dropped to his knees and leaned over her, practically cheek to cheek, praying to God he'd feel a flutter of breath against his skin. If she died, here, now, he'd have no one to blame but himself for exposing her to such illness. How had things spiraled so out of control?

Faint as a faery's whisper, a warm wisp of air kissed his face. He sank back on his haunches, blowing out a long breath. She'd be all right. Of course she would. He'd settle for nothing less. Besides, when the babe had first taken ill, hadn't little Emma appeared as close to death's door as—

Emma!

He shot to his feet and stalked out of the room. The child was likely even now squalling up a storm for having been left alone in the carriage.

Hawker would have his neck for being so careless with the babe.

A few patrons dotted the public room. Their eyes burned through his riding cloak as he blazed past them and stormed out the front door. As soon as the wood slapped shut behind him, he stopped. Ten yards ahead, where the carriage should have been, nothing but empty gravel met his gaze. Had a dull-witted stable boy retired the coach without first checking inside?

He veered left, his boots pounding the ground with each stride. Hopefully Emma still slept in her basket and she'd be no worse for the wear of having been left behind.

Breezing through the wide stable doors, he swept the area with a wild gaze, all the while listening with his whole body for a whimper or a cry. A few hooves stamped the ground. Straw rustled. Pilgrim's ears flicked and her nose raised at his entrance. He'd have to tend to her later.

Over in one corner, two ostlers rehashed their exploits of the night before as they worked on brushing down some horses. But other than their chatter and the normal sounds of a working stable, not a single baby wail rent the air.

Samuel swung right and closed in on the yellow carriage. Had Emma slept through the ordeal, then? He yanked open the door and peered in. No basket. No baby.

Blast!

Wheeling about, he stomped over to the men. "Have you seen a babe in a basket? She was in that carriage over there." He hitched his thumb over his shoulder.

Only one paused from his work, his head shaking. "No, sir. Weren't no little 'un in there, leastwise not when the coach were brought in."

Samuel's chest tightened. He tipped his hat to the man and beat a trail back outside. Had the postilion taken her inside the inn? But if so, why hadn't he seen the man or Emma in the taproom?

Fear for the child's safety punched him in the gut, and he increased his pace, eating up the ground with long-legged steps. This time he shot toward the back entrance of the inn, rather than the front. A stone stairwell led to the lower level, and he flew down the flagstones.

He'd start at the bottom and work his way to the top. If he had to tear the inn apart floor by floor, so be it. He *would* find the child. He had to.

But what if he didn't?

Please, God.

Pushing down doubt, he shoved the door open—and a blessed, barking cough pealed out from a room down the corridor. He dashed along the smoky passageway and flew into a large kitchen. Near a wall lined with shelves of crockery, a plump woman on a stool patted Emma on the back, little puffs of flour wafting off her sleeves with the movement.

Samuel's shoulders sagged, tension draining.

At the center of the room, the cook looked up from where she stood chopping a chicken, and aimed the butcher knife at him. "Guests aren't allowed down here. Best be off with you, then."

"That's my child." He nodded toward the babe and advanced.

At the sound of his voice, Emma turned, her rosy cheeks splitting wide in a grin. She flailed a chubby fist toward him, greeting him with a rattling coo.

He reached for the babe and nodded at the woman. "Thank you."

The woman handed Emma over with a cancerous gaze. "For shame, sir! Leaving a little one unattended, and an ill one at that."

The cook chimed in from her post at the table. "Aye. What's this world coming to when a father leaves behind his baby like a forgotten loaf of bread?"

It was reasonable to believe the cook assumed he was Emma's father. Unreasonable, however, was the queer catch of his breath and lonely ache in his soul—especially when Emma reached for his hat and tugged it sideways. What would it feel like to hold a child of his own?

One by one, he removed Emma's fingers from the brim of his hat and retreated, as much from the strange notion as from the cook, who yet brandished her big knife. "I assure you, ladies, that it was necessary. Good day."

He ducked out the door, the last of the cook's words stabbing him in the back.

"That child needs a mother."

He winced. She couldn't be more right. Emma did need a mother, and well did he know it. Going to live with an aunt didn't guarantee a happy ending, a lesson he'd learned the hard way long ago.

Gaining the servant's stairway, he ascended, keeping a strong hold on the girl wriggling against his shoulder. No doubt she'd be hungry soon. Thunderation! Should he turn back and once again face the two women of wrath to beg a bowl of porridge?

He paused at the top of the stairs, but as luck would have it, the wire-haired innkeeper swung around a corner and headed his way.

The man's eyes narrowed as he drew close. "This part of the inn is not for guests. Have you lost your way, sir?"

"No, just retrieving something I lost. Could you send up a bowl of porridge, some tea, and a mug of warm milk?"

The innkeeper eyed him for a moment. "I could, but I have yet to see a coin from you."

Really? The man wanted to quibble over coins while he stood here with a squirming babe? He dug in his pocket with his free hand while Emma once again yanked his hat sideways, cutting off half his vision. Even so, he held out a shilling—one of his last. "Will this suffice for now?"

The innkeeper snatched it, the offering easing the creases on his brow. "Aye."

"Good." Samuel brushed past him and worked his way upward to Miss Gilbert's room. Once inside, he set Emma down and pulled off his hat, giving the worn felt to her. The girl immediately bit into the brim, her big blue eyes smiling up at him.

Samuel couldn't stop his own smile from wavering across his lips. Emma was a charmer—and Hawker was a fool for having sent her away.

Turning from Emma, he eyed Miss Gilbert. She lay exactly where he'd left her, cheeks unnaturally flushed, eyes closed. His smile faded—then disappeared altogether when she suddenly thrashed her head side to side.

"No. No! Do not shut me away. Not again!" Her eyes flew open, glassy and abnormally bright. "Please, I beg you. . ." She looked right at him but not really. Whatever she saw wasn't him. "Why, Papa? Why did you send me off alone?"

Her *father* sent her on this journey alone? Samuel fisted his hands, a fire hotter than Abby's fever burning through him. He'd ask what sort of man would do that to his daughter—except he knew all too well.

Her voice softened to a whimper. "You just left. Did not even say goodbye. Do you not love me?"

Her words knocked him sideways, his gut hardening to a sickening knot. It wasn't right, this pain of hers, this anguish, and now he finally understood her determined flight to Penrith.

Dropping to his knees at her side, he blew out his tension through his nose and brushed back the damp hair sticking to her face. "Shh, Miss Gilbert. All is well. You're not alone. I'll not leave you."

At his assurance, her eyes rolled back and she went limp. Alarmed, Samuel bent closer, praying to God for breath and life. So fair a frame should not have to bear the fire of such a fever—especially for one who'd apparently come from a hellish existence.

God, please! Would that I might take this illness in her stead. Grant her peace, God. Grant her Your peace.

Minutes passed, and thankfully, Miss Gilbert's breathing evened. Perspiration yet dotted her brow, but she lay serenely enough that he pulled back.

With Miss Gilbert quieted, food on the way, and the child entertained, Samuel left the lady's bedside and sank onto a chair. Scrubbing a hand over his face, he took care not to touch the tender part of his nose. He'd been on some hair-raising journeys in his time. But this one? His hand dropped to his lap. This one was beginning to trouble him the most. It scared him, this growing need to protect the woman and the child as if they were his own.

And he wasn't afraid of anything.

Chapter Fifteen

Abby's eyes opened to blurry outlines in a fuzzy world. Was this another dream? She blinked and—slowly—all the blobby shapes began to separate into individual objects. The table by her bed. The basin atop it. The man sleeping on a chair with a babe sprawled across his chest.

What? She blinked again. This might be a dream, for never would she have imagined the sweet way Captain Thatcher nestled Emma in his arms. His stubbly cheek rested against the top of the baby's head, a contrast of fair and rugged, dark and light. Asleep, the hard lines of the captain's face softened, erasing cares and years and burdens so that he was a young man again—albeit a bit battered. His nose yet sported a gash, and a purple bruise spread from his temple to his eye.

Abby shifted, and a cloth fell from her forehead. She reached for it and pulled the nearly dried bit of rag away, trying in vain to remember if she'd been the one to put it there. Had she forgotten, or had the captain been bathing her brow? Either way, the treatment had apparently worked, for she no longer shivered or sweated with a fever.

Emboldened, she risked a swallow. No sharp pain. No more fire burned, no tenderness or swelling. Only a slight ache remained.

"How do you fare?" The captain's low voice crept across the room, his eyes open now and studying her with a worried gaze.

"Better—" Her voice garbled, and she cleared her throat. "The room no longer spins."

And it didn't, leastwise not while she was lying prone. Tentatively, Abby pushed up to sit—and still no dizziness swooped in. Light did, though. A sunray cut through the length of the room, beaming in a straight line from between the nearly closed draperies to her eyes. Judging by the slope of it, she estimated the day was well spent. Had she slept several hours, then?

Turning from the brilliance, she faced the captain. "You must think me a pampered princess. I am sorry to have wasted the day away."

"It's been two."

Stunned, her lips parted, but no words came out. *Two* days? Surely she'd heard wrong. "Pardon me, but what did you say?"

Emma stirred, rubbing her face against the captain's shirt. Then she planted her chubby little hands against his broad chest and pushed up, craning her neck to peer at Abby. A coo burbled out of her.

The captain rose. In three strides, he swiped up a chunk of bread from off a table near the window, then settled the girl on the floor with it. Emma gnawed the crust—until he started to walk away. Big tears shimmered in her eyes, and her mouth opened in a wail.

Without a word, Captain Thatcher turned back and pulled his hat off the table, then handed it to the girl. Immediately, Emma crushed it to her chest, forgetting all about her upset.

Abby couldn't help but smile at the scene. Whether he'd admit it or not, a big heart beat beneath the captain's wrinkled waistcoat.

He dragged the chair to the side of the bed and faced her. "We arrived yesterday afternoon. You slept the night through and most of today."

La! Then she had heard right. Abby sank into the pillow, the reality of the captain's words seeping in. Surely by now Sir Jonathan was worried sick by her late arrival and was out searching the highways and byways for her. "I stalled our journey," she murmured, then looked up at the weary captain. "And left you alone to tend to Emma."

"And you."

Her nose wrinkled in confusion. If she'd been sleeping the whole time, what kind of tending could she have possibly needed?

"What do you mean?"

He scratched the side of his chin, the raspy noise a reminder of his manhood. "You were delirious into the early hours of the night. Thrashing about. Mumbling about your Sir Fanciness."

"It is Sir Jonathan and—" She gasped. The *early* hours of the night? "Do not tell me, Captain, that you spent the entire night alone with me in my room."

"You were ill." His hand dropped, and he shrugged. "I couldn't very well leave you by yourself."

Did the man have no sense of propriety whatsoever? She pressed her lips to keep from gaping. "You could not have hired a serving girl to sit with me?"

A storm brewed in his eyes, a dark warning that she'd pushed him too far. "Believe it or not, lady, the day I set out for work on the heath, I wasn't expecting a journey to the north, especially not one that would take more than a fortnight. I don't carry as much coin on me as your Sir Fancy—"

"Jonathan!"

She winced at her shrill tone, shrewish as her stepmother's. By all that was righteous, was she turning into the ill-tempered woman?

The captain flattened his palm against her brow. True concern pulled at the sides of his mouth. "Is the fever returning?"

"No." She pushed his hand away, overly aware of the warmth of his skin against hers. "I should not have spoken so forcefully. Forgive me for such ingratitude. I thank you for your care, truly, but I have a reputation to uphold. If anyone should find us thus and report back to the baronet, he would not have me."

The truth tasted bitter. Whether Sir Jonathan loved her or not, his social station demanded he avoid any hint of scandal. He was taking a big enough risk marrying her, a nobody with naught to offer but her dowry.

Captain Thatcher's jaw hardened. "That, Miss Gilbert, would be his loss."

No. He was wrong. It would be entirely her loss, for she had nothing to go back home to.

"You do not understand." Her throat tightened, and for a moment she feared that the illness really was returning. There was no way the captain could grasp how horrid her life had been, dressed in the trappings of a beloved daughter yet living each day reviled and berated. Just thinking of going back to her stepmother's sharp tongue and her sisters' digging remarks sent a shiver across her shoulders.

"After last night, I understand far more than you credit." The captain's gaze burned into hers. "You are running from an unhappy existence toward a man you hope will value you for the gem that you are."

She sucked in a sharp breath, unsure what shocked the most—that he could so easily sum her up in so few words. . .or that he'd earnestly called her a gem. But no. It was neither. What really stunned was the casual way he meted out truth with no pretense or guile whatsoever.

But that didn't mean she'd admit to it. Not to him. Not to anyone.

She lifted her chin. "Suffice it to say, Captain, that a lady never—ever—shares a room with a man who is not her husband, illness or not."

He said nothing for a long while, then ever so slowly, he nodded. "All right. Don't fret. It's highly unlikely anyone here holds the ear of your baronet, so rest assured not a soul will go telling him of your sordid night alone with me. Besides, no one knows us, and frankly, I doubt that anyone cares."

A sharp rap on the door belied his words.

Though still fully dressed in her gown of yesterday, Abby yanked the counterpane up to her chin. Heaven help her. Ill or not, were she to be found in a bedchamber with a man, it would be her ruination.

Samuel sprang to his feet. Scoundrels didn't usually knock so politely, but that didn't stop him from unsheathing his knife. He'd not be caught off guard again—especially not with a woman and child within range of harm.

He cracked open the door and peeked out, every sense heightened. Nothing met his gaze—leastwise not at eye level. Standing only as tall as his waist, a smudge-faced boy gawked up at him. The lad retreated a step when their gazes locked.

"Y–you be Cap'n Thatcher?"

He frowned. Such trepidation didn't usually bother him, but this time it nicked him in the heart. Since when had he grown tired of being feared? It was a protection. A shield. His frown deepened. So much time spent with Miss Gilbert and Emma was changing him in ways he couldn't fathom.

He scanned the length of the corridor behind the boy, on the off chance the lad was a setup. No one lurked about nor were any doors cracked open. Nothing moved, save for a tree branch casting a shadow on the wall from a window at the end of the passageway.

Satisfied for now, he finally answered. "I'm Thatcher."

"Then this be for you, sir." The boy held up a folded slip of paper.

The instant his fingers pinched the note, the lad whipped around and tore down the passageway. His untucked shirttail flew behind him and was the last thing to disappear down the stairway.

Samuel stared a moment longer, making sure no ill surprises popped up, then tucked his knife back into his boot and closed the door.

By now, Miss Gilbert sat on the edge of the bed, gripping the coverlet with both hands. Little Emma rumbled a cough and started crawling his way.

"Who was it?"

The lady's voice was a shiver. It wasn't right, this fear he'd brought upon her. She never should have been caught up in this mess. A pox upon Shankhart!

Samuel allowed a small smile, hoping to calm her worry. "It was just a boy. Don't fret."

The coverlet dipped an inch. "What did he want?"

He left the question dangling in the air. Sometimes the better part of valor was silence. Turning the paper over, he scanned for a name, a seal, anything to hint as to who'd sent the note, but it was blank on both sides.

A tug on his trousers drew his attention away as Emma pulled herself up on his leg. He stood poised to snatch her should she totter backward and crack her head. She wobbled—yet held tight to his leg, baby chatter burbling past her lips. She'd be fine.

He focused back on the note. Unfolding the paper, he read three hastily scratched words, barely legible:

I see you.

One by one, the hairs at the nape of his neck stood out like wires. Without moving a muscle, his eyes darted around the room. He knew in his head no one could possibly see him inside these four walls, but that didn't stop his heart from racing. The weight of a thousand pairs of unseen eyes pressed down on him, making it hard to breathe. For the sake of Emma and Miss Gilbert, he fought the urge to rave about like a madman, knife bared, looking for a killer who wasn't there.

"Despite your earlier reassurance, Captain, apparently someone knows you are here. Or is the message for me?"

Would to God that it wasn't! He crumpled the paper and shoved it into his pocket, then forced a soothing tone to his voice. "No, it's nothing."

Liar!

The dip of Miss Gilbert's brow concurred.

Bending, he peeled Emma's fingers from his trousers and eased her bottom to the floor. As soon as she sat steady, he strode to the window and slid back an edge of the drape with one finger.

Their first-floor chamber overlooked the front of the inn. There were no outbuildings from this view, so no one could possibly be secreted inside a shadowy corner, peering out a window at him, or worse, aiming a muzzle. Only a stand of trees stood opposite the drive, maybe ten yards off. He narrowed his eyes, staring so hard his eyes watered. Branches. Greenery. Nothing large enough to suggest a villain hunkered down for a shot at him.

Behind him, footsteps padded on the floor. "Clearly there is more to that note than you are telling me. What did it say?"

He pulled back his hand and the drapes fell shut, sealing them off from the world outside. A blessing and a curse, that.

Turning, he faced Miss Gilbert, hating that he couldn't tell her the truth—and hating the truth even more. Her skin glowed white, a contrast from yesterday's flaming patches of colour on her cheeks. She was definitely on the mend, but had all of her strength returned?

"Do you feel equal to watching Emma?" he asked.

A small crease lined her brow. "You are frightening me, Captain."

"There is nothing to fear. I only need to step out for a while."

Her big brown eyes searched his face. "Why?"

He clenched his jaw. He'd rather take on a rock-fisted brawler bent on smashing his brains out than answer that question.

So he parried with one of his own. "Do you trust me?"

Her nose scrunched, as if the query smelled of something rotten. Which it did. Truly, it wasn't fair of him to twist the conversation back onto her like this, but it was necessary.

Her lips parted, closed, then parted again. "Yes, Captain. I do trust you. Implicitly."

The conviction in her tone was stunning enough, but the veracity in her gaze stole his breath.

He reached out, tentatively. She held still. Assured she wouldn't flinch or recoil, he stroked his knuckle along her cheek. Skin soft as the babe's warmed beneath his touch, more delicate and velvety than he imagined.

"Believe me when I say, Miss Gilbert, that I will allow nothing bad to happen to you or Emma." The words came out husky, and he swallowed against the thickness in his throat.

"Very well." She nodded and pulled back. "I shall tend Emma."

Hard to tell what shook him more, the foreboding note or the loss of their connection. Giving himself a mental shake—what *was* he thinking to have caressed her so?—he sidestepped the woman and gathered his hat from off the floor. He jammed it on his head, then shrugged into his coat and grabbed his gun. Hopefully he wouldn't need it.

Behind him, a hand rested on his sleeve.

"Be careful, Captain."

This time he pulled away, unsure if he should feel angry that she plagued him to be cautious or touched that she cared enough to warn him. He settled on neither, choosing to ignore the host of foreign emotions the woman kindled in his gut.

He stopped at the door and tipped his head at her. "Stay in the room."

Then he slipped out of the chamber and stole down the corridor, using all his powers of stealth. Keeping to the edge of the stairs—less chance for squeaking a loose board—he descended into the public room. Two men shared a pipe in one corner, but he quickly discounted any danger they might pose. Both were grey-headed and incapable of wrestling with a cat let alone him. The rest of the tables sat empty.

Near the kitchen door, a boy strolled out, chewing on a pastry. . . the lad who'd delivered the note.

Samuel collared the boy before he could see him coming. He guided the lad to a shadowy corner, away from prying eyes. But to be extra cautious, he kept his tone quiet as he crouched to eye level. "Who gave you that message?"

Fear rampaged over the boy's face. "D-dunno," he stuttered.

Samuel narrowed his eyes. "How can that be? Was it a ghost?"

"No, sir." The boy shrank until his back hit the wall. "Never seen him afore, that's all."

"So, it was a man, hmm?"

The boy nodded. "He gave me a shilling to bring that note to you."

Suspicion prickled across his shoulders. Most would only pay a ha'penny or maybe a thruppence to have a note delivered. But a whole shilling? The sender was either very careless with his money—or had a good supply of coin. Had Shankhart mended and tracked him here so soon? Or had he sent one of his henchmen to torment him?

"This man, tell me of him."

The boy's lower lip trembled, but to his credit, his voice didn't crack. "Can't, sir."

"Why not?"

"I din't see him. He stayed in the shadows, out in the stable."

Samuel shoved his hand into his pocket and pulled out one of his last shillings—for he'd not be bested by a scoundrel even in the paying of a lad.

"For your trouble." He held out the coin.

Eyes widening, the boy snatched the money quick as a pauper—which he wasn't. Not anymore. It was he who was well on his way to the workhouse if he kept parting with the sparse amount he had left.

He rose, and the boy scurried past him with a hasty, "Thank ye!"

Leaving the inn behind, Samuel strode across the backyard, pulling out his gun yet keeping it concealed. It wouldn't do to go scaring any ostlers lurking about the stable, but neither would he run headlong into an ambush.

He slid around the door on silent feet, immediately easing into a shadow. No one moved, for no one was about. Not here in the large work area, anyway. The scene was eerily reminiscent of a week ago when he'd gone in search of Miss Gilbert back at the Laughing Dog.

Satisfied no one hid beneath the workbench or behind a line of tack hanging on a wall, he padded over to the long corridor lined with stalls and began methodically searching each one. The first two were empty, standing ready to house the next horses arriving at the inn. A beauty of a black Belgian eyed him warily in the third. And at the fourth, where Pilgrim lodged, a roar ripped out of his throat.

"No!"

White-hot rage flamed in his gut as he flung open the half door and dashed inside, trading his gun for his knife. Pilgrim lay on her side, hooves tied, rope biting tight into the horsey flesh of her forelegs. A single crude word was painted in whitewash on her belly:

SOON

Samuel sliced through the ropes, barely able to thank God that his horse yet breathed, so keen was the fury burning through him.

If war was what Shankhart wanted, he just got his wish.

Chapter Sixteen

A knife to the kidneys. A shot to the head. Maybe even a fast drop from a short rope. Samuel scowled. No, none of those were good enough.

He slackened the reins as Pilgrim tramped along the rocky trail. If God called him home today, he feared the gates of heaven might not open to him—not with such molten anger simmering inside his veins. It was wrong, of course, to clutch on to these cruel thoughts of vengeance against Shankhart, but sweet mercy! He was a mortal, was he not? Flesh and blood. More sinner than saint, for though he tried, he could not let go of his rage. Not when his best horse yet favored her front foreleg where the rope had sliced into it, nor when he witnessed the fear in Miss Gilbert's eyes. And especially not when he thought of the threat hanging over all their heads. Shankhart or his lackeys could strike at any moment—or not at all. . .and that was almost worse.

Keeping the carriage well within sight, Samuel eased Pilgrim down the rise. For two days he'd had to temper their pace, slowing their progress, hoping and praying all the while that the gouge on his horse's leg would heal quickly. Besides, Miss Gilbert and little Emma were still on the mend themselves, so the sluggish pace suited. Leastwise, that's what he told himself. But were he honest, the real reason he plodded along and kept to the shadows was to remain vigilant while nursing the hatred he bore toward Shankhart. Next time they met, he'd have no qualms about shooting the blackguard right through the heart.

He hung his head, conviction bubbling sour at the back of his throat.

God, have mercy, on Shankhart and on me.

A rumble of thunder lifted his head, and he studied the horizon. While the entire day had been sullen, now the pewter sky deepened to an unholy blackness. A dark bank of clouds advanced like a shield wall and would soon bear down upon their heads. He sniffed, then frowned as a pungent tang hit his nostrils. Earthy. Acrid. Pilgrim's ears twitched, indicating the horse sensed the same.

This was more than a summer rain. A tempest was about to break, as potent and ugly as his rage.

Carefully, Samuel urged Pilgrim to up the pace. By his best judgment, they were halfway between inns, so even if they did turn around, they'd not outrun the storm by the time they reached shelter. Yet pressing on only brought them closer to the menacing—

Lightning struck. Deafeningly close. The zing of it raised the hair on his arms. The accompanying boom reverberated in his chest. Pilgrim reared, and Samuel held tight, flattening forward against the horse's neck while working to get his mount under control.

Ahead, the carriage horses bolted.

Blast it!

Samuel dug in his heels, coaxing Pilgrim into a controlled run. He trailed the bouncing coach by twenty yards, wishing to heaven he could give Pilgrim free rein, but any faster and he'd lame his friend for certain.

Another crack boomed. The carriage lurched sideways, careening over rocks. Crashing into ruts.

God, protect Miss Gilbert and little Emma.

The space between him and the coach lessened in increments, until miraculously, the carriage stopped. Samuel heaved back on the reins, halting Pilgrim barely a pace or two behind it. Thankfully, the thing was still in one piece—but a very lopsided piece at that. The carriage listed hard to the right, the entire back end jutting down toward the rear left wheel.

Samuel swung off Pilgrim and neared the broken coach just as the postilion rounded the side and joined him. They both crouched as the wind picked up and the first stabs of rain fired down from the sky.

The postilion's curse rang out with the next peal of thunder. "I knew this carriage weren't sound! But did old man Herrick listen to me? No, not a bit of it. Carpin' crow! I should've insisted on a different coach."

Samuel was inclined to agree. Only God knew how many years and miles this carriage had seen. Judging by the looks of it, far too many. He narrowed his eyes and trailed his finger along the curve of the spring—leastwise as far as he was able. The bolt holding the spring arm had completely sheared off so that the casing had ripped loose.

Rising, he met the postilion's gaze. "Is there shelter nearby?"

The man made a grab for his hat as the next gust of wind lifted it. Holding tightly to the black felt, he bobbed his head. "Farmer Bigby, up past Bramble Creek."

Samuel tugged down the brim of his own hat as the sky turned to an unnatural shade of greenish grey. Hopefully Bramble Creek wasn't far off. "We best make haste, then. Unhook the horses. I'll see to the lady and—"

"No need, Captain. Emma and I are accounted for."

The sweet voice in his ear was as startling as the next peal of thunder. He jerked aside. Barely an arm's length away stood Miss Gilbert, Emma blinking wide-eyed in her arms. "How did you. . . ?"

He shook his head. No sense asking how she'd managed to crawl out of a crook-sloped hulk of a carriage with a baby in tow, for such was the wonder of Miss Abigail Gilbert. Glancing about, he spied a boulder just about the right size to employ as a mounting block.

"Come along. This storm is about to break in earnest."

She followed, but not without questions. "What about the carriage? Will you be able to fix it? Where are we going?"

He stopped and reached for Emma, letting Miss Gilbert's queries blow away in the wind. Clutching the child to his chest with one arm, he offered Miss Gilbert his hand to aid her atop the rock. "Climb up."

She frowned at his upturned palm. "Surely you are not suggesting I ride your horse."

Big plops of rain began to hammer harder, popping like grape-shot as they hit his riding cloak. He grabbed her hand. "It's not a suggestion."

"But I cannot manage your horse!" She pulled back.

He held tight. "I'm not expecting you to. Now mount."

Fear flashed in her eyes. Odd. Surely being a gentlewoman, she had riding experience. Didn't she? He squeezed her fingers. "Don't worry, Miss Gilbert. I'll be with you the whole time. I'll keep you and Emma safe, I vow it."

"Do not tell me you intend to ride along with me." Her nostrils flared, indignation as thick in her tone as the humidity in the air.

"Propriety be hanged, lady! Do you see this lightning? If we don't get on my horse soon, you'll have more than proper etiquette to worry about. Now grab the saddle and hike yourself up."

Thunder boomed an accompaniment to his order, and a breath later, the sky ripped open, unleashing a downpour. Without another word, Miss Gilbert heaved herself atop Pilgrim. He handed her Emma, then swung up behind them. For a moment, he fumbled with the wet tie on his riding coat, then whipped it off and flung it around the lady and child, covering most of her and all of Emma. They'd still get wet, but not nearly as much.

Miss Gilbert turned her head, her warm breath puffing against his cheek. "Thank you, but now you will be wet and cold."

Wet, yes, but cold? Not a chance, not with the feel of her body tucked against his.

"This way." The postilion shouted above the roar of wind.

Samuel urged Pilgrim into line behind the man, who'd tethered the other carriage horse to his mount. As they worked their way along a cow trail, the storm pitched wicked gusts of wind and rain, sharp and frigid.

But Samuel paid the harsh weather no heed. How could he? The only thing he could feel was the woman pressed against his chest. The softness of her. The heat of her body. The way she fit so perfectly against him.

Though he ought not, Samuel leaned closer and inhaled her orange-water scent, the sweet fragrance mixing with the wildness of the storm. If he bent any nearer, his lips would be against the bare flesh of her neck, and the craving to taste that skin charged through him, settling low in his belly.

He tensed. What was this strange urge? He'd doubled-up with women before, hauling them to safety more times than he could count. Such was his job.

He clutched the reins tighter as a new realization slapped him hard. This wasn't a job anymore. Not with this woman.

Involuntarily, his arms tightened against her, encircling her, drawing her close, sheltering her from the storm—or so he told himself. Were he honest, the physical reaction stemmed from so much more. And that scared him more than facing Shankhart. For the first time in his life, he was unsure what to do with or how to manage the mounting desire to make a woman—*this* woman—his own.

He frowned—yet he didn't pull away. He couldn't. Such was the magnetism of Miss Gilbert. If her baronet could read his thoughts, the man would more than reconsider his proposal.

He'd challenge Samuel to a duel of honor.

Abby clutched the squirming Emma tightly against her chest. How terrifying it must be to endure such a tempest cloaked in the darkness of the captain's riding coat. She ought to be squirming with fright herself, seated atop the man's fearsome horse, riding headlong into rain that cut sideways.

But oddly, fear wasn't a consideration, not with the captain's strong arms holding her firmly in place. She shifted as the horse climbed a rise, and the captain's strength pulsed through her. He guided them through the blackest of storms as if nothing but a few pesky drops of water fell from the sky.

With each step of the horse, she tried not to feel the ride of his body behind her. A worthless effort. She could think of nothing else but the hard muscles pressed against her back or the touch of his thighs bumping into her. It was licentious, this position. She ought to lean forward, put what distance she could between him and her. But God help her, she didn't want to. Didn't *ever* want to, such was the draw of the man.

Heedless of propriety, she turned her face and pressed her cheek against his chest, seeking a measure of shelter from the pelting rain. Without his cloak, the soaked fabric of his shirt and waistcoat moulded against his flesh, and she breathed in his scent of horse and leather and possibility. What would it be like to be loved by the untamed Captain Thatcher? Tingles shivered through her, and in response, he tucked his chin, protecting the top of her head.

Using the wriggling Emma as an excuse, she leaned into him, telling herself she needed such closeness to balance as the horse fought for footing against the storm. It was wrong, though, and she knew it. If her stepmother witnessed her brazen behaviour, she'd be struck with more than a tongue-lashing. The surety of a stinging slap needled the cheek not shielded by the captain's warmth, and Abby forced herself to turn away and face the rain instead.

She blinked as water blinded her view. What a cow-eyed schoolgirl she'd become. What was wrong with her? Inwardly, she scolded herself as soundly as her stepmother might. Yet surely, once she arrived at Brakewell Hall and reached the arms of Sir Jonathan, all these unbidden feelings for Captain Thatcher would vanish. Yes, that was it. Of course they would. She entertained naught but a silly infatuation for the man because she'd paid him to look out for her. Any woman in her place would feel the same. In fact, had Fanny remained, the woman would've been positively moonstruck in his presence.

That settled, she eased little Emma around and rubbed the child's back with one hand, a motion that soothed her as well. Shortly thereafter, the postilion ahead of them halted, and they dismounted in front of a whitewashed croft. Hardly bigger than the nearby stable, the squat building braved the onslaught like a stalwart sailor, used to lashing winds and driving rain. Loosened by a wild gust, a few pieces of the thatched roof near the corner waved a greeting.

Not so the man who flung open the door. He welcomed them with the barrel of a musket.

Immediately, the captain sidestepped in front of her and Emma, blocking them with his wide shoulders.

"Be ye daft?" A woman's shrill voice from inside the cottage blended with the howl of the storm. " 'T'ain't fit for beasts out there, let alone travelers. Let them in, man!"

Captain Thatcher raised both hands, his wet frock coat riding the strong lines of his back. "We mean no harm. We only ask for shelter."

Abby huddled closer to him, seeking haven from the captain's big frame just in case the crofter wouldn't allow them in. A few grumbles later, the man pushed the door wider and stepped aside. And thank goodness, because Emma started to cry.

The captain ushered her and the child in first, keeping close behind them as they entered. Abby warmed immediately from his watchful care and from escaping the cold rain. The postilion followed suit.

And the woman howled again. "Why, stuff my goose! That be you, Darby Cleaver?"

Doffing his hat, the postilion shook his head like a dog, water droplets flying everywhere. "Aye, m'um. We broke down on the road just afore the storm picked up."

"See?" The woman turned to her husband, planting her fists on her hips. "And you about to send them to glory."

"Wheest!" The man blew air through his teeth, his hook nose bunching from the effort. He lowered his gun—though he didn't let go of it—and pinched the woman's cheek. "Just protectin' my fair beauty."

"Ach! Off with ye." She flicked her fingers at him, yet despite the action, the warmth in her voice radiated volumes of love.

As she bounced Emma, quieting the child somewhat, Abby studied the woman. A ruffled cap, which at some point might've been white, clung to the top of the woman's head. Lines carved into her face at the sides of her mouth and near the creases of her eyes. Those eyes might have shone a brilliant blue once but were now bleached to the colour of a sun-washed August sky. The woman wasn't old, but neither was she young. Rather, she was timeless, her apron holding in an eternity of love and life and laughter. She was the kind of woman with whom you could share a pot of tea and your deepest secrets. Abby's heart swelled. Would this be what her mother might've looked like had she lived?

As if the woman sensed her perusal, she swooped over to Abby and corralled her with an arm about the shoulders, pulling her away from the captain's side. "Come along, child. We'll get ye and yer little one into some dry clothes, then some hot broth is in order, I think."

Abby tried to keep up, but with wet skirts sticking to her legs and the woman's brisk gait, she was glad for the fleshy arm guiding her across the small main room. Dry clothes would be heaven, but anything more seemed like an imposition. She glanced sideways at the woman. "Please do not trouble yourself about the broth."

Just then a sharp cough barked out of Emma, and Abby recanted. Though the child had made amazing progress in regaining her health, it wouldn't do to extend a calling card for her illness to repay a visit.

"On second thought, some broth would be nice." She smiled. "And thank you."

The men's low talk about horse stabling and carriage repair faded as the woman ushered her into a back room. A bed with a rumpled mantle filled nearly the whole space, save for a small table with a candle, a crooked chair in the corner, and a battered chest against one wall with a shelf above it.

The woman flung open the chest's lid and yanked out a shift and a gown, both the colour of sand. Straightening, she faced Abby and shoved out her offering with one hand while collecting Emma with the other. "No doubt the garments will be too big and not nearly as fine as yer used to, but all the same, they will serve ye well until we get yer gown dried. I'll see to yer wee one while you change."

The woman bustled past her and laid Emma on the bed. For a moment, Abby froze, wondering where exactly she was supposed to shed her clothes and don the dry ones. But as a shiver shimmied across her shoulders, all modesty fled, and she began the arduous task of peeling off the drenched fabric.

"Thank you for your hospitality, Mrs. . . . ?" She fished for the woman's name while she worked.

"La, child! No such formalities under this humble roof. The name's Wenna. And you be?"

Wenna? Ahh. . .so that explained the leftover Cornish lilt in the woman's voice. But what in the world was the woman doing this far north?

Shoving the wet pile aside with her foot, Abby reached for the fresh shift. "I am Abigail Gilbert, but please, call me Abby."

"Well then, Abby, pleased I am to—"

A desperate wail squealed out of Emma, cutting the woman off. Despite Wenna's murmurs and shushings, the child would have none of it as she wrangled Emma into what was likely one of her husband's shirts. Strange, that. Usually Emma was such a placid little girl.

Wenna swung the child up into her arms and faced her, bouncing Emma as she spoke. "As soon as you're dressed, let's get you, your fine man, and your youngling fed and put up for the night. We'll tuck ol' Darby Cleaver out in the byre and the rest o' ye can sleep upstairs in my boy's loft." She jerked her head toward the rafters. " 'T'ain't much, but 'tis snug and kept at the ready for my Georgie to return."

Heat crawled up Abby's neck, though she was hard-pressed to decide if it was from the woman's misunderstanding that Captain Thatcher was "her fine man" or from the niggling wish that she might want him to be. She ducked inside the billowing fabric and pulled the ample cloth over her body, mulling over what to say.

"I appreciate your offer, truly." As soon as her head popped out of the gown, she smiled. "But there is no need to put yourself out. We are more than grateful for the shelter you are providing while the storm rages, but as soon as it breaks, we shall be on our way."

"Ach! None of it." The woman wagged her head and juggled the fretting Emma to her other shoulder. "That storm's like to bluster and blow till the wee hours. Ye'll be staying the night, no doubt, and I'll not hear another word on it."

Abby bit her lip as the woman bustled past her, humming a folk tune to quiet Emma. It had been bad enough back in Stratford when the surgeon had assumed her union with the captain, but they hadn't had to share a roof with him. How was she to tell the headstrong Wenna they weren't married?

She followed the woman's swishing skirts, scrambling for the right way to broach the subject, and settled on simply being direct. "We are not married."

Wenna stopped and turned so quickly, Emma's head bobbed from the ride. "What's that you say?"

"The captain and I. . .well. . ." Abby withered beneath the woman's narrowed eyes. Perhaps the direct approach hadn't been the best idea, but she couldn't rescind it now. So, she lifted her chin. "We are not married, but I can explain—"

The woman's hand shot up, cutting her off. "Faith and honor! Then ye can't be staying here after all!"

Chapter Seventeen

Samuel stopped on the threshold of the croft's front door. Outside, sheets of rain swallowed Farmer Bigby and the postilion, Darby Cleaver, as they dashed toward the stable, horses in tow, Pilgrim last in line. His horse needed his attention, especially that wound on her foreleg, yet Samuel turned back and shut the door behind him. Pilgrim would have to wait, for a bigger squall was about to break in here. The remnants of the older woman's harsh tone yet resounded from wall to wall. What the devil had Miss Gilbert done to offend her so?

The lady in question clutched her hands in front of her, dressed in a gown two sizes too large. Miss Gilbert's dark hair curled past her shoulders, wet and loose as a wayward girl's. Patches of colour pinked her cheeks, and her big eyes blinked wide. A smile twitched Samuel's lips. Even garbed in homespun, the woman was a beauty.

"Please, Wenna, hear me out." She dared a step closer to the farmer's wife—Wenna, apparently—and Emma nearly launched out of the woman's arms to get to her. But Miss Gilbert kept her gaze fixed on Wenna and measured out her words, slow and even. "I assure you that we bring no shame to this house. Captain Thatcher is my hired guardian, nothing more. Believe me when I say that there is not a nobler man on the face of this earth."

Samuel planted his feet to keep from staggering. He'd taken blows to the chest before, even fell out a first-story window once, landing flat on his back in a pile of crates, but none of those incidents stole his breath quite like Miss Gilbert's passionate defense.

The older woman humphed. "That may be, but this child is yours."

She handed over the weeping Emma, who immediately buried her face into Miss Gilbert's neck and quit crying.

Before Miss Gilbert could respond, Wenna folded her arms, clearly not done with the battle. "I'll not be condoning no unwed mothers, no matter how fancy yer clothes be. You can stay the night, but off with the likes of ye come morning, and may God have mercy on yer soul."

Miss Gilbert's face flamed. So did the anger in Samuel's gut. While he couldn't fault the farmer's wife for jumping to such a torrid conclusion, neither could he allow it to stand unchallenged.

He stalked over to the women, his boots hitting the planks harder than necessary, and pulled up next to Miss Gilbert. Drawing from years of experience, he faced down Wenna with a stern set to his jaw. "The lady is innocent of your charge, madam. The child belongs to a friend of mine, who wishes us to deliver her to his sister. Your censure is not only unmerited but ill-mannered, for Miss Gilbert's character is above reproach. An apology is required."

Rain beat against the windows, and the glass rattled in the frames. On the hearth, an occasional ember popped out from the fire. Other than that, silence reigned, for Wenna stood mute. Her shoulders deflated in increments as his words sank in, until finally, her hands flew to her cheeks and her washed-out eyes sought Miss Gilbert's. "Mercy and grace! And me, going on so, grizzling like a badger. I beg your pardon, miss. It weren't kind o' me to think such a thing, let alone say it aloud."

Her gaze drifted to him, the droop of her floppy cap as repentant as the woman. "Nor ought I have thought poorly of you, Captain. I'll catch a scolding from my husband when he hears of it, for sure and for certain."

The sheepish tuck of Wenna's chin radiated her shame and subsequent angst over her husband's expected upbraiding. Amusement flickered through Samuel that for such a headstrong woman, the farmer's wife cared deeply about her man's opinion of her.

A small smile lifted his lips. "Then we shan't tell him."

"Well said!" Miss Gilbert laughed. "And I agree. All is forgiven,

Wenna. It was naught but a silly misunderstanding. How about I settle Emma on the floor then help you with the broth, hmm?"

"Aye, and I'll be glad for the help." A relieved grin curved the woman's mouth. "When those men come in, no doubt they'll be hungry as the horses they've settled, eh?"

Wenna winked up at him, then scurried over to the hearth, apron strings riding the current of air behind her.

Miss Gilbert turned to him, and once again his breath hitched as their gazes locked. Admiration ran deep in those brown eyes. Deep and pure. Ahh, but he could get used to that look, to the resultant twinge that charged through him from heart to gut, arousing a hunger for more. It was heady, this new craving, this reckless yearning to pull her into his arms and hold her close.

And altogether far too dangerous.

He scowled and stalked away, leaving the queer feelings shut tight inside the cottage as he strode into the storm. The drenching rain slapped him hard in the face, and he relished the sting of it. Better to lose himself in a torrent than hand over his heart to a woman.

Inside the small byre, Cleaver and Bigby yet worked to remove the coach horses' tack. Pilgrim stood to the side, casting him a poisonous eye as he pulled off his hat and shook the water from it. He patted his old friend on the neck, and Pilgrim tossed her head, making a point. "Now, now. . .you didn't think I'd leave you for long, did you?"

Crouching, he ran his fingers gingerly along the animal's foreleg, inspecting the muscles and examining the wound. Despite the harried ride through the storm, the rain had washed the gash clean, and as he peered closer, he thanked God silently that pink skin formed at the edges. A day or two more of salve and slow going, and Pilgrim would be set to rights.

Rising, he unbuckled the girth strap and called over his shoulder to the other men. "How safe is that road where we left the carriage?"

Bigby turned his head, the shorn hairs on his scalp giving the stout fellow the appearance of a great, bristly scrub brush. His large ears added to the picture, looking like handles. If you tipped the man over, he could be used to scour the floor with the top of his head. "Why do ye think I answered the door with the tip o' me musket? Been a great load o' thievin' hereabouts lately. But ne'er fear. Ye and yer lady are safe as can be now."

Thieves? He sighed. If only it were that simple. Hefting the saddle off Pilgrim, he faced the farmer. "Maybe so, but the lady's chest, all her belongings, are ripe for the picking."

Cleaver spewed out a curse as he eased off the coach horse's bridle. "It'd be a half-witted fool to plunder on a night like this."

True, but all the same, a glower weighted Samuel's brow. He'd seen one too many half-witted fools in his time, and the worst were those bent on wrongdoing. He set the saddle on the stone floor near the door, then doubled back. "All the same, soon as this storm lets up, I'd appreciate the use of your wagon outside to collect Miss Gilbert's chest."

"I'll not be refusin' ye, but neither will I venture out on this wicked night." Bigby cocked his head at him as if he were the half-wit. "Have at it on yer own, if ye like."

He nodded and returned to Pilgrim. Hauling the lady's chest on his own would be an arduous task, but a necessary one. Not only would it save the lady from a possible theft, but it would also erase any ties to them and their location.

Ties that Shankhart or his toadies might come across.

Abby pulled off the borrowed gown and folded it while Emma watched from the bed, flat on her back and chewing on her toes. It'd been a long day for the girl, and as a yawn stretched Abby's own jaw, she had to admit it'd been long for her as well.

Farmer Bigby had entertained them well into the evening with stories around the hearth, a pleasing way to pass the time while the tempest continued to rage outside. The captain, however, had seemed distant after his defense of her virtue. He'd been polite and answered when spoken to, yet Abby got the distinct impression he'd listened more to the storm than to what was going on inside the cottage walls, and the lack of his attention was a great, gaping loss.

What sort of a frivolous female was she turning into?

Casting the strange thoughts and feelings aside, she laid Wenna's gown over the back of a chair, taking care not to bump into the small table next to it and disturb the contents. The blue porcelain washbowl already sported a chip in the rim, and Wenna had made it clear that her son's belongings were not to be moved. Abby glanced at the shaving kit next to the bowl, candlelight cutting a steel-grey line along the edge of the razor. All of the man's accoutrements stood at the ready, but how long had it been since he'd used them? On a peg nearby, a white shirt hung against the wall like a ghost in the night shadows, just waiting to drape over its owner's shoulders. Though the room was sparsely furnished, the spirit of the Bigbys' son permeated everything, so pristinely did Wenna preserve it in anticipation of his return.

Cupping her hand, Abby blew out the candle, a splash of wax burning her skin from the force. All the love and hope embodied in that hung shirt and dish of soap standing at the ready sliced into her heart. No doubt her stepmother had charged the servants at home with scrubbing down her former bedroom, washing away any possible traces that Abby had ever inhabited the space. Would the woman go so far as to order the housekeeper to remove her small portrait from atop her father's desk? Would her father even miss it if she did? She frowned as she stared at the spectre of a shirt in the darkness. What would it feel like to be as loved and missed as the Bigbys' son?

She padded over to the bed, huffing out a long breath and expelling the ache in her soul lest any bitterness take root. Grousing over past ill treatment was a waste of time. Was she not on her way to a man who would cherish her? One who was even now likely fretting like a wild man over her delayed arrival?

Emma reached for her with both arms, and Abby pulled the child close, kissing the crown of her head. Snuggling them both beneath the counterpane, she traced a finger along the downy skin of Emma's cheek. However many days she had left with this sweet girl, Emma would know love and know it well.

"Sleep sweet, precious one," she whispered.

Emma's long lashes fanned against her cheeks, and Abby couldn't help but close her own eyes and dream of a dark-eyed man who, more often than not, hid beneath the brim of his hat.

What seemed like only minutes later, raised voices growled downstairs, rudely pulling her from the depths of slumber. Abby blinked her eyes open, surprised to see morning light streaming in from the loft's single window.

Rising, she shrugged into Wenna's gown once again, straining her ears to decipher the heated words bandied about below her. The captain's low tones only occasionally added to the mix. What could he possibly be quarreling about so early in the day?

Emma rolled over on the bed and made a crawling dash toward the edge. Abby snatched her up, noticing her bottom end sagged heavier than normal. "My, my, little one! You are as wet as the green grass outside."

Emma gurgled a reply and smacked her lips—signaling she cared more about a warm drink of milk than her soiled clout.

Carefully, Abby picked their way down the ladder leading to ground level. As soon as her feet hit the wooden planks, Wenna turned from the hearth.

"Ach! I knew they'd wake ye." She aimed her finger at the bickering men near the door. "Take yer squabbling outside. Ye've gone and waked the ladies!"

Wenna's husband flicked his hand in the air, batting away his wife's words as if they were no more than a swarm of gnats. But even so, he yanked open the door. "Come along, Captain. We'll check on that horse o' yers afore church. Cleaver, ye can do as ye like, and may God have mercy on yer soul."

"Bah!" The postilion jammed on his hat and stalked past all of them, muttering under his breath.

The captain shot her a look before he followed Farmer Bigby out the door, his brown eyes a mix of humour and irritation.

Abby lifted a brow at Wenna. "What was that all about?"

Wenna chuckled as she hefted a pot of porridge to the scarred wooden table. "The Cleavers ne'er were the kind to grace a pew with their backsides. 'T'aint setting right with ol' Darby that my man and yer captain see fit to worship as is fitting fer a Sunday morn. He were all fired up to get to work on that broken carriage of yours. But don't ye fret none about it." She wiped her hands on her ever-present apron and reached for Emma. "Let's get you and the little one fed, then off we'll be to church."

Emma let out a wail, and Wenna shifted the babe to her shoulder. "I'll get this one into some dry wraps, and you can don yer fine gown again. It's waiting for ye on that stool near the fire. Unless you prefer a fresh one?" She tipped her chin, indicating something behind Abby.

Abby turned, and her jaw dropped. Her mud-spattered hulk of a chest sat safely against the wall. "How did that get here?"

"Yer captain slogged through the mud late last night soon as the rain let up, and like as not had a devil of a time o' cleaning his boots when 'twas all said and done."

Warmth shot through her, and she was glad Wenna turned away with the crying Emma so she'd not witness the red flushing her cheeks. How thoughtful of the stoic captain!

By the time they were both changed and fed, Emma's tears ceased, and Abby carried her outside to a world washed fresh and smelling of meadowsweet. Wenna hooked her arm through her husband's, coaxing him away from the captain with a warning that if they didn't quit jawing, they'd all be late and have to suffer the vicar's evil eye. Abby followed behind the pair, not wishing to earn such a reprimand from Wenna, and the captain fell into step at her side.

"Hand over Emma. She's too much for you to bear on a hike through the woods." He reached for Emma, and the girl fairly leapt into his arms.

Abby smiled at the twitch of the captain's jaw, a valiant attempt to hide his own grin, no doubt. Whether he admitted it aloud or not, clearly the man was smitten with the child. Beneath that gruff exterior, a heart of compassion beat pure and strong.

Keeping to the gravelly part of the path, she lifted her hem as they skirted a puddle. Good thing she had the option to change into a fresh gown when they returned. The trek to and from church might very well leave the bottom of this one soaked and muddy. She peered up at the captain. "Thank you for retrieving my chest. It must have been a frightful task in the dark and wet."

He shrugged. "I've seen worse."

Her gaze fixed on the crescent scar near his temple. Indeed. What kind of troubles had this man seen?

Emma made a grab for his hat, and he gently pulled her grasping fingers away from the brim, then turned her around and cradled her in the crook of one arm. She bounced, clearly enjoying the ride, and Abby smiled at the scene. The captain managed little Emma with such tenderness, it was hard to reconcile with his frequent dour moods and steely looks. Surely he must owe Emma's father some kind of enormous debt.

Abby's gaze drifted from the bouncing Emma back to the man. "I am curious, Captain. . .had not Emma's father been one of your particular friends, would you have taken the girl into your care anyway?"

He cocked his head as they walked, a single brow lifting beneath his worn hat. "Tell me, Miss Gilbert, if you had the opportunity to do good for someone, would you not do so without a second thought?"

She hid a smile. She would—and had—time and again. Fixing her sister's embroidery when it turned knotty. Playing shuttlecock with her brother when no one else could be bothered. Bearing her stepmother's tirades with naught but a kind word in return.

"Yes," she answered. "I suppose I would."

"There is no supposing." His dark eyes sought hers. "I see it daily in your care of Emma."

She grinned. "Emma makes it easy, for she is a sweet little lamb."

As if Emma understood the praise, her cherub cheeks turned her way, a happy squeal bubbling out of her. Emma *was* sweet and far too easy to love.

But as they walked along the trail to morning worship, Abby's grin faded. Despite it being hardly a fortnight since the captain had hefted Emma into her arms, already the girl had made an indelible mark on her heart.

One that would bleed when they handed Emma over to her aunt.

Chapter Eighteen

Samuel put all his muscle into pounding the final nail into the newly fashioned springboard. It wouldn't last long, formed out of rowan wood instead of steel, but it ought to at least get them by until they reached the next inn and could change carriages. He set down the hammer, then offered the layered strip of board over to Cleaver. "Want to ride out and see if this fits?"

The postilion nodded, his earlier ill feelings about the morning's delay pacified by a thick slice of Wenna's partridge pie when they'd returned from church. "Aye, and if so, I'll be back for your muscle to help put it on."

Cleaver's exit ushered a small breeze into the stable, but not enough to stop a drip of sweat from trickling down Samuel's brow. He swiped it away, shoving back the damp hair sticking to his skin. How long had it been since he'd made the effort to visit a barber?

He paused a moment to roll up his sleeves, chiding himself for not thinking of doing so sooner, then glanced over to where Bigby shaved down a thick strap of leather to attach the springboard—if it fit.

"You need my help?" he asked.

"Nay. I'm near to finished."

Good. If God's grace held, they'd have the carriage fixed by dark and be on their way come morning. A blessing that, yet one he held lightly. Putting too much stock in an expected outcome was never a good idea.

Grabbing a currycomb off the workbench, he sought out Pilgrim, who stood tethered just outside the door. The horse bobbed her head at his approach, then went back to munching on the green shoots nearest the stable wall.

"Someday, my friend," he breathed out in a soothing tone, matching the words to the pace of his strokes. "Someday soon, God willing, you'll not be driven so hard. No more heaths to roam. No highwaymen to hunt. Only sky and fields and wind. Just you and I and a stretch of land as far as the eye can see."

The chant was familiar, a common litany he used when grooming his horse, but this time it struck him as empty. Lonely, somehow. As friendless as a solitary tree left to weather on its own in a vast sweep of moorland.

Shoving the odd thought aside, he crouched and studied the wound on Pilgrim's foreleg. Pink skin, not inflamed or swollen, knit the injury together. Soon new hair would cover the damage, leaving the gash naught but a memory.

Even so, Samuel scowled. The damage never should have happened in the first place. He stalked back into the stable and flung the currycomb onto the bench, drawing in a deep breath to calm the ever-present rage that flared whenever he thought of the wicked man.

"The day off did yer horse good, no doubt. Aye?"

Bigby's bass tone crept up on him from behind, and he turned to face the man. "Aye."

"Then what's got yer blood still aboil?"

Samuel clenched his jaw, wielding silence like a great, grey blade. More often than not, the tactic worked, causing the inquirer to back down from the sheer discomfort of the moment.

Yet Bigby stepped closer, peering at him right in the eye. "There's no hiding it, lad. Ye've got a fire in yer belly"—he aimed a stubby finger at his gut—"and secrets enough to keep that blaze stoked hot."

He forced his brows to keep from raising. The farmer was bold, yet with an outspoken wife like Wenna, he likely had to be.

"Maybe." Samuel folded his arms and widened his stance. "Or maybe not."

Bigby chuckled, his ale belly jiggling beneath his work apron.

" 'T'aint no maybe about it, though I respect yer silence. Never have known me a lawman what didn't hold his cards close."

Samuel sucked in air through his teeth. How the blazes had the canny farmer figured that out? Not that he'd admit to it, though. He narrowed his eyes, prepared to scan the slightest twitch on the man's face. "What makes you think I'm a lawman?"

"The gleam o' yer tipstaff." Bigby nodded toward Samuel's hip.

Samuel's gaze followed the movement, only to see the hem of his waistcoat hitched up on the brass end of the wooden baton he kept tucked in his waistband at all times. In one swift movement, he yanked the fabric over the instrument.

Bigby's ready smile faded, mirth replaced by pity in his watery blue eyes. "Ahh, son, don't let the worst of man ruin the best o' you."

Hah! The sentiment, while likely well intentioned, stuck in his craw like a glob of gristle. The old fellow had no idea of what he spoke—or to whom he was speaking. Living here in the heart of England, secluded by hedgerows and fields of wheat and rye, Bigby couldn't possibly understand all the vile crimes he'd seen or the depth of depravity no one should have to witness. . .all embodied in the slit-eyed, square face of Shankhart Robbins. The mere thought of the man coiled his hands into fists.

Samuel turned away, finished with the ludicrous conversation.

But a strong grip on his shoulder stopped him. "Ye keep holding on to such anger, Captain, and it'll do you in."

He wrenched from the man's grip. "This has nothing to do with me. There's danger out there on the road, one Miss Gilbert and young Emma shouldn't have to face."

The farmer jutted his jaw. "Ye're a God-fearin' man. Leave that danger to Him."

Pah! If only it were that simple. "All that woman and child have is me and my gun standing between them and a man more ruthless than I've ever known."

"Yer not God." Bigby's voice lowered to an ominous tone. "So quit tryin' to be."

He stared at the man, seeing yet not seeing as the words barreled into him, booming as loudly in his heart as if God Himself thundered the message down from heaven.

"Yer not God, so quit tryin' to be."

Sweet everlasting! Was that what he'd been doing?

Shame left a nasty taste at the back of his throat. When it came down to it, he was no better than Shankhart. Not really. Just two sides of the same pence. While pride drove the highwayman to boast of his conquests of the innocent, was it really any different than the smugness Samuel harboured in his own heart every time he hauled in a villain? For ill or for good, did not pride always precede destruction? And by harbouring unforgiveness, was he not destroying himself, just as the farmer suggested?

Oh God. . . He swallowed hard.

Bigby cuffed him on the arm. "Don't take it too hard, Captain. It's to yer credit that ye care for the woman and child, but ye can safely leave them in God's hands. Not that He can't use yer gun, though, mind ye. There's no sin in wanting to protect them. The fault lies when ye think ye're their *sole* protector. Aye?"

The sharp edge of the farmer's words cut deep. He'd taken beatings before, but none so brutal as this. His shoulders sagged. His head. His soul.

Forgive me, Lord. The old man couldn't be more right, and for that I beg Your forgiveness.

Bigby shuffled his feet, his big boots rustling wisps of straw littering the ground. "But it's well beyond caring now, ain't it, Captain? Leastwise where the lady's concerned. Have ye told her?"

Samuel jerked up his head, stunned by the man's continued perception. Were the farmer in need of an occupation, Bow Street could well use his abilities. Donning a mask of indifference, he stared the man down. "There's nothing to tell."

Bigby chuckled. "Why, it's plain as a bleatin' goat stuck in a briar patch that ye love the woman. What's keepin' ye from claiming her? She's a right fine female."

Love? He clenched his jaw tight lest he gape. Surely that wasn't what these foreign urgings were. Were they?

No, he wouldn't—he *couldn't*—allow it.

He pivoted and snatched up a hoof pick from the bench, Pilgrim's mute company much preferred.

But Bigby was a hound with a bone, his footsteps dogging his every move. "The woman deserves to know, lad."

"I'm not the man for her," he rumbled.

"Ye ought to let her be the judge o' that."

He clenched the pick so hard, the metal shook in his hand. Even if this burning in his heart were love, there was no way he could admit such an offense to Miss Gilbert. For an offense it surely would be. He couldn't compare to a baronet, not in wealth or stature, and surely not in temperament. He was no fine dandy, serene and mollycoddling.

And even *if* he did have feelings for her, would Miss Gilbert return them? An impossibility, of course, but on the slightest chance that she did, he could offer her nothing save a rugged life with a very broken man. And oh, blessed heavens, she merited more than that.

He shook his head, refusing to turn around and face the farmer's all-seeing eyes. "There's too much at risk."

"Flit! Did not our own Lord risk His very life for the likes o' us? It's more noble to love, even if it's not returned, than to live without it. Why, 'tis one o' the greatest of all the commandments, man!"

"You don't understand. She's promised to another."

"Ahh, but she's not yet married to the man now, is she?"

Samuel scowled. The farmer mucked up so many sentiments, he couldn't begin to name them were he asked to at gunpoint. It was safer by far to embrace the anger he'd kept company with these past years.

"No." He spit out the word, then turned once again to face the farmer. "I will deliver her to her baronet, and that's the end of it."

"For her, maybe, but not for you." Bigby arched a brow at him. "Ye'll be heart-sore a good long time, I reckon. It's a cold ache. An empty one. And well I know it, leastwise till my Georgie comes home." Bigby's gaze strayed out the stable doors, focusing on some undefined point in the distance. "Aye, ought to be any day now, ol' Georgie will be riding up the road to home." The farmer's face softened, erasing years of toil and worry. How long had the man been missing his son? And why had the boy not returned?

"Where is he?" Samuel asked.

"Wanted to see the world afore he settled into farming alongside me. Georgie picked up and joined the queen's finest."

Samuel cocked his head. "Navy?"

"Aye. Sailed fer America the spring of '13, proud as a full-feathered peacock to patrol and keep safe the waters of Lake Erie. Ought to be home any day now."

A sick twinge tightened Samuel's gut. The year '13 had been notorious for British losses in the fledgling country of America, especially in the north. "Do you know the name of his ship?"

"The *Queen Charlotte*." Bigby shifted his gaze back to him. "Georgie's last letter home were from late August o' that year, saying he were proud to be on deck of one o' the best in the fleet." The man's bushy brows drew together. "Been nigh on two years though, since. He's like to be too busy to put pen to parchment, I reckon, but he ought to be home any day now."

Despite the summer heat, a chill leached into Samuel's bones. He nodded, then escaped out to Pilgrim. A report of the damages from that particular year had crossed the magistrate's desk. Devastating damage—especially on Lake Erie. If George Bigby had indeed been aboard the *Queen Charlotte*, he was either captured or missing. Or worse. . .killed. Samuel gathered up Pilgrim's front hoof and glowered. Ought he tell the Bigbys what he knew?

Or let them go on staring down that road, watching with love in their eyes for a man who may never come back?

Abby jabbed the needle into the fabric of the breeches she was mending, promising herself she'd not look out the window. Not again. She'd already been caught in the act of staring at Captain Thatcher as he brushed his horse. Not that Wenna had said anything—which might've been worse. The knowing gleam in the woman's eyes had unleashed Abby's imagination to entertain all sorts of accusations and innuendoes. Which was silly, of course. There was nothing between her and the captain, so the woman could have nothing to say on the matter. Truly.

Ignoring the squeeze of her heart, Abby wove the thread in and out, forming a tight seam.

"Ye're a fine hand with a needle. Ye'd ne'er be in want of employment should ye need to get by on yer own, and that's a fact." Wenna winked at her from her chair near the hearth. No fire crackled today, for the late June afternoon was warm enough.

But even so, heat flared in Abby's belly from the woman's praise. Of all the years she'd spent sewing in her stepmother's and sisters' company, not once could she remember such a kind word—and to this day she prayed to forget all the harsher cuts.

"That seam is as puckery as those little lines by your mouth, Abby."

"Keep your back straight when you sew. La! You hunch like a decrepit fishwife."

"Do you see Mary and Jane creasing their brows while they embroider? No man will want you with such wrinkles, girl!"

She straightened in her chair, correcting her posture out of habit, and glanced down at Emma, who yet slept sweetly in her basket. Would that Emma might never bear the same hurtful scars she suffered.

Outside the window, a movement from the corner of her eye snagged her attention. A shadowy figure. Dark and tall. Commanding enough to warrant a second and third look.

Don't do it. Don't give in.

But the pull of the man was too strong. Abby turned her face to the glass, making sure to keep her needle moving, and stared out at the fine lines of the captain.

He bent near his horse, shirtsleeves rolled up. The thick muscles on his forearm flexed as he worked to clean something out of his horse's hoof. His waistcoat stretched across his back, the flesh beneath rippling with his effort. He could conquer the world, this man, were he of a mind to. Did he know it? Or did the latent humility that was so much a part of him keep him unaware of his inherent power?

For a moment, she allowed herself to relive the feel of his arms pulling her close, the heat of his body as he'd shared his horse with her and Emma during the storm. He'd sheltered. He'd protected. He'd been soaked to the skin from wrapping her and Emma in his riding cloak.

"He's a good man, that one."

Her thought exactly—but Wenna's voice.

Abby jerked her gaze back to her sewing, dipping her head slightly so the woman wouldn't see the flaming of her cheeks. A big knot snarled her thread, and she was glad for the distraction to pick at.

She stabbed the knot with the tip of her needle, working to free the twisted mess. "Captain Thatcher is a good man. Were it not for him, I shudder to think of what might have happened to me."

Indeed. He'd rescued her and Fanny from highwaymen. Come to her aid in the stable from that brute of a false guardian. When she'd fallen ill, he'd been the one to nurse her back to health. And countless times he had put her and Emma's comforts ahead of his own. She wrangled the knot, which only seemed to tighten it further, and sighed. The captain had saved her from trouble so many times, she would have to beg Sir Jonathan to give him more compensation than what had been promised.

"If ye'll humour an old woman?" Wenna nipped her own thread with her teeth and added the repaired shirt she'd been working on to a growing pile of garments. Despite the woman's earlier praise, her worn yet nimble fingers put Abby's skills to shame. It was Wenna herself who could get by on her own with all the sewing she did for the manor house and tenant farmers hereabouts.

But Wenna didn't reach for the next torn shirt. Instead, she fixed her gaze on Abby. "Why are ye running off to marry another when there's one who cares for ye right in front of yer face? With all the pretty girls in church service this morning, the captain had eyes for none but ye."

She chuckled at the woman's misguided notion. "No, Wenna, 'tis not like that at all. I pay Captain Thatcher for his care, and being the noble guardian that he is, I am sure he was merely keeping an eye out for me. He would do the same for anyone."

"Pish! Ye really believe that?"

"Without a doubt." What a silly notion!

Finally, the threads on her knot parted. Abby licked her thumb and forefinger, then ran them along the kinked strands to straighten them out. "Besides," she continued, lest Wenna think any more on the topic of her and the captain, "I am promised to another and am on my way to happiness, you see."

She smiled at the woman.

"Are ye?" Wenna frowned. "Tell me of that man, then."

"Sir Jonathan Aberley is a baronet, lord of Brakewell Hall, a manor home on two-hundred-plus acres near Penrith. I have it on good authority that he is well respected." She tugged at the thread, fighting against another knot, the kinks from the former tangle straining to overtake the smoothness she'd worked to achieve.

Wenna's eyebrows arched. "That be nice, miss, but that doesn't tell me much about the man."

The words were an unnerving echo of the same Samuel had voiced to her not long ago, and suddenly she was glad for the threat of a snarl in her thread, for it meant she didn't have to look over at Wenna. It was hard to remember what the baronet was like, and even harder to keep believing he was truly in love with her—but she must.

She pulled back her shoulders and stabbed the needle into the knot. "Sir Jonathan has dark hair. Brown, I think. He is taller than I, and he dances quite well."

There. She pulled the thread through, victorious with the stitch and her description.

"Fine qualities, all." Wenna leaned forward in her chair, her gaze seeking Abby's. "But what captures yer fancy about the man?"

Abby dipped her head, focusing on the worn bit of breeches as if her life depended on it. How was she to answer that? How could she possibly fancy a man she hardly knew? One sweep around a ballroom while changing partners at intervals was barely grounds to know what it was about Sir Jonathan that she might admire.

But Wenna's eyes bore into her. She could feel it. Searching. Probing. She'd have to answer.

"He asked my father for my hand," she said simply.

"I'm wondering if it's you he wants or yer dowry," Wenna mumbled.

Leastwise that's what it sounded like. Abby lifted her chin, her brows pulling tight. "Pardon?"

The emotions on Wenna's face pieced together like a homespun quilt. Patches of pity coloured the woman's cheekbones. Concern basted tucks at the sides of her mouth. Yet compassion blanketed her tone as she softened her voice. "Allow me to be plain with ye, Miss Abby. Yer baronet may very well want ye. Who am I to say? But that's not solid ground for ye to be committing the rest o' yer life to him. A hungry lion might pursue ye with the same eagerness, but to devour, not to love."

The needle slipped, pricking her fingertip as sharply as Wenna's words stabbed her heart. Immediately, she pinched her thumb against the pierced flesh, stopping a drop of blood, and frowned at Wenna. "Why are you telling me this?"

"Flit, child! I'd hate to see ye throw away yer life on a man who didn't care enough to come and get you himself. Allowing ye to traipse the countryside on yer own. Not even providing a guard to keep ye safe."

The truth she'd been trying to ignore for so long stung the back of her eyes, and the world turned watery. Blinking, she stared at the fabric on her lap.

Footsteps padded, and an arm wrapped around her shoulder, giving her a little squeeze.

"Here be the way of it, miss. Ye say ye're on yer way to happiness, when all along it's been right under yer very nose. The truth is, ye *are* wanted, by the Creator of the stars, no less. Ye don't have to run across the country to find love when every minute of every day it's being offered to ye in God's wide, open arms. Do ye know that, girl?"

Setting down her sewing, she pulled from Wenna's touch and stood. Did the woman really think she was that much of a heathen? "Of course I know God loves me. I have been to church every Sunday of my life."

"Ahh, but do ye *know* the truth of God's love in yer heart, daughter? Have ye been in His presence, dropped to yer knees by the power o' His love?"

Slowly, she turned and faced the woman, afraid to ask what she must—but more afraid not to. "What do you mean?"

"Ahh, child." The ruffle of Wenna's mobcap dipped along with her brows. "It seems ye're setting yer expectations on earthly things, such as yer happiness with yer baronet. But ye'll not find it there. Not in man. Not in any man. Until ye're fully satisfied with the love God gives ye, freely and without question, ye'll not be satisfied at all."

Abby sucked in a breath, stunned. Was that what she'd been doing? Striving so hard to find love—first in her family and now in the man she was to marry—that she'd ignored what God had to offer? She pressed a hand to her stomach, the sick feeling beneath her touch a testament to the truth. But how to change? How to really *know* God's love, as Wenna said?

"I—" She cleared her throat and dared a peek at Wenna, bracing herself for the sympathy that was sure to glisten in the woman's eyes.

"I do not know how," she admitted.

A huge smile brightened Wenna's face. "Well, God be praised! Then yer one step closer."

Abby frowned. "What do you mean?"

"It's not by yer own strivin' that ye'll find God's love. All ye have to do is ask. Our faithful God will do the rest." Picking up Abby's sewing, Wenna shooed her with her other hand toward the door. "Go and talk to yer Creator. I'll finish up these breeches and mind the wee one for ye."

She shook her head, astounded by the woman's suggestion. "It cannot be that simple."

Wenna's grin widened. "If little Emma were to lift her arms to you, would ye not gather her to yer breast and hold her?"

Unbidden, Abby's gaze drifted to the sleeping babe as the woman's words sank in. Could it truly be that simple?

Slowly, she turned toward the door. There was only one way to find out.

Chapter Nineteen

"You shouldn't be out here alone."

A charge ran through Abby at the deep timbre of the captain's voice behind her back, and her eyes shot open. Even more jarring were the last rays of daylight painting Farmer Bigby's field a golden green. How could that be? It seemed like only minutes had passed as she'd poured out her fears, her longings, and all the hurts she'd thought were buried deep enough to never remember. But from the moment she'd whispered, "God, are You there?" time had stopped. Tears had flowed. And a peace she'd never before experienced watered, soothed, and healed the cracked soil of her soul.

Clutching the rough wooden gate, she stared out at the turnip field a moment more, the land a verdant sea of thick leaves. Nothing had changed in the time she'd been out here. Yet everything had. How could she possibly tell the captain she wasn't alone—and never would be again?

Her lips curved into a smile, and she turned to face him, surprised to see he stood but a few paces away, with Emma riding atop his shoulders. "Do not concern yourself, Captain. I am perfectly safe."

"No one is ever safe this side of heaven, Miss Gilbert." His jaw hardened, tightening as if all his bones strained beneath the weight of the sentiment.

Compassion swelled in Abby's heart. She reached toward him, as if by touch alone she might transfer some of her newly found peace and confidence in God.

But at the sudden cock of his head and narrowing of his eyes, she realized this was not a man who welcomed pity, but rather might slap her hand away. Reaching higher, she tucked in a stray strand of hair, hoping he'd think that'd been her intent all along.

Emma laughed, her sudden outburst causing several sparrows to take flight from a nearby hedge. The girl shoved Captain Thatcher's hat brim over his eyes, and with one big swoop, he freed her from her perch on his shoulders and swung her to the ground. She clung on to his big hands, refusing to let go, and bounced on her toes.

Abby's grin grew. "She looks as though she is ready to take her first step." Crouching, she held out her arms. "Come, sweet one!"

The captain squatted as well, then breaking free of Emma's grip, shot out his arms in case the child teetered one way or the other.

Emma's eyes widened, and for a breathless eternity, she wobbled. Slowly, one leg lifted then landed, the momentum tilting her body forward. Abby leaned forward too, lest Emma fall face-first in the dirt. But the girl's other leg jerked ahead, and in one more stilted step, Emma squealed and lunged into Abby's arms.

"Well done, little one!" Abby laughed, nuzzling her cheek against the crown of Emma's head, then she turned the girl around. "Try it again, dear heart. Walk to the captain."

When Emma balanced upright, Abby let her go, stretching out her arms so that her fingertips were barely a hand span away from Captain Thatcher's. If Emma did fall, she'd not have far to go. Once again, the child took off, her legs a bit jerky, her little hands flailing in the air. Gleeful gurgles burbled out of her mouth. The big, strong captain stood at the ready to catch her should she miss her footing.

And suddenly Abby's eyes stung with tears. Was this not the very picture of how God had just held out His arms to her during her fledgling steps toward Him?

Emma laughed again, but with too much gusto. She veered sideways like a tightrope walker, off-balanced on one leg. Abby gasped and, in reflex, lunged ahead. But no need. The captain swept little Emma up and stood, swinging her around and chuckling.

Chuckling?

Both Abby's brows rose. Surprisingly, laughter suited this man, erasing the sharp lines and angles that usually hardened his face. He looked years younger and entirely too attractive.

Planting his feet, the captain swung Emma back up to his shoulders and gazed down at Abby. "Soon there'll be no containing her." He gripped the girl's legs tighter as she bounced against him. "You'll have your work cut out for you until we reach Manchester."

She smoothed her damp palms along her skirt, focusing on his words instead of his handsome face. "A labour I gladly accept."

His eyes glimmered with approval, or dare she hope. . .admiration? A sudden yearning welled in her to have this man look upon her with his full heart in his gaze, cherishing her above all other women.

She turned away, cheeks heating at such a wayward thought. Surely it had only been the angle of the sun painting him in a charitable warm glow. Nothing more.

The captain strode past her, leading the way to the main road, then paused and waited for her to catch up. As she fell into step beside him, Emma bent from her perch and shoved a chubby fist her way. Abby kissed the girl's fingers, and Emma cooed.

The captain slid her a sideways glance. "You'll miss Emma when she's gone, I think."

He couldn't be more right. In truth, it would be harder to part with the sweet girl than it had been to say goodbye to her own family.

"I will miss her," she admitted. "Dreadfully. Though I am not her mother, she has stolen my heart. I cannot imagine the pain the Bigbys must have felt when parting with their son, nor how happy their reunion shall be when he returns."

All humour fled from the captain's face, more sudden and drastic than yesterday's storm. What on earth had she said to exact such a change? Did he harbour some secret about Emma? Emma's mother? The Bigbys?

She dared a light touch on his sleeve. Hard muscles rippled beneath his shirt, and he glowered down at her hand. She almost pulled back, but by will alone she kept her hold, determined to be as courageous as him. "There is something you are not telling me, Captain. What is it?"

His boot sent a rock skittering, yet he said nothing.

She squeezed his arm. "Well? You should know by now, your silence will not work with me."

A muscle jumped on his neck, and he muttered something too low for her to hear.

"A little louder, if you please."

His face turned to her, his eyes once again lost in the ever-present shadow of his hat. "You know, with your persistence, you'd make a fine officer yourself."

"I shall take that as a compliment, sir." She grinned. "But I will not be put off."

He blew out a long breath and faced forward again. For several paces, she wondered if the conversation was over before it began. Far too aware of the silence—and how warm and solid his flesh felt beneath her fingertips—she pulled back her hand.

Finally, he murmured, "All right. Since you insist, it's about the Bigbys' son, George. I suspect he won't be coming home."

She pursed her lips. How could he possibly know that? "Surely the man is not an acquaintance of yours. Is he?"

"No, but I am familiar with the ship he served on."

An ominous undertone moved swiftly through his words, and despite the heat of the afternoon, a shiver skittered across Abby's shoulders. She turned to him and stopped, the movement halting his steps.

"What do you know, Captain?"

Emma rested her cheek against his hat, her sweet cherub face a stark contrast to the captain's flinty stare. "His ship—the *Queen Charlotte*—was taken by the Americans two years back. The captain was killed, as were many of the crew. Some may have escaped. The rest were chained as prisoners. If George hasn't made it home by now, he isn't coming."

The truth knocked her as off-kilter as Emma's earlier misstep. How awful! How horribly cruel. Even now if she closed her eyes, she could envision the man's shaving kit, his shirt and trousers, his tin mirror shined and ready for his return. Wenna would be crushed by the weight of such a sorrow. And what of Mr. Bigby? The man not only desired but *needed* his son to help him on the farm. The pain of knowing George wouldn't be back could send the old man to his deathbed.

She peered up at the captain. "But you do not know this for certain. Do you? Can you say beyond a shadow of doubt that George was killed or captured? Why could he not have been one of those who escaped?"

"I'm no stranger to war, Miss Gilbert. If he made it out of there, he'd be home by now. The chances of that man returning are little to none." His lips pressed into a grim line. "And the Bigbys deserve to know."

Her jaw dropped. "You would cause them great pain for something that may not be true?"

"Is it not more cruel to let them live out their days staring down the road for a son who might never come back?"

"No, it is not, for I know what that feels like. You can have no idea how empty it is to be told what you hope for is not within reach. My stepmother certainly taught me that truth well, for despite my hope of a loving relationship with her, she squelched my efforts at every turn. Worse, she belittled my attempts." Righteous anger flared in her chest, and she lifted her chin. "So you will pardon me, Captain, when I insist that it is never cruel to live with hope, even the smallest portion. It is a weak comparison, but if someone came along and stole your hope of buying some land, farming your own fields, how would that make you feel? Hmm? Tell me."

A shadow darkened his face, and he wheeled about so quickly, Emma swung sideways. He pulled her down to his chest, saying nothing.

Abby bit her lip. Had she pushed him too far? Then so be it. She'd rather irritate the man than have hope snatched away from the Bigbys.

She upped her pace to gain his side. "Will you at least consider what I have said?"

For a long while, he didn't answer. Maybe he wouldn't at all, but could she fault him? The passion she'd just let slip likely made her sound like a raving lunatic.

They rounded the last curve in the road, and as the cottage came into sight, the captain slanted her a sideways glance. "Very well. I will consider it."

She hid a smile. Why that felt like such a victory was a mystery, but did not God work in mysterious ways? Was God even now working in the captain's heart? Glancing up at the leafy canopy, she silently prayed.

Lord, give this man wisdom to know what, if anything, to say to the Bigbys—

Her appeal ended abruptly as the captain shoved Emma into her arms, then stepped in front of her, blocking them both.

Abby froze, clutching Emma, wanting yet fearing to raise to her toes and stare over the captain's shoulder. What danger had he spied?

"Captain, what—?"

He spun around, jamming his finger against her lips. Without a word, he commanded her to stay put, and then he pivoted back and stalked ahead.

Every sense on high alert, Samuel's gaze snapped from the fallen branch in the middle of the road to the tree line at the side of the road. A maze of dark trunks, thick enough to conceal an enemy, spread as far as he could see—which was a precious short distance. Even so, he scoured the ivy blanketing the ground, looking for a trail, flattened greenery, anything to hint at an entrance or escape route someone might've taken when putting that chunk of wood on the road. But the woodland appeared as unspoiled as the day God had called it into being. Clearly no one had trampled through this swath of undergrowth recently.

Even so, he pulled out his gun. Tree branches didn't fall for no reason, not in the middle of the road where nothing but sky opened overhead. It surely hadn't gotten there by itself.

Choosing his steps carefully, he advanced, his gaze bouncing between the forest on one side and the hedgerow on the other. Sparrows chattered and flitted inside the shrubbery, quivering the leaves. The topmost canopy of trees swayed in a gentle breeze. Other than that and a few squirrels scurrying about, nothing moved. He frowned. Whoever had been here was long gone now—*if* anyone had been. Was he looking for demons when none threatened? Could the branch simply have fallen and rolled?

Lowering to his haunches, he studied the piece of wood, as long as his arm and just as thick. One end was jagged, crumbled by rot. The other stretched out fingers of dead wood. Thunder and turf! He could've sworn the thing hadn't been here when he'd passed by on his way to find Miss Gilbert, but maybe—just maybe—it had?

He felt sick in his gut. Perhaps he had been distracted by Emma or overly preoccupied with how to tell the Bigbys about George. Neither were a good excuse, though, and suddenly his pistol weighed heavy in his hand. What kind of captain of the horse patrol would pass by such an obvious hunk of wood without even noticing it?

Footsteps padded behind him. The rustle of a gown. The cooing of the child. Soon a question about his erratic behaviour would shoot him in the back. How was he to explain pulling a gun on nothing but an insignificant hunk of tree limb?

Angry at himself, he shoved his gun back into his belt and swiped up the branch. He was about to toss the thing aside when he froze. Something didn't feel right. But what?

Slowly, keeping his back to the advancing woman, he turned the wood over. Three crude letters scarred the wood, formed by cutting away the ash-coloured bark to the lighter flesh beneath:

YOU

You? He narrowed his eyes. For all the effort and stealth it took to put this message in his path, that's all it said? Or had the sender been scared off before finishing the message? His gaze drifted back to the tree line. Still, he detected nothing out of place. Whoever had delivered this curious dispatch was good at what he did, a professional, likely well paid from deep pockets.

And there were none deeper than Shankhart's.

"What is it?"

The whispered question shivered behind him. He hefted the branch and flung it into the woods, then turned. "Nothing." He forced a pleasant tone and a sheepish tilt to his head. "My mistake."

Miss Gilbert pursed her lips, a small crescent dimpling her chin. Either she didn't believe him or she inwardly condemned him to madness.

"While I appreciate how seriously you take your responsibility toward me and Emma, Captain, did you really feel it necessary to pull out your gun for naught but a fallen branch?"

He shrugged. "As I said, my mistake."

"Hmm. Obviously you are expecting trouble."

Sweet heavens! How could this woman read him so thoroughly?

"Yes," he admitted, then turned about and called over his shoulder. "We'll suffer Mrs. Bigby's wrath if I don't get you back for dinner."

Thankfully, they hadn't far to go, for Miss Gilbert shot out questions in rapid fire—and he thanked God for years of experience in dodging bullets. As soon as they stepped through the cottage door, Wenna pulled Miss Gilbert aside, enlisting her help in serving up bowls of pottage.

The rest of the evening passed by uneventfully, though he kept a sharp ear for any telltale noises outside, purposely manning the chair nearest the window for such a purpose. While the Bigbys, Cleaver, and Miss Gilbert chatted amongst themselves, his mind wore ruts with alternately trying to decide if he ought to say anything about George and his unlikely return, and the message on the log and what it could mean.

". . .morning, Captain?"

He snapped his gaze across the small room, where Miss Gilbert's brown eyes pinned him in place. Clearly she'd been speaking to him, but he'd not heard a word. "Pardon?"

"I asked if we are to leave early in the morning."

"Yes. Daybreak." Standing, he swiped his hat off a peg on the wall, jammed it on his head, then dipped a farewell. "Good night."

He strode to the door—and the floorboards creaked behind him. His hand paused on the latch when the faint scent of orange blossom curled over his shoulder.

"You did the right thing," Miss Gilbert murmured low.

His brow folded, and he turned, surprised to see she stood hardly a breath away. "What's that?"

She stepped closer, pressing her hand against his sleeve. "You let the Bigbys keep their hope. You are a good man, Captain, and I thank you."

The admiration glimmering in her gaze crawled in deep. And her touch. . . Lord have mercy. Against his better judgment, he leaned into it, and his heart skipped a beat. Ahh, but he was starting to crave this woman's nearness. Her warmth. Her smile. All the delicate fierceness that made up the petite form of Abby Gilbert.

Abby? Heat settled low in his belly. Since when did her Christian name come so easily to mind?

Without a word, he turned and fled into the night, glad for the slap of cool air against his face. The sooner he delivered Abby—Miss Gilbert—to her baronet, the better.

Chapter Twenty

Outside the stable, crickets chirruped. Inside, Cleaver snored. Samuel lay wide-eyed, annoyed by both.

Some nights just weren't meant for sleeping. He'd learned that lesson as a young lad, when long after his father's shouts had ended and his mother's weeping had subsided, he'd lain awake. Staring in the darkness. Wishing he were somewhere else. This night was no different save for the reason—a brown-eyed vision chasing off his sleep. Even now he could hear the thick emotion in Abby Gilbert's voice as if she lay right next to him.

"You are a good man, Captain."

Rising slightly, he punched the straw into a thicker wad and whumped back down. Good man. Him? Oh, not that he didn't yearn to be—try to be—but that same little boy who lived deep inside him still huddled in a corner of his heart, crushed by his father's words of long ago.

"Get your worthless backside out o' my house! I'm done with you."

And so, at only eleven, he'd left to live on the streets, vowing to never turn into the same drunken bully as his father.

Though no one could see it, a small smile curved his lips. Apparently, leastwise in Abby Gilbert's eyes, he'd succeeded. And that one, singular truth prodded him to flip over yet again. He should run from the tenderness he'd heard in her voice, flee the fondness he'd read in her eyes. He knew it in his head, the same as he knew he should've left his father's house sooner than he did. But in his heart, ahh, that misguided organ. . . His heart demanded he not only stay but also win

Abby over to him alone.

He flung his arm across his eyes. It wasn't good, this growing attraction he harboured for the woman, not when she belonged to another. Though Farmer Bigby had told him—hardly two paces away from where he now lay—to love with abandon, whether returned or not, somehow it felt wrong. Abby Gilbert deserved more than a worn-out lawman with enemies skulking around every corner. She should have a quiet home filled with love and peace, especially after escaping such a dismal existence with a family that neither cared for nor valued her. Indeed, a man of means such as her baronet was exactly what she merited, not a broken horse patrol captain...and the sooner he got her to her baronet, the better, before he did something stupid like fall in love and ruin her chances with the man.

He punched the straw again and tossed to his other side, then stilled, listening past Cleaver's heavy breathing. A solitary bird chirped. Then another. Soon the farmer's rooster would cock-a-doodle-do the official start of morning.

Weary to the marrow of his bones, Samuel stood and arched his back, working out a kink with a satisfying pop. He moved on to his neck, stretching one way and the other until it cracked. One stall over, Pilgrim stuck out her head, eyeing Samuel's movement. A horsey smirk twitched the animal's nose, mocking his creaking body. Condemning him as an old man. Samuel smirked back. He couldn't agree more.

Grabbing his riding cloak off the workbench, he threw it over his arm and snatched up his hat. Then he stalked over to where Cleaver yet lay snoring and nudged the postilion with his boot. "Time to move."

Cleaver bolted upright, bits of straw sticking to his coat like a poorly stuffed scarecrow. After a curse and a "What the...," his gaze followed the length of Samuel's leg up to his body, then finally to his face. "Oh," he yawned. "Aye."

Outside, early-morning vapors rose like prayers, blurring the countryside into a mystical softness. Samuel glanced at the sky, pregnant with the promise of morning. Still a deep grey, but no clouds. A good day to travel. A better day to put space between them and whoever left that carved message in the branch yesterday.

The next hour passed in a flurry of hitching horses, reloading Miss Gilbert's chest, and downing as much porridge as Wenna could possibly ladle into their bowls. Emma surprised them all by finally allowing the farmer's wife to hold her without crying, though it lasted for only a moment before she wrenched around and shot out her arms toward Abby.

Thunderation! She should be Miss Gilbert to him, not Abby!

After helping her and Emma into the carriage, he strode over to Pilgrim. Farmer Bigby followed him while Wenna darted to the coach's side to say her goodbyes at the window.

The farmer clapped him on the back. "Keep in mind what I said, Captain. Don't let that one"—he hitched his thumb over his shoulder, aiming at the carriage—"slip from your hands."

Samuel turned his back on the man and his advice and swung up onto his horse. Grabbing Pilgrim's reins in a loose hold, he looked down at Bigby, purposely changing the subject. "Thank you for your hospitality. You and your wife have been more than generous."

"Just sharin' what the good Lord provides." Bigby squinted up at him. "Godspeed, Captain."

Samuel gave the man a sharp nod, then trotted ahead, getting a lead on the carriage horses. No branches in the road would miss his observation today. In fact, just to be safe, he sped ahead, intending to scout the length of the Bigbys' curvy route all the way to the main thoroughfare.

Leftover mist clung low to the ground, but only in spare hollows where the land dipped at the sides of the road. As the sun rose higher, nothing but shimmery dewdrops remained. Samuel gazed past the beauty, scowling as he urged Pilgrim onward. It didn't seem right to ignore God's handiwork in favor of looking for evil, yet that was his job, *always* his job. And by all that was righteous, how it wore on him. It wouldn't be soon enough to receive the baronet's payment and retire on his own piece of land.

Pilgrim's ears twitched. Samuel stiffened and listened beyond the thudding of his own horse's hooves. Rounding the last bend to the main thoroughfare, he peered into the distance—and saw what had snagged his and Pilgrim's attention.

To the east, a cloud of dust rose above the brush along the main thoroughfare. A horse and rider. And by the looks of it, coming fast. The sight wasn't that unusual. Maybe someone rode hard for a surgeon. Or perhaps the rider tore hell-bent for a midwife, his first child on the way. Any number of innocent reasons could drive a person to move at such a frenzy this early in the day.

But when the rider turned off the main road and onto the Bigbys' lane, all his speculations darkened to a dangerous shade. No one should be eating up ground that quickly to get to an old farmer and his wife.

Unless the rider wasn't coming for them.

In one swift movement, Samuel snatched out his gun and dug in his heels. Pilgrim shot ahead. Thirty yards away from the approaching rider, he angled Pilgrim sideways and stopped the horse perpendicular in the middle of the road. A blockade of sorts—made all the more deadly when he jerked up his arm and steadied the pistol muzzle on the crook of his elbow.

"Stop!" he yelled.

The rider didn't.

No choice, then. Samuel pulled off a warning shot—the *only* warning he'd give.

With one hand, the rider yanked on his reins. Too hard. The horse reared, and the man fell.

Samuel leapt off Pilgrim, pulling his knife with one hand and flipping his gun around with the other to use the grip as a bludgeon. All the while, he sprinted to where the rider rolled to a stop. He planted his feet wide, ready for anything. "Who are you?"

The man pelted him with curses. "You'd better have a good reason for threatening me on my home land!"

Samuel cocked his head, wary yet curious. *Home* land?

The man shoved up one-handed to his knees, still calling down brimstone and all manner of other oaths upon Samuel's head. His other sleeve was empty, pinned to his chest. And when Samuel caught full sight of the man's face, he gasped.

A jagged scar crawled like an earthworm from his chin to his cheek, stopping briefly at an eye patch, then emerged out the other end to disappear into his scalp. But it wasn't the wound that punched Samuel in the gut. It was the man's ears, sticking out like handles on his head, and a hook nose that might serve as a sparrow's perch. . .the very image of a young Farmer Bigby.

George? No wonder the man hadn't returned home in two years. With those wounds, it was a wonder he'd returned home at all.

Samuel lowered his gun and knife, yet kept a grip on them in case he was wrong. "Do you live in the farm cottage down the lane?"

The man glowered up at him. "Not that it's any of your business, but aye."

Samuel stored his weapons and offered his hand, relieved he'd been wrong about George not coming back—and even more relieved that he'd said nothing about his suspicions to the Bigbys.

George slapped his offer away and rose to his feet, a bit wobbly but on his own power.

Allowing the man a moment to collect himself, Samuel turned and snagged the lead of George's horse, then returned the animal to his master.

George snatched the lead from his hand. "Who the devil are you, and why gun me down?"

If looks could kill, Samuel would be bleeding out on the dirt. He lifted his hands and backed away, edging toward Pilgrim. "I beg your pardon, Mr. Bigby. I made a mistake. Please, continue on your way."

George narrowed his eye. "Do I know you?"

"No." Just then, the carriage rounded the bend, and Samuel tipped his head in that direction. "We were simply passing by, and your family took us in. I daresay you will be a welcome surprise. Once again, my apologies."

He swung up on Pilgrim and cantered down the road, chagrined by his blunder. Of course his drastic precaution had been a necessary evil. What were the odds of George Bigby returning home on the very day he rode out looking for trouble? His offense had been the right thing to do. The *only* thing to do.

So why did his gut twist and his heart burn?

Putting pressure on the reins, he guided his horse onto the main road. Thank God he hadn't shot the man. From now on, he'd be more careful. Use a bit more discernment before pulling out his gun and—

"Easy," he rumbled and put pressure on the reins, halting Pilgrim at the side of the road, hardly believing his eyes.

There, on a rise of thicket grass that led up into a stand of trees, strategically placed rocks spelled out letters, three feet high. Two feet wide. Vindicating his gun-pulling. The single, ominous word kidney-punched him:

DIE

A morbid enough message, but when added to the previous two he'd already received, his pulse took off at a breakneck speed.

Soon. You. Die.

Abby fanned herself with her hand, debating yet again if she ought to ask the driver to stop so she could retrieve an actual fan from her chest at the back of the coach. Oh, why hadn't she thought to remove it when the big chest had sat in the Bigbys' cottage? Even with both carriage windows down, the air stifled, making her want to crawl out of such a heated cage. Or maybe it was Emma who she really wanted to escape. Ever since discovering her mobility yesterday, the girl was a scrambling squirrel.

Instant remorse pinched Abby's conscience, and for at least the twentieth time in the past hour, she shot out her arm to block Emma from diving off the seat.

"Gee!" Emma squealed and bounced, then, thankfully, lunged for the opposite window and pulled herself up to peer out.

Abby leaned back against the seat, closing her eyes as the wheels rumbled along. Was this what it felt like to be a mother? To be driven to such extremes, loving wholeheartedly *and* desperately wishing for a minute alone? Or was she being selfish? Either way, God bless each and every self-sacrificing mother on the planet.

Exhaling her frustration, she tucked up a hank of hair loosened by Emma's grasping fingers. The child truly had at least four arms, each of them out of control. With a last look to make sure Emma's feet were safely anchored away from the edge of the seat, Abby leaned sideways and poked her head outside the opposite window, not caring that she probably looked like a beagle riding with its ears flapping in the breeze. Propriety be hanged! The wind on her face was so worth it.

Ahead, the captain rode tall on Pilgrim and glanced over his shoulder as if he detected her breach of decorum. But he didn't see her. Not really. She'd learned that hours ago when she'd waved at him and received no response. Ever since they'd left the Bigbys' cottage early this morning, he'd been looking back, and sideways, and straining to see up front—where he'd been riding all day.

Abby narrowed her eyes and studied his broad shoulders. In the heat of the afternoon, he'd forsaken his riding cloak, shoving it into the leather bag he kept strapped behind his saddle. He rode loose, his body rolling with the horse's movement, his muscles slack. Still, it didn't fool her. Pulling a gun on nothing but a branch. Pitching rocks away from the side of the road. Scanning his surroundings like a spinster bent on finding a husband. Something festered inside that man. Something he wouldn't tell her, no matter how many times she peppered him with questions.

A squeal ripped out of Emma. "Ah-be-da! Ah-be-da!"

Abby pulled her head back inside the carriage, curious yet dreading what might've caught Emma's attention. *Ah-be-da* could be any number of things. Scooting sideways on the seat, Abby neared the child and peered past her.

The road gave way to a large field, and on the opposite end of the big clearing, all manner of coloured tents, flags, people, and animals spread out. As the road curved and they drew closer, the sounds of music and laughter, hawkers clamoring about their wares, and showmen begging for an audience all filled the air. Abby smiled. Ah-be-da, indeed! She'd always wanted to visit a country fair.

Once again, she shoved her head out the window. "Stop the carriage!"

The postilion slowed the coach to a stop and barely had the step out for her to exit when the captain rode up, his usual glower in place as he swung from his mount.

"We're nearly to the inn. Why stop here?"

She peeled Emma's fingers from her face, then turned the child around and angled her head toward the merriment. "The fair, of course."

His dark gaze drifted to the revelry, then cut back to hers, sharp as a knife. "No. Absolutely not."

Truly, he needn't have said anything. The steely set of his jaw and stiff way he held his neck screamed he'd rather be drawn and quartered than escort her and Emma to a fair.

Abby pursed her lips. Good thing opposition was a commodity she'd learned long ago to trade in deftly. She blinked up at him, determined to win the battle. "While you have enjoyed the fresh air all day, Emma and I have been slowly cooking inside the carriage. She needs this outing, Captain. As do I."

A tic twitched at the side of his eye. "It's not safe."

"Maybe not, but that is why I hired you, hmm?"

He glanced around, his eyes slowly grazing the entire length of the fairgrounds. His mouth flattened into a straight line, and he shook his head. "It's a bad idea."

Abby shifted Emma to her hip, stalling for time. How was she to convince him? Her sisters would've fluttered their eyelashes or maybe let loose a single, fat tear, but that wouldn't work with this man.

So she met his gaze, hard and even, and softened her tone. "Please, Captain? Despite any dangers you may perceive, I know that Emma and I shall be perfectly safe in your company."

As if on cue, Emma stretched out her arms toward him. "Ah-be-da?"

Finally, he broke.

A growl rumbled in his chest, and he pulled Emma from her arms.

"Very well. But we're not staying long." He turned toward the postilion. "See to my horse and the lady's belongings, then secure us two rooms. Also, arrange a carriage and fresh horses for the morning. We'll settle with you later."

"Aye, Captain." The driver dipped his head.

Abby hid a smile, lest Captain Thatcher saw how much her victory pleased her.

The captain set off toward the rows of merchants displaying their wares, likely assuming that would fancy her most. Given that she had lived in the great harbour of Southampton, where such merchandise shipped in daily, he couldn't have been more wrong.

She tapped his sleeve. "Might we go see the performers?"

One of his brows lifted. "Truly? A woman who scorns shopping?"

This time she allowed her smile to run free. "I have no need of anything at the moment."

His other brow shot up as well. "As you wish."

They roamed past food vendors, and though her stomach pinched at the savory scents of spiced nuts and meat pies, she'd not give in to the temptation. Eating was an everyday occurrence, and she didn't want to waste one minute on such a mundane activity when she could be watching musicians and jugglers, slack rope walkers and tumblers.

The captain paid scant attention to any of it, his gaze never landing long enough to enjoy the performances. But that was his loss. Abby clapped and exclaimed along with the rest of the crowd. And Emma squealed with delight, especially when a monkey in a jester's suit did backflips all the way up to the captain's legs.

Abby grinned at the child. "Did you like that, sweet one—oh!"

Her gaze shot downward at a tug on her skirt. Big brown eyes gazed up at her, set wide into a furry little face. How dear!

But then she gasped when the monkey scampered up her gown, all the way to her shoulders. He reached behind her ear and pulled out a shiny, gold coin, holding it out for the crowd to see. Those around her gasped. Some laughed. The captain narrowed his eyes.

The monkey's handler, dressed in matching harlequin silk, stepped up to her and extended his arm with a flourish. The furry scamp leapt from her shoulder to dangle off the man's sleeve with one paw. With the other, the monkey offered her the coin.

His handler laughed. "Why, he likes ye, miss. Take it!"

She peered up at the captain. Not that she needed his permission, but did he suspect anything untoward about the transaction?

At his single nod, she bent and took the coin. "Thank you."

The crowd cheered, and both the monkey and his master doffed their hats and held them out.

Pennies clinked into the red velvet as patrons passed by. Abby reached into her reticule and fished out a thruppence, then tossed it in along with the monkey's gold coin. No doubt the traveling entertainers could use the money far more than she needed.

"Thank you, miss." The handler winked at her.

"No, no. Thank you."

She turned back to the captain, and for the first time that day, something other than suspicion glimmered in his eyes. "You are a generous soul, Miss Gilbert."

"As are you, more than you will admit to. I know you do not wish to be here, but I thank you for escorting me and Emma. I have never had such a wonderful time." She grinned up at him.

And he smiled right back at her.

For her.

Suddenly shy, Abby bit her lip, trying to ignore the tripping of her heart—until a barrel-bellied man stepped up to them, waving a red rose:

"The rose is fair but fairer still,
true love that binds and twines the will,
of lovers' hearts, and melds to one.
Try your luck and beat Big John!"

He pointed toward a raised platform not far from where they stood, where a shirtless man sat at a table at center. His greased brown flesh glistened in the sun, enhancing the muscles rippling on his chest and in his arms.

The man in front of them angled his head at the captain. "Best Big John in a fair-and-square arm wrestle and win your lady a flower, *if* your arm is as strong as your love."

Heat flared on Abby's face. "Oh, but you are mistaken. I am not his—"

"All right." The captain shoved Emma into her arms and stalked off.

Abby stared at his broad back, clutching Emma, unsure if she should follow or faint. Was the dour Captain Thatcher seriously going to take part in a frivolous fair game?

Just for her?

Chapter Twenty-One

A shadow kept pace with them. Off to the left. Stopping when they did. Moving at their speed. Yet every time Samuel snapped his gaze that way, he was met only by innocent stares.

He thrust Emma into Miss Gilbert's arms and shot into the crowd. Not that he was eager to arm wrestle, but that platform would give him a broader view. He took the stairs two at a time, and at the top, he spun back to scan the edge of the people gathering closer.

Two young boys chased a pig past people's legs, sending a ripple through the swarm. Miss Gilbert, clutching Emma, shouldered her way through men and women alike, plowing a furrow right up to the front of the platform, God bless her. A long-limbed man with a brilliant green cap darted through the throng, taking bets for the upcoming wrestling match. Samuel frowned. Though he couldn't ask for a better vantage point, no one seemed suspicious, leastwise in this direction.

He pivoted, and—there. Possibly. Behind an apple vendor's stack of empty crates, he could barely make out a dark shape. Was someone hiding? After this morning's blunder, he'd need clear cause to go chasing a man down. He tugged the brim of his hat lower against the late-afternoon sun, shading his eyes, and—

"Don't back out now, man! Yer lady is a-watchin'."

An arm around his shoulders corralled him away from the edge of the platform and propelled him into a chair. Opposite him, a monster of a man assessed him as he might a carcass on the side of the road, his eyes like two black pebbles pushed deep into the sockets. He reeked of sweat and ale and far too much arrogance. Samuel jutted his chin. If he had the time, he'd be more than happy to school that pride right off the man's face.

The other man—the one who'd propositioned him in the first place—stepped to the front of the platform and faced the crowd with upstretched arms, beckoning with fluttering fingertips. "Step close, ladies and gents! See if Big John Banyan will retain his title, or if this fellow here"—he swept his arm toward Samuel—"will win his love a red, red rose. Is love strong enough to vanquish such solid brawn and muscle?"

Hoots and hollers—and even a few whistles—blew through the crowd like a gust of wind. Ignoring all the hubbub and Big John, Samuel jerked his gaze over his shoulder to catch another glimpse of those crates while the announcer kept on trumpeting about the match.

"That's it! Gather 'round! Don't be shy. Here's your chance to win and win big. But before ye place your wagers, ye ought to know, Big John ain't ne'er lost a match, not a one. Gentlemen, begin on my mark."

Samuel offered his arm without a glance, too busy studying the apple vendor's stand to even flinch when Big John's anvil-sized hand clamped on to his.

"Go!"

The black shape behind the crates moved. So did his arm. Just a second more and he'd see the face of whoever—

His shoulder wrenched, and he snapped his attention back to Big John. A wicked smile slashed across the brute's face, like a badly carved gourd on All Hallows' Eve. And no wonder. Samuel's arm was a breath away from being smashed into the tabletop right there in front of God and man. He'd look like a half-weaned stripling if he lost this quickly.

Ahh, but he didn't intend to lose at all, not if he could help it. True, Big John had at least ten stone on him, all bulging and steely, but for all the man's muscle, he was a compact fellow—and most importantly, his forearm was shorter than Samuel's.

Samuel gritted his teeth and twisted his wrist, turning his palm toward his face and slightly edging his opponent's hand into a direction he couldn't defend. Then, manipulating that angle, Samuel rotated his body, lining up his shoulder with the spot on the table he wanted to grind Big John's arm into. His muscles burned. This wouldn't be easy.

With a quick prayer, a sharp thrust, and using all his body weight for leverage, Samuel whumped the man's arm over and pinned it to the oak.

The crowd roared. Big John's coal-black eyes burned like embers, his whole beefy face reddening to a deep shade of astonishment and rage.

Samuel sprang from his chair, craning his neck to peer at the apple crates. Sunlight leached through the slats. Each of them. Whoever had been there was gone now. Could've been nothing. In fact, he *hoped* it was nothing—and that was a new feeling. Lighter, somehow. He flexed his aching hand, ignoring the quivering muscles in his arm, while behind him, angry voices simmered into a hot, bubbling mix.

"He's a bleatin' cheater! Big John shoulda won!"

"Undefeated? My ever-loving backside! I want my money back!"

"This match were fixed, I tell ye!"

Alarm crept up his backbone. He'd seen riots before, humanity frothed up into foaming-mouthed dogs. Snarling. Snapping. Devouring. Abby and Emma wouldn't stand a chance in a mob like that, not once fists started flying.

He darted toward the stairs, plucking the rose from the announcer's hand. The man probably didn't even notice. He stood with his arms akimbo, his mouth opening and closing like a landed trout.

As soon as Samuel's feet hit the dirt, he shouldered his way over to Abby and grabbed her hand. "Come along," he shouted above the raised voices.

She followed without complaint, keeping close to his back. Once free of the crowd, he kept going and didn't release her hand until they neared a roped-off area, where a man led a spirited white Barbary horse on a spangled strip of leather.

Abby shifted Emma to her hip and smiled up into his face. "Well done, Captain! Such showmanship. For a moment, I feared you might lose."

"Have I not told you to never fear when I am around? Tip your head a bit. Here is your prize."

He snapped off the long stem of the flower—crushed beyond salvation, anyway—and tucked the rose behind her ear, securing it between her bonnet and hair. But as he began to pull away, his fingers grazed the skin of her neck, and he sucked in a breath. He'd never felt anything so soft. So warm. So vibrant and pulsing with life.

Without thinking, he ran his thumb along the line of her jaw and brushed over her mouth. Heat flashed through him. What would it be like to touch those lips with his own? To pull her close and taste the sweetness and fullness of her?

Blessed heavens! What was he thinking?

He yanked back his hand and retreated a step, his heart beating loud in his ears.

Colour deepened on her cheeks, matching the red rose nestled against her dark hair. "Thank you, Captain. I am honored."

Her eyes gleamed with all the brilliance of a starry night, emotion shimmering in those brown depths. . .emotion stirred by him.

He swallowed—hard—and set his jaw. "We should leave."

And they should. Danger lurked somewhere on these fairgrounds —and in his own heart, for there was no denying it anymore.

He was in love with Abby Gilbert.

He turned away, then jumped back a step as a pig squealed past his feet. The two boys he'd seen earlier kicked up clods of dirt as they tore after it, arms outstretched, hollering all the way. The animal raced its stubby legs into the makeshift horse pen, and the boys followed right along, ducking under the rope.

Samuel's stomach rolled, churning a warning all the way to the back of his throat. That Barbary had been high-strung enough simply being led around the paddock. If the pig got too close—

It darted between handler and horse. The Barbary reared, breaking free of the man's hold. Thankfully, the boys scattered before the deadly hooves crushed their skulls to bits. The handler reached for the horse's lead, but the animal jerked from his reach and raced ahead.

Straight toward Abby and Emma.

Emma squirmed and screeched, her flailing arms knocking Abby's bonnet down over her eyes. At times, the child sounded just like a squealing piglet, especially when fatigued. The captain was right. This would be a good time to leave the madness of the fair.

Shuffling Emma to her other hip, Abby pushed up the brim of her bonnet, then gasped as the captain barreled into her, violently knocking her sideways. She stumbled away, frantically trying to regain her balance so she and Emma wouldn't topple to the ground. Why would he—?

A horse screamed. Close. Too close. She spun toward the sound. Then froze, horrified. The captain stood in the exact spot where she'd been.

And horse hooves plummeted toward his head.

He twisted, but a hoof caught him in the shoulder. The captain hurtled to the dirt with a whump. So did the horse's front legs, narrowly missing his face.

She gasped for air—then quit breathing altogether as the horse reared again.

Abby shrieked. Emma bawled. A few men rushed over, the horse's handler among them, but they stopped a safe distance from the wild animal, their arms flailing helplessly. Hot fury burned in Abby's heart. Why didn't they help the captain? Surely something could be done!

The dangerous hooves plummeted once more.

With all that was in her, Abby desperately wanted to close her eyes. Shut out the shocking gore that was sure to happen. But God help her, she stared, frozen, unable to blink let alone breathe.

God, no! Please!

With the deadly hooves inches away from the captain's head, he rolled and sprang up. Before the horse's legs landed, the captain grabbed the bridle with one hand. His other snagged the lead. He spoke into the animal's ear as he pulled the horse aside, leading it in a tight circle. Again and again. Finally, the frenzied horse calmed, and so did Abby's heartbeat.

Applause rippled around her, and she glanced sideways. A crowd had gathered. Surely they didn't think this was a show. . .did they?

The captain led the horse to his handler and offered over the lead without a word. The man took it, wide-eyed, slack-jawed. Was he amazed at the captain's skill or woefully shocked by his own lack?

"Well, now." The handler cleared his throat and tossed back his shoulders. "That was quite a show of horsemanship. I've a job for you, if you will have it. We could use a man like you."

"No thanks, I've already got one." He turned his back on the man and strode toward her.

Once again, her heart took off at a gallop. Dust coated the captain's shoulders and his suit coat. A hank of dark hair hung over one of his eyes, and sweat cut a trail down the dirt on his face. But even worn and beaten, his step was sure. His head held high. His dark gaze belonging to her alone. It didn't take any more to convince her that no matter the odds, this man could move a mountain by the strength of his will alone.

He stooped to pick up his hat, then stopped in front of her, shoved his wayward hair back, and jammed the worn felt onto his head.

Emma reached out a plump hand toward him, still sniffling from her crying bout. Abby shifted her away from him. The last thing he needed right now was to hold a wriggling child.

"Yet again you saved my life, Captain. You saved *our* lives."

"That's what you hired me for." He swiped his mouth with the back of his hand, rubbing off leftover dirt, as if he'd simply taken a tumble on the ground instead of nearly getting killed.

Which only endeared him to her more. If Sir Jonathan turned out to be half the man as Captain Thatcher, she couldn't help but live happily ever after.

"You are far too modest, sir. I thank you for risking your life for ours." Just like Emma, she reached toward him, wanting—*needing*—to feel the solid muscle beneath his sleeve. She'd nearly lost this man, and the thought sent a ripple through her soul.

Her hand landed lightly on his upper arm—and he winced.

She pulled back. "You are hurt!"

He looked away, scanning the ground around them. "Just a bruise, likely. It's getting late. Have you seen enough of the fair?"

A shiver shimmied across her shoulders. "More than enough."

His gaze shot back to hers, and he held out his arms. "Then hand over Emma, and let's be on our way."

She shook her head. "After what you have just been through, I cannot allow you to—"

"I insist." He pulled Emma from her arms, and Abby couldn't help but note that he held her far away from his injured shoulder. She frowned. The big oaf. That was more than just a bruise.

Before she could protest any further, he pivoted and set off through the merrymakers. By the time they got to the inn, the hunger pangs in her stomach surely ached as much as the captain's shoulder.

After a dinner of pease pudding and bacon, throughout which the captain said hardly more than five or six words, both she and Emma yawned. Strange that the captain didn't seem weary, especially after his ordeal. While stoic, he didn't sag in his chair, nor did his eyes droop. He sat as alert as ever.

Narrowing her gaze, Abby studied him. Not fatigued, but definitely preoccupied. By what?

He stood and pushed back his chair, then gathered Emma against his chest. "I'll see you ladies to your room."

Abby followed his broad back toward the stairway. The chatter of the taproom lessened as they ascended to the first floor, and faded even more as he led her down to the farthest door at the end of the passageway. It was a tight little corridor, not much wider than the captain's shoulders. When he turned and handed over Emma, his arm brushed against hers.

Though propriety dictated she shy away, she didn't. Nor did she move so he could open the door. There was something precious about this moment. Something she didn't want to give up so soon. She peered up at him, memorizing the strong line of his nose, his firm mouth, the defined cut of his jaw. Even the small scrape to his chin that he must've earned while capturing the wild horse charmed her.

Finally, fully, he met her gaze. Curiosity darkened his eyes to the shade of polished mahogany, and he angled his head. "You look at me as if I might disappear. What are you thinking?"

"I would ask the same of you, Captain. You hardly put two words together during dinner. Clearly there is something on your mind. What is it?"

His jaw worked, yet no sound came out. Emma laid her head against Abby's shoulder, signaling she was ready for sleep.

But Abby held her ground. She'd learned long ago how to outwait a stubborn mule.

The captain sighed, his breath warm and feathering against her cheek. "Has anyone ever told you how persistent you are?"

"You have. Many times." She tipped her chin. "And though your bluster makes it sound as if that is a bad thing, I get the distinct impression that you somehow admire me for it."

His Adam's apple bobbed. "Would it matter?"

She frowned. "Would what matter?"

"If I admired you." He bent close, his brown eyes searching parts of her she'd never shared with anyone. . .until now.

Sudden warmth flooded her from head to toe, and she held her breath. The truth was that this man's good opinion of her *did* matter, more than she could possibly understand. She leaned toward him, and despite the barrier of a small child in her arms, she craved the captain's touch, desiring far more than his admiration.

She froze. What was she thinking? She had no right to share any part of her heart with the captain. But how could she take back what she'd already given?

"I—" All the words she should say, the denial of him she must give, stuck in her throat, and she swallowed.

He rested his worn, calloused finger on her lips. "There is no need to answer. I shouldn't have asked the question to begin with. Good night, Miss Gilbert." He edged past her and stalked down the corridor.

She stared at his retreating form, clutching Emma. Each of his steps away from her was a great, gaping loss, like someone carving a hole in her chest in the exact area that her heart ought to be.

"Good night," she whispered, the words tasting as dry as ashes in her mouth.

As hard as it was going to be to say goodbye to Emma in two days, she suspected that when the time came, it was going to be impossible to voice a farewell to the captain.

Chapter Twenty-Two

The next days flew by, far too fast for Abby's liking. Her mouth twisted with the irony of it as she stared out at the Manchester streets. How eager she'd been a lifetime ago when Fanny had accompanied her, zealous to cover as many miles as possible in a day. Now if she could grab the hands of time and stop them, she would.

The carriage bumped over cobblestones then dipped into a pot-hole. She held Emma closer on her lap, her arm wrapped snug around the girl's tummy. Surprisingly, Emma sat still and had for some time. It was almost as if the girl knew her life was about to change and was as reluctant to let go of Abby as Abby was to release her to a family unknown.

She pressed a kiss atop Emma's head, then looked out the window, trying to guess which house might be the girl's new home. Rusty brick row houses paraded by, straight as a school matron's posture. They were neat and tidy, but the doors opened right onto the street. There'd be no green grass for Emma to run around on, no space for her to explore, and oh, how she loved to move. Hopefully they wouldn't stop here.

The coach turned, leaving the brick houses behind, and relief loosened the muscles in Abby's shoulders. Emma deserved a cottage house, one with a great field and possibly a pony, where she could grow up running free and breathing fresh air. That was an impossibility here in the city, of course, but at least they might pull up in front of a town house with a small patch of yard.

But the carriage turned again, this time onto a narrower lane stinking of eggs and fish brine. Abby scrunched her nose. Surely this was only a shortcut on the way to a better part of town.

It wasn't. The farther they traveled, the closer the sides of the road drew, choking out light and air and hope. Houses leaned one against the other, like drunken sailors holding each other upright. If one fell, the rest would lie down and never get up again. Abby grimaced, silently praying for mercy on Emma's behalf. She'd hate to leave the girl in one of these hovels.

Thankfully, the carriage made a sharp right, and she flung out her hand to balance against the wall. Emma laughed, and after one more kiss to the little one's downy head, Abby once again looked out the window as the coach jolted to a stop—and her heart dropped to her shoes.

The captain flipped down the stairs and opened the door. When he offered his hand, Abby debated if she ought to shrink back and hide Emma behind her skirts.

His dark gaze met her hesitation, commanding her to come out with nothing more than the tilt of his head. She stepped down into an alley courtyard, surrounded on three sides by buildings made up of weathered boards that were held together more by misguided will than nails. Ropes crisscrossed overhead, from one window to another. Those that had glass were cracked. Patched garments hung like graveclothes over the lines, colourless sleeves dangling, grey trousers languishing. . . or were those rags? None of the clothes rippled with movement, for not a breath of a breeze crawled into this hole.

She peeked up at the captain. "Are you certain you wrote down the correct address?"

His jaw hardened, and he nodded. Without a word, he handed Emma to her and retrieved the girl's basket and small traveling bag. Three steps later, she stood by the captain's side as he pounded his fist on a pitted door. Abby felt dirty just looking at the place. Maybe no one would answer, and they wouldn't have to—

The door opened a crack. A smudge-faced boy with a black eye peered out, saying nothing.

Captain Thatcher stared down at him. "I'm looking for Margaret

Gruber. Is she your mother? Is she at home?"

The lad's nose twitched, then he shut the door—or tried to. The captain shoved the toe of his boot in the gap.

Inside, a reed-thin voice leached out the opening. "Who is it, Tim?"

The boy stiffened. He darted a look over his shoulder, then licked his lips. "Ain't s'posed to allow no one in. Father's orders."

Captain Thatcher took a step closer and bellowed into the house. "Margaret Gruber? I'm here on behalf of your brother, James Hawker. I'm a lawman, madam. You have nothing to fear."

Tim glowered up at him, the purple around his eye deepening to a shade of fury no young lad should own.

"Let him in, Timmy." The voice inside was little more than a whisper.

"But we ain't s'posed to—"

"You heard your mother." The captain used his stern tone, and Abby straightened her own spine in response.

With a scowl better suited to an overworked longshoreman, Tim flung the door open and retreated into darkness. The captain followed, and for a moment, Abby hesitated at the threshold, holding Emma tight, afraid to enter. Afraid for the girl's future. Afraid of the thick dread knotting her stomach.

Pudgy little fingers cupped her chin, pulling her face down. Emma's big blue eyes stared up at her. "Ah-be-da?"

Abby's throat tightened at the only word Emma knew—whatever it meant. Swallowing back tears, she willed herself to be strong. If she started to cry, no doubt Emma would wail, and the captain would surely have no patience for such a display.

She brushed back the girl's reddish-blond hair and whispered, "Ah-be-da, little one."

Summoning all her courage, Abby stepped into a room not much bigger than a crypt. Daylight barely seeped through a soot-filmed window, casting shadows over a few sticks of furniture. A table stood at center, which was really just some planks propped atop two crates. An off-kilter bench, large enough to seat only two, sat next to a small hearth. On the floor in one corner lay a poorly stuffed sack with a threadbare lump of fabric balled atop it. Their bed, perhaps? Tim stood next to it, arms crossed. A strange stance of protection for naught but a wad of bedding. . .unless he had some treasure hidden there? But where was the owner of the thin voice? There were no other rooms and no ladder leading up to a loft.

The captain strode to the foot of the mattress. "Are you Margaret Gruber?"

Abby dared a few more steps into the room, narrowing her eyes upon the crude bed. What she'd mistaken for fabric slowly moved, lengthening, rising. A waif of a woman sat up, one arm pressed tight against her stomach. Stringy hair hung down over parchment skin, her eyes deep set and yellow. Her lip was split as if someone had punched her in the teeth.

"I am Margaret," she rasped. "What of my brother? Is James well?"

Abby huddled closer to the captain's back, seeking solace that she knew he couldn't provide. Everything inside her screamed to make him turn around, to plead with him to take her and Emma out of here, to ride hard and far away from this place of despair. Not that he'd listen, though. It was his duty to carry out his friend's wishes, and above all, the captain was a man of honor.

But none of that mattered to Abby. Not now. Not ever. How could she possibly leave Emma in the care of a woman who was little more than a collection of bones and blue veins?

"Your brother is. . .he lives." There was only a slight hitch in the captain's words, but enough that Abby caught the slip. He knew something about the man, something he wouldn't share with the woman. "James charged me with delivering his only child into your care."

The captain glanced at Abby over his shoulder, and with a nod of his head, he indicated it was time to hand over Emma.

Abby's gut clenched, feeling as sick as the woman on the pallet looked. She'd known all along this moment was coming. Tried to separate her heart from the babe she'd learned to love as her own flesh and blood. But now that it was here?

She turned and fled out the door, clutching tightly to Emma.

Of all the foolhardy moves!

Samuel dropped Emma's basket and bag and took off, chasing Abby's blue-striped skirt outside. What on God's green earth was the woman thinking? That wasn't a kitten she held. Emma was not a pet she could cosset and make her own.

He grabbed Abby by the shoulder and spun her around. "What do you think you're doing?"

Her brows folded into a fierce frown. "We cannot leave Emma in that place. We cannot!"

The words were choked. Desperate. As ragged and ruined as the pathetic scrabble of a courtyard they stood in.

Samuel yanked off his hat and raked a hand through his hair, tugging hard and relishing the sting. It was a stalling tactic, one he employed on those rare times he felt helpless, and sweet blessed heavens, his hands were tied in this wretched situation. He let loose a breath, praying for the right words to convince Abby—and himself—that leaving Emma here was the right thing to do. That there was no other option.

For there wasn't.

He tugged his hat back onto his head, just as Emma reached out to him.

"Ah-be-da?"

His gut clenched, sickened by the guileless blue eyes staring up at him. Trust lifted the girl's brow. Innocence as pure as that of a newborn foal radiated from her. His hands curled into fists. How could he possibly go through with this?

Steeling his jaw, he gently pushed Emma's hand away and looked only at Abby. "I know this is hard. This isn't what I want for Emma either, but the child is not ours. We cannot keep her from her kin. Say goodbye."

"But—"

"Say goodbye!" He snapped out the command, hating himself for his harshness, hating even more the instant tears shimmering in Abby's eyes.

The small shards of his heart that were left broke into a million jagged-edged pieces as Abby lifted the child, face-to-face, and wept openly. Little gasps for air punctuated her words.

"Goodbye, little one. You be a good girl for your new"—her face contorted and she gulped—"for your new family."

Emma planted her palms on each of Abby's cheeks, pulling their faces together.

And Samuel clenched every muscle in his body to keep from crying himself.

God, how am I to bear this? Give me strength, Lord. Give me Your strength.

From an act of sheer will, he pulled Emma from Abby's arms, refusing to look at the girl, staring only at Abby's teary gaze. "Stay out here if you like." His voice lowered an octave, and in truth, it was a wonder he could force out the words at all. "I'll be back shortly."

He wheeled about. Footsteps padded behind him, each tamp of leather against gravel accusing him. She blamed him for doing this—yet she needn't have. The nightmares that were sure to follow this day would sear his soul for years to come.

His step faltered as he neared the door. He'd had to do hard things before. It came with the job. Dragging mangled bodies out of crashed coaches. Hunting down killers who'd think nothing of slicing open his throat. But stepping back into the rat hole the Grubers called a home topped them all.

Sucking in a breath for courage, he strode into the dim interior. For the first time ever, the gloomy shadows that wrapped around him didn't comfort, and he suspected they never would again.

He stalked over to the pallet in the corner and held Emma out. "This is Emmaline Hawker, your niece."

Hawker's sister looked up at him, her face softening, and for the briefest moment, the ravages of whatever disease she suffered from lessened. "Ahh, such a lamb. Give her to me."

"No, Mother!" The boy dropped to all fours, pleading with the woman practically nose to nose. "You can't. Send them away before Father returns."

Samuel tensed—and suddenly he was ten years old again. Begging his mother to snatch up his sister and run away with him. Tugging at her apron to get her out of the house before his father came home, drunk, loud, and swinging his fists. Cold sweat beaded on his forehead. The similarities here were far too many. What kind of wicked jest was this?

Margaret patted a bony hand atop the boy's head. "It is my brother's wish. I owe him this, at least."

Samuel eyed the woman as Emma kicked her legs, angling to be free. What had Hawker done for his sister that she felt so beholden to him?

Tim sank back to his haunches as his mother held up her arms to receive Emma. The neck hole of the woman's thin shift drooped with the movement. Paste-coloured skin peeked out, dotted with red spots.

Samuel bit back a curse, knowing full well but not wanting to admit what the woman suffered from. . .wasting fever. He'd wager ten to one on it. Margaret Gruber would be dead within a week. Two, if she were lucky—which she wasn't. Luck didn't live in this wretched backstreet fleapit.

Clenching his teeth so hard that his jaw cracked, he stooped and handed Emma down to the woman, not releasing her until Margaret Gruber's skeletal arms wrapped around her.

Emma craned her neck, gawking up at him. One of her hands snaked up in the air, reaching for him. "Be-dah?"

He shook his head, refusing the request, and betrayal wailed out of the girl's mouth, punching the air from his lungs.

Folding his arms, he turned to the boy, vainly trying to shut out Emma's cries. "Where is your father?"

Tim didn't bother standing. He stayed crouched, only his eyes moving. "Out selling apples."

Apples? Samuel frowned. Only cripples sold—

"What's this?" A foghorn of a voice entered just before a thump-step, thump-step drew up behind him.

Samuel swung about, and Abby darted to his side. Two steel-grey eyes bored into his. The man was his height, slightly smaller of frame, and propped up by a rag-topped crutch shoved beneath one armpit. Only one leg and the stick of hickory held him up. A sour stench wafted off him. From a morning of drinking or from whatever it was he held in a canvas sack.

The man's cold gaze slid from him to Abby, drifted down to where Hawker's sister tried to shush a snotty-nosed Emma, and finally landed hard on Tim. Purple crept up the man's neck. "I told you, boy, ne'er to let anyone in."

Samuel sidestepped, blocking Tim from his father's deadly stare. "The boy had no choice in the matter. I am Captain Thatcher, principal officer of the Bow Street magistrate."

Gruber bared his teeth like a wolf. If hatred were a living thing, the size and breadth of the monster living inside the man would devour them all.

"What's a filthy runner doing up in these parts? Not enough men to harass in London? Bloody thief catcher. Bootlicker to the crown, that's what you are."

Samuel rolled with the jabs. He'd heard worse. These weren't even particularly creative. He met the man's stare head-on. "I was charged to deliver your niece into your wife's care."

Curses thickened the air, punctuated by the thwack of the man's bag landing on the table. "I can't feed a squalling brat! I can barely feed these two worthless sacks of horse—"

"Mind your tongue," Samuel growled. "There are ladies present."

Scarlet spread up the man's neck and bled across his pockmarked face. "I'll not be told what to do in my own home, *runner*."

"You will as long as I'm here." Pulling free of Abby, Samuel stepped up to the bully and squared his shoulders.

Footsteps trembled behind him. Abby gained his side and fumbled with the strings of her reticule, drawing all their attention. She dumped the contents into her palm, the coins jingling into a small pile, then held out the offering to Gruber. "Here. Use this for Emma's care, for all of your family's care, that she may not be a hardship to you."

The man snatched the money away so quickly, he wobbled on his crutch. "All right. But soon as this is gone"—he looked past him and Abby, narrowing his eyes on his family huddled in the corner—"the child will be eating from your portions, not mine."

Fury quaked through Samuel, shaking him to the marrow of his bones. Should not a husband, a father, *any* man born in the image of God die to self for the sake of a loved one? Ahh, but there was the truth of it. Gruber loved no one but himself—just like the man who'd sired him thirty-odd years back.

Gruber shoved the coins into his pocket then turned on him. "Well, runner? Have you further business with me?"

Aye, he'd like to give the mongrel a sound thrashing. Teach him what it was like to be knocked about for no reason other than the whim of the moment. Samuel's fists tightened into iron knots. He could use a real bloody knuckle toss-around right about now, and in his younger days, nothing would've held him back. But Emma's mewls did. So did the trembling of Abby's skirts.

"No," he ground out.

Gruber's mouth twisted into a snarl. "Then shove off."

Without another word, Samuel wrapped his arm around Abby's shoulders and guided her toward the door, forcing each step. There was nothing else to do. He never should have given Hawker his word.

And Emma's wailing cries drove home that ugly truth, each one stabbing him in the back.

Chapter Twenty-Three

Merry chatter bubbled in the taproom, boxing Abby's ears. Laughter clanged in her head, overly loud. This inn was a rash. The *world* was a rash. Irritating. Rubbing her raw. How could everyone be so cheerful when all was not right?

She stabbed a piece of roasted pork and popped it into her mouth, knowing the thing would stick in her throat, as had the few bites she'd barely managed before. All she wanted to hear was Emma's coos or babbles. She'd even listen to the girl's cries and count herself blessed. But never again would she hear that little one's sweet voice.

The pork landed like a rock in her stomach, and Abby set down her fork. Who was she kidding? She ought to rummage through her chest and pull out her mourning crepe until her heart healed. But would it ever? And if it did, would that not be dishonoring to the child whom she'd come to love so much? It seemed a hideous blasphemy to simply forget Emma like a castoff mantle.

A pang of guilt churned the meat in her belly. She hadn't grieved the loss of her own family as profoundly as this.

Across from her, the captain shoveled in his last bite then pushed away his plate. Amazing that he could eat so heartily. Did he not miss Emma as keenly as she?

Abby searched the captain's face for an answer. His dark gaze met hers, but nothing moved behind his eyes. He was a house shuttered tight against any unwelcome visitors.

"A farthing for your thoughts, Captain."

"Trust me," he grumbled. "They're not worth that much."

"They must be of some kind of value. You've hoarded them since we delivered Emma."

Leaning back in his chair, he folded his arms across his chest, a stance she knew too well. He had no intention of answering.

So it astonished her when he opened his mouth. "You are—"

"I know." She cut him off with a flutter of her fingers. "I am persistent. And *you* should know by now that I will not rest until I hear what it is that worries you so."

His lips clamped shut, pressing into a firm line.

Abby shoved down a sigh, for she knew that expression intimately as well. The captain was done with the conversation before it even began. His stubborn streak was as long and broad as her persistence. She might as well bid him good night now, for they were at a stalemate. Pulling the napkin from her lap, she set it on the table and edged back her chair.

But before she could rise, the captain's voice rumbled low, catching her off guard once again. She scooted closer to the table, straining to hear over the clatter of forks scraping against plates and dinner conversations much more pleasant than this would surely be.

"I have no idea why I'm telling you this." He looked past her for a moment, as if he searched for words at a far table in the room. Then his gaze shot back to hers, swift and sharp as any arrow. "It's Emma. She'll die there, in that house. I might as well have killed her with my own hands."

Abby bit her lip, unsure of what to say, how to comfort the pain riding ragged in his voice. Yet she must say something. Put him at ease somehow.

She clenched her hands in her lap, hoping to squeeze out some form of consolation. "Surely God will watch over her."

There. She'd done it, said something...but what exactly had she said? Even to herself her words sounded small in the big room—or maybe it was the sentiment that felt so absurdly tiny in the face of such a loss.

The captain apparently agreed. His jaw hardened, and his eyes narrowed upon her, making her feel even more minute and ridiculous.

Tipping his chin, he looked down the length of his nose at her. "The only thing sure is that man Gruber will run them all into the ground."

She stiffened. No. She couldn't believe that. She wouldn't.

She met his rock-hard stare with one of her own. "You do not know that, Captain. Can you not hope for the best?"

He snorted. "Can you?"

He shoved back his chair and stalked toward the front door, leaving her alone to fight the monster of a question he'd loosed upon her. Coward!

She jumped up and followed him outside. Sconces burned brilliantly against the night, set at intervals on the brick wall of the inn, welcoming any late travelers. The captain, however, strode beyond the yellow glow, his boots pounding hard on the courtyard's gravel. He stopped when he reached a stone wall, standing as high as his waist, then bent and propped his elbows on it. But he didn't turn as she drew up behind him, though he had to know she stood close. He just stood there, staring into the darkness, no acknowledgment whatsoever.

Abby clenched her hands, her nails digging little crescents into her palms, angry with the obstinate man. Angry with herself too. What had gotten into her? Now that she was here, what was she to say to the captain's broad back? That he was wrong? That Emma was even now likely tucked safely into a soft bed with a full tummy?

Despite the chill of the evening, fury burned all the hotter in her chest. Deep down, the truth roiled her few bites of pork roast to rancid bits. The captain was right. Though she'd been trying all afternoon to hope for the best, going so far as to search the scriptures before dinner, she couldn't do it. She was anxious, despairing, and annoyed with searching for hope. No, worse. She was chained and fettered by a lack of it, unable to move or breathe.

She clenched her fists tighter until her arms shook. How was she to be hopeful when the outcome for Emma would be a life of poverty? Or death? No. There was no possible way she could churn up any morsel of hope for the girl she loved.

"But I can, child."

She tensed, every muscle in her locking tight. Had she heard right? But how could the captain know what she'd been thinking? Why call her a child? And how on earth did he propose to help restore her hope when he rarely partook of the sentiment?

She dared a step nearer to him. "What did you say?"

He glanced back at her. "There is nothing to say except go to bed, Miss Gilbert."

She cocked her head. She could've sworn she'd heard—

"Hope in Me, child. Emma is Mine, as are you."

Wonderful. Now she was hearing things. Tiny prickles ran down her arms, raising gooseflesh. Had she not begged all afternoon for guidance and wisdom, to hear some measure of comfort from God's mouth alone?

She lifted her face to the black sky.

Is that You, Lord? Is that Your voice I hear?

She stood there for a long time, the captain's broad back to her, stars blinking down on them both. No more whispers came, but that didn't stop an urgent prayer from welling up in her soul.

Oh God, will You take my ugly hope of You protecting little Emma and change it into a peaceful hope? A strong one? Maybe even a joyful hope? Because I do believe, with all my heart, that Christ is the Victor, that You are Emma's Protector no matter what, and in that truth will I abide.

The same peace she'd felt days ago draped over her shoulders, and against all reason, she knew—she *knew*—that somehow Emma's future would shine as brightly as the stars twinkling overhead.

In the dark, the captain's shoulders bent, his silhouette black upon black. "I shouldn't have left her there." The words were quiet, more of a groan, really. His bleak confession dared her to drift back into despair.

She laid a hand on those bent shoulders, wishing with all that was within her to relieve some of the weight this man carried. "You did what you promised, Captain, and that is always a good thing."

"Maybe." He turned to face her. "But maybe I never should have promised such a thing in the first place."

Sidestepping her, he stalked toward the inn and disappeared through the door.

For once, she didn't follow him. She planted her feet and looked up to the heavens. It was going to be a long night for the captain—and for her. She had a lot of praying to do on his behalf.

Regrets always attacked worst in the darkness. Springing out from the midnight shadows. Drawing blood as the witching hours slowly ticked off. By the time Samuel swung his leg over Pilgrim the next morning and led the carriage through the streets of Manchester, he was battle sore and bone weary from an evening of wrestling with guilt.

He shouldn't have left Emma at the Grubers'.

He shouldn't have taken her on in the first place.

And he definitely shouldn't have said anything to Abby about it.

Scrubbing his hand over his face, he fought a yawn. He couldn't afford this fatigue, for it might cost his and Abby's life if Shankhart or his men were about. And they would be, sooner or later. If only he had enough funds to buy another gun, arm the driver, or even hire on another man to ride with them.

Shops thinned out as he neared the Manchester city limits. Beyond, fields stretched into a green patchwork. He urged Pilgrim with a nudge to her side to up the pace. Soon they'd pass by a gibbet with some blackguard's body in a state of decomposition, swinging in the breeze, which was no proper sight for Abby to witness should she chance a glance out the carriage window.

Clouds smothered the countryside, punching down from the sky like mighty grey fists. A bleak day, as dreary and miserable as his mood. Abby had been right when she'd called him a dour old naysayer.

Off to his left, in the field, a boy cried out. Samuel narrowed his eyes. A big man held the lad in the air by the collar with one hand. The other clutched a switch, striking the boy on the backside. Again and again. Far too many times for whatever crime the lad had committed, if any. Men like that often didn't need an excuse to torture those younger and smaller, those like Emma. *Oh Emma. . .*

His throat closed, and he lifted his face to the sullen sky. "God, what have I done? Emma won't last long in that place. Some guardian I turned out to be."

"Peace, My son. I am her Protector."

The truth of the unspoken words hit like a hammer to the head, stunning, smarting, and rankling in a most unholy fashion. He clenched the reins to keep from raising a fist to the heavens. "But how? How will You protect a child I left defenseless with a monster?"

"*You.*"

He cocked his head, suddenly unsure of his sanity. But more words whispered on the wind.

"*You are my means.*"

Sweet heavens! He was going mad. Surely a righteous God would not condone him breaking a vow. "But I swore to bring her there. I promised—"

The boy's cries stopped. So did his heart. The truth of his own prayer zapped through him from head to toe, leaving a line of prickles in its wake. He had promised to deliver Emma to Hawker's sister, and so he'd fulfilled his pledge.

But he'd never once said he'd leave her there forever.

He tugged Pilgrim's reins, stopping the big bay, feeling lighter. Freer. And more determined than ever to rescue Emma. But first he swung his gaze back to the field and narrowed his eyes toward the boy, intent on helping him.

Half a smile lifted his lips. The lad had wriggled free and was even now hightailing it out of the barley, the big man with the switch losing ground as the boy sprinted. The cruel master wouldn't catch him again, not today, and maybe not ever if the boy kept running.

Clicking his tongue, Samuel guided Pilgrim in a tight circle, then bolted back to the carriage and pulled up next to the postilion with a raised hand.

"Turn around," he ordered.

Alarm widened the man's eyes. "Something wrong, Captain?"

"Not anymore." He kicked Pilgrim into a canter, purposely avoiding the bewildered look on Abby's face as he rode past the carriage window.

It took every last bit of his self-control to keep from galloping. Tearing into a town as if the devil were at his heels was asking for attention, and that was never a good thing.

The Grubers lived near the cotton mills, where the rich broke the backs of the poorest of the poor, working them to death and making profit during the sparse years they laboured. Soot blackened the nearby buildings, windows, hearts, and souls. But this day as Samuel rode into the alley on Mudlark Lane, the oppression of the bleak courtyard didn't smother him. In fact, he sprang off Pilgrim as if he'd lost ten years.

The postilion eased the coach to a stop, and Samuel strode over to the man. "Turn the carriage around and wait."

"Aye, Captain." He gave him a sharp nod.

And Abby gave him a sharp look as she stuck her head out the open window. "What are we doing back here? Are you going to—"

He shot up his hand, staving her off. "Stay in the carriage, Miss Gilbert."

"But—"

Thankfully, the postilion ordered the horses to walk on, carrying away Abby's questions and protests.

Samuel drew near the door, rage lighting a fire in him as Emma's pitiful cries leached through the thin wood. If Gruber had harmed that girl, may God have mercy on the man—for he surely wouldn't.

He pounded his fist against the door, rattling the wood like bones in a coffin. "Open up! Captain Thatcher here."

Emma screamed. "Ah-be-da!"

That did it. He rammed his shoulder against the door, forcing it open. The wood smacked into the wall, startling Emma, and she stared up at him from where she sat on the floor, mouth open, face smudged, and her bonnet gone. The clean gown Abby had dressed her in the day before was now soiled with ash, grease, and the contents from an overflowing clout.

But he didn't care. Samuel swept her up and cradled her against his chest, rubbing his cheek against the top of her head. Her fingers clawed into his waistcoat in a grip that would be impossible to pry off.

"Ah-be-da, little one," he whispered against her hair.

With a last, shuddering breath, she quit crying.

Samuel lifted his face, surveying the small room. His gaze landed near the hearth, where Margaret Gruber lay on the floor still as a stone, despite the commotion of a man breaking into her home and snatching up the babe in her care.

He pulled off his hat and peeled Emma from his chest, setting the child down with the old piece of worn felt—her favorite plaything. Two paces later, he dropped to his knees and bent over what might very well be Margaret Gruber's corpse. Strands of greasy hair hung over her sharp cheekbones, her skin the colour of wax. Her eyes stayed shut, and though he looked, he couldn't really detect any rise or fall of her chest.

"Mrs. Gruber?" He pressed his fingers against the side of her neck. A weak pulse fluttered beneath his touch, for now, anyway.

He scooped her up, her body weighing hardly more than Emma's, and as he laid her on the flattened sack of straw in the corner, her eyes flickered open.

"Captain?" Her voice was a wisp against her cracked lips. The air rattled in her lungs. But she'd recognized him, a small victory, that, but a victory nonetheless.

"Yes, madam, it's me. Let me get you a drink."

He collected a dipper of greenish water from a pail with scum climbing up the insides. Not good, but better than nothing...hopefully.

Emma scooted over, grabbing onto his leg and pulling herself upright, so that he had to hobble back to Mrs. Gruber with the child attached. Once again he pried Emma's hands from him, then aided the sick woman to sit, lending her his strength as she drank.

"Mmm," she murmured as she took little sips and finally downed it all. Her yellowed eyes blinked up to his. "Thank you. I am much revived."

He eased her back down and set the dipper aside while Emma pounded on his back, cooing. Then he faced Mrs. Gruber. "Is there anything more I can do for you?"

"No, I. . ." She swallowed, her throat bobbing with the effort, but when she spoke again, her voice came out much clearer. "You came at a fortunate time. I was trying to stop Emma from getting too near the hearth, but I. . .I couldn't do it." Her brow folded, and she swallowed again. "Why are you here?"

"I'm taking the girl." With one arm, he swept Emma from behind his back and drew her forward. "I'm taking Emma back to your brother."

The woman's eyes glistened. From sadness or a return of her fever? "But James wished me to care for her."

He hugged Emma tighter in the curl of his arm. "We both know you can't, madam."

"You don't understand. I owe him this." Thin tears broke loose, just a few, for she likely couldn't produce more. "My brother is the one who got us out of debtors' prison."

Samuel stifled a scowl. Would that Hawker could've saved his sister from her brute of a husband as well.

"Mrs. Gruber," he softened his tone, "I am certain that if your brother knew you were ailing, he'd not have sent Emma in the first place. I shouldn't have left her here yesterday. The burden is too much for you to bear."

"You are"—her voice hitched, and she gulped in a breath—"very kind, sir."

Reaching with his free arm, he pushed back the matted hair from her brow, wishing he could do more for her. But it was too late. It would be a miracle if she lasted till nightfall.

"Rest now," he whispered. "I'll gather Emma's things and let myself out."

Her hand shot out, grabbing his arm with more strength than he'd credited. "Thank you."

Torment twisted her face, stabbing him in the heart. It wasn't fair, this ruined life of death and destruction. "May God bless you, Margaret Gruber."

Her lips parted, and for one spectacular moment, a brilliant smile lit her face, erasing the ravages of disease and hard living. "He already has, Captain, for I am assured I will go to a better place because of Christ."

Her eyes closed, and she drifted into a peaceful sleep.

Blowing out a long breath, Samuel gripped Emma tighter and stood, hauling her up along with him. Her basket lay overturned on the floor near the door, and her bag of belongings spilled out clouts and tiny gowns onto the table. Samuel scooped both up in his empty hand and strode to the door—just as it opened.

Tim stood on the threshold, blood dripping a trail from his nose to his upper lip, then smeared across his cheek where he'd obviously been swiping at it with his sleeve.

"Best be on yer way, sir." He ran his arm across his nose once again. "My father's not far behind."

Fury throbbed a vein in Samuel's temple. No doubt the boy had his cullion of a father to thank for that bloody nose. He set down the basket and crouched, keeping a good hold on Emma. Then he fished in his pocket, pulling out the last of his coins and the end of his hope to purchase any land in the near future.

"Hold out your hand, Tim."

The boy sniffled and cocked his head, but slowly he obeyed. Good boy. Too good for the likes of Gruber.

Samuel pressed the money into the boy's hand and held on.

The boy's blue eyes searched his, questions creasing his forehead as blood continued to ooze from his nostrils.

Samuel squeezed his hand. "Take this money and hide it. It's a tough truth, but you need to know. Your mother isn't long for this world. She'll be lucky to make it another day. When she's gone, leave here. Immediately. Use these coins to take a coach to Warrington. When you get off, seek out Farmer Bigby, about six miles from town. Tell him you have my recommendation. You'll be safe there. Do you understand?"

Slowly, the boy nodded. "Aye, sir."

"Good." Samuel released him and snatched up Emma's things. Indeed, no place this side of heaven was truly safe, but that never stopped God from being a protector. And maybe—just maybe—God had allowed him, a tired, worn-out lawman, to make the world a little safer for one young boy.

Chapter Twenty-Four

Eyes watched them—and had been since they'd left Manchester two days ago. Close but unseen. Ever present. Samuel couldn't prove it, despite his best efforts, but the queer twist in his gut was all the evidence he needed.

So he alternated between scouting ahead of the carriage, then doubling back and trailing behind, as he now rode. To his right, fields stretched just beyond an abrupt dip that led to a small river. To his left, death. In what had been a vibrant pine forest, charred trees stood like skeletons. The larger ones, at any rate. The rest scattered the blackened ground like dead men's bones, eerily rising up from the grave in spots where boulders lifted the ends of them into burnt pikes.

Pilgrim's ears twitched, and Samuel bent forward, patting the horse's neck. "Easy, girl. That fire's long gone."

He straightened and continued plodding along. Prudence demanded he up his pace, but even so, he held Pilgrim to a slow and steady stride. Within the hour, the manor home of Sir Jonathan Aberley would loom large on the horizon and steal Abby away from him. Forever. The thought of it cut deep in his soul. While it would be a relief to deliver her safely, he could not make himself hasten to that hideous end. He wasn't ready to part with her—and never would be. He'd grown accustomed to the woman, and he'd miss her as sorely as he would his arm or his leg. Somehow over these past weeks, she'd scaled his best defenses and become a part of him.

But in his heart he knew it was time to let her go. Release her into God's care and that of the baronet He'd provided for her. True, the man hardly knew her and likely didn't love her—yet—but he soon would once he learned of Abby's family background and saw how precious the woman truly was.

Shadows stretched longer as the sun sank lower in the sky. Would that he could stop time from passing, that he wouldn't be traveling this same road tomorrow in the opposite direction with Emma shored up in front of him. After a quick stop at the Bigbys' to check on Tim—for surely the lad would be smart enough to go there—he'd make the trek back to Hawker's. And when he dropped off Emma, he'd be alone.

More alone than he'd ever been in his life.

Ahead, the carriage stopped, and he pressed his heels into Pilgrim's side, shooting forward. The way the road bent, this was not a good place to loiter. Any manner of danger could come at them with little warning. Half-wit driver! He'd had reservations about the postilion's aptitude the first time he met the fellow. It was a foul twist of fate that the fellow had been the only available postilion.

Drawing near, Samuel rolled his shoulders, vainly trying to ease some of the tension eating at him. A felled tree blocked part of the road in front of the coach, a valid enough reason to slow the horses—but not stop them. The man could easily have driven around the impediment. And why the deuce had he dismounted and was even now walking away from the carriage, toward him?

Samuel halted Pilgrim in front of the fellow. He was a jittery man, like too many nerves were bundled inside his skin and were wild to break free. Or maybe it was because the man's lanky arms and legs didn't quite fit his stub of a body, and the spidery feel of it drove him to constant movement. Either way, Samuel didn't like it.

Samuel stared down at him. "What's the trouble?"

The man flicked a glance over his shoulder, indicating the felled tree. "Road's blocked, Captain."

Pilgrim shied sideways, and Samuel heeled her in with a jerk on the reins, irritated more at the man than the horse. The driver could try the patience of a frock-coated saint. "I see that. I can also see there's enough clearance to go around it."

"Yes, but. . ." His arms jerked up in an overzealous shrug.

Samuel shoved down a growl. "But what, man? Drive around it! This is not a good place to stop."

The driver stepped closer, putting distance between himself and the back of the carriage. "I've, um. . ." He cleared his throat, then lowered his voice for Samuel alone to hear. "I've some *personal* business to attend to down by the riverbank, if you know what I mean."

Sudden understanding flared. No wonder the man seemed particularly animated—which only peeved him all the more. He gave the fellow a sharp nod and edged Pilgrim aside. "Be quick about it."

The man darted off and skittered down the embankment.

"Why are we stopping?" Abby's head poked through the carriage window, her brown eyes seeking his.

Samuel eased his horse ahead several paces, keeping the riverbank in his line of sight. "The driver needed a respite."

The words, spoken aloud, circled back and slapped him in the face. Any postilion worth his salt wouldn't need to stop, especially this close to arriving at their destination—even one as half-witted as their particular driver.

He reached for his gun.

"Captain?" Alarm pinched the edges of Abby's voice. "Why are you—?"

Two shots cracked the air. Blistering pain ripped into his upper arm, and his gun flew from his grip.

"Get down!" he shouted. He turned Pilgrim toward the wood line, reaching for his knife with the only arm that worked.

Too late.

A blade sliced into his thigh and a demon from hell reached for his arm, yanking him down.

The world exploded, spattering Abby's cheek with hot droplets. Blood. The *captain's* blood. Her heart stopped. So did her breath. She froze, helpless, staring at a living nightmare outside the window.

A grey-cloaked monster of a man pulled the captain from his horse, and he whumped to the ground. Another man stood a few paces back, trading his gun for a knife. Fear stabbed her in the chest. The captain could die here, now, right in front of her eyes.

God, no. . .please!

A screech rang in her ear, and it took her a moment to realize the echoes weren't from her own throat. She ripped her gaze away from the fight outside to a tearful Emma. The girl had pulled herself up on Abby's arm, standing on the seat, eye level with her—and a clear target if another shot should fire out.

Grabbing the child, Abby plummeted to the floor, huddling them both into the small space. Curses blasphemed the air. A growl. Several grunts of fresh pain. Abby clung to Emma as tightly as the girl dug her fingers into Abby's neck.

"Shh," she breathed out, hoping to calm Emma. What a farce. How could she expect the girl to settle down when chaos clashed and gnashed just beyond the thin carriage wall?

The captain roared—and Abby's heart sank. For all she knew, that could be his death cry. . .and she'd done nothing to help him. What kind of coward trembled in a heap on a floor when the man she loved—*loved!*—was in the fight of his life?

She pried Emma's fingers off her neck and tucked the girl into the corner. "Stay!" she ordered.

Turning away from the child, she swept a desperate gaze around the carriage, ignoring the crazed beat of her pulse and the madness of what she intended to do. What could she use to help the captain? What might serve as a weapon?

Her eyes landed on the curtain rod just above the window on the door. If she snuck up behind one of the captain's attackers, one good wallop with that iron bar could dent the brute's skull. It might work. No, it *had* to work.

She shot toward the door—then gasped. A horse and rider tore up from the riverbank, riding straight toward her. Behind her, Emma's cries crescendoed. Abby bit the inside of her cheek, stopping her own scream.

The captain would have to hold his own for now.

She dropped back down, shoving Emma aside and sorry for the harshness. Propping her spine against the wall, Abby curled up her legs, prepared to kick wildly and slam open the door at the slightest hint of movement on the handle. Timing was key. Too soon and she'd open the thing wide, giving the man access without an effort. Too late and he'd grab ahold of her, pulling her out for whatever wicked deed he had in mind. Either way would not be good.

She fixed her gaze on the brass door handle, watching for movement. Narrowing her universe down to a small hunk of metal that, at the slightest quiver, would mean life or death.

And prayed as never before in all her life.

Chapter Twenty-Five

Samuel's face mashed into the ground, gravel cutting his cheek. Fire burned in his arm, and life seeped out of his thigh. But he couldn't give in to pain now. Lying there meant death, for him *and* for Abby and Emma.

Harnessing momentum, he rolled, then slashed his blade in a wide arc as he rose to his feet. The knife caught. Slicing through flesh and muscle. Coming away slick and sticky.

His attacker stumbled back and fell, spewing out curses and clutching his belly—or what was left of it, anyway.

Ten paces behind the felled man, a guttural cry tore across the afternoon, from a cavernous mouth on a misshapen head.

Shankhart.

Samuel sucked in air. So this was it, then. Kill or be killed. . .unless he could get the better of the man and haul him in.

Oh Lord, make it so.

The brute barreled forward, his gaze narrowed on Samuel. "You're a dead man, runner!"

"God numbers my days, Robbins. Not you." He charged to meet him, knife at the ready, and at the last minute before contact, swerved sideways, forcing Shankhart to spin toward him—leading the villain away from the carriage and toward the charred wood line.

Putting most of his weight on his good leg, Samuel pivoted and crouched, grasping the hilt of his knife tighter. Already he felt his strength draining down his leg and spilling onto the ground. He'd not last long. That gash on his thigh had to be deep, but he dare not pull his gaze from Robbins.

A little help here, God, if You please.

Curses belched like hot tar out of Shankhart, and he edged sideways. Samuel did too. It was a macabre dance, this circling of mortals and murder, working their way off the road and into the ruined woods. Each of them took measure of the other. Looking for an opening. Ticking off weaknesses. If he could strike Shankhart on the upper part of his body, find the place where that bullet of a few weeks ago had torn flesh, he might gain the advantage. And judging by the way the man favored his left arm, up near that shoulder would be the best place to thrust his blade.

Robbins lunged. Samuel threw himself back, and his boot hit a rock, knocking him off-balance. With a wild swoop of his arms, he caught himself before a sharp spire of pine sticking up from the ground could skewer him through the back.

He barely recovered when Robbins slashed again, carving into him, the metal snagging the flesh of his arm—the same one the bullet lodged in.

Samuel roared.

Shankhart struck again. The beast was unstoppable, his blade cutting through the air like lightning. Samuel feinted one way, then as Robbins lurched forward, he darted back the other, slicing the man on the meaty part of his shoulder.

They both spun, exchanging places, and before Shankhart could strike again, Samuel stabbed upward.

Shankhart jumped back, just as Samuel had moments before, and the man's foot hit the same rock. But the force of Robbins's recoil was too much. The ungainly bulk of him too off-center. Flailing his arms for balance came too late. The notorious highwayman arced backward.

And the blackened point of a charred pine branch speared through his back and jutted out his chest, just below the rib cage.

Sickened, Samuel spun away, shutting out the grisly sight—but not able to keep from hearing the last gurgle of Shankhart's final breath. That awful death rattle would haunt him for years to come.

God, have mercy on that man's soul. . .but even as he prayed it, Samuel knew it was too late for the black-hearted sinner—and that was a fate worse than death.

He staggered from the thought as he wiped off his knife. It was always like this, the heave of his stomach, the squeeze in his chest, every time a criminal died unrepentant, no matter how abominable their offenses.

Sucking air through his teeth, he hobbled from the gruesome scene, spent and worn. Darkness closed in at the edges of his vision, and he blinked, desperate to remain conscious. But he had to. If he fell here, he'd never stand again. All he had to do was get to the carriage. Stumble or crawl the distance if he must. Once Abby tied up the gaping flesh on his leg and staunched the flow on his arm, he could think more clearly. Assess what action to take next. Or maybe close his eyes for one blessed moment and rest. Had he ever been so tired in all his life?

Fighting to remain upright, he pressed on. Every step ignited fresh agony as he worked his way from the wood's edge. He bypassed the other blackguard lying still on the dirt, permanently curled into clutching a gut that spilled onto the road.

A movement caught Samuel's eye, but not from that man. On the river side of the byway, a foreign horse stood on the rise leading down to the water. Four paces away, its rider stalked toward the carriage, the man's hand rising to yank open the door. His other hand clutched a pistol.

Sweet blazing stars! Were all the forces of hell against him today?

Biting back a growl, Samuel used every skill he owned to silently scoop up his gun where it lay in the dirt. Sweat broke loose, dripping down his brow and stinging his eyes. White-hot pain blistered from his knee to his waist. He gritted his teeth to keep from crying out as he fumbled to reload his gun. The fabric of his sleeve stuck to his skin, heavy with blood, and his fingers shook. No, his whole body did, coaxing him to lie down and give up the ghost.

Focus. Focus!

He cocked open the hammer and, with a quivering arm, lifted the gun.

But not soon enough. The man's hand already gripped the door handle and—

The door exploded open, slamming into the man's face and jerking him backward. His arms shot out. His gun plummeted to the ground.

Samuel took aim and pulled the trigger.

The man crumpled like a wadded-up rag, clutching his knee and howling on the dirt.

For the first time in the past eternity, Samuel heaved a sigh of relief as he strode over to the man and clouted him in the head with the butt of his gun, just to be on the safe side. No sense giving the fellow an opportunity to put a hole in him when he wasn't looking. Then he stepped back and scanned the area for movement of any more attackers.

Abby climbed down from the carriage, her skirts giving the man on the ground a wide berth as she raced over to Samuel's side.

"Oh Captain." Her voice was as wobbly as he felt. Tears shimmered in her eyes, wide open with pity and fear. "You are hurt!"

Despite the effort, he smirked. "A little. Are you unharmed? Is Emma safe?"

"Yes, but you—" A small cry cut off her words, followed by a gasping breath.

"I'll mend." He wavered on his feet, his own body calling him a liar. "If you could just. . ."

Just what? His thoughts scattered like chaff. He swiped the back of his hand across his brow, hoping the movement might straighten out his tangled thinking. "You should. . ."

He gave himself a mental shake. *Hold it together, man!*

"Captain?" Abby eyed him, fear glinting in her eyes.

Beyond her shoulder, a dark shape rose from the river embankment. Or was he seeing things? At this point, anything was possible. With another swipe, he shoved the hair from his brow, praying to God it would push away the confusion as well.

He narrowed his eyes and stared past Abby.

Blood-smeared and pale, the captain swayed as if he might topple to the ground. He looked over her shoulder as if she weren't there. Did he know she was? Could he still think straight? Or was his spirit even now packing bags, about to depart?

Abby clenched her jaw. Not if she could help it. She reached for him, hoping to guide him gently to the ground and get that leg and arm of his to stop bleeding.

He sprang to life, sweeping her behind him and pulling out his knife, the movement so sudden, she teetered on her own feet.

"Stop right there!" His voice was a bear's growl, and she retreated a step from the fierceness of it.

"Put your hands up where I can see them," he commanded.

A debate raged fierce inside her. Huddle down behind the captain's broad back and hide from whatever danger approached? Or peek around his shoulder to see what threat loomed?

"Be-dah!" Emma's shriek tore out of the open carriage door. If the girl toppled out headfirst, she could break her little neck.

That did it. Abby rose to her toes. If she had to, she'd snatch up a rock and fight alongside the captain.

She blinked, confused. Ahead, the postilion stood wide-eyed, fear draining the colour from his face. Slowly, he lifted his long arms high into the air, like he might grab the sky and pull it down over their heads. "I don't want no trouble, Captain."

"Seems you've avoided that so far, like you knew it was coming." The captain's words stabbed the air, and with each one, the postilion winced. "You did, didn't you? You knew Robbins was going to attack."

"I—I—I—" The man stuttered to a stop.

"Didn't you!" the captain boomed.

"I did." A guilty tot couldn't have looked more penitent for having been caught with his hand inside a biscuit tin. Even from this distance, Abby could see his Adam's apple bob.

The captain advanced. "How much were you paid to endanger the life of a woman and child?"

"It's not like that." The driver retreated a step, terror etching lines on his face. "I didn't—"

"I ought to cut you down where you stand."

Abby frowned. Didn't he see the man's fear? Couldn't he understand that the postilion posed no threat? After a glance at the carriage to make sure Emma was yet inside, Abby gathered up her skirt hem and bolted forward. "Captain, please. Put down your knife."

He waved her away, blood glossy on his hand and dripping off his fingers.

"I didn't make a farthing. I swear it!" The postilion looked from the captain to her. "They said they'd kill my wife, miss, and my little ones, if I didn't stop your carriage here. I don't wish any ill on you, on *any* of you. That's why I run off. I couldn't bear to witness any violence against ye."

Desperation shook the man's words and his lanky legs, rippling the fabric of his trousers from his boots all the way up to his riding jacket.

Even so, a low rumble vibrated in the captain's throat. His knife raised higher, sunlight cutting a line off its sharp edge.

Abby darted between the men. "You heard the driver, Captain. His family was in danger. You would have done the same for me and Emma. You *have* done the same for me and Emma, time and again."

She dared a few steps closer, blocking the postilion from view. "Put your weapon away. We are safe now, Emma and I. You have kept us safe."

His brow creased into a hundred questions. "You are safe?" he mumbled.

Her heart broke at the bewilderment in his tone. She'd never heard such uncertainty from this man of muscle and confidence. She forced a smile, hoping it looked more than just a baring of her teeth. "I am safe."

"Thank God," he breathed out.

His knife dropped. His arm lowered. And the mighty captain sank to his knees in the dirt.

Abby reached him as he pitched forward, dropping down to her own knees and catching him in her arms. The sudden weight of him knocked her back a bit, and she cast a wild glance over her shoulder. "Help me!"

The postilion snapped into action, relieving her of the bloody burden and easing the captain to sit on his own.

Turning her back on them both, Abby lifted the bottom of her gown and frantically tore at the petticoat beneath, ripping off a strip. Then another. And another. And if that wasn't enough, then to the devil with propriety and she'd start ripping her gown. Anything to stop the captain's bleeding.

She sucked in a breath for courage then knelt by the captain's injured leg. Blood oozed out like a cancer that would not be stopped. If she didn't get the bleeding stopped soon, he'd die. Pushing away the thought, she hefted up his leg so that his knee bent. He didn't cry out, but his fingers grabbed great handfuls of dirt, white-knuckled.

She started wrapping slowly at first, tugging the fabric tight despite the captain's grunts. Then as the gaping flesh pressed together, she worked faster, winding the makeshift bandage around his thigh. While she worked, he spoke to the postilion, charging him with tying up the brigand felled by his gun and tossing him into the outside seat of the carriage. The baronet could send some of his men to bury the other two.

The postilion didn't have to be told twice. He dashed off, and Abby scooted from the captain's leg to his arm.

He twisted away. "Leave it. It's not. . ." He sucked in air. "The shot needs to come out."

"But it still bleeds!"

"I know." He closed his eyes, a wave of pain creasing lines near his temples. "Just. . .leave it."

An argument rose to her lips, but she pressed her mouth flat. He needed a physician, not a quarrel. She shoved her shoulder beneath his armpit on his uninjured arm. "We will stand on three. Ready?"

At his nod, she counted off, and somehow, staggering and grunting, she got them both to their feet and over to the carriage, just as the postilion jumped down from where he'd tied up the other fellow on the back seat.

"Help me get him in."

"Aye, miss."

Between the two of them and with the last of the captain's strength, they hefted him inside. Before Abby climbed up, she raced around the back of the carriage and retrieved the captain's hat from the dirt where it lay, as beaten and ruined as he was.

The driver lent her a hand up, and before she ducked inside, she turned to him. "Thank you. Please see to the captain's horse, then make haste to Brakewell Hall. There is no time to spare."

He nodded. "You can count on me, miss."

She edged past the captain's sprawled legs and reached for Emma. The girl had clutched his arm and pulled herself up to stand—thank God it was the uninjured one she'd grabbed.

"Here, love." She handed the girl the captain's hat—still her favorite plaything—and settled her on the floor in the corner. Then she turned back to the captain and sank beside him on the seat.

His eyes watched her. Barely. His head lolled back against the wall as if he hadn't the strength to lift it—and likely he didn't. His skin was ashen. His breath wispy and smelling of copper.

"Oh Captain!" Whatever strength she'd mustered before failed her now, and a sob rose in her throat. "Please, stay with me. Stay right here with me and Emma."

One side of his mouth curved, and slowly, so gradually that she didn't notice it at first, his hand rose, and his worn knuckle brushed along her cheek. "Abby," he whispered. "Sweet Abby."

Her name on his lips was a kiss, and she gasped from the intimacy of it. Did he truly think of her so? She leaned closer, memorizing the feel of his hand now cupping her jaw, her gaze searching his.

Without warning, his hand dropped, and his eyes closed.

No! She pressed her ear against his chest, praying, hoping, weeping that she'd hear his heart beat. That he'd live to someday call her Abby again.

The carriage jolted into motion, the wheels overloud against the gravel. Stopping up her other ear, she pressed closer, straining with her whole body to listen for a sound—*any* sound—beneath his shirt.

And. . .nothing.

Tears broke. *She* broke, grief and rage swirling a great, dark tempest in her soul. She clutched the captain's shirt with both hands and buried her whole face in his waistcoat. "Do not die, Captain!" she sobbed. "Do not leave me. Please, I cannot bear it."

A hint of a sound rattled in his lungs. Small, but it was something. . . wasn't it? She lifted her head and was startled to see his brown gaze burning into hers.

"Not Captain," he rasped. "My name is Samuel."

Then his eyes rolled back into his head.

Chapter Twenty-Six

This wasn't how Abby imagined she'd arrive at her future husband's manor, with a baby on her shoulder, a criminal tied up at the back of the carriage, and the man she loved bleeding to death on the seat next to her.

Oh Samuel.

His Christian name lingered bittersweet in her mind, and she pinched the bridge of her nose, warding off another bout of tears. Likely she already looked a hideous, puffy mess, bloodstained and bedraggled—not the sort of bride the baronet would expect. Or maybe not even welcome. And he must. For the captain's sake, Sir Jonathan *must* take them in immediately.

The coach lurched to a stop in front of Brakewell Hall. While she waited for the postilion to lower the step, she hefted the sleeping Emma and gazed one more time at the captain's still form. Not once since he'd spoken his name had his eyes opened. His chest continued to rise and fall, thank God, but though she longed for it, no more whispers passed his lips. Her heart twisted. Would she ever hear his commanding voice again?

No, better not to think such a morbid question. Better to simply focus on what needed to be done, here and now. It was her turn to be the strong one, and she would be. She owed him that much, at least.

She handed Emma down to the postilion's waiting arms, then carefully worked her way out into the darkness. Night had fallen, and she stepped gingerly onto a drive composed of gravel and weeds, her leather soles landing with a muffled crunch.

Golden light poured out the manor's ground-level windows, most open to usher in the evening air. Gossamer curtain panels hovered like passing ghosts near the glass. A few of the shutters hung crooked, or maybe it was only the play of night shadows. Hard to tell, especially with Emma rousing. If Abby didn't collect her immediately, the baronet would be greeted with a howling child.

She reached for the girl, yet she needn't have—the driver all but thrust Emma into her arms. "Shh, sweet one. Go back to sleep."

Emma rubbed her face into the crook of her neck, and thankfully, her little body once again went limp. Abby clutched her tightly and strode ahead. The sooner a physician attended the captain, the better his chances of survival.

Three stairs led up to a stone landing, where she stopped in front of a big wooden door streaked dark from weather and years. She rapped the knocker hard against the brass plate. Again and again. And wouldn't stop pounding until—

The door flew open, ripping the knocker from her grasp so forcefully, she stumbled forward. In front of her towered a man wearing midnight blue livery and a disgusted scowl. Judging by the wide cuffs on his sleeves and overly long cut of his coat, he was either a rebellious butler refusing to change with the times or he simply didn't mind that his dress was outmoded and unbefitting of a baronet. Neither was a good portent—of him or Sir Jonathan.

But neither did she care. Abby lifted her chin. "Please, I must speak with Sir Jonathan at once."

His lips tightened, and the longer he studied her, the flatter his mouth drew into a disapproving line. "The foundling hospital is in Penrith proper. Continue down the road."

The door started to close—but not if she could help it. Shielding the sleeping Emma, Abby wedged her body into the narrowing gap. The wood smacked into her shoulder blade, but the effort was worth the pain. The door stayed open.

Splotches of red mottled the butler's face. "Step aside this instant!"

She frowned up at the man. "You are making a grave mistake. I am not this child's mother. I am Abigail Gilbert, soon to be Sir Jonathan's wife. He is expecting me, and I implore you to summon him at once."

His gaze grazed over her, from head to toes, then back up again. Wrinkle upon wrinkle gathered on his nose as he sniffed in disdain. "The baronet's intended is a lady, not a disheveled imposter with a child on her hip. If you do not step aside, madam, I will be forced to bodily remove you."

She narrowed her eyes, hoping desperately to mimic the same kind of imperious stare that the captain oft employed. "Do you really wish to risk that I am not who I say I am? For I will be the lady of this manor soon, and when that happens, you will be out of a job—unless you let me in. Do you understand?"

Something moved behind his eyes, a hesitation of sorts. Ahh, but he was a dogged, bullheaded man. By faith! She didn't have time for this—*Samuel* didn't have time for this! But she held her ground, waiting, hoping, praying.

"Very well," he grunted. "We will let the master settle this." He opened the door wide, yet grumbled under his breath.

Ignoring the butler's rude manners—for now—she entered a small foyer, expecting to follow the man to a sitting room, but he stopped and turned to her at the entryway's arch, blocking her advance. "Wait here."

He stalked down the corridor, the breach of etiquette stunning, but not surprising. If the butler truly did believe her to be naught but an unwed mother in search of charity, he likely also supposed she'd pilfer the silver or secret the knickknacks into the folds of her gown.

While she waited, she shifted the dead weight of Emma to a better position and prayed for God's mercy on the captain. All the times she'd told him to hope for the best, expect the best, haunted her now. . . yet trust she would. Nothing that happened took God by surprise or was beyond His reach to heal. She'd cling to that. She must.

Turning, she peered out the narrow glass pane at the side of the door. A useless endeavor. The night was so black. But somehow, just staring at the dark shape of the carriage where Samuel lay was a connection to him—one that comforted.

"Miss Gilbert?"

She whirled.

Striding toward her was a Greek god clad in green velvet. Abby swallowed, suddenly shy. Though she'd remembered Sir Jonathan to be a handsome man, it'd been so long ago since she'd seen him, and then for such a brief time. Here in the flesh, he stood taller than she recollected. His eyes blazed bluer. His shoulders stretched wider. His smile flashed more brilliant than humanly possible.

He stretched out his arms as he approached, the butler tagging at his heels. "So you have finally arrived." A few paces from her, he slowed, then stopped, his gaze fixed on Emma. "What is this? A child?"

Behind him, the butler edged closer, eyes glinting with interest in the sconce light. The talk belowstairs tonight would be rabid, no doubt.

Abby closed the distance between her and Sir Jonathan, lowering her voice for his ears alone. "I will explain everything in private, but first, please send for your physician."

"Are you ill?" His head reared back as if the air between them were diseased. "Or is it the child?"

"Neither. We are both well. But there is an officer dreadfully wounded out in my carriage who will die without immediate attention."

Spoken aloud, the gruesome words taunted mercilessly. Though she'd wrestled with the possibility in her mind the entire drive here, voicing the awful words to the baronet somehow breathed life into them. Samuel could die—could be drawing his last breath even now—and the thought of living in a world without him burned a fresh wave of tears in her eyes.

Sir Jonathan cocked his head, no doubt studying her very physical reaction, then called over his shoulder. "See to the injured officer in the carriage, Banks. Have Mencott tend him."

"Yes, sir." The butler—Banks—pivoted and strode down the long hallway, not fast enough for Abby's liking, but at least he moved toward getting Samuel some help.

"Come." Sir Jonathan swept out his hand. "You are overwrought."

La! He couldn't be more right. Clutching Emma—who by now sagged in her arms like a leaden weight—Abby followed the baronet past the foyer and through the first door. Two large settees flanked a wide hearth. A single table with an oil lamp rested between them. Off in the corner, several cushioned chairs huddled near one another, and in the other, a sedentary dumbwaiter stood like a three-tiered sentinel, with various coloured bottles and crystal glasses on the shelves. No artwork adorned the walls. No trinkets sat on the mantel. Apparently Sir Jonathan cared nothing about displaying his wealth. . .unless, perhaps, his funds were tight? Abby shook her head, confused. Neither her father nor stepmother had made mention of any lack.

"Be seated while I ring for a maid," he instructed.

She sank onto the nearest settee, glad for the support. Emma stirred, lifting her head. Truly, it was a wonder she'd slept this long. Tendrils of damp hair stuck to her brow, and Abby pushed them back. The child craned her neck for a moment, but seeing nothing of interest, she nuzzled her cheek against Abby's shoulder and popped her thumb in her mouth.

Across the room, Sir Jonathan busied himself with a decanter, pouring amber liquid into a tumbler. His long legs were clad in well-tailored buff trousers, and above that, his green dress coat narrowed at the waist and broadened at the shoulders. His sandy hair was brushed back neatly, the curled ends riding just above a hint of his cream-coloured cravat. There was no denying he cut a dashing figure, a desirable one, this man who would be hers.

Hers?

A strange thought, that, though it shouldn't be. For so long she'd looked forward to this moment. To finally be near the man who loved her. But now that it was here, it didn't quite feel right, like a gown that fit properly yet somehow looked ill-suited when glancing at a reflection of it in a mirror.

But that was a trifle compared to the injured captain. Careful not to jostle Emma, she edged forward on the cushion. "Are you certain your butler will carry out your instructions posthaste? Time is of the essence in the matter of the captain. I should like to attend him until the physician arrives."

"Banks is a bit rough around the edges, but he will do as I say, my dear. And as for you, a drink to calm your nerves is first in order, I think." His words were honeyed, his step even more fluid as he turned and crossed the room, holding out a drink for her.

Abby shook her head. While her brother liked his brandy and her sisters hid sherry bottles in their rooms, she'd never acquired a taste for strong drink—and wasn't about to start now.

The baronet crouched, face-to-face. "I insist."

She tensed. Of all the times the captain had commanded her to do something, never once had she felt so coerced as she did now.

"You are wound too tightly, sweet Abigail. This will do you good, hmm? You have been through much and are rightly disturbed." He angled his head, the glass in his hand never wavering. "I wish your first night beneath my roof to be pleasant."

Slowly, she reached for the tumbler. Of course he was right. After the events of this day, she was out of sorts. It was kind of him to notice and wish to ease her distress.

The horrid liquid burned a hot trail down her throat, and she spluttered, shoving the glass away from her. Ack! How could anyone drink that?

Frowning, Sir Jonathan took the tumbler and retreated to the dumbwaiter. Turning his back to her, he poured another glass.

Glad for the moment of privacy, Abby ran her hand across her lips, wiping away any last burning remnants, then resettled Emma on her other shoulder.

Sir Jonathan tossed back his head, slugging down his entire drink, then refilled his glass and joined her on the sofa—on the side farthest from Emma.

His leg brushed against hers, and a hint of a smile curved his lips. "I expected you a fortnight ago, my dear. It appears you have had an eventful journey." He tipped his glass toward Emma, then took a long pull on his drink.

Abby bit her lip and leaned away from him. The man was a tippler. Had her father known of his habits before agreeing to give the baronet her hand? Then again, most men drank, often to excess. . .didn't they?

Yet she'd never once smelled hard liquor on the captain's breath.

Behind a second set of doors, leading to what she could only assume would be a dining room, a burst of laughter leached through the gap near the floor. Abby's gaze bounced from Sir Jonathan to the sound, then back to him. "Am I interrupting something?"

He shrugged. "Some friends are here for a house party. I would invite you to join us but. . ." He eyed the bloodstained traveling gown. "Well, you were going to tell me about the child, were you not?"

A party? His bride-to-be was more than a fortnight late in arrival and he dined with friends instead of frantically searching for her? Abby closed her eyes for a moment, desperately trying to calm the riotous thoughts stabbing one right after the other—for surely these thoughts were all wrong. There had to be an explanation for the baronet's apparent callousness.

"Abigail? Are you certain you are well?" Sir Jonathan's hand rested warm on her thigh, his fingers giving her a little squeeze.

Her eyes flew open at his touch. Betrothed or not, the captain would have never taken such a brazen liberty. But when her gaze met Sir Jonathan's, concern etched crinkles at the side of his eyes—not desire. He loved her. He did. She *was* overwrought.

"I am well," she assured him, inching from his grasp. "How Emma came to be in my care is too long of a tale for me to tell tonight. The short of it is that the man I hired to be my guardian—a captain in the service of the Bow Street magistrate—agreed to deliver this little one to her home, just as he agreed to deliver me to mine."

"Hmm." Sir Jonathan tossed back the rest of his drink and set the glass on the floor. "And that man—that guardian of yours. . .he is the one who is critically wounded?"

"He is." Her heart squeezed. Hopefully even now the captain was resting in a cushioned bed, kept warm by a coverlet, kept company by a. . . By whom? No one knew him here. No one cared.

She stood so quickly, Emma startled. "I hate for the captain to be left alone until your physician arrives, and I assure you that I am much refreshed now. If you would direct me to his room, I should like to wait there. I owe him that. He has saved my life, several times. He has saved *our* lives." She hugged Emma tighter.

"Has he?" Sir Jonathan eyed her as he rose to his feet, his chiseled face a mask hiding what he might think of her singular request. "Then I suppose I also owe him my gratitude for bringing my bride here in one piece."

He reached for her, brushing a lock of wayward hair from her cheek. "Yet you need not concern yourself on the captain's behalf any further. My man Mencott is attending him. All that matters is that you are here now, safe and sound. We have a wedding to prepare for, do we not?"

"But I—"

"You rang, sir?" A maid entered, cutting her off.

Sir Jonathan pulled away and faced the woman. "Have a fire laid in the green room. I will see the lady up there directly. Oh, and take this child to Mrs. Horner. Tell her to make provision for the girl until she leaves, which may be a day or two."

"Yes, sir." The young woman bobbed her head, then marched over to retrieve Emma.

Abby threw a wild glance at her future husband, clutching Emma so tightly, the girl squirmed. Didn't he see how attached she was to the child? "I prefer Emma to remain with me. I am afraid she shall give anyone else a difficult time."

"I assure you, my love, Mrs. Horner is quite capable."

"But she does not know Emma like I do." A sob caught in her throat. *She* was the only mother Emma had for now, not some stranger of a housekeeper. She patted Emma's back and lifted her chin. "The child is new here, as am I, and we would both do better if—"

"I think not, darling." Though he softened the blow with an endearment, it still nearly knocked her from her feet. "We would not want people getting the wrong impression of my soon-to-be wife, would we? Tongues will wag if you insist on favoring the babe as your own. You have my word that the child will be well cared for, and if you wish, we will house her in the very room our own children will one day occupy. You may visit her as often as you like."

A headache started, throbbing a painful beat in her temple. As much as she didn't want to part with Emma, how could she prevent it? She *wasn't* Emma's mother, and though her heart yearned otherwise, she could never be. The baronet was right. It wouldn't be proper for her to be seen caring for a child that wasn't his.

Heart breaking afresh, she planted a kiss on Emma's downy head, then handed her gently into the maid's waiting arms. As the young woman strode from the room, Emma peered over her shoulder. Her little face screwed up into a big wail, the cry colliding discordantly with another burst of laughter from the dining room.

Abby grabbed great handfuls of her skirt, unsure of what to do. She felt like throwing up. Throwing things wildly. Throwing her body down onto the floor and pounding the carpet with her fists.

"Come." Sir Jonathan's arm wrapped around her shoulders. "I shall see you to your room. Clearly you are in need of a good night's rest."

That much was true. She was tired. More than tired. Her bones wanted to lie down and never get up again.

She allowed Sir Jonathan to guide her across the carpet. This was surely not the romantic reunion she'd hoped for—nor likely what Sir Jonathan had expected either. She peered up at his clean-shaven face, the fine cut of his jaw every woman's dream, and tried to ignore that he wasn't her dream. Not really. She'd grown to prefer the captain's shadowy stubble.

Shaking off the inappropriate image, she forced a pleasant tone to her voice. "I apologize, Sir Jonathan, for arriving in such a distressing fashion. I shall make it up to you, somehow. I promise."

He turned to her, tipping her chin with the crook of his finger, and his blue gaze searched hers, intimately deep. "Drop the *sir*, my sweet, for I am your Jonathan. And yes," he drawled, "you will make it up, no doubt."

She froze. All the times she'd stood this close to Samuel had felt like a warm embrace. Somehow, this didn't.

"Pardon me, sir." A male voice entered the room this time, and they both turned.

The servant standing at the door dipped his head. "Banks says to tell you that Mencott has things under control. The captain is attended and the other man has been secured until the constable arrives."

"Other man?" He shot her an arched brow.

"Yes, sir," the servant continued. "Apparently the captain apprehended a criminal during their scuffle. The driver says the man also dropped two other brigands on the road back near Thacka Beck and we ought to send a few men to bury the poor souls."

"I see. Tell Graves and Hawthorne to go. You are dismissed." The baronet waved him away.

The servant hesitated. "There is one more thing, sir. Lady Pelham asks for you."

"Does she?" Sir Jonathan glanced at Abby for a moment, then unexpectedly, pulled her into his arms and brushed his lips lightly across her forehead, right there in front of God and the servant. "If you will excuse me, my dear, duty calls," he whispered against her skin. "I am sure you understand."

He strode from the room, leaving her wobbling. Before he disappeared down the corridor, he called over his shoulder. "See Miss Gilbert to the green room."

Abby stood barely breathing. Sir Jonathan was wrong. Horribly wrong. She didn't understand anything. Not the gnawing angst in her heart for Samuel. Not the ache in her arms, longing to hold Emma.

And she surely didn't understand why the man who claimed to love her attended to another woman when he should be at her side.

Chapter Twenty-Seven

Sleep came hard, but when it did, it crashed into Abby like a load of falling bricks. She woke the next morning to grey light, a head that still pounded, and an insane urge to run through the manor, collect Emma, and lay them both down by the captain's side. Only by breathing in his scent of leather and horses and, yes, even gunpowder, would she feel at home here in this foreign manor. The baronet had forbidden her from attending him last night, but today was a new day—and she *would* see Samuel, one way or another.

Without waiting for the aid of a lady's maid, she hurried into her traveling gown of the day before and tried to rub off the worst of the bloodstains and grime. A quick splash of water on her face and some pins in her hair was the extent of her toilette. It was the best she could do, anyway, for her chest had not yet been delivered to her, nor even her traveling bag. She frowned as she brushed out the wrinkles in her gown with the palms of her hands. The captain had slogged through a storm to make sure she had use of both her bag and her chest, and the memory squeezed her heart.

She dashed to the door and set off down the corridor. When the passageway ended, leaving no choice but to go right or left, she paused and stared down the length of one then the other. The bare wooden walls and planked flooring of each mirrored the other. Oh, why had she not paid better attention last night?

She hesitated a moment, then veered right. Halfway down that corridor, she turned right again and entered a wider hallway. Remnants of what might've been flocked wallpaper spread like diseased arms. Smoke stains streaked up to the rafters, where darkness collected into black clouds. Not far ahead, a staircase with a warped balustrade led downward, and above it, a large, round window blistered out from the ceiling toward the sky. Light seeped in, barely. Ivy and moss covered most of the glass.

Abby narrowed her eyes as she neared the first step. A tattered carpet runner clung to the wooden risers in spots—the only spots that hadn't been mouse chewed. Flecks of plaster and mould collected in the corners. She'd have to be careful where she put her feet. *This* was a baronet's home? Why hadn't his servants cleaned here? The home she'd left wasn't as large, but for all her stepmother's faults, she made sure to keep a tidy house.

Gripping the bannister with one hand and hefting the hem of her gown with the other, she picked her way downward. Of only two things was she certain. She definitely hadn't come this way the night before. And the need to see the captain's and Emma's familiar faces was now as vital as air.

Her feet touched the ground floor, and she stopped and turned in a circle. Cracks ran through the tiles like black veins. Three doors, all closed, punctuated the walls. She strode toward the double set, for surely that would lead into the main part of the house.

The handle of one was broken off, and the other wouldn't turn. Bother! Working her way back up the stairs and trying a different route would waste more time. She frowned. There was nothing for it, then.

Turning a bit, she sucked in air for strength and rammed her shoulder against the wood as she'd once seen the captain do. The door gave way with a groan, but only a little. So, she did it again. And again. Pain shot through her bones, and eventually, with effort and grunts, the wood inched open just enough for her to peer through.

Oh my. . .

Absently, Abby rubbed her shoulder as she stared at weeds run amok, choking the remains of charred stone walls. Window holes gaped like empty eye sockets on one side. The other crumbled to nothing but a hump where a wall should've been. Grey clouds were the only ceiling.

Grabbing the handle with a tight grip, she yanked the door shut, closing out the sickening sight. Hopefully nothing other than the manor had been hurt during that blaze. Sympathy welled in her empty belly. In light of the destruction she'd just witnessed, the rest of the home didn't seem nearly as austere as she'd first judged it last night. Poor Sir Jonathan, to have suffered what surely must have been a devastating loss.

She hurried as fast as she dared across the ruined tiles and chose a different door. This one swung open easily. The pounding in her temples eased a bit as she stepped into a narrow yet well-kept corridor. A smaller staircase led down to her left, plain and hardly the width of her hem. A servants' stair. She pressed on, and when the corridor turned into a wider, well-lit passage, hope rose—especially when the murmur of a woman's and man's voices wafted out through an open door only paces ahead.

A servant exited as she neared—the same fellow who'd seen her to her room the previous evening. He dipped his head in greeting and scurried past her, clutching a silver urn in a white cloth.

Abby upped her pace, eager to see Sir Jonathan—though a twinge of guilt pinched her for her motivation. She ought to be keen on breakfasting with him as her future lover, but all she could think of was asking him how the captain fared and where she might find him. What kind of bride did that?

God, forgive me.

Forcing a pleasant smile, she swept into the room and scanned it from corner to corner, then froze when the only gaze that met hers was green and overly curious.

A black-haired lady sat at the head of a dining table, looking at Abby over the rim of a rose-petal teacup. She was a trim little pixie, sitting there in a white organza day dress, making Abby feel like an overgrown slattern in a wrinkled sack of a gown. The woman's green eyes held secrets, hiding them deep while probing Abby for hers. It was an unsettling scrutiny, as if the lady searched for a weak spot, a broken wing perhaps, so that she might reach out and break the other.

Shoving aside such uncharitable thoughts, Abby bobbed a small curtsey, trying desperately not to let her smile slip. "Good morning. I am Abigail Gilbert."

The lady set down her cup yet didn't rise, nor did she dip her head as custom required. She merely arched a brow and continued her inspection. "Good morning, Miss Gilbert. I am Lady Pelham. You appear to be looking for someone—a tall, handsome someone, perhaps?"

Her smile faded as the woman's bold implication sank in. "I am, actually. Have you seen Sir Jonathan this morning?"

"Heavens no!" Lady Pelham laughed, and while Abby wished she could dislike the sound as much as she disliked this woman, she couldn't. The lady's merry chuckle was entirely intoxicating.

"Unless there is a hunt, Jon—*Sir* Jonathan does not rise until well in the afternoon." The lady reached out a slim hand and patted the chair adjacent to her. "Come. Take a seat. I shall pour you some coffee. . . unless you prefer tea?"

Abby glanced over her shoulder, debating what to do. Stay and possibly find out from this lady where the captain was? Or search the grounds for him on her own? Yet it had been luck and not her skill that had brought her to this room.

She crossed to the offered chair and sat at the edge of the cushion. She'd query the lady and go from there. "I will have whatever you are having."

"La!" The lady grinned. "You are an easy kitten to please. I see why the baronet chose you. We shall be the best of friends, shall we not?"

Best friends? With this woman? Abby pressed her lips tight as the woman poured steaming brown liquid into a teacup and passed it over. The scent of bergamot hit her nose as Abby lifted the cup to her lips. Better to occupy her mouth than to answer that question.

Lady Pelham sat back and studied her afresh. "There are many questions in your eyes, Kitty. I know! Let us play a game. I will answer yours without you having to speak a word. Would you like that?"

Abby set down her cup. No, she wouldn't like that at all. "I do not think—"

"Excellent! Then the game begins." Lady Pelham clapped her hands and stood, circling the table while she talked. "Though I have told you my name, you no doubt wonder who I am, do you not? That is an easy one to answer. I am Sir Jonathan's cousin, so you shall have to get used to seeing much of me." She paused opposite Abby and tossed her a glance. "We are very close, you know."

Her hands fluttered out and she continued following the curve of the table. "Of course you cannot help but wonder at the state of the manor. I would, and in fact did, the first time I came to visit. The home is a bit sparse and the west wing is in dire need of repair, but soon after your marriage that will all change, and the manor will be restored to its former glory. It has been in the family for seven generations now." She stopped directly behind Abby and bent, breathing into her ear. "Did you know that?"

Abby tensed. Why had her father not told her of this? Had he even known?

Lady Pelham laughed again and circled the table a second time, running her index finger along the chair backs as she went. "Of course you must have many questions about your soon-to-be husband, hmm? Fortunately for you, he is not too complicated. Sir Jonathan prefers green, so I suggest you have gowns made in varying shades of it. He does not take snuff, likes his brandy warmed, and on the rare occasion when his temper runs short, he has an endearing little tic near his left eye."

Abby clenched her hands in her lap. While the information was helpful, it rubbed her against the grain. She should be finding out this information on her own, not from another woman. And it was getting her nowhere closer to finding out about the captain or Emma.

She pushed back her chair and stood, done with the game. "Lady Pelham, I—"

The lady held up her hand, eyes twinkling. "No need to thank me yet, Kitty. There is more you are likely dying to know. The butler, Banks, is a goat. Cook is a magician. And the housekeeper, Mrs. Horner, is never—*ever*—to be trifled with. The rest of the staff members are spineless bootlickers."

Abby gripped the back of the chair. "While I appreciate your—"

"Tut, tut! Save that gratitude, for you will want to know who else you will cross paths with today. There are several guests in residence, whom I am sure you will meet, if not this morning, then at dinner tonight. They are Colonel Wilkins and Amelia, his wife; Parker Granby; and Parson Durge, though he is not really a parson." Lady Pelham finished her circle and sank into her seat, a pleased grin lighting her face. "Well, how did I do? Does that answer all of your questions?"

Abby skewered Lady Pelham with a direct stare. "It answers all save one."

"Good! Then the game continues." The lady leaned forward, folding her hands on the table as if she held court. "Pray, what is it you want to know?"

"When I arrived last night, I was not alone. I—"

"Ahh, yes! I nearly forgot to mention the mysterious injured captain, the wounded brigand, and the young girl. You would like to know where they are, hmm?" The lady laughed again, but this time the merriment of it chafed, and Abby stiffened.

"Oh, do not look so surprised, Kitty. I daresay I know more about what goes on beneath this roof than Sir Jonathan does."

Abby clenched her jaw, trapping a salty remark. If she offended the woman now, she'd cut off her main source of information—as catty as it was. Though it sickened her to have to rely on Lady Pelham's intelligence, she had no choice. "Yes, I should like to check on both the captain and the girl."

The lady smiled indulgently and pointed toward the floor. "The child is in Mrs. Horner's care, belowstairs, just past the kitchen. The captain, I am afraid, has been put out in the stable."

Anger flared hot in her belly. The stable? They put the beaten and bleeding captain out with the animals? Why would he not be housed in the manor? Why offer such rude accommodation, unless. . . Her heart stopped as an ugly realization hit her hard.

Only a corpse would be kept in an outbuilding.

Tears burned her eyes and she spun, unwilling to let Lady Pelham witness her reaction. "Thank you," she forced out before her throat closed. Then she sped to the door.

"Leaving so soon, Kitty? You have not yet taken a bite to eat."

Abby stumbled into the corridor. Eat? She could barely breathe—and might never again if Samuel was stretched out in a burial shroud in the stable.

Even half-dead, Samuel could tell a lot about a man by the way he handled three things: old age, trousers that wouldn't stay up, and strangers. Judging by his slit-eyed observation of the grey-haired man across the room, the fellow was a saint. The man's tread had been purposely light since he'd entered the small chamber. He'd set down a mug on a trestle table without a sound, clearly trying to keep noise to a minimum. Rheumatism gnarled his knuckles into craggy walnuts, growing all the larger as he patiently adjusted the leather braces holding up his breeches. But he didn't wince or moan or make any sound at all—until his gaze landed on Samuel.

"Well, well! Ye're not dead, then, eh Captain?" The man retrieved the mug and the only chair in the room.

Samuel pushed up to sit, and a groan ripped out of his throat. Fire burned in his arm and agony flared even hotter in his leg. He sucked in air like a landed fish. Sweet blessed heavens! Death would've been far less painful than this.

"Where am I?" he gruffed out.

The old man dragged the chair across the floor, then straddled it at Samuel's bedside. "This here be the stable house of Brakewell Hall, home to Sir Jonathan Aberley. Ye're in my quarters. I'm Winslow Mencott, stable master, at yer service." He dipped his head in introduction.

Ahh. . .slowly things started to make sense. The lingering dreams of whickering horses and stomping hooves. The familiar scent of horseflesh and oiled harnesses that were as much a part of the room as the gap-spaced boards and cobwebs on the high windows. Apparently the baronet kept strict rules about broken bodies and blood sullying his fine manor home.

Samuel scrubbed a hand over his face, and stubble rasped against his palm. When was the last time he'd shaved?

"How long have I been out?" he asked.

"Tish! Not long enough. I reckon ye could use a good sleep. Ye lost a lot o' blood, man." Mencott leaned close and offered the mug. "Here, drink this. 'Tis my old mother's recipe."

Thirst unleashed at the man's suggestion, and Samuel gripped the cup. He swigged back a big swallow, and a queer stench met his nose—which would've stopped him were his body not a desert and this the only watering hole to be found. Several mouthfuls drained down his throat before the flavor of the swill registered. Dead badgers soaked in lye would've tasted better than this swampy liquid.

He turned aside and spit the nasty concoction onto the floor, the accompanying stab of pain from the quick movement worth the effort. He shoved the mug back toward Mencott. "Are you trying to kill me?"

Chuckling, Mencott retrieved the cup and set it on the floor. "Looks like somebody else already gave that a go and failed. Far be it from me to finish the job."

Samuel rubbed his mouth with the back of his hand, thankful for the truth in Mencott's words. He *had* survived. The ordeal with Shankhart was finished. He'd come away broken but not dead, and Abby and Emma were. . .well, surely since he was here at Brakewell Hall, they must've arrived safely along with him. Hadn't they?

He eyed Mencott. "The woman and child that I traveled with, are they safe?"

"Aye. They're up at the house." He tipped his head toward the door, as if the manor home lay just on the other side of the wood.

Reaching with his uninjured arm, Samuel rubbed a knot out of his shoulder. The assurance of Abby's and Emma's welfare eased some of the tension in his muscles, but not all.

"And my horse?" he inquired.

"Ahh, now she's a real beauty." Mencott nodded, his gaze drifting, and no wonder. Pilgrim was the sort of animal that few horse lovers could forget once they laid eyes on her. Even mud-spattered and burr-speckled, Pilgrim was the finest animal Samuel had ever owned.

"Brushed her down me'self, I did. Gave her the best provender we have." Mencott glanced over his shoulder, then leaned closer. "But don't let the baronet get wind of it. He buys only so much of the choice feed for his racehorse. The rest get last year's hay."

Samuel nodded, irritated that the baronet didn't see fit to provide quality feed for all of his stock, yet pleased for Mencott's favor upon Pilgrim. He shifted on the bed and stifled a wince from a stabbing reminder that his leg was torn up. At this point, Pilgrim no doubt fared better than him and was itching to get back on the road. Which they should. He'd never intended to house beneath the baronet's roof to begin with. His heart faltered at the thought of leaving Abby behind, but truly, his mission was finished. He'd delivered her safe and sound. It would be wise to collect his payment and Emma, then head back south—and no doubt the baronet would agree.

"Thank you, Mencott, for all you've done. I won't trouble you any further." He swung his legs over the edge of the bed and gritted his teeth. Pain sliced deep as the bone in his thigh, and a universe of stars flashed across his vision. He blinked them away, clutching the side of the mattress so tightly, the small scar on his hand from the orphan boy he'd rescued an eternity ago whitened to a thin line. If he kept this up, he'd be nothing but scar upon scar.

Mencott reared back his head. "Now, Captain, I wouldn't do that if I were you."

He grunted. How many times had he heard that in his life?

Filling his lungs with air, he rose. So did the fires of hell, up his leg and straight to his gut, pushing nausea to his throat. The room spun. Darkness closed in.

And he crumpled like dead wood fallen from a tree.

Mencott's sinewy arm caught him and eased him back to the

mattress. "It's too soon, man. Rest yer bones another few days. If that leg o' yours takes to flamin', ye'll lose it."

Samuel groaned. The truth of the man's words hit him like a bludgeon, and his stomach lurched. He might as well lose his life as a leg. He would *not* join the ranks of the empty-eyed cripples begging for pennies in some waste-filled gutter of London's streets.

Mencott adjusted the thin pillow behind Samuel's back, then leaned over him. "I'll bring ye up some breakfast directly, if ye think ye can keep from spewing it out on the floor."

Weary beyond his years, Samuel nodded. "Aye, as long as you keep that drink away from me, I'll be fine."

Chuckling, the man retreated and shut the door behind him. Samuel let his head sink back against the cushion and closed his eyes, desperate to end another wave of dizziness.

Moments later, a knock rapped on the door. His eyes shot wide as the wood cracked open a few inches. Out of habit, he reached for his knife—a moot endeavor. His fingers met nothing but the cloth of his shirt.

"Captain, may I enter?" Abby's voice crept out from behind the door, and his breath hitched at the sweet sound. Traitorous body.

He dragged the thin coverlet up to his waist, covering his bare legs. Hopefully some servant somewhere was patching his ruined trousers.

"You can now."

The words barely passed his lips when the door flew open, then banged shut as Abby raced to his bedside. Her gown flounced into a big poof as she dropped to her knees. Emotions he couldn't begin to name rippled across her face, one after the other, too fast to identify. She grabbed his hand in both of hers and pressed it against her cheek. "Oh Captain, I was so afraid. I thought you were. . .dead—"

Her voice caught, and for a flicker of a moment, the shimmering of a hundred suns welled in her eyes. Tears broke loose then, in a torrent, one after the other, baptizing their entwined fingers.

He swallowed a huge lump in his throat, and though pain slashed an intense trail from shoulder to fingers, he reached with his injured arm and wiped away her tears with his thumb.

"Shh," he soothed. "Don't fret on my account. I'm not that easy to get rid of."

She nuzzled her face into his palm. "I thank God for that, and for you."

Warmth spread across his chest—but this time not from pain. He could die satisfied now, having known the admiration of such a fine woman. Did the baronet have any idea what kind of a jewel he was about to marry?

The thought slapped him hard. Despite the very real attraction between him and Abby, the ugly truth remained that she still belonged to another.

Slowly, he pulled his fingers away from hers, diverting her from his retreat with a question. "How is Emma faring?"

Abby drew in a shaky breath. "I have not seen her yet this morn."

Strange, that. Unless. . . He cocked his head. "Emma did not stay the night with you?"

"No. The baronet did not. . .well, he did not think it prudent for me to remain as Emma's caretaker." Sorrow tightened little lines at the sides of her mouth, but then just as quickly, a small smile erased them. "He did say, however, that I may visit her as much as I like, which I intend to do as soon as I leave here."

"Perhaps you can bring her by, then. Looks like I'll be laid up for a day or two." He flicked his fingers toward his wounded leg.

"I would be happy to." Abby smiled. "Emma would like that."

He grunted. "It's the hat, not the man, that the child prefers."

"You are wrong, you know. It is entirely the man that enchants." Her voice thickened, and her smile faded. The blush of a June rose flushed her cheeks.

A charge shot through him. Abby Gilbert mesmerized like none other. He'd remember her like this. Forever. Brown eyes shining into his. A wayward spiral of hair dangling down to her stately neck. The curve of her collarbone kissing the bodice of her blood-flecked gown.

Hold on. *Blood-flecked?*

He leaned forward, cupping her chin and studying her face. "How are you faring? And speak the truth. For I know this is the same gown you wore yesterday. Do not tell me your baronet put you up in the stable as well."

"Of course not." She frowned. "I have a lovely accommodation, and I cannot complain."

He tilted her face higher, looking deep into her eyes, to where the soul could not deceive. "So, you are happy?"

"I—I am. . ."

Little liar! Such a ragged tone did not denote happiness—*and* she never finished the sentence.

The door flung open, nearly as forcefully as when Abby had entered. Pulling away from his touch, Abby shot to her feet.

A man strolled in, clad in a worsted woolen dress coat and ivory trousers. A white cravat spilled out of his collar, as unsullied as the smooth skin on his hands. Clearly the man didn't work for a living. His blue gaze was direct and disturbing, like too much power given over to a tot, dissecting both Samuel and Abby with one glance.

The man closed the distance between him and Abby, then he draped his arm around her waist. "I thought I might find you here, my dear." He pecked a kiss on the top of her head, then stared down at Samuel. "It is a pleasure to finally meet you, sir. The illustrious Captain Thatcher, I take it?"

The muscles on Samuel's neck hardened to steel, and it was all he could do to answer in a calm fashion without flying from the bed—injuries and all—and pry the man's hand off Abby's body. "I am he."

A thin smile flicked across the man's lips. "My bride here speaks highly of you." He pulled Abby closer. "I am Sir Jonathan Aberley, baronet."

Of course he was. The pompous dandy.

Instantly he regretted the harsh thought. How many times had Abby admonished him to hope for the best? Expect the best? And oh, how dearly he did wish for the best for her sake. Besides, did it not bode well for her that the man paid her such loving attention? Surely the baronet would make an attentive husband—which is exactly what Abby deserved.

Samuel dipped his head in polite respect toward the man. "I have heard much of you as well, sir, and I thank you for your charity while I mend. I assure you I will not be here long."

"I should think not. A man of your profession," he drawled out the word as if it were a dirty sheet to be boiled, "is likely used to such inconveniences. You are, no doubt, adept at maneuvering about while wounded, are you not?"

He met the man's pointed stare and upped the intensity of it. "I am."

"Well then, we shall let you get back to your. . .er, *mending*, as you put it." His hand slipped from Abby's waist to capture her hand. "Come, my dear. Let us leave the captain in peace."

"But—"

Before she could finish whatever it was she wanted to say, the baronet swept her to the door, where she cast Samuel a backward glance as the man ushered her outside.

As soon as the door shut, Samuel grabbed the pillow and threw it to the floor, then whumped flat on his back, glad for the blinding pain cutting him to shreds. This wasn't right. None of it. Not his torn-up leg or the hole in his arm. Not the insane urge pumping strong through his veins to steal Abby away from a life that would provide her with ease and security.

And especially not the animosity curling his hands into fists with the desire to thrash Sir Jonathan Aberley, baronet.

Chapter Twenty-Eight

Abby gripped her skirt hem up in one hand, taking care not to trip headlong down the stone stairs. At the rate Sir Jonathan whisked her along, such a fate was a real possibility. What was his hurry?

He stopped once they reached the gravel of the stable yard, and turned to her, running his hands up and down her arms. The intimate gesture ought to make her heart flutter, her cheeks warm, but the only twinge she felt was a slight irritation that she'd not gotten to say good-bye to the captain.

"Such a strange little mouse you are, rising early, scurrying off to the stables." Sir Jonathan lifted his chin and stared down the length of his nose. "When we are wed, you shall lounge about all day, drinking chocolate and eating dainties, as befits a woman of your station."

Her brow puckered. Not even her coddled stepmother loafed around in her nightgown all hours of the day. "But there will be a household to run—*your* household. I cannot do that from my bedchamber."

"Oh, I think it can be managed." He winked and dropped his hands, then held out his arm. "Come, let us take a turn about the garden."

"I would like that," she murmured halfheartedly, then glanced past his shoulder toward the manor. Surely by now, Emma was beyond consolable. It must be frightening for her in new surroundings with new people.

Abby lifted her face to Sir Jonathan's. "But first I would like to see Emma."

Reaching for her fingers, he placed them on his sleeve. "In due time, my sweet. I would have you to myself a moment more." He patted her hand, then guided her across the gravel, away from the house.

It was a pleasant morning, truly. July sun kissed the earth. Bluebirds sang. Crickets chirped. Yet it took all Abby's strength to keep from screaming. Why did she feel so patronized by this man? Was it not a natural desire for him to wish to spend time alone with his bride? Should she not be grateful for his attention?

Shame settled thick on her shoulders. Her stepmother had been right. She was a thankless wretch.

Oh God, forgive me.

She snuck a peek at Sir Jonathan. He stood a head taller than her—almost as tall as the captain. She curved her lips into a pleasant smile. "I am surprised to find you up so early. Lady Pelham says you rarely rise before noon."

His teeth flashed white as he chuckled. "Lady Pelham paints her version of the truth with wide strokes. Get too near her, and you shall be splattered."

Her smile faltered. What was that supposed to mean? She tucked away the strange remark to mull on later. "Well, this much is true. The lady seems very fond of you."

"Does she?" Stooping, Sir Jonathan swiped up a wild daisy midstride and handed it to her.

Abby's smile disappeared altogether. He had to know his cousin admired him. She'd discovered as much in a five-minute conversation with the woman. Did Sir Jonathan perhaps harbour feelings for Lady Pelham as well? Yet if he did, how could Abby possibly cast a stone when, in her own heart, she longed to be kneeling at the bedside of a rough and rugged lawman?

She pulled her hand from Sir Jonathan's sleeve and twirled the daisy in her fingers. "I was also surprised to find Captain Thatcher lodged above the stable. I realize parts of the manor are in need of repair, but is there not a more comfortable room to which he might be moved?"

Sir Jonathan turned onto a pea-gravel path, too narrow for them to walk side by side. She followed at his back, noting for the first time the colour of his dress coat. Green. At least that much of Lady Pelham's information had been correct. But must he wear the same shade every day?

"It is easier, my dear, for Mencott to attend your captain by housing him in the stable master's quarters. He is in the best possible place for now."

She bit her lip. Why was her thinking so contrary? Clearly Sir Jonathan really did care about the captain. She lifted the daisy to the sunlight, admiring the white petals and thoughtfulness behind the gift.

"It is kind of you to show such hospitality. I should have known you would move him to the manor once he is mobile."

"Nothing of the sort. Once the man is able to stand without keeling over, we shall say our goodbyes."

The baronet's words blended with the sharp trill of a woodcock, both grating to her ears. Of course the captain would be leaving—but that didn't mean she had to think about it right now.

She dropped the daisy into the dirt. It was naught but a weed anyway and blended in with the rest. Most of the garden was overgrown with ivy and lamb's ears running rampant. She'd seen better tended plots on Fisherman's Row in Southampton.

The narrow path ended, opening onto a stretch of ankle-high grass that swept back to the manor. Once again, Sir Jonathan offered his arm and smiled down at her, sunlight glinting off the blue in his eyes. A woman could get lost in that gaze, that handsome face, the strong lines of his jaw and dimpled chin.

But not her. She rested her fingers as lightly as possible on his sleeve.

He covered his hand over hers, his touch cool. "Now that you have finally arrived, I expect you are anxious for the wedding. With the banns already read in my parish and in yours, there is no need to wait. Does the day after next suit?"

"So soon?" She gasped, then pinched her lips shut. Such a churlish response might put him off, and then where would she be? Packing to go back to her awful family?

She blinked up at him, feigning innocence as the cause for her hesitation. "But you see, Sir Jonathan—"

"*Jonathan.*" He squeezed her fingers.

"Jonathan." She pushed out the name. "I cannot possibly be ready in only two days. I have not yet finished my trousseau. I was hoping for a day or two in Penrith to purchase the last of my needs."

He arched a brow at her. "Have you extra money for such trifles?"

"Yes, my father gave me a goodly sum."

"I see." He stopped and, facing her, captured both her hands in his. "Well, you must transfer that money to my safekeeping. No wife of mine need trouble herself over worldly matters such as finance. That is what a husband is for, darling. I will accompany you to town, of course." He leaned close and whispered against the top of her head. "I should like to see what fancies you in the shops."

A shiver crept down her back, and she told herself the sensation must be a good response to his affection. Yes, naturally her body would react in such a fashion. Any woman would tremble to have a handsome man speak such intimate words to her alone.

Even so, she pulled back a bit. "Might we go visit Emma now?"

His blue eyes narrowed. "You seem inordinately attached to the child."

"I am the only mother she has ever known. Granted, it has only been for a few weeks, but we have been through a lot together." A smile curved her lips as memory after memory surfaced. Emma's first steps. Her *ah-be-da* baby gibberish. The smell of her salty-sweet skin after sleeping hard against Abby's shoulder.

She squeezed his fingers, as if by touch alone she might make him believe. "You will adore Emma as well. Once she gets to know you—"

"You forget, my sweet." He dropped her hands and pinched her cheek. "I have houseguests to attend to. The men and I are taking in a spot of fishing today. See to the child, if you must, but I expect you to be dressed and down for dinner by seven. Will you do that for me?"

The conversation moved from Emma to fishing to dinner so fast, she stuttered. "I—I. . .of course. I look forward to it."

And she should. Dinner with the man who would be her husband in the manor that would be her home was a dream come true.

But deep down in her heart, she wished she were back on the road with the captain, looking forward to a homely meal in a smoky pub with a sleeping baby on her shoulder.

Dinner with Sir Jonathan and his guests did not change that sentiment. The four-course meal lodged like a brick in Abby's stomach as she sat on the sofa in the drawing room. Next to her, the colonel's wife, Mrs. Wilkins, chattered away like a magpie. Abby picked at a thread on the hem of her sleeve to prevent her hands from stopping her ears. The woman hadn't come up for air since she'd latched arms with Abby immediately following the baked apple pudding.

As the woman droned on, Abby's gaze drifted to the corner of the room, where Colonel Wilkins and Parker Granby engaged themselves in a quiet hand of picquet. The colonel was a man of few words, as was Mr. Granby, and both were likely quite pleased Mrs. Wilkins had found a new victim to regale.

Opposite them, Parson Durge—aptly nicknamed for his strange penchant to wear a black cassock over his trousers—bent over another table close to Abby's side of the sofa. He held a large magnifying glass in one hand as he studied a book on entomology, exclaiming aloud now and then on some wonderful quirk of insect lore.

But none of these guests interested Abby nearly as much as Sir Jonathan and Lady Pelham. They congregated near the pianoforte, riffling through sheet music. An innocent enough occupation, especially since they stood a good arm's length apart. All the same, Abby frowned. Other than a gut feeling and several offhand remarks by Lady Pelham, she had no evidence of anything illicit between the two. Still, suspicion gnawed away in the corner of her mind that far more than kinship drew them together.

"...wouldn't you say, Miss Gilbert?"

Abby snapped her attention back to the colonel's wife, painfully aware she'd neglected the last several minutes of the woman's conversation. "I. . .er. . ." How was she to answer a question she hadn't heard without offending the older lady?

Think. Think!

Forcing a fake yawn, she lifted her fingers to her lips. May God—and Mrs. Wilkins—forgive her. "I beg your pardon, Mrs. Wilkins, but with the excitement of finally arriving here yesterday after such a long journey, I confess I am still a bit fatigued."

"Of course you are." Mrs. Wilkins leaned over and patted Abby's knee, the movement wafting a somewhat musty smell of overripe melons. Everything about the woman was beyond seasonal, from the outmoded cut of her floral gown to the tight pull of her grey hair, styled in a fashion that died twenty years ago.

"It was a champion thing of you to travel so frugally, my dear. Rented chaises are so unreliable. Perhaps once the manor is restored, Sir Jonathan will once again be able to own a carriage of his own."

Ignoring the woman's queer odour, Abby dipped her head closer and lowered her voice. "Are you saying the baronet has no carriage?"

Mrs. Wilkins shook her head so quickly, her silver earbobs jiggled. "Not a one."

Abby pursed her lips, thinking back on her earlier visit to the captain above the stable. While she'd not entered the bottom half, she'd swear in a court of law that she'd heard horsey whickers and shuffling hooves.

"Yet he owns horses," she thought aloud.

"Only for racing." Mrs. Wilkins glanced aside to the pianoforte, then scooted nearer to Abby. "I think you should know, dear, that the baronet's luck is dismal. However, I am sure that will all change now you have arrived. I had always hoped a valiant woman would come along to save the baronet from his money woes."

Abby pressed her lips flat to keep from gaping. Did Sir Jonathan really love her, or did he love the dowry she came with? Had he chosen her that night at the MacNamaras' ball because she'd captivated him or because he'd learned she was the daughter of a wealthy merchant?

Resonant laughter pulled her gaze back to the pianoforte.

Whatever jest had been shared between Sir Jonathan and Lady Pelham heightened the colour on the lady's cheeks, painting her face a becoming shade of scarlet. Her green eyes twinkled in the sconce light, her black hair framing her pixie face in perfect spiral curls. She was a picture, this woman. A masterpiece. The sort to beguile and mesmerize any warm-blooded man.

Parson Durge's book slammed shut, and Abby startled from the sharp *thwap* of it. In four great strides, the man left the table and took up residence next to Abby on the sofa. Still clutching his magnifying glass, he gestured in the air with it, emphasizing his words. "Did you know, ladies, that the female praying mantis eats her mate? Head first. In fact, some begin eating the male's head before the mating process is finished."

"Oh dear!" Mrs. Wilkins gasped. "Such scandalous talk!"

Abby blinked. She'd suffered through many a gathering of her stepmother's eccentric guests, but Parson Durge outshone them all.

He drew the glass close to his eye—enlarging the brown orb well out of proportion—and stared at her as if she were a beetle to be dissected. "I would say, Miss Gilbert, that you have saved Sir Jonathan from a very painful fate. The mantis Lady Pelham would have shown him no such mercy."

So she wasn't the only one to harbour such suspicions about Sir Jonathan and the lady's relationship. But true or not, it wouldn't do them any good for rumours to travel outside the walls of Brakewell Hall. Gossip, once birthed, often grew into a deadly cancer.

She forced a pleasant smile to her lips. "Pardon me for disagreeing, Mr. Durge, but you are misinformed. The lady is Sir Jonathan's cousin. They could not marry even if either were so inclined."

The parson's bug-eyed stare swung toward Mrs. Wilkins, and the two exchanged a glance. Without another word, he rose and strode back to his book, the hem of his cassock swaying with each step.

Mrs. Wilkins reached for her teacup on the small sofa table, averting her gaze. Was she afraid Abby would take her to task as well?

"I am sure, Miss Gilbert, all the parson meant to say is that it is a good thing you are doing, that *you* are a good woman."

Heat warmed Abby's cheeks. Had she jumped to a conclusion? Was she overly sensitive?

"What is this? Are we speaking of my bride's goodness?" Sir Jonathan approached and held out his hand to her—and Abby's face flushed all the hotter. How much of the conversation had he overheard?

Accepting his offer, she placed her hand in his, and he pulled her to her feet, then bowed over her fingers and kissed a benediction atop them. As he straightened, his voice curled out in a low caress. "You are goodness and light, you know. Kind to a fault."

All eyes turned their way, the parson's magnified behind glass, Lady Pelham's brow arched with avid interest. Even the card-playing duo swiveled their gazes away from their game.

Abby pulled back her hand and ran her fingers down her skirt, abhorring all the attention. "Thank you, Sir Jonathan, but there is nothing special about me. I am certain that if you had the opportunity to do good for someone, you would, without a second thought."

"Ahh, such precious naivete." He chuckled and waved a hand in the air. "One must always count the cost and determine how much such an act would cut into profits, be that monetarily or emotionally. You will never be a success if you give away more than you have, my sweet."

Her brow crumpled. "I do not mean to be disagreeable, but did not our Lord do that very thing? He gave His life, defeating hell and death. I can think of no greater success than that."

"Yes, well," he snorted, "if you believe such tales to be true."

"You do not?" A sudden coldness sank in her belly.

Sir Jonathan threw back his head, his laughter shaming. "Such gravity for a dinner party? Come." He held out his arm. "Lady Pelham has agreed to play for us. Let us sing and save such dreary topics for a rainy day, hmm?"

A slap across the face couldn't have stunned her more. What kind of irreverent man was she engaged to? The urge to run into the night and seek the quiet, solid sanctuary of the captain's company coursed through her veins, growing stronger with each beat of her heart.

Bypassing his arm, she pressed her fingers to her lips, once again feigning a yawn. "Forgive me, Sir Jonathan, but I am really rather weary. Perhaps another time."

She flashed a smile at the rest of the guests. "I bid you all good evening."

Murmurs of good night followed her to the door, and when she finally stepped into the corridor, some of the tension of the long evening fled from her shoulders—

Until a deep voice warmed her ear.

"I will see you to your room." Sir Jonathan looped his arm around her waist and guided her toward the stairway.

She clenched her hands against an irrational desire to bat away his touch and peered up at him with a tight smile. "No need. I do not wish to rob your guests of their host."

"It is no inconvenience whatsoever, my sweet." His fingers pressed against her side. A possessive type of embrace. The kind she'd hoped for ever since Father had spoken of Sir Jonathan's offer of marriage.

Even so, she pulled away and grabbed the bannister.

Undaunted, he kept pace at her side. "I have arranged for a ride into Penrith five days hence. Will that suit?"

"Yes. I should like that."

"Good. Then we shall wed the day after your purchases arrive."

Her slipper hit the riser on the last step, and she stumbled onto the first-floor landing.

The baronet's arm shot out, steadying her. "Take care, darling. I would not want you tumbling down the stairs."

Though he spoke of concern, a shadow of foreboding draped over her.

He pulled her close again, this time tightening his grip. His thigh brushed against her gown as he led her toward her room. His hand rubbed up and down her waist. Being alone with this man in the garden was one thing, but here? In the shadows of a sconce-lit passageway? A chill shivered down her spine, the involuntary reaction nothing at all like what she'd experienced when standing close to the captain. Though she had no familiarity with intimacy or passion, she was certain the odd sensation had nothing to do with physical desire.

They stopped in front of her door, and before a "good night" could pass her lips, the baronet swept her into his arms.

She gasped. "I really do not think—"

His mouth came down hard on hers. Wet. Hot. His long arms wrapped around her like steel bands, entrapping her. She wanted—*needed*—air. Space. Freedom. But his hands cupped the back of her neck, forcing her head up so that he could deepen the kiss.

She'd heard tales of her sisters' stolen kisses, but none of them had mentioned the clenching of one's gut or sudden rise of nausea.

"I have been waiting a long time for this," Sir Jonathan whispered against her skin as his lips trailed down the curve of her neck. His hands drifted, moving down her back, to her waist, to her—

She planted her hands on his chest and shoved him away with all the strength she possessed. "Sir Jonathan, please! We are not yet married, sir."

His blue eyes smouldered to a smoky shade. "You will be mine within the week. Why trifle over a few days?"

He reached for her again.

She arched away, searching for the doorknob behind her. "Yet I insist. Good night, sir."

As soon as her fingers met brass, she yanked open the door and darted inside, slamming it shut before he could follow. Shaking, she leaned against the wood and braced herself, on the off chance he might try to gain entry.

Silence hung thick and heavy, the tick of the mantel clock and beat of her heart overloud in her ears. Had he gone?

"Soon, my innocent dove." The baronet's muffled voice leached through the door.

She stiffened.

"*Very* soon." His husky words seeped into her like an unholy prophecy.

A breath later, his footsteps padded down the corridor, then disappeared altogether.

Abby pressed her fingers against her lips, hating that the baronet had taken such a bold liberty. Hating even more that as his soon-to-be bride, she would have no choice but to welcome such advances.

But most of all, she hated the unstoppable desire to find out what it would feel like to be kissed so passionately by the captain. . .for that could never be.

Chapter Twenty-Nine

Time and the full-hearted embraces of a child were the best elixirs in the world, diminishing Abby's revulsion of the baronet's advance four days ago. Thankfully, since then, Sir Jonathan had been nothing but the utmost gentleman—seating her first at dinner and making it a point to include her in the conversations of his guests. Most importantly, he kept his caresses to a simple brush of his fingertips against her cheek or a light peck atop her hand when seeing her to her room at night. Perhaps she had been a bit harsh with him. After all, he'd merely been showing his eagerness to have her as his bride. What woman wouldn't want that kind of attention?

And so she fell into a pattern of sorts. Her days were filled with enjoying Emma's silly grins and sloppy kisses as they spent afternoons with the captain. Her evenings were occupied by the baronet and his houseguests. All in all, it was a perfectly pleasant existence—save for the nettling feeling that would not go away whenever Lady Pelham entered the room.

Abby shoved aside all thoughts of the woman and swung Emma to her other hip, then pushed open the back door to the stable yard. Sunlight washed the world in a golden glow, and she squinted. It took a moment for her vision to adjust to the brightness—and when it did, she did a double take.

Across the yard, the captain hobbled down the stable's stone stairway—without use of the makeshift crutch old Mencott had fashioned for him.

She clutched Emma tighter and dashed across the gravel. "Oh, you are doing better!"

Emma squealed, from the wild ride *and* the sight of the captain. And Abby didn't blame her. It was all she could do to suppress her own squeal.

Abby caught up to him as his boots hit the cobbles. He said nothing, but he didn't have to. The flash of a wince tightening his face said enough.

She stifled a sigh. Every day he pushed himself too much, asked more from his body than it could give. And each time pain flickered in his eyes, another piece of her heart broke off.

She frowned. "Shall I help you back upstairs?"

"I am not a fragile flower, *lady*." He winked—knowing full well the name ruffled her—and reached for Emma.

Abby twisted aside, keeping the girl beyond his grasp. "Do you really think it is a good idea to hold this squirming worm?"

"You worry too much," he grunted. "Life is more than good ideas. It's the risks that return greater results."

He stepped to the other side of her and pulled Emma from her arms, swinging the child up high into the air. "How's my girl?"

"Ah-pa!" Emma shrieked, and when he lowered her, she wrapped her arms around him and giggled into his neck.

Joyful tears filled Abby's eyes, blurring the scene. She'd never tire of watching this man love this girl and vice versa—especially since they'd nearly lost him. Swallowing, she dabbed away the dampness at the corners of her eyes with her knuckle.

The movement pulled the captain's gaze toward her. "Are you all right?"

"I am." She grinned and swept her hand toward the old workbench just outside the stable doors. "Shall we sit and let Emma play?"

He shook his head. Emma giggled and planted her hands on his cheeks. "I came down here to stretch my leg, not sun myself like a lazy alley cat."

"Do you mind if Emma and I join you?"

"Not at all." He peeled Emma's hands away, but each time he

succeeded in releasing one and reached for the other, she slapped her freed palm right back again.

Abby's grin grew. "Good. I would have joined you even had you denied me. Come, little one."

Before the captain could protest, she retrieved Emma and swung her down to the ground, keeping tight hold of the girl's hands. Emma bounced a moment, then kicked out one chubby leg after the other, eager to walk. Abby followed behind, now and then letting go so Emma could practice walking on her own.

The captain's hobbling step joined her side. "She grows more every day."

"That she does. Mrs. Horner tells me she is quite the handful, especially when I am not around." She gazed up at him. "Will you be able to manage her on your own when you take her back to her father? I will not be traveling along to care for her, you know."

His lips twitched into a smirk, his silence and the accompanying scolding from an overhead martin speaking volumes.

Heat crept up her neck. "I suppose that was a ridiculous question. You round up highwaymen and bring them in. One small girl should be no challenge for you."

"I think, Miss Gilbert, that you're finally getting to know me." A slow smile brightened his face, and sight of the rare appearance tingled in her belly.

As they rounded the back of the stable and moved onto the grassy path leading to the garden, laughter floated on the air. Abby's jaw tightened reflexively at the merry chuckle, for the origin was unmistakable.

On the far side of a vast stretch of creeping ivy, a green-coated man and a blue-skirted woman batted a shuttlecock between them. Lady Pelham and the baronet, unattended by anyone else, appeared to all the world as if they were a happily married couple.

A hot mix of shame and anger boiled in the back of Abby's throat. Why couldn't Sir Jonathan employ better discretion? She swooped up Emma and turned to the captain, intent on suggesting they take a different route before he witnessed the sight.

But too late. He narrowed his eyes at the pair.

Abby forced a light tone to her voice. "Emma would like to see your horse, I think. Shall we go back to the stable?"

His gaze swung to her, a dark glint deepening the brown of his eyes. "Tell me, Miss Gilbert, how are your wedding plans coming along?"

"Oh. . .um. . ." Shifting the kicking Emma to her hip, she sidestepped him and headed back toward the stable, calling over her shoulder, "I am not quite ready yet."

Despite his injured leg, he caught up to her. "I should think you'd be more than ready. Your baronet was all you could talk about on our journey here. Or is it, perhaps, your groom is the one who is *not quite ready?*"

La! Neither of them were. But after the hardship of the cross-country journey, she couldn't very well admit aloud that the captain's astute guardianship all the way across England may have been in vain. Besides, once she married the baronet, of course he would send Lady Pelham away.

Wouldn't he?

She flipped Emma around, allowing the girl to face forward, and wrapped her arms tight against Emma's middle. "Do not be silly, Captain. There are a few more necessaries I must purchase in Penrith, that is all. Then everything will be set for the wedding."

He eyed her as he might a potential criminal, searching for truth between the thin spaces of her words. She looked away, the scrutiny too much to bear.

"Who is the lady with your baronet?"

The directness of his question startled her, and her step faltered. His strong hand gripped her arm, righting her.

She pulled back, scorning her own awkwardness. "Lady Pelham. She is his cousin."

"Hmm." The gravelly sound grumbling in his throat indicted and condemned without a word.

Frowning, she stopped and turned to him. "What does that mean?"

"Maybe nothing. Or maybe everything." A murderous shadow darkened his gaze. "The baronet. . .is he treating you well?"

Instantly her mind slid to the stolen kiss. The force of Sir Jonathan's embrace had been brutal. His lips had devoured her like an animal, not a loving and tender suitor.

Abby nuzzled her cheek against the top of Emma's head, banishing the ugly memory to the past where it should be buried. After all, the baronet had not been untoward since then. So why did it still chafe to be in his presence, while being with Samuel felt so comfortable?

She lifted her face to the captain. "Sir Jonathan is all politeness and decorum, and I have nothing more to say on the matter."

A muscle on his jaw pulsed as he studied her, indicating some kind of mental battle raged inside his head. She didn't dare look away, though. Any semblance of retreat on her part might label her a liar. And who knew what he'd do if he believed the baronet was mistreating her, for she'd witnessed the captain's raw strength when unleashed.

Finally, he blew out a long breath. "I should head back."

Her brows pinched together. Was his face paler? His breath laboured? Had he overtaxed himself? "How are you faring?"

"I'm fine. I promised Mencott I'd help him mend some of the tack, that's all." He reached out and rubbed his hand over Emma's head, mussing her hair. A slight smile lifted the corners of his mouth, but when he pulled back, it faded—then completely sobered as he stared into Abby's eyes. "You know we'll be leaving soon, Emma and I."

"I. . .I know." Her throat closed, the admission tasting as bitter as horseradish. She didn't want either of them to leave. Ever.

A wild impulse rose to her lips, and without thinking any further on it, she blurted, "Say you will come to dinner tonight, at the house. We have so little time left, you and I, and I do not want to waste a minute of it."

Reaching, he kneaded a muscle at the back of his neck. "That's probably not a good idea."

"Did you not just tell me life is more than good ideas? That it is the risks that return greater results?" She nodded toward the manor. "This will soon be my home as much as the baronet's, and I should think I may invite whomever I like to dine with us. After all, his friends are here. I deserve to have mine as well."

"Well, I am glad to see your spunk is still intact." A grin broke over his face like a ray of August sunshine—the effect stunning and ruggedly handsome.

Three smiles in the space of a quarter hour? That *was* a victory.

"So you will come?" She rose to her toes. "Please?"

He sighed. "Just this once."

He stalked off without another word, his step determined but a bit stilted each time he put weight on his injured leg.

Abby squeezed Emma tighter and whispered against her downy hair. "What will we do without him, little one, when he leaves us behind?"

Slowly, Abby lifted her head. That was a battle for another day.

For now she must convince the baronet to allow the captain to dine with him and his guests.

A firing line would've been easier to face.

Samuel tugged at his collar and slipped a covert glance across the table at Abby. Which fork would she pick up? Ever since sitting down in the baronet's dining room, the long line of silver flatware in front of him blasted grapeshot into his confidence. He had no idea so many different-sized forks or spoons existed, let alone which one to employ for which course. This type of dainty banqueting was better suited to Brentwood or Moore. Oh, sweet mercy. If they could see him now, sitting here sweating over the selection of a butter knife, they'd laugh him halfway across the continent.

Just as he fingered the farthest utensil on the left, the man across from him speared him with a direct gaze.

"I don't suppose a man like you is used to this sort of gathering."

Samuel set his jaw to keep from grinding his teeth. It took a lot of gall for the long-gowned fellow to pretend to know what a man should or should not be like. When Abby had introduced him as Mr. Durge instead of parson, Samuel had thought she might've made a slip of the tongue. But after listening to the fellow's colourful language and heretical ideas, no doubt remained. Mr. Durge was no saint and, in fact, blasphemed the clergy by wearing a cassock.

He met the fellow's gaze. "What kind of man would that be, sir?"

"I am sure you do not need me to spell it out."

"By all means, enlighten me."

The man narrowed his eyes, a wicked flash sparking like that of a cat about to bat around a mouse. "The kind of man, Captain, to eat with a fork and knife at a fine linen table, set with imported porcelain. Surely this is an oddity for you."

Samuel upped the intensity of his stare, a skill he'd honed over the years of interrogating criminals. At this point, offense was his best defense—and he intended to be as offensive as possible. "You're right. Usually I gnaw raw meat off a bone, bare handed. I'm surprised the baronet allowed me in here."

Next to him, a strangling choke burbled in Mrs. Wilkins's throat, and she shot out a jeweled hand for her water glass.

Nervous laughter tittered out of Abby. "Oh Captain, such a jest! I assure you all"—she swept her gaze around the table—"that I have never once seen the captain gnawing on bones of any sort."

Next to her, at the head of the table, Sir Jonathan Aberley leaned aside and caressed Abby's shoulder with a possessive touch. "You cannot expect a man who deals in ruffians and rogues to maintain sweet manners, my dear."

The fish in Samuel's gut sank like a lead weight. He'd like to show the baronet some of his manners, right at the end of his fist—especially if the man's fingers slid any closer to the bare skin just above Abby's bodice.

Seated at the so-called parson's elbow, a living, breathing weasel perked up. Parker Granby, his eyes two black beads set close to a nose better used as a parakeet perch, angled his head toward him. "Well, I, for one, would not want to ride roughshod along the highways and byways of the wilds. It must be a hard life, I imagine."

"Must it?" Samuel stabbed a bite of meat and lifted it to his mouth. "Fresh air quite agrees with me."

"Yes, well, I suppose simple pleasures are to be enjoyed now and then." A sneer rippled across Granby's lips. "I find that the simple are often the most content, unruffled by avarice or ambition."

Samuel bit down hard on the chunk of meat. A bullet taken sideways often did the most damage. Clearly this fellow was an adept marksman with his mockery, and this was exactly why he preferred the dust of the road to the carping of upper society.

Abby gasped and leaned back in her chair, shooting her own daggered look at Mr. Granby. "Surely you are not suggesting the captain is a simple man, sir."

"I should think not, Miss Gilbert." Mr. Granby speared a bite of his food. "I hardly know him."

Patches of colour deepened on Abby's cheeks, and it took all of Samuel's restraint to keep from leaping over the table and popping the man smack in the middle of his weaselly nose. Baiting him was one thing. Toying with Abby, quite another. One more word from the fellow and—

A light touch on his sleeve jerked his gaze to the right.

Lady Pelham angled toward him, a single black curl caressing her shoulder like the snake she was. God forgive him for such a harsh judgment, but it'd only taken a few minutes to see beyond her polished façade into the reptilian scales of her soul.

"Tell me of your home, Captain." Her lips parted into a sultry smile. "I find London to be an exceedingly exciting city."

Of course she did. Most strumpets thrived there. He reached for his glass and eyed her over the rim. "I don't live in London."

"But you are a runner." She launched the derogatory term more accurately than a French mortar shell. "Do you not operate out of Bow Street?"

"I do." He slugged back a drink of wine, then set the glass on the tablecloth, relishing the burn down his throat. "Yet I house in Hammersmith."

"Oh. . .I see," she drawled.

He gritted his teeth. By the curl of the lady's lip, what she saw was a poor man unable to pay the high rent in the city—which goaded even more, because she was right.

Two servants moved in, removing plates and setting down bowls of greenish soup. The pleasant twang of lemon and parsley erased some of the bitterness of the lady's words, but not all.

The baronet picked up a wide spoon and indicated Abby with the tip of it. "My bride here informs me that you are quite proficient with a gun."

Samuel's gaze shot to Abby, who took a sudden interest in her soup. Why on earth would she have said such a thing to the baronet?

Opposite the baronet, at the far end of the table, Colonel Wilkins planted his elbows on each side of his bowl and laced his fingers over it, his interest clearly piqued. "What do you shoot, Captain?"

He gazed at the grey-haired fellow. If the parson was not really a clergyman, was this fellow truly a colonel? Only one way to find out. "I carry a nine-inch land pattern, sixty-two calibre."

One of the Colonel's thick, white eyebrows lifted. "Ahh, light dragoons, perhaps?"

So the man did have military experience. Samuel nodded. "The Nineteenth."

"Well!" The colonel blustered and dropped his hands to his lap. "I am surprised you survived. If I recall correctly, that regiment was not known for their quick thinking."

The slur lit a blaze in his belly, driving heat up his neck and over his ears. "Wellesley would've lost Assaye were it not for our detachment."

"Yet you must admit, Captain, that the assault was not of your own contrivance, but under orders from my colleague, Colonel Maxwell."

"That has little to do with it," he gritted out. *He* was the one on the front line. *He* was the one dodging a rain of deadly fire, losing brothers, facing hell—and bearing a crescent mark on his cheek to remind him daily of the carnage.

"I should think it has everything to do with it." The colonel dabbed at the corner of his mouth with a napkin. "Last time I checked, a colonel outranks a mere captain."

Beneath the table, Samuel's hands curled into fists. This was not to be borne.

The baronet tapped his spoon against his goblet. "Back to the subject at hand, gentlemen. I myself have little use for pistols. Real damage is done with a Girandoni, though they are not for the faint of heart. Have you ever tried one, Captain?"

Samuel swung his gaze back to Sir Jonathan, unsure which man aggravated him more—the pretentious baronet or the know-it-all colonel. Though he might as well add the pretend parson and Granby to the mix.

"No, sir, I have not," he answered, and for good reason. That particular rifle was expensive, accurate, deadly—and frowned upon by most militia, for the usage of such most often targeted officers, a grievous breach of the rules of war.

"I thought as much." Sir Jonathan bent to sip a mouthful of his soup, then set down his spoon and leaned back in his chair. "Besides being costly, such a weapon requires special training to operate. No slur intended, Captain, but the Girandoni is not a firearm for the common man. If you like, I will show one to you after dinner, for I do not suppose you have ever had the opportunity."

That did it. One more insult and he'd take them all on—and revel in the pleasure of bloodying their arrogant noses.

"Thank you, but no need to trouble yourself." He pushed back his chair and tossed his napkin onto the table. "If you'll excuse me, it's been a long day."

Made even longer by this lot.

He stalked out, leaving behind murmurs and hissed breaths, hating that his injured leg slowed him down. The sooner he made it out of Brakewell Hall, the better. If that was the company Abby wished to keep, then God help her. He'd rather share a crust of stale bread in the stable with Mencott than suffer one more minute with those finely dressed vultures.

Taking care to favor his stitched-up thigh, he hobbled out into the middle of the stable yard and faced the sky. A three-quarter moon cast a white glow in the blackness, blotting out the nearby stars with its brilliance. Samuel closed his eyes and filled his lungs with the damp night air, then slowly blew it all out, easing some of the tension in his shoulders—until footsteps once again cinched his muscles.

He turned. Abby's ivory gown soaked up moonlight as she floated toward him, a being of light in the darkness. She stopped in front of him, saying nothing, bringing her sweet scent of orange blossom water and lazy summer afternoons. He watched her warily as her eyes welled and pity swam laps in their depths.

Pity? For him?

Disgust rolled through him all over again. Folding his arms, he steeled himself against her tears. "Go back to your dinner party, Miss Gilbert."

She shook her head. "They had no right to say such things."

"Why not?" He snorted. "Everything they said was true."

A ruffled hen couldn't have looked more perturbed as she planted her fists on her hips and lifted to her toes. "You do *not* gnaw on bones with your bare hands!"

"All right, I'll give you that." He threw back his shoulders. "*Almost* all they said was true."

"What they said were lies! They painted you a barbarian. An animal."

He advanced, going toe to toe, eye to eye, and stared her down. "Maybe I am," he growled.

Most women would've tucked tail and run, or called him out for the beast he really was. At the very least, they'd have burst into tears. But not this stubborn little sprite. Slowly, she reached up a slim hand and caressed his cheek, her touch hot against his skin.

He stiffened.

"No, Samuel," she whispered, a thousand possibilities thickening her words. She lifted her face higher, her mouth a breath away from his. "You are not anything like they insinuated, and I thank God for that. You, Samuel Thatcher, are the most compassionate man I have ever met."

The veracity in her gaze, the huskiness of her voice, the way her fingers slid over his face, pulling him closer. . .it was too much. More than a mortal man could bear.

"Abby," he breathed out.

Then he pulled her into his arms and fit his mouth onto hers.

The heat of an August sun burned through him. She tasted sweet, spicy, hinting of promises and distant horizons. He'd kissed women before, and kissed them well, but this? He staggered, fully intoxicated, moulding his body against hers. This was dizzying. Heady. Dangerous. Especially when she moaned his name and grabbed great handfuls of his suit coat, burrowing into him.

Alarms tolled in his head, but the thrumming in his veins and throbbing in his body overrode reason. His mouth traveled from her lips, to the curve of her neck, then lower, tracing a line to her collarbone, to the very flesh that would not—*could* not—ever belong to him. Unless. . .did he dare?

"Samuel." She arched against him, a passionate invitation—one neither of them had any right to issue or accept.

Sobering, he pulled away, breathing hard. Her chest heaved as well, and slowly, she lifted one trembling hand to her lips. Was she remembering? Wanting more?

Or regretting?

The need to know cut into him like a knife. What were her feelings toward him, her *real* feelings, not just some physical response to a well-placed kiss? He drew in a deep breath, desperately trying to regain equilibrium, and pinned her in place with his gaze.

The fire blazing in her eyes lit with a passion to match his own.

"Promise me, Thatcher! When you find a woman you love, you'll not waste one second. You'll go after her with all your heart because one day, ahh, one day. . .it will be too late, and you'll be left with nothing but regrets."

Hawker's words barreled back with stark clarity. It'd been easy enough to agree with his friend then, but now? There was no more denying that he loved this woman, but how could he possibly pursue her when he hadn't even a shilling in his pocket? No, asking her to be his wife was out of the question, for now, anyway—but that didn't mean he had to leave her here in this nest of vipers, not if she wanted out. And if she did wish to leave, maybe someday—with a bit of hard work and the smile of God—he would have the chance to make her his.

"I'm only going to ask you this once, Abby, so take care with your answer."

Her hand dropped, her eyes shimmering wide and frightened. "Very well."

"Do you want me to take you away from here?" He measured the words out like a lifeline. "Emma and I will be leaving soon. Do you want to leave as well?"

Her mouth opened, then closed. Moonlight brushed over her face, draining the colour from her skin.

"I. . ." Her throat bobbed. "I—"

A sob broke off her words, and gathering up her skirts, she spun and sprinted back toward the manor.

"Abby!"

He sucked in a breath. Was that ragged voice bouncing off the cobbles truly his, or some wounded animal heaving a death groan?

The door slammed. Abby vanished. He stood speechless, breathless, hopeless.

Crushed.

Movement at an upstairs window snagged his attention, and his gaze climbed the stone wall of Brakewell Hall. In a candlelit window, the back of a green dress coat stepped away from the glass.

Samuel stiffened, what was left of his heart nothing but ashes now. Had all Abby's talk of a loving family and home life been but a means to urge him to deliver her safely here?

He gritted his teeth. If the baronet, that pompous coxcomb, was the man that Miss Gilbert truly wanted, she could have him.

Chapter Thirty

The morning breeze wafted through the open stable doors, unreasonable in its carefree tussling of Samuel's hair. Scowling, he tossed back his head, shaking the annoying swath away from his face. He should've thought to grab his hat.

With a nod to Mencott, who perched on a stool near the workbench, Samuel grabbed a currycomb with one hand and snatched up Pilgrim's lead in the other. As he guided the horse out into the sun, pain stretched a tight line across his thigh, but not the sort that broke a bead of sweat on his brow. Not anymore. Thank God he was on the mend, and none too soon. After last night, even the thought of seeing Abby again was an exquisite agony.

Just outside the door, he looped Pilgrim's lead to an iron ring, then patted her on the neck. "You are a constant, my friend. A true and faithful companion."

Pilgrim shoved her horsey nose against his shoulder, then perked up her head, ears twitching.

Samuel wheeled about.

Sir Jonathan Aberley clipped across the cobbles, the buckles on his black leather shoes catching the light and bouncing it back. "Good morning, Captain."

Out of respect for the man's station—and nothing more—Samuel dipped his head. "Sir Jonathan."

The man stopped several paces from him, a pair of kidskin gloves held loosely in one hand. With the other, he shielded his eyes and glanced up at the sky. "Yes, indeed, it is quite a fine morning today, is it not?"

Samuel cocked his head. Never once had the baronet sought him out like this. Something was up—and more than likely it had to do with what the man had seen out the window last evening. . .a topic he'd rather not discuss. Ever. He turned back to Pilgrim with a grunt and started brushing.

Behind him, footsteps thudded, and the baronet circled into Samuel's line of sight. "This is a beauty of a bay you have here."

Shoving back a sigh, Samuel dropped his hand idle at his side. "I think we both know you're not here to appreciate my horse or supply me with a commentary on the weather."

The baronet's gaze hardened, his mask of pretense falling to the dirt. "You are correct. I have come on Abigail's behalf."

Samuel gripped the currycomb tighter. Why would she send Sir Jonathan to do her bidding? She wasn't one to avoid confrontation. Unless, for some reason, she wasn't able to venture out here.

A ripple of unease spread like unsettled waters in his chest, making it hard to breathe. Merciful heavens, had she taken ill? Had she somehow been injured?

"Is she all right?" he asked.

The baronet's brow pinched. "She is no longer your concern. You appear sufficiently able to ride, so I suggest you collect the child and leave at once. In short, Captain, Abigail wishes you gone, as do I."

She wishes you gone. She wishes you gone. She wishes. . .

The words buzzed like angry hornets, stinging mercilessly. A bayonet to the belly would've been a kinder act than this abrupt dismissal. After all they'd been through, the danger, the passion, she hadn't the decency to part from him herself? The currycomb in his hand shook beneath his death grip.

"Very well," he ground out, surprised the words could even form the way his jaw locked. "But first I'll thank you to pay me what is owed."

Pursing his lips, the baronet slowly pulled his gloves onto his hands, working each finger hole snug against his flesh. "I should think your room and board are sufficient payment."

The muscles on Samuel's neck hardened to steel. He needed that money, now more than ever after having given the boy in Manchester the last of his coins. "Miss Gilbert and I agreed that I would be paid—"

"And so you have been, Captain." The man's gaze jerked to his. "You have been compensated in the medical services rendered by my stable master, in the roof over your head these past six days, and in the food filling your belly. Not to mention the care and feeding of your squalling brat. I will not give you a penny more, nor will I allow you to continue to suckle at my breast. I want you off my property within the hour. Is that quite clear?"

Astounding. Absolutely astounding. The man was more tight-fistedly bold than most cutthroats roaming the roads.

"Quite." Samuel shot the word like a bullet, wickedly wishing it were a deadly ball of lead.

"Good." The baronet flexed his hands in his skin-tight gloves, a sneer slashing across his face.

Without another word, he skirted both Samuel and the horse and strode into the stable.

Closing his eyes, Samuel clenched his jaw, sickened that it had come to this. He'd done hard things before, performed distasteful duties and inglorious tasks. But traveling halfway across the country, his body held together by catgut and willpower, with nothing but a baby he must keep fed and dry, well. . .that would surely be a challenge, even for him.

But not nearly as demanding as trying to forget the betrayal dealt him by a brown-eyed snip of a woman and the arrogant rogue she'd chosen over him.

Hope for the best? Expect the best? No. He never would again.

Abby ran her finger aimlessly over a bolt of muslin. Early-afternoon light slanted through the linen draper's large window, highlighting the fine green-and-gold stripes on the fabric. Any woman would be proud to own a length of such fine material, but she didn't reach to loosen the strings on her reticule. It was a fruitless pursuit, this shopping. She'd not made one purchase for her upcoming marriage the entire morning she'd been in Penrith. How deep would the baronet's scowl be if she returned empty handed to Brakewell Hall? He'd been so insistent she take Lady Pelham's carriage to finish purchasing her needs for the wedding, practically shoving her out the door right after breakfast . . .alone. . .though earlier he'd said he'd accompany her. Not that she minded, but why the sudden change of heart?

A sigh deflated her. This should be a happy outing, an exciting one. Not all brides were as fortunate as her to be marrying a baronet, shopping with his blessing.

So why the dead weight hanging heavy on her chest, smothering the life from her?

Pulling back her hand, she fought the urge to once again lift her fingers to her lips and remember all over again—though she needn't, really. The taste of the captain's kiss lingered like a lover in her mind. She'd never forget the feel of his arms moulding her against him, the heat of his body, or his exotic spicy flavor. A delicious twinge rippled through her belly. She'd found a home in his embrace, a sense of belonging, and something more. Something eternal. Samuel's kiss had been an unspoken promise that he would cherish her more than his own life, even beyond the grave.

Which was nothing at all like what she'd felt in Sir Jonathan's arms.

The shop clerk closed the ledger she'd been tallying in and wove past a table of lace. An inquiring smile lifted the older lady's mouth. "Have you made a decision, miss?"

The question hit her broadside, and she gasped. Indeed, she *had* made a decision—a forbidden and altogether irresistible decision—one she should've told Samuel and the baronet long ago.

Her own grin spread wide and free on her face. "I have, thank you."

Then she turned and bolted out to the carriage.

"Brakewell Hall, with all haste," she told the driver as she gripped his hand. "Deliver me to the stable yard, please."

"Aye, miss." The man nodded as he helped her up, a curious tilt to his head. Likely Lady Pelham had never instructed him so, or returned from a shopping excursion without excessive packages or parcels.

But no matter. Abby was going home. Home! To a dark-eyed, sometimes grim-jawed captain who, more often than not, was a sort of gruffly man—but the only man she wanted. Though the road leading out of Penrith was worn smooth and the wheels turned easily, she couldn't help but bounce on the seat, imagining the flash of a smile on Samuel's handsome face as she flung her arms about his neck. She could practically hear his laugh rumbling deep in his chest when she told him she loved him and to please take her away with him and Emma.

Turning her face, she gazed out the window at the passing greenery, anticipation fluttering her heart, not unlike the eagerness she'd felt when leaving behind her home in Southampton. Of course her stepmother and father would be horrified at her wayward behaviour, running off with a captain of the horse patrol, but so be it. They'd made their choices, lived their lives as they'd seen fit. It was time, for once, that she did so as well, for had not God Himself extended His love to her by offering the deepest desire of her heart—a loving home with Samuel?

When the carriage barely slowed, she leapt from her seat, practically crawling out of her skin for the door to open and release her to her future. The second her feet touched ground, she hiked her skirts and ran up the stone steps to the stable master's quarters.

"Samuel?" She gave the door a cursory rap then, without waiting for an answer, shoved it open.

A wedge of sunlight cut in through the opening, highlighting a swath of dust motes in the air. She rushed over the threshold, then stopped. Blankets fit snug on the cot where the captain had lain. The crutch he'd used leaned forgotten against the wall. No leather pack of belongings troubled the floor by his bed. She frowned. Why did it look so empty? So forlorn? So. . .final. A shiver spidered down her spine.

Abby straightened her shoulders, casting off the ridiculous

foreboding. Silly girl! He was likely in the garden, stretching his legs, or perhaps testing his strength by taking Pilgrim for a ride. In the meantime, she'd see to Emma and prepare the child to leave.

Shutting the door firmly behind her, she retraced her steps down to the stable yard, then stopped short as Mr. Mencott swung around the corner and blocked her path.

"Miss Gilbert." He nodded. "Is there anything I can help you with?"

"I was looking for the captain. Have you seen him?"

Yanking out a handkerchief, the old man ran the soiled cloth across his brow, then tucked the thing away. "You haven't heard, then, eh? The captain is gone."

"Gone?" The word stuck sideways in her throat. "What do you mean?"

"Sir Jonathan and him had words this morn. The captain and the child left shortly thereafter and—miss? Miss!"

The older man's voice faded as she tore across the cobbles to the manor's back door. She flung it open and dashed down the corridor, loosening her hat and her hairpins in the mad race. By the time she neared the sitting room door, where the baronet's deep voice and Lady Pelham's laughter rang out, her hair broke loose and fell to her shoulders, her bonnet hung down her back by the ribbon at her neck. Regardless of her crazed appearance, she bolted into the room.

Green eyes batted up at her. Lady Pelham sat like a princess on the settee, carefully balancing a teacup. Sir Jonathan stood behind with one hand draped across her shoulder, bending so that his lips nearly touched her neck.

He straightened, a quirk to his brow. "Well, it looks as though your shopping trip nearly did you in, my sweet."

Swallowing a red-hot rage, Abby stormed to the middle of the room and skewered the lady with a glower. "Excuse me, Lady Pelham, but I would have a word with Sir Jonathan. Alone."

"Hmm. . .perhaps the kitten does have claws." The lady set down her teacup and rose, then cast Sir Jonathan a look over her shoulder. "Until later."

"Mmm," he murmured, his gaze following Lady Pelham as she sashayed past Abby. Once she exited, he sidestepped the sofa and crossed the rug to stand in front of Abby. The lady's lavender scent clung to him like a second skin.

His gaze bore into hers, iciness flashing in those blue depths. "I have been very patient with you, darling, but it is bad form for you to dismiss one of my guests so casually."

"Yet you dismissed my dearest friend!" Her voice shook, and she breathed in deeply to steady herself. "What did you say to the captain to make him leave so abruptly?"

"That is what this is about? Your precious captain?"

He pulled her to him so quickly, his mouth coming down hard on hers, that her protest stuck in her throat. Squirming, she planted her hands on his chest and shoved with all her fury.

"Stop it!"

She jerked back her arm to slap him, but he caught her wrist and held fast.

"Listen, you little fool." He shoved his face into hers. "I saw you and the captain last night, in the stable yard. You should be thankful I sent him away instead of you."

She staggered. Of all the hypocritical, double standards! "And what of you and Lady Pelham? You are not cousins! Were you going to tell me that before or after the wedding, *darling*?" She drew out the word like the slice of a knife.

"Ahh..." A dangerous smile slashed across his face. "It comes down to managing our indiscretions so soon, then? Very well. It will be easier not to pretend."

Though she'd known it all along, the admission hit her hard, stealing her breath. "Why?" The question shook out of her, sounding as forlorn as a lost little girl even to her own ears. She tipped her chin and forced steel into her tone. "Why did you ask to marry me if you had no intention of loving me?"

"Love?" His laughter bounced off the walls, mocking her from every direction. "What has love to do with status and a fine home? It was a fair enough trade, my dear. Your dowry for my name. Your family certainly did not raise any objections and, in fact, were quite eager for the arrangement—as were you, if I recall."

She stiffened, horrified. What a naive little lamb she'd been. "I had no idea," she ground out. "I thought you cared for me, that you cherished *me*!"

"Oh kitten." Pity was tied by a thread to the end of his endearment, and the lines on his face softened. He brushed away the hair that'd fallen across one of her eyes, and his fingers lingered near her ear. "You are upset. Let us put this behind us. I very well might come to love you. Stranger things have happened."

Her jaw dropped. She stared into his hollow blue eyes, hopelessly and completely speechless. What was one to say when a dream finally heaved its last, shuddering breath?

But no. The impeccably dressed man in front of her was not her dream at all—and honestly, never had been.

She shook her head, disentangling her hair from his grasp. "I cannot go through with this. I *will* not. I am done with waiting for love to find me, when all along it was within my grasp."

He grabbed her arm before she could sidestep him. "Do not do this, Abigail." For the first time since she'd known him, panic whined in his voice. "Do not throw away what you have for what you think you want. It is never a good idea to base one's life on the whim of passion."

A whim? Was that the only value he put on love? Compassion rose up, tightening her throat. How awful it must be to live with such a shallow understanding of the very thing that caused a heart to beat.

"Someone once told me that life is more than good ideas. It is the risks that return greater results. I hope, sir, that one day you too will learn to risk all for love, for that is what our Lord did for us." She pulled from his grasp.

"You are more an innocent than I credited." His brow folded into a sneer, then as suddenly, faded. "But you are young, and you will learn.

Come. You are weary. I shall walk you to your chamber and you may rest. Things will look different after a good sleep."

"No. All the sleep in the world will not change my mind." She lifted her chin. "I bid you goodbye, Sir Jonathan."

His eyes narrowed. "This is no small thing you are doing, Abigail. If you walk out that door, your father will hear of this. Do not think for one second it will go well for you. We have an understanding, he and I, and you will be sent back here immediately. You *will* be my wife, so save yourself the trouble of an unnecessary journey."

Without another word, she turned and strode from his threat, hopefully hiding the hitch in her step as his words hit home. He was right. Leaving behind Brakewell Hall and facing her father when he returned from the continent was no small thing.

And neither would be finding Samuel and Emma on her own.

Chapter Thirty-One

Rain showered down, unrelenting in its ability to drip off Samuel's hat and find a crevice to crawl under, usually between his collar and shirt. Emma sat on the wet ground next to a pine tree, crying, while he scrambled to collect boughs to make some meagre refuge. Their first night on the road, and it had to rain?

He scowled. He should've expected as much. All of Abby's "hope for the best" folderol was a load of manure. Life was hard, hope was for dreamers, and the dirt of the highway was the best he could expect for the next ten years.

One by one, he propped up bough after bough, crafting a lean-to—until Emma crawled over and threw herself against his leg, catching him off-balance. Flailing his arms, he managed to stay upright, but the shelter didn't. His arm caught against one of the branches, and the whole thing imploded into a soggy heap of pine needles and sticks.

Emma pulled herself up his trousers and wailed into the storm. He didn't blame her. He felt like howling himself.

Blowing out a disgusted sigh, he scooped up the child and held her close to his chest, wincing at the pain in his leg, his arm, his soul. She burrowed into his waistcoat, sobbing. And he couldn't fault her, not one bit. Bedding down with an empty stomach in the wilds of the woods was not for the weak of heart—and certainly not for a child.

"Very well, little one." He kissed the top of her wet head. "Let's get you dry and fed."

He trudged to the tree where he'd tethered Pilgrim and unloosened the length of rope. Hefting himself and Emma into the saddle cost him a stitch in his thigh and a grunt, but he made it, then maneuvered the horse in a tight roundabout and set off for the road.

The rain made for hard going, Emma nearly slipping from his grasp several times, all a sickening but apt picture of his life. He'd tried to hold on to hope—for funding, for a farm of his own. . .for Abby—but look where all those fine thoughts had gotten him. Riding a mud-slicked horse with a crying baby, penniless and injured.

Where's that peace You promised, God? I could use a smidgeon of it now.

He tucked his head against a sideways blast of wind, no better off on his journey back to London than when he'd started out that fateful day on the heath. No, that wasn't true. He was worse off, his heart more jaded, his faith more ragged.

God, have mercy.

Strengthening his grip on Emma, he urged Pilgrim onward, willing his broken spirit to do the same. Two sodden miles later, he neared a coaching inn and turned into the front drive—where it appeared half the population of the county congregated, or at least their carriages and horses did. The Blue Bell was apparently the place to be on this wet and wicked eve.

He slid from Pilgrim, and keeping a tight hold on Emma, he tied his faithful mount to an iron ring on a post. He'd have to see to his horse later. For now, he pushed open the studded oak door of the Blue Bell and strode into chaos.

The taproom boiled with people. Men lifted mugs, calling for refills. Women chattered, some tittered. One of them held a yipping pup with a red bow on its head. Emma twisted in his arms, craning her neck to stare at the ruckus. Her whimpering subsided as she forgot her soiled clout and empty belly—but that wouldn't last long.

With Emma clinging tight around his neck, Samuel plowed through the merrymakers toward a man in an apron, who now and then barked orders to a red-cheeked serving girl.

"Pardon." He tapped the man on the shoulder and loosened Emma's grip, drawing in a much-needed breath. "Have you a mug of milk and a corner of the stable to spare?"

"Aye." The man pivoted, long flaps of skin on each side of his chin wagging with the movement. He held out a meaty palm. "Five shillings."

Five? For a small patch of straw? Robbery! Samuel scowled at the man's open hand. Even if he had the coins in his pocket, he wouldn't share them willingly with such a greedy goblin. The fellow was nothing more than a highwayman garbed in the trappings of an innkeeper.

He slipped his gaze up to the man's shrewd face. "A trade would be more to your benefit, I think. I am skilled with horses, and judging by the amount of patrons packed in here, I suspect you could use a hand out back."

"You're right. I do need some help." Reaching behind his back, the man fumbled with the ties of his apron. "This is an unexpected mob, and I'm short a serving wench." He yanked off the soiled fabric and held it out. "Bring the child to the kitchen and get to work."

Samuel shook his head and recoiled a step. "I don't think—"

The innkeeper shoved the apron closer, cocking his head like a raven before it pecked. "Take the offer or leave. I've not the time to cater to you."

A growl lodged in his throat. He didn't know the first thing about serving mugs of ale or plates of beef, nor did he want to—but once again Emma's whimpering surged, making his decision for him.

He grabbed the apron and stalked into the kitchen, savoring the ache in his leg. Pain was better to focus on than anger, and he had a whole lot of rage simmering in his gut. A pox on Sir Jonathan Aberley, the miserly cur.

Inside the large room, a wide-hipped woman bent over a steaming pot at the hearth, stirring with a wooden paddle. Cooks were notoriously ill-tempered, and no wonder. Considering the dark stains spreading out from her armpits, she'd likely been bucking cinders and heat all day. Samuel shied away from her and instead pursued the red-cheeked miss, who breezed in through the door.

"Pardon me, but—"

"No time." She snatched up six bowls of stew—*six!*—and balanced them in her arms as she whirled back toward the taproom.

He followed. "Could you just direct—?"

"I couldn't just *anything* right now."

She darted out the door and disappeared into the crowd beyond.

Well, so much for a polite approach. Shifting Emma to his other arm, Samuel stalked over to the cook. "I'm to serve," he declared as if he were addressing a new recruit. "This child needs milk and a safe corner in which to stay."

The woman stiffened, her shoulders flinging back like a crossbow ready to shoot. She whirled from the pot and pierced him and Emma with a narrow-eyed stare—one that could curdle cold milk.

"Are you daft, man? I'm a cook, not a nursemaid."

He swung out his free arm, indicating the bowls of pottage lined up on the table, cooling as they waited to be served. "Yet you need the help."

The red on her face deepened to burgundy. If she blew, it wouldn't be pretty. He held his ground, steeling himself for what might be a blood-drawing battle.

"More sausages, Mary!" the innkeeper hollered in through the kitchen door. "And keep that stew flowing or it'll be the devil to pay."

"Pah!" The woman reached for another apron on a peg, then shoved it toward Samuel. "Use this to tie the child to the cabinet leg in the corner and give her a bowl of the cooled pottage. Milk will have to wait."

She turned so quickly, the hem of her skirt puffed up a cloud of spilled flour.

Samuel snapped into action, anxious for this night of humiliation to be over. He secured Emma to the cabinet, giving her a bit of lead for movement, but not much. She stared up at him with shimmering blue eyes, accusing him in ways that cut deep.

Squatting, he lifted her face with the crook of his finger. "My pardon, Emma. You are of more value than being tethered like a horse, but chin up and bear it, hmm? Can you do that for me?"

Her lower lip quivered—a sure sign she was about to go on a

full-fledged crying jag.

He shot up and snatched a dish of stew from the table behind him, then handed it to her with a wooden spoon.

Emma wobbled for a moment, then threw down the spoon and planted her face in the bowl, coming up with a smile and stew dripping down her chin. A messy triumph, but a triumph nonetheless.

Heaving a sigh, he tied the apron the innkeeper had given him around his waist and sucked in a breath. Chin up and bear it, indeed.

He stalked into the public room, armed with grim determination and two bowls of pottage. At the very least, no one should know him in this part of the country. A blessing, that. Should his fellow officer Bexley catch wind of him prancing about in an apron, there'd be no end to the jesting.

Three hours later, he wore more broth than he'd served, the pains shooting up his legs howled like angry beasts, and he'd heard a rash of inventive curses more creative than the time he'd run a night watch at the Wapping docks. But slowly, finally, the taproom emptied of patrons. Sloop-shouldered and weary beyond measure, he trudged into the kitchen, where the other serving girl hung her apron on a peg then slipped out the back door with a nod to Cook.

"Well, well. . ." The cook eyed him. "Still standing, are ye?"

"Barely," he breathed out as he glanced at Emma. The girl had curled into a ball and slept with the overturned bowl as a pillow. Stew matted her hair into clumps.

He reached to unloosen the knotted apron ties at his back, when the innkeeper's voice bellowed through the kitchen door. "One more to be served."

Samuel clenched his jaw. Would this woeful day never end?

The cook's gaze shot to his. "There's but a scraping of deviled kidneys and spoonful of pork jelly for you to offer. That's all that's left."

He nodded. Hopefully this far into the evening, the late rider would be more anxious to visit a soft mattress than to fill his gut.

Samuel strode into the public room, his brows raising as he approached the table nearest the door. It wasn't a man who demanded service after all, but a straight-backed bit of skirt perched on a chair. His own empty belly cinched. A woman wouldn't be traveling alone at this time of night, so no doubt her companion would soon join her. What kind of wrath would he have to parry when they found out the only food to be had was nothing but scraps? Thunder and turf! He'd rather face a bare-fisted bandit keening for a knockdown than a hungry, quarrelsome woman.

He neared the table and, with the last of his willpower, forced a soothing tone to his voice. "Pardon, miss, but the kitchen is—"

She turned, and the air punched from his lungs. Two brown eyes bore into his, blinking with shock.

Abby gripped the table with one hand, stunned. She hadn't expected to catch up with Samuel so soon—and certainly not with an apron tied around his waist.

She swallowed her surprise and raised her eyebrows. "What are you doing wearing an apron?"

A shadow darkened his face, heralding a coming storm. "What are you doing here with your baronet?"

The question seethed through his bared teeth, indicting and condemning her in the same breath—and it rankled her to the core.

She'd done nothing wrong! She was the one who'd risked everything by leaving Brakewell Hall, pushing herself to travel far past sunset, stopping at every inn along the way. He had no right to stand so rigidly imperious, making her feel more of a wayward imp than ever her stepmother had. This was not the reception she'd expected. Why did he not welcome her with open arms?

"I travel alone." She emphasized each word then jutted her chin.

Lamplight slid along the captain's hardened jaw. "You should know better, and so should your man."

"He is not—"

"Enough!" The captain's face tightened into a mask of steel. "What trickery is this? Why would Sir Jonathan Aberley, *baronet*, allow his bride to roam the roads at night?"

The headache she'd been ignoring all evening broke loose and banged around in her skull. So be it. If a quarrel was what the captain wanted, then she was in a mood to serve. She poked him in the chest with her finger. "The baronet has nothing to do with this. You are the reason I am out here—you and Emma, and—Emma! Where is she?"

He grew dangerously still. "Even now you doubt my ability to care for the girl?"

"You know that is not what I mean!" she huffed. Why was he being so obstinate? Where was the man of the previous evening, all tenderness and passion?

"Emma is asleep in the kitchen, if you must know, but why come all this way on your own? Unless. . ." He ducked his head like a bull about to charge. "Feeling guilty about not delivering on your promise, are you?"

She scrunched her nose, a most unladylike action, but it was not to be helped. Promise? She'd not even given him an answer last night let alone vowed anything. "What are you talking about?"

"Playing the innocent ill becomes you, Miss Gilbert. Just pay me what is owed and be on your way."

"Owe?" That's what this was about? Money? She frowned. "After what the baronet already paid you—"

"Oh yes. Six days of food and lodging. Quite generous, that baronet of yours." His brown eyes turned to stone—so did his voice. "Which is why I'm standing here in an apron. So Emma can have supper and a dry place to sleep."

She sucked in a sharp breath. He'd not been paid. Not one ha'penny. And after all his hard work, suffering, bleeding. . .oh my. What a horrid mess this had all become.

She rubbed her temples, the pounding in her head worsening, then gestured toward the chair next to her. "Please, sit. There are things we must discuss."

A pot clanged in the kitchen, and he glanced toward the door. For a moment she wondered if he would stay at all or might dash off. And he had every right to, after the unjust treatment he'd been given.

Eyeing her warily, he scraped back the chair and angled it to face her. His posture remained taut as a sail in the wind, but beneath it all, she could tell he hoarded fatigue. Surely his arm must ache, and his leg, especially after standing for who knew how many hours, rushing between the now empty taproom and the kitchen. . .all because Sir Jonathan had sent him away penniless.

She swallowed down the lump in her throat. "Look, I do not know why the baronet did not pay you nor what he said to make you leave Brakewell Hall with such haste, but believe me, I had no part in it."

His eyes narrowed, yet he said nothing. What in the world was he thinking? Why did he not respond?

"Please, Captain. Why did you leave without saying goodbye?"

He winced. A sign he was softening, perhaps?

So, she prodded him. "What did the baronet tell you?"

"You should know. You're the one who sent him to me to say you wished me gone."

She flinched, his icy reception of her suddenly making sense. Of all the wicked, scheming plots the baronet had manufactured— offering marriage to her because of her dowry or claiming Lady Pelham as his cousin—this one was by far the worst.

"I would never wish you gone. Never! I was dreading the day that you and Emma would have to leave."

He stared at her, a terrible stare that could cleave truth and lies from the most protected of hearts, and finally his chest deflated as he blew out a long breath. Unfolding his arms, he leaned forward and planted his elbows on his knees. "All right. Tell me what happened with you and your baronet."

She bristled. "Please, stop calling him that. Sir Jonathan is not mine, nor ever shall be."

"But he is the man you chose, that night we. . ." His gaze drifted to her lips.

Heat climbed up her neck and spread over her cheeks. "I never said such a thing."

His eyes snapped back to hers. "Neither did you say you wanted me to take you away, nor that you wanted to leave."

"I did not say anything!" She threw up her hands. "I was so torn, so conflicted, that I ran off without giving you an answer. You told me to think carefully before I answered, remember? I needed time for that."

"You needed time to talk yourself out of loving the baronet?"

"No, Samuel." Her voice broke, and she leaned toward him, laying her hand over his. "I needed time to listen to my heart. Do you not know? Can you not see? It is you that I love, *only* you. Despite the baronet's title, you are the true nobleman, not him."

His breath hitched, yet he pulled away. Something unsettling charged the air between them, rife with words that should've been spoken long ago. Her throat closed. Was it too late? Had any feelings he might've had toward her cooled and vanished like a mist?

Sorrow pulled at the corners of his mouth. "Oh Abby. . ."

Whatever words he'd intended to say languished into silence. Was he struggling to turn her away? To tell her goodbye? Hot tears burned behind her eyes at the possibility.

"Forgive me," she murmured, then licked her lips, her mouth impossibly dry. "I see my declaration is unwelcome. I should not have spoken so boldly."

"No." He stood and averted his gaze, his face twisting into a grief no man should have to bear. "It is I who is the real criminal here. I stole your heart from a man who could provide for you. I had no right to ask you to give that up for me."

"You cannot have stolen what was freely given."

"Go back, Miss Gilbert, while you still can. Go back to a man who can give you what you deserve."

"Don't you see? I am *never* going back." She shot to her feet and cupped his face in her hands, forcing him to look at her. "You are the man who can give me what I deserve."

His jaw flexed beneath her touch, the rasp of his whiskers prickly against her palms, and for a moment, he said nothing, merely studied her with that same unnerving, brown gaze of his.

Finally, he spoke. "Then you do not know what you truly deserve." He pulled away. "If you will not return to Brakewell Hall, then I will see you safely to London."

Turning, he stalked into the kitchen, each of his steps driving another nail into her heart. She stood alone in the big room, with nothing but unanswered questions and a hole in her chest, bleeding out the last of her hopes and dreams. Apparently love was never meant to be hers. Her stepmother had been right all along.

She was a stupid girl.

Chapter Thirty-Two

Samuel pounded each step hard into the gravel of the Blue Bell's courtyard, relishing the pain in his leg. He deserved it, this torment, and the closer he drew to the carriage where Abby waited with Emma, the deeper he dug in his boots—especially when Abby turned at his approach.

Grey morning light draped her figure, the cloudy day as sullen as the stiffness in her spine and hurt in her eyes. He'd caused that injury. His words. His resolve. Yet by all that was holy, he'd had no choice in the matter! He couldn't provide for her. At the moment, he couldn't even provide for himself. But as he closed the distance between them, with the waft of her citrusy scent and the way her gown rode soft along the curves of her body, he wanted her so badly, his teeth ached.

Stopping in front of her, he schooled his face into a blank slate. It would do neither of them any good to unleash his true feelings. "Are you ready?"

Emma popped her thumb into her mouth and turned her face away from him. Was he to be shunned by the child as well?

Abby threw back her shoulders. "I am, but what about Emma?"

He ground his jaw, hating the iciness in her voice, hating even more the estrangement hanging thick between them. But it wasn't to be helped, not until he could figure out a way to care for her. His best hope at the moment was to take her to Brentwood's and see if his wife might keep Abby on to help tend their brood. Abby was certainly good with children, and he could properly court her there while he earned some money out on the heath. Or maybe, if God and Brentwood smiled upon him, he could take on a few of those lucrative security jobs of Brentwood's. And if not. . .well, he would turn London upside down if need be to find Abby a safe place. Anything to keep from returning her to a family who didn't love her until he could claim her as his own.

Emma reached up with her free hand and rubbed Abby's cheek, as if by instinct the child sought to console her.

"We'll stop at the Gable Inn and return Emma to her father." He turned on his heel to retrieve Pilgrim. Let the driver help her into the carriage, for no doubt she'd slap away his hand should he offer.

And she probably would have. For the next five days, Abby held herself aloof, shutting him out at every possible turn. The one time he did hold up his gloved hand to aid her into the coach, she'd gazed at his fingers as if he held out a black adder, then she'd sniffed and hefted herself up unaided. Each night at dinner, she ate in her room with Emma, her door securely locked. When they stopped to change out the horses and the driver, she handed Emma over to him and took care of her personal needs without a word. The tension was taut enough to stretch across a river gorge and walk upon it from one bank to another.

And with each mile they traveled, the worse he felt. Should he tell her of his plans before he even asked Brentwood if it was a possibility? Would it not be cruel to dangle such a hope before her?

Clicking his tongue, he guided Pilgrim onto the last stretch of road leading to the Gable Inn, helpless to stop the raging in his soul. He was less than a man. He was a beast, for any man worth his salt could provide for a wife. But not him. He'd had to rely each day on the graces of Abby's purse strings for the food in his belly and the roof over his head—*and* over hers and Emma's.

Self-loathing and the grime of travel crawled into every crevice of his skin as he swung off Pilgrim. He brushed away the worst of the dirt on his trousers while waiting for the carriage to catch up.

In front of him, the Gable Inn stood as proud as ever. He tethered his mount to the front post, busying his hands until he heard the carriage door open and Abby's footsteps draw near. He turned, and the shimmer of tears in her eyes nearly dropped him to his knees.

She clutched Emma to her breast, nuzzling the child's head with her cheek. "Shall I say my goodbye here?"

His chest squeezed. He knew this moment was going to be hard, but now that it was here, he realized just how wrong he'd been. It would be impossible for Abby to let the child go without tearing out yet another piece of her heart.

"No, come with me." He strode to the stable yard, biting down so hard, his jaw crackled.

God, please, have mercy. Abby can't do this. I can't do this!

But sweet blazing fireballs, what else was he to do?

Filling his lungs with air, he prayed for courage and strode into the coolness of the Gable's big stable. Ahead, a familiar set of broad shoulders hunched on a stool near a workbench.

"Hawker, we're back."

The large man turned at Samuel's approach, the sour stink of an unwashed body and cheap rum clinging to him like a Shoreditch harlot. He narrowed his red-rimmed eyes. "Thatcher? What are you doing here?"

Abby stepped beside him. Hawker's terrible gaze landed on Emma and hardened. Emma stared back, then turned and burrowed against Abby's shoulder, rubbing her face into Abby's neck.

"What's *she* doing here?" Hawker bellowed.

Samuel clenched his hands. Lord, but this would not go well. He took a step away from Abby, in case his old friend should snap and go on a rampage.

"It's about your sister, my friend. She. . ." He swallowed. How to say this gently? "Well, she died peacefully."

Hawker sat deadly still, his face tightening to granite. Samuel held his ground, unsure if the man would spring or just sit there and never move again.

Slowly, Hawker rose, his stilted steps crushing straw beneath his boots. He held out one hand toward Emma, but a pace away, he stopped and dropped his arm. A ragged sigh ripped from him, blowing out a demon or two.

Then his bloodshot gaze swung to Samuel. "No, I can't keep her. I won't. When I look at the girl, all I see is her mother, the woman I'm drinking myself into the ground trying to forget. You take her. You and your lady. She's your child now."

Samuel shook his head. "But you can't—"

"Don't tell me what I can't do!"

Hawker dodged past him and stalked into the light, leaving him and Abby in the shadows of the stable, a cloud of questions in the air too numerous to even think about answering.

Abby turned and blinked at him. Her mouth parted, yet no words came out. How could they? He hardly knew what to say himself.

So he pivoted and strode outside as well, as big a coward as his friend. "Hawker, wait—"

"Well, stars and thunder, Captain! And here I was thinking I'd have to haul my hide halfway across England to find you." Officer Bexley's familiar voice pulled up alongside him, and his patrolman clouted him on the back. "Good to see you alive."

Turning, Samuel frowned, unsure which he needed to attend first—the retreating Hawker or the interest in Bexley's eyes as Abby joined Samuel's side.

Bex cocked a brow his way. "It seems, Captain, that you hunted down more than just Shankhart, eh?"

"Now's not a good time, Bex," he breathed out. "What do you want?"

Bexley lifted his meaty hand and scratched behind his ear, one corner of his mouth turning up. "The magistrate says you're to return at once. He's got something for you. Says it's urgent."

Samuel grimaced. Sure he did. A contract to shackle him for the next ten years. . .but if that meant enough income to marry Abby, then so be it. She was worth having no matter what job came his way.

Abby's gaze pinged between them both and finally landed on him. "Emma and I will wait in the carriage, Captain."

She whirled, the hem of her gown swishing with her steps.

Bex watched her go, his brows pulling into a line. "Why is the lady still with you? Unless. . . Ahh." A slow smile spread across his face, stretching from one edge of his side whiskers to the other. "Ho ho! You've gone and fallen for a skirt?" A chuckle shook his big shoulders, drawing the attention of a passing ostler.

Samuel ground his teeth, needing to explain but wanting to ignore—especially when Bexley slugged him in the arm.

"Never thought to see this happen. And a child to boot? You old hound!"

Samuel's fists shook with the effort of holding back from punching Bexley straight to kingdom come.

His laughter spent, Bexley folded his arms. "Makes sense though, I suppose, now that you're a man of means."

Samuel angled his head, studying the man. "What say you?"

"Huh? Oh, I suppose you've not heard, eh? Wrapping up the Shankhart affair and all. Remember that lad you rescued off the heath? The one we nearly left behind but you found?"

How could he forget? The lad's scratches had scarred the back of his hand. "The orphan, yes?"

Bex nodded. "Turns out the boy isn't an orphan after all. He's the son of a wealthy fellow, an earl or some sort, who was out of the country on business. The lad was en route to the man's estate for safe-keeping in his absence. Apparently their hired guardian took a fall and broke his arm. Not wishing to be delayed, the foolish women decided to go it on their own across the heath with naught but their driver and manservant, thinking to hire a new guardian at the next inn."

Samuel shook his head. Funny how one seemingly small decision could affect the lives—or deaths—of so many.

"When the boy never arrived," Bex continued, "the boy's father offered quite a reward for his return. The magistrate got wind of it and checked into the missing lad of Devonshire. You were the one what found him, so you get the reward. But the earl isn't long for London, and peers don't like to be kept waiting. That's why I was sent to fetch you. The man wishes to reward you in person."

The words circled slowly, coming to roost as gingerly as the sparrows atop the peak of the Gable's roof.

But he didn't believe a word of it.

He narrowed his eyes at Bex. "This is a poor jest."

Another laugh rumbled in Bexley's throat. "'Tis no jest. You're a moneyed man now, or soon will be. Why, I figure ye ought to have more than enough to buy that land you been scarpin' about."

Moneyed? Him? He clenched his jaw to keep it from dropping and lifted his gaze to the sky, shame burning a hole in his gut.

Forgive me, God, for casting aside hope and wallowing in a lack of faith. You have answered my prayers for mercy time and again. Truly, Lord, Your goodness knows no bounds.

Then he took off at a dead run.

Tears came easily these days, as prolific and never ending as a spring rain. Sucking in a shaky breath, Abby fought back another round, tired of weeping. Tired of life. Tired of everything.

She cuddled Emma closer to her breast, next to the place where her heart used to be, and strode past the carriage to a green patch of lawn in front of the Gable. Who knew how long it would take for the captain to sort things out with Emma's father—if things could be sorted at all. The man had seemed adamant in his rejection of his daughter, and oh, how Abby ached for the girl. She knew firsthand what it felt like to be spurned so cruelly by a parent who should have loved her. What was to become of Emma? The uncertainty of the girl's future was as nebulous as her own.

"Oh little one." Tucking her chin, Abby murmured against the top of Emma's head. "We are an unwanted pair, are we not?"

Emma squirmed. "Ah-ma?"

"Yes, my sweet." A sob welled in Abby's throat, choking her voice. "I will ever and always be your *ah-ma*, no matter what happens."

The child was too wriggly to hold on to any longer, so she let her down and pulled out a small felt rabbit from her reticule—the one and only purchase she'd made while wedding shopping in Penrith. Emma clapped her hands and reached for the toy, having no idea that her fate was likely even now being decided by the captain and her father—or would be, after the captain finished his business with the bearlike man who had joined him.

Oh Samuel. Would that we might have been able to come to an understanding of our own—a lifetime of an understanding.

But that hadn't happened, nor ever would. She sighed. The captain had spoken little the past five days. Not that she'd given him much of a chance. What was the point? Clearly he'd decided she was not the woman for him, and once his mind was made up, there was no turning him.

While Emma played at her feet, alternately gnawing on the little bunny then lifting it up to the sunlight, Abby leaned back against a tree and stared out at the road. How different things had been a month ago when she'd first traveled that dusty path. She'd been a naive girl then, full of hopes and dreams, so certain of a happily ever after.

She flattened her lips. And now look at her, backtracking to a home she'd vowed never again to see. Already she could envision the pinch of her stepmother's face and hear the screech in her voice once she found out Abby had refused the baronet. Her father would likely wash his hands of her, pensioning her off in some small cottage as a spinster to grow old all alone. Despite the warmth of the summer afternoon, she chilled to the core.

No, that would never happen, not if she could help it. She was good with children. Perhaps in London, she might find occupation as a governess—though without references, that might be a stretch. Better yet, Wenna had commented on her skill with a needle. Employment in a dress shop might be a more attainable situation. But how to keep herself until such a job might be found?

Absently, she reached up and fumbled for the watch brooch beneath her bodice. Her throat tightened as she rubbed her thumb over the glass face. Could she truly part with this last piece of her mother to begin a new life?

Boot steps crushing gravel broke into her misery, pulling her gaze as the sound grew louder. Captain Thatcher dashed past the carriage and closed in on her and Emma. Something had been decided, though she wasn't sure she wanted to know what exactly.

Bracing herself, Abby stepped away from the tree trunk and straightened her shoulders. For Emma's sake, she'd stay strong, no matter the outcome.

The captain stopped in front of her and yanked off his hat, then wiped his brow with the back of his hand. His brown gaze held hers, yet he said nothing. He stood silent, the afternoon breeze lifting wisps of his dark hair, his fingers turning his worn felt hat in a slow circle. A muscle clenched on his jaw. Whatever he had to say clearly cost him in ways she couldn't begin to understand. Did he fear to tell her, perhaps, that Emma was to be given over to a foundling home?

Abby glanced down at the sweet girl, then back up to him. "Has something been decided?"

He shook his head. "Not yet."

"Thank God," she breathed out, but a wave of uneasiness still washed over her. He hadn't hurried over here for no reason, for the captain was ever a man of intention. She angled her face. "Then why are you here? Should you not be speaking with Emma's father?"

"No, you're the one I need to talk to."

His fingers continued to pinch his hat, moving it inch by inch, 'round and 'round. Emma threw her rabbit and crawled over to it, then threw it again. And again.

Another carriage rolled in, passing them by and stopping at the inn's front door, and still the captain said no more.

"Well?" Abby prodded.

He blew out a sigh. His head dipped, and he pinned his gaze on the ground, as if he might find whatever it was he wanted to say lying there in the dirt.

Abby tensed, uneasiness prickling the skin at the nape of her neck. What was this? The captain wasn't one to mince words. He was a man of action, of command. One who said what he must and hanged the consequences.

"You frighten me, sir."

He jerked his face up, pain etching lines at the corners of his mouth. "Forgive me. I know my silence has caused you much hurt, Miss Gilbert, and for that I am grieved. But I hope to put an end to it here and now."

"And how do you propose to do that?"

"By asking you to marry me."

Her jaw dropped. Her breath stopped, clogging somewhere in her throat. Surely she had not heard him correctly.

"Pardon?" her voice squeaked.

He turned away and crouched by Emma, handing her his hat, then rose and swung back to Abby, catching both her hands in his big, calloused fingers.

"That night you came to me at the Blue Bell and told me you loved me, I could hardly fathom it. Lord knows I am not an easy man to love. But you, sweet Abby. . ." His lips thinned, and he shook his head. "You have held my heart in your hands from the day you stood brave and tall on the heath, threatened by highwaymen yet holding your ground. There can never be another woman for me but you. The truth of it is I love you, Abigail Gilbert, and I will never love another."

The healing balm of his words slipped into the cracks, the hurts, the years of dry ground that had longed to hear such endearments—until one single question stopped the flow.

She narrowed her eyes. "Why did you not tell me this five nights ago?"

"I. . ." He squeezed her fingers, gentle, firm, warm, as if to drive home some unspoken point. "I didn't want to get your hopes up, not until we reached London. I wanted to find you a home with one of my colleagues first. Give you a safe place to stay while I earned money for lodgings of our own."

Lodgings of our own?

Samuel's words nestled into her heart. All this time, when she had thought he had rejected her, he was only planning how to care for her. *Her.* The immense weight of responsibility he must have carried the past few days swept over her. Because he loved her.

"But things are different now. *I* am different, and there is no more need to wait. So. . ." He cleared his throat and looked at her almost sheepishly—a first, that. A very handsome first. "Will you have me? Will you be my wife?"

Tears filled her eyes, turning the world to yet another watery mess. "Oh Samuel," she barely managed to choke out.

A slow smile flashed across his austere face, instantly changing him into a young man full of life and vigor and love. "So your answer, my lady, is yes?"

Pulling free of his grasp, she lifted to her toes and planted a resounding kiss on his lips. Satisfied, she stepped back and grinned. "Yes!"

Low laughter rumbled at their side, and they both turned.

The bear of a man who'd rode in to find Samuel chuckled at them both. "If Brentwood or Moore could see this."

"Indeed, my friend." Samuel laughed too. "Would that they could." Then he glanced at her, a sultry gleam in his brown eyes, and once again caught up her hand in his. "I will never be the same, you know. You have made me very happy."

She beamed at him. "Do you realize, Captain, that you have just taken on my guardianship for the rest of your life?"

"I would have it no other way."

Emma clapped her hands, and Abby's heart soared.

"Neither would I, my love." She lifted Samuel's fingers to her lips and pressed her mouth against his knuckles. "Neither would I."

Epilogue

Abby set down her sewing and shifted in her chair, preparing to rise. Nowadays simply standing took all her effort. But before she pushed upward, Emma dashed across the room, ginger curls flying, and plowed into Abby's legs.

"Baby sleep?" Emma pressed her cheek against Abby's swollen middle.

A resounding kick from inside pushed back against the girl's sudden attack.

"No, Emma." Abby smiled. "The baby is most definitely *not* sleeping. Be a good girl, now, and gather your Bibby. It is time we begin making dinner for your father."

"Papa!" Emma squealed, then spun on her heels and ran to the corner of the bedchamber where she'd left a heap of blankets and a cloth baby doll. Ever since Samuel had brought home the little toy last week—which Emma promptly named Bibby—the girl had hardly let the doll out of her sight. Lord only knew what Emma would do when she had a real babe to hold.

Abby pressed her hand against her big belly as she stood, struggling for balance. Sweeping aside the sheer window curtain, she peered out at the hay field, and her heart instantly melted. Ahh, but she'd never tire of watching the long lines of Samuel's body stride across the land. He'd thrived since they'd moved here, wrangling with dirt and sun and rain instead of cutthroats. He smiled frequently, laughed often, and his brooding good looks took on an even more handsome shine.

Lowering her hand, she let the curtain drop. He'd reach the house soon, likely bringing with him an appetite. Heat flushed over her cheeks, and a slow grin curved her lips. No doubt he'd want more than dinner.

Her grin suddenly faded as a knock on the front door carried in past the sitting room. They didn't receive many guests out here in the country, especially not in the minutes before dark.

She hurried as fast as her large girth allowed, Emma running on her tiptoes right alongside her, and opened the front door—

Then wished she hadn't. Her stomach lurched, and she leaned one hand against the doorframe.

A man in a dark blue riding coat stood on the stoop, the grime of the road dusting his shoulders. His blue eyes were all too familiar, for she looked into the same shade each day.

"Mr. Hawker?" The name barely made it past her lips. What in the world was Emma's father doing here? Now?

"Mrs. Thatcher." He dipped his head toward her, then pinned his gaze on Emma. "May I see her?"

A chill cut straight to Abby's heart. She'd feared this day. Awakened at nights in a sweat, fighting with the counterpane from a nightmare such as this. Though Samuel often reassured her otherwise, she'd always suspected Emma was only theirs on loan, a gift that would be snatched away some future day.

And now the future was here, standing at her door in a black felt hat and riding boots.

She drew in a breath for courage and fumbled for Emma's little hand. "Of course you may. Will you come in?"

Without pulling his gaze from the girl, he shook his head and crouched, eye to eye with Emma. He fumbled in his coat pocket and retrieved a small, hand-carved horse, then held it out. "For you."

Emma's eyes widened. "Horsie?" she breathed, then glanced up at Abby.

"Yes, Emma. A horse for you." She bit her lip before her voice broke.

"Horsie!" Emma shrieked and snatched the toy from her father's hand.

Mr. Hawker reached out and patted the girl on her head, then rose. "Is your husband here?"

For one wicked moment, a lie bristled on her tongue. If she told the man Samuel was away, he'd leave and Emma could stay. . .but that would only delay the inevitable.

She pulled back her shoulders, hoping good posture would provide some measure of courage. "You should find my husband out back. He was nearing the house only moments ago."

Mr. Hawker tucked his chin. "Thank you, madam."

He strode away, and Abby pressed the door shut behind him, a bit wobbly on her feet but this time not from pregnancy. Emma galloped around the sofa in a circle with her new toy, squealing, "Go, horsie! Go!"

Abby skirted her and sank to the sofa cushion. Would this be the last she'd hear of Emma's sweet laughter? Had last night been the final time she'd ever tuck her into bed? Had the plate of cheese and bread she'd shared with the girl at noon been her last meal with her?

God, no! How am I to part with her?

The loss was too great, and she hunched over, bowed by the weight of such a dreadful prospect. Her chest squeezed, feeling as hollow as if a giant hand had reached in and yanked out the roots of her deep, rich love for Emma, a love that'd been growing ever since the day Samuel had handed the girl over to her.

The door jolted open, and Samuel poked his head inside. "Bring Emma outside, please."

Tears burned in her eyes. Was this shearing pain in her heart what it felt like to lose a child? She rubbed both hands on her belly and stood. Though another was on the way, there would be no consolation for losing Emma.

With a bravery she didn't feel, she held out her hand and forced a light tone to her voice. "Come, Emma."

Emma trotted over to her, horse in hand, and wrapped her small fingers around Abby's. "Go? Ride?"

"No, my sweet. At least, I hope not—" A sob cut off her words. Her head pounded as she delivered Emma outside, fighting to keep a great, wailing cry from breaking loose.

Samuel and Emma's father turned at their approach, and once again, Mr. Hawker crouched. "Come, child. Come to me."

Emma looked from the new horse in her hand to the man and apparently decided it was worth the risk to allow him to gather her in his arms since he'd brought her a toy. He walked off with her, but not far.

Abby turned to Samuel, unable to contain the misery welling inside her for one second longer. "Oh Samuel!"

His brow folded as he studied her, then suddenly softened. He pulled her to him and pressed a kiss against her forehead, smoothing back her hair with his big hands. "All is well, my love. He merely wants to say goodbye."

Her breath hitched, especially when the babe inside gave another good kick—as was the child's custom whenever Samuel held her close.

She pulled back and tipped her face up at her husband. "But where is Mr. Hawker going? Why such a formal parting?"

"He sails for America, and thank God for that. I feared he'd drink himself to death, but he's finally decided to leave his past and pain behind and start a new life."

"And Emma?" Abby held her breath, dreading but needing to know what would become of her girl.

A grin flashed across Samuel's tanned face, vanquishing any fear she might ever bring to him. "She stays with us." He reached out and placed his hand on the bulge of her belly. "Emma will be the finest older sister our son could ever know."

Closing her eyes, she breathed in blessed relief and thanked God. Then she snapped her eyes open and arched a brow at Samuel. "Do not be so sure it is a boy, husband. You might very well have a daughter."

"If it is"—he smirked—"then I will be sorely outnumbered."

Boot steps neared them, and they both turned. Mr. Hawker set Emma down, and the girl ran right into Samuel, wrapping her arms around his legs. He stood solid, a broad beam holding up both of their worlds.

Mr. Hawker's blue eyes—so hauntingly the same as Emma's—stared directly at Abby. "You're doing a fine job of raising her, ma'am." Then he dipped his head at Samuel. "Thatcher, take good care of your family, all of them. Goodbye."

Samuel nodded. "Goodbye, Hawker. Godspeed."

Emma's father wheeled about and retrieved his horse, swinging up into the saddle the same time as Samuel swung Emma up into his arms.

He winked at Abby. "He needn't have told me that, you know. I will care for my girls until my last breath."

Abby grinned. "And *if* you have a son?"

"And *when* I have a son"—he bent and kissed her on the nose—"I shall teach him to care for my girls as well." Settling Emma up on his shoulders, he reached for Abby's hand. "But until that day, I guess I'll have to do as your sole guardian."

"I would have none other." She grinned. "For you, husband, are the most noble of guardians a woman could have."

Historical Notes

One of my favorite parts of writing historical fiction is the research. I love learning tidbits and weaving them into the story. Here are a few pertinent facts I came across in the writing of *The Noble Guardian*.

Highwayman

A highwayman is simply a thief who steals—usually at gunpoint—from travelers on the road. Not all, but some of those attacks turned deadly, the robbers not wishing to leave anyone behind who could identify them. Others wore masks for the same purpose. Hounslow Heath was a notorious haunt for highwaymen because criminals would choose remote stretches of highways that supplied regular traffic going to and from major destinations. Dick Turpin is one of the most notorious English highwaymen, a villain who roamed the wilds in the 1730s.

The Magistrates of Bow Street (especially Richard Ford)

Bow Street Runners began with only a handful of men under the direction of Magistrate Henry Fielding in the 1750s. The force grew to eventually branch out into a horse patrol in 1805. This consisted of around sixty men who were charged with guarding the principal roads within sixty miles of London. Their most successful achievement was to rid Hounslow Heath of highwaymen.

In *Brentwood's Ward*, *The Innkeeper's Daughter*, and even in this story, an update is given on Magistrate Richard Ford. There really was a Bow Street magistrate with this name, but alas, he died on May 3, 1806, at age forty-seven. For the sake of this story, however, I chose to keep him alive a bit longer *and* give him a wife. The magistrate mentioned in this story, Sir Nathaniel Conant, served from 1813 to 1820.

Physicians vs. Surgeons vs. Apothecaries

During the Regency era there was a clear distinction between physicians, surgeons, and apothecaries. Only physicians were labeled with the title of doctor, and they usually attended only wealthy families. They were the gentlemen of caregivers and were deemed socially acceptable.

Surgeons, on the other hand, were the general practitioners of the day, so they didn't get such a high and lofty title but merely went by *mister* instead of *doctor*. Because surgeons performed "physical labor" by treating patients, they occupied a lower rung on the social ladder. Apothecaries were the pharmacists who concocted and dispensed drugs.

Croup and Putrid Throat

What we think of today as croup—barking cough and wheezing breaths—isn't necessarily what people of yesteryear believed it to be. In fact, croup was a catch-all phrase that could be applied to many illnesses at the time, such as the deadly diphtheria. The most common treatment during the Regency era was white horehound syrup, which was used to alleviate any cough or lung issues. It is known to have a pleasant taste.

Putrid throat is another historical all-inclusive phrase that meant a severely inflamed throat that put off an odor and included tissue destruction. Generally a high fever, delirium, and hallucinations also accompanied such an illness. Most likely this was either strep throat or, once again, diphtheria. Back in the day, diphtheria was a very common cause of death.

Coaching Inns

Before the advent of the railroad, the best way to travel across country was by carriage. Though not everyone owned a carriage because the upkeep of horses was expensive, travelers could still rent a carriage and horses at coaching inns. In fact, that was the main function of a coaching inn (besides providing lodging). Inns hired out fresh horses, post-chaises (sometimes called traveling chariots), and drivers, who were called postilions. Inns were anywhere from seven to ten miles apart and could be any size, ranging from small, family-run affairs to large, several-storied buildings manned by plenty of staff.

Bibliography

Beattie, J. M. *The First English Detectives: The Bow Street Runners and the Policing of London, 1750–1840*, reprint ed. Oxford, England: Oxford University Press, 2014.

Bleiler, E. F., ed. *Richmond: Scenes in the Life of a Bow Street Runner, Drawn Up from His Private Memoranda*. Mineola, NY: Dover Publications, 1976.

Cox, David J. *A Certain Share of Low Cunning: A History of the Bow Street Runners, 1792–1839*, 1st ed. London: Willan, 2010.

Harper, Charles G. *The Old Inns of Old England: A Picturesque Account of the Ancient and Storied Hostelries of Our Own Country*, vol. 1. London: Forgotten Books, 2017.

Protz, Roger. *Historic Coaching Inns of the Great North Road: A Guide to Travelling the Legendary Highway*. St. Albans, England: CAMRA Books, 2017.

Tristam, W. Outram. *Coaching Days and Coaching Ways*. Amazon Digital Services LLC, May 1, 2011. First published 1893.

Acknowledgments

While writing is a solitary profession, a book is never written alone. I have so many to credit with holding my sweaty hand on this writerly journey. Here are a few of those that make up my tribe. . .

Critique Partners: Yvonne Anderson, Julie Klassen, Kelly Klepfer, Lisa Ludwig, Ane Mulligan, Shannon McNear, Chawna Schroeder, MaryLu Tyndall

First Reader: Dani Snyder

The Team at Barbour: Mary Burns, Liesl Davenport, Nola Haney, Annie Tipton, Shalyn Sattler, Bill Westfall, Laura Young, and editor Becky Durost Fish

Awesome Readers & Bloggers (just a smattering of the many): Perrianne Askew, Crystal Caudill, Elisabeth Espinoza, Robin Mason, Deborha Mitchell, Trisha Robertson, Susan Gibson Snodgrass, the Tantalizing Tea Ladies

Cheerleading Friends: Linda Ahlmann, Stephanie Gustafson, Cheryl & Grant Higgins, Sal Morth, Darrie & Maria Nelson

And last but not least, my family: Mark, Joshua, Aaron, Callie & Ryan, Mariah

But the biggest of all shout-outs is to you, dear readers, who faithfully read story after story.

More than likely I've inadvertently left off someone important to mention, so if that's you, consider yourself heartily thanked because to one and all, I am grateful.

About the Author

Michelle Griep's been writing since she first discovered blank wall space and Crayolas. She is the Christy Award–winning author of historical romances—*A Tale of Two Hearts, The Captured Bride, The Innkeeper's Daughter, 12 Days at Bleakly Manor, The Captive Heart, Brentwood's Ward, A Heart Deceived,* and *Gallimore*—but also leaped the historical fence into the realm of contemporary with the zany romantic mystery *Out of the Frying Pan.* If you'd like to keep up with her escapades, find her at www.michellegriep.com or stalk her on Facebook, Twitter, and Pinterest.

And hey! Guess what? She loves to hear from readers! Feel free to drop her a note at michellegriep@gmail.com.

Other Books by Michelle

Brentwood's Ward
The Innkeeper's Daughter
The Captive Heart
The Captured Bride
12 Days at Bleakly Manor
A Tale of Two Hearts